W9-CPF-444

3 1321 00561 5557

WITHDRAWN

Legacy of Fools

MISSY HORSFALL
& SUSAN STEVENS

BARBOUR
PUBLISHING

© 2012 by Missy Horsfall and Susan Stevens

ISBN 978-1-61626-545-8

eBook Editions:
Adobe Digital Edition (.epub) 978-1-60742-770-4
Kindle and MobiPocket Edition (.prc) 978-1-60742-771-1

All rights reserved. No part of this publication may be reproduced or transmitted in any form or by any means without written permission of the publisher.

Scripture quotations are taken from the New King James version of the Bible. Copyright © 1982 by Thomas Nelson, Inc. Used by permission. All rights reserved.

Scripture quotations marked NIV are taken from the HOLY BIBLE, NEW INTERNATIONAL VERSION®. NIV®. Copyright © 1973, 1978, 1984, 2011 by Biblica, Inc.™ Used by permission. All rights reserved worldwide.

Scripture quotations marked MSG are from *THE MESSAGE*. Copyright © by Eugene H. Peterson 1993, 1994, 1995, 1996, 2000, 2001, 2002. Used by permission of NavPress Publishing Group.

Scripture quotations marked NLT are taken from the *Holy Bible*. New Living Translation copyright © 1996, 2004, 2007 by Tyndale House Foundation. Used by permission of Tyndale House Publishers, Inc. Carol Stream, Illinois 60188. All rights reserved.

This book is a work of fiction. Names, characters, places, and incidents are either products of the author's imagination or used fictitiously. Any similarity to actual people, organizations, and/or events is purely coincidental.

Cover design: Kirk DouPonce, DogEared Design

Published by Barbour Publishing, Inc., P.O. Box 719, Uhrichsville, OH 44683, www.barbourbooks.com

Our mission is to publish and distribute inspirational products offering exceptional value and biblical encouragement to the masses.

 Member of the
Evangelical Christian
Publishers Association

Printed in the United States of America.

TINLEY PARK PUBLIC LIBRARY

A NOTE TO OUR READERS

The topic of sexual abuse is an intense and complicated one. If we had given any deeper thought to how difficult it would be to address all aspects of it, this book in all likelihood would never have been written.

We are indebted to Victoria Kepler Didato, not only for her expertise, but also for her heart and her sensitivity to victims and offenders alike. Vicky, you shine as an example of God's unconditional love. Any mistakes or inconsistencies in our representation of the therapeutic process are ours alone.

We are also grateful to the many women (and men) who have shared their journeys of healing with us and whose lives have been transformed by God's restorative love. Lest we do a great disservice to these remarkable individuals, or to other survivors who have suffered, we would like to make it clear that healing is a lifelong process.

Legacy of Fools is fictional. It is in no way intended to be a statement of how recovery should or will happen. The devastating effects of sexual abuse impact every area of its victims' and offenders' lives—physical, emotional, mental, and spiritual. The message of this book is that no man—or woman—is beyond the reach of God's grace and mercy. We do not suggest that a quick fix is realistic, nor do we intend to diminish the difficult and painful task most survivors face in dealing with their pasts or the consequences that offenders must face even after God's redemption. We do not wish to imply that forgiveness is instantaneous, nor do we intend to say that all who have been abused need therapy. Forgiveness is a process, and faith an individual journey.

To all survivors of sexual abuse and their offenders and those who love them: it is our prayer and hearts' desire to extend hope to you and to all who read this book. May each of you meet Jehovah Rapha, "the Lord who heals."

DEDICATION

From Susan's Heart

To Missy, who never stopped believing in the dream. You are amazing to work with. Thank you for keeping me motivated.

To Elaine Grant, Denise Ramser, Emily Horsfall Smith, Freda Martin, and Darcy Miller who diligently read the rough draft and gave us valuable insight—thank you.

We are grateful also to Gary Raber for answering all our insurance fraud questions.

A special thanks to Alice Henderson who took us behind the scenes of educational IT and gave Catherine a career worthy of a calling. Thank you for believing in me.

Thank you to my Circle of Friends who included me without batting an eye.

For my part, this book is dedicated to the memory of Ryan Vitt, a man who struggled much like Eric and Marty, who won the battle, obtained the victory, and is now beholding Jesus face-to-face. Cousin, I love you.

From Missy's Heart

This one is for my beloved granddaughters, Adalie, Isabel, Clara, and Sara Ann—and the generations to come. May your legacy be one of bringing Him glory.

To Ned—for always. To my precious children—J.T., Beth, Ryan, Lydia, Eric, and Emily. You are my joy.

Susan, you're the best writing partner in the world! Thanks for hanging in there with me. It's been amazing watching Him at work in and through you.

And to my wonderful Circle of Friends—thanks for giving me "a place to belong." I love doing life with each one of you.

The curse of the LORD is on the house of the wicked,
but He blesses the home of the just.
Surely He scorns the scornful, but gives grace to the humble.
The wise shall inherit glory,
but shame shall be the legacy of fools.
PROVERBS 3:33–35 NKJV

Chapter One

When I grow up, I wanna be famous. . ."

Eric Bennington watched his daughter sing at the top of her lungs and thrust her hand with the Wii controller toward the ceiling before crossing her body a half beat behind the music. Despite her enthusiasm, she had no sense of rhythm—just like her old man. He wanted to laugh but didn't. Lindsay took this singing and dancing stuff way too seriously for that. She had circled his calendar for the release date of the new dance game and made him promise to be one of the first in line to buy it.

"Dad! It's your move."

Eric jerked to attention and smiled at his daughter even as he shook his head. "I'm terrible at this, you know."

"No, Daddy. You can do it."

He began to gyrate as best as he could to the music, but he wasn't any better on his turn than she had been. How had he let his daughter talk him into this? Only because there was no one around to see him make a fool of himself. He darted a glance to the side and saw Lindsay clapping and cheering him on. He looked back in time to miss his next step and trip over his other left foot.

"Whoa, kiddo! That's it. I've had enough!" Eric flopped on the couch and tried to control his breathing. He wiped away beads of sweat from across his hairline. Maybe he could call that his workout for the day.

"That was fun! Wanna bowl now?" Lindsay bounced on the cushion beside him.

Eric shook his head. He groaned and rose from the couch. "We'd better turn off the Wii." He tugged on her braid. "It's time to go."

"Aww, Daaad."

"Sorry—but your mom's expecting us."

"Can we get an ice cream cone on the way?" She pulled on his hand and batted her big, blue eyes at him.

Eric laughed. The little squirt knew exactly how to get what she wanted. "Why not?"

They stopped at the Twisty Treat, and he bought her the double scoop mint chocolate chip she requested and a butter pecan for himself. They sat at the stone picnic table and watched as a family drove up in a station wagon. Several children tumbled out of the car and ran toward the concession window. Eric licked at the drips running down the side of his waffle cone onto his fingers and only partially listened to Lindsay chattering on about how she was sure she would be the shortstop on her softball team this year because the coach had told her so. He nodded and made all the reassuring responses, but his heart and mind weren't really listening. He was too worried about what he had to tell his daughter. It was the last thing that he really wanted to do.

Lindsay had suffered so much in the last two years; he hated being the one to cause her more pain. During the last couple of years, they'd adjusted to the divorce. All of them had come to terms with being a part-time family living in two separate houses, but this new wrinkle was going to be difficult for both of them—and how could a nine-year-old possibly understand the complications of their family relationships when even he couldn't at thirty-nine?

He wiped at his sticky fingers and mopped up the dab of ice cream on Lindsay's chin then threw away the napkin. He couldn't procrastinate any longer. He had to tell her, no matter how hard it was going to be for both of them.

"Daddy, please don't go."

Lindsay's arms tightened around his neck. Two fat tears pooled in her eyes and rolled down her face, leaving a streak in the smudge of dirt on her cheek. Eric gently wiped it away. He shifted to relieve the stress on his right knee and tightened his arm around Lindsay. "Please don't cry."

"Daddy, why can't we be a family like we used to be?"

Why indeed? Eric was feeling older by the minute. "Sweetie, you already know why we can't be a family like we used to be."

The kid-swapping schedule he and Catherine had worked out was crazy, but it was the only one that made all their lives work. Explaining their new living situation to Lindsay had been harder than he'd imagined.

"But why can't Marty and me be together? How come we have to keep living apart? I want Marty and me to go back and forth like we did before." Those two fat tears became a river running down her cheeks.

"Shhh. It's okay, honey. It'll be all right." He kissed the top of her head and fought his own tears. It wasn't all right. It would never be right for them not to be together. He cursed the judge's decision that had brought them to this impossible situation then corrected himself. It wasn't the judge's fault; it was his son's.

Marty. What was he going to do with that kid?

"Why can't we, Daddy?"

"You know that Marty got into trouble last year, and you know that part of his punishment was to not be with you for a while.

I explained all this before, honey. Mommy and I think it will be best if Marty comes to live with me for a while."

Well, his mother and the judge seemed to think it was best, but he kept his personal thoughts from his daughter.

Lindsay squeezed his neck, and Eric loosened her grip.

"We talked about this, Linds."

"But I thought that I would get to spend a lot of the summer with Gran, and now..."

"We'll see what we can do. It's not like we won't spend time together. I'll still come and see you." He eased her away from him and smoothed her damp hair away from her forehead. "Now, you're going to have to be brave for your old dad and good for your mom, okay?"

Lindsay swiped the tears off her cheek with the back of her hand and gave a reluctant nod. Eric gave her a gentle swat on the seat of her jean shorts. "Okay, then, go on in, and let your mother know I'm here."

His daughter kicked a pebble across the sidewalk then paused halfway to the front door and turned around. She placed a hand on her jutted hip, looking exactly like her mother did when she wanted to cajole him into doing what she wanted. "When will I get to come see you again?"

Eric unbent his stiff knee and straightened himself until he was upright. With the mess their lives were in right now, it didn't seem like it would be anytime soon, but he didn't want to tell his daughter that. He cleared his throat then replied with a forced cheerfulness. "I can't say right now, honey, but I'm sure it won't be too long. And don't forget that even if you can't live with me while I have Marty, I'll still come see you, and you'll come stay with me sometimes."

"Promise?"

Eric drew his fingers across his heart and nodded. "I promise."

He watched her run up the front steps, her crooked braid

swinging over her shoulder. He still hadn't mastered the art of styling her hair. He shrugged his shoulders. Linds didn't seem to mind. The door slammed shut, and Eric turned to lean his arms on the hood of his Jeep. He was as weary as he had ever been in his life.

How had things unraveled so badly? Two years ago he had come home from work to find his house empty, his wife and children gone. "Irreconcilable differences" her divorce papers claimed. If nothing else, it seemed they agreed they couldn't get along.

"Marty's coming. He's getting his stuff." Catherine's voice was soft, but her words were clipped.

Eric shoved away from the Jeep and turned around. She'd come from the garage. No wonder he hadn't heard the front door.

His eyes tracked over his ex-wife, and he felt a familiar pull of desire. She was dressed in a dark blue business suit with a light pink blouse and matching shoes. He swallowed and shifted his eyes back to her heart-shaped face.

He rested his hip against the car and folded his arms. How could she have changed so much through the years and still look exactly like the day he met her? His world evaporated and reshaped into the past. He'd just finished his tour of duty, and his last military buzz cut hadn't grown out yet. He had been looking for a distraction before heading back home and seeking employment. One of his army buddies had set her up as his blind date. He'd only wanted a night of fun: what he found was an instant attraction to a petite china doll who had surprised him with her feisty spirit.

"I'm not crazy about military guys." She had stared him down, and with a tilt of her head and hands on her hips she had dared him to change her mind.

He'd felt dizzy and more than a little out of control. It was a heady feeling after the years of mental discipline to keep his emotions reigned in. He smiled wide. "Hmm. I love a good challenge. Win or lose, the game should be fun."

Somewhere along the way they had lost his buddy and his date, who turned out to be Catherine's sister. They'd argued and laughed the whole night about everything from their favorite bands to what to have for dessert. Before the weekend was over, Eric had fallen hard. However, convincing her to fall for him had been another matter. He had pursued her with all the passion that was in his heart, and the day he had slipped the silver band on her finger, he knew she was his forever. Or so he had thought. They'd had some great times—some good years—so what had changed? When had it grown sour?

One thing that hadn't changed was his attraction for her. She was still gorgeous—and still tiny even after two children. The sheen of Cat's blond hair glinted in the glare of the sun, and she held up a hand to shield her eyes—or was it to ward off the unseemly advances of the evil prince? Eric swallowed a bitter laugh. If she felt uncomfortable with his stare, too bad. She was a beautiful woman, and he had the right to look at her even if. . . Eric stopped that train of thought. He had enough problems in his life without going there.

Catherine's dress shoes tapped against the asphalt as she stepped closer to him. "This is best, you know. Marty needs his father right now. He's fighting me every step of the way. It's time you dealt with his problems for a while."

A flare of anger heated Eric's belly. What did she think he'd been doing for the last year and a half? The court case, the child custody swapping, not to mention paying for therapy sessions and trying to explain to their daughter why they had to keep her brother away from her. If Catherine had kept better control of Marty in the first place. . .

"God knows I've been a better parent than you!" Catherine's shrill voice told him she'd heard his mumbled words. Electric blue eyes glared at him. The seething anger would have contorted anyone else's face, but Catherine's fury just seemed to light her from the inside. On more than one occasion he had intentionally egged her on just to watch her Irish blood boil and see that fire light her face. Besides, she made up with the same passion in which she fought. Eric shook his head to come back to the present. That had been a long time ago, and now he just wanted a truce.

If God knew anything, He knew none of this was Eric's choosing. She was the one who had wanted out, not him. He ran his hand over his mouth and tugged on his beard to keep from saying something he'd regret. The spikes of his whiskers poked his hand, and he counted to twelve before he replied. "What do you expect me to do, Cat?"

Her full lips thinned before she answered. "Just be there for your son, Eric."

"I have been there for *my* son. I was there when he was born. I was there when we brought him home from the hospital. I was ther—"

She interrupted him. "That's not what I meant, and you know it. You need to support him."

"I have supported him! I supported him when we were a family. I support him with child support. I supported him with court fees and attorney fees and—"

"Try some emotional support! Try not to belittle him and the efforts he's making."

"Belittle him! When have I ever done that?"

"When have. . . ?" Catherine threw up her hands before letting them fall at her side. "Ever since he was a little boy, Eric. You locked him out of your heart years ago!" Before Eric could respond, she held up her hand. "Forget it!" She shook her head. "I'm wasting my breath. We've already been down that road." She stepped closer until the pointy end of her pink heels was touching his worn work boots. "If you need to blame someone, go ahead and blame me. Blame yourself, even. But quit blaming your son.

He didn't do anything wrong."

Eric clenched his jaw. "Really? What about all the stupid stunts he's pulled? How about breaking curfew and ducking out on his last therapy session? How about—"

How about him getting caught with his own six-year-old cousin? Eric slammed the brakes on his runaway thoughts, wishing he could slam something else as well. This was a Movie of the Week, a Jerry Springer special; it didn't happen in real life. Not to his family. But it had happened, and now he had to deal with the fallout.

He folded his arms and waited, but when she finally spoke, the firecracker had fizzled to a sparkler. "Eric, he's a child screaming for attention. Don't you get it?" Catherine rubbed her hands over her eyes as her voice slid to a tired sigh. She slumped against the fender and watched him for a long moment, but he refused to be the one to break the tense silence. Her eyes roamed across his face as if searching for something. "Where is the man I fell in love with fifteen years ago? What did you do with him?"

You killed him. You ripped the heart right out of him. She'd skinned, gutted, and hung his emotions out to dry. "Quit changing the subject. This isn't about me, Catherine." Eric strode to the driver's side of the vehicle and opened the door.

Catherine followed him, sparks spitting from her eyes again. "It never is. Frankly, I'm tired of covering for you. Don't miss any more of his counseling sessions, Eric. No more stupid excuses, or I'll go talk to the judge personally!"

Eric muttered under his breath. "Why does it always have to end like this? Just go get your son, Cat." He slid behind the wheel, but Catherine stopped him from closing the door. Her fingernails dug into the flesh on his wrist as if trying to punctuate the point she was trying to get across.

"Marty is your son, too. Maybe it's time you started acting like a father to him." She slammed the door of the car and retreated toward the house. "Marty!" Catherine's voice reverberated all the way to the inside of the car. "Your father's ready to go."

Eric turned the key and pushed the gas pedal, revving the engine.

Acting like a father to Marty. Now there's an idea. Catherine just didn't get it. He'd tried. Six months after Catherine had walked out with the kids, and a mere three weeks after their divorce was finalized, a Sunday school teacher had turned in his son for molesting his younger cousin. "It's not what it looked like," was his son's only defense, and the then twelve-year-old Christopher Martin Bennington had been detained in the county detention center and their entire lives had been plunged into a soap opera.

Child Social Services had come and ripped his sister Lindsay from her home, briefly placed her in the custody of the court while he and Catherine had been investigated; then Lindsay had been sent to live with him until the sentence had been handed down. It had been good to have Lindsay home with him again. Marty had been put on probation and issued a severe fine along with payment of the court costs, which he was required to pay with money that he had earned. As a part of his sentencing, it was mandatory that he seek counseling at the expense of his parents. Make that at the expense of his father. They had joint, but rotating, custody of the kids. Now Catherine had made claim that Eric needed more custody time with Marty, and the judge had agreed. Marty now had six months to go until the judge would review his case. It couldn't come fast enough for Eric.

He was just about to blow the horn when Marty appeared in a ragged T-shirt and a pair of jeans that had seen better days. Long bangs hung over his eyes, and the rest of his hair was pulled back in a ponytail, exposing the shaved underside of his head. Eric shook his head. He could remember his son's first haircut. Catherine had trimmed the long strands of white-blond hair and saved them in his baby book.

As Marty came down the steps, in his mind Eric could still see the little boy running to greet him when he'd gotten home from work, mitt in hand, begging his daddy to play ball with him. No mitt in his hand now. Just a duffel bag that he threw in the back of the vehicle. Marty slammed the door then climbed into the passenger seat.

"Got everything?"

"Yeah."

Eric waited, but Marty kept his head turned toward the window. "Buckle up." That got a response. Eric pushed in the clutch and ignored his son's rolling eyes and impatient sigh.

"Wait!"

Now what? Before Eric could ask, Marty was out the door and halfway up the drive at a loping run. It was Eric's turn to sigh. He began to take the car out of gear, but in his impatience dumped the clutch and stalled it out. He was just restarting the car when Marty reappeared with his iPod.

"Almost forgot my tunes." Marty bent his head to adjust his seat-belt strap, and Eric noticed something shining through his bangs.

"What's that?" He shoved the hair away from his son's eyebrow. A circle of silver pierced the skin above his eye. "Your mom let you do that?"

Marty jerked away. "Mom didn't let me do nothin'. It's my body. I decide what to do with it."

That was the problem. The boy did what he felt like without thought or regard to anyone else. Eric clenched the steering wheel. It was a waste of breath to argue with him, but everything in him wanted to make him see the foolishness of his behavior. He opened his mouth to respond to Marty, but he had put his earphones in and tuned everything else out.

Eric was left with a view of the back of his ponytail bobbing in beat to the music.

It seemed it was too late now. Eric could only wonder if it was too late for any kind of communication with the boy. He shifted the Jeep into REVERSE.

It was going to be a long drive home.

Chapter Two

Catherine closed the front door and rested her forehead against it. Why was this so hard? She knew that she had made the right decision, but every encounter with Eric made her doubt herself. She heard his car start again, and she pulled back the curtain on the skylight beside the door and watched him back out of the driveway. Marty was slumped down in the passenger seat. Catherine swallowed the lump that formed in her throat. Guilt mixed with the sense of relief she was feeling in not having to deal with Marty's drama.

"It's not fair!" Marty had yelled at her only hours ago when Catherine had explained that he was going to live with his dad while Lindsay came here. There were no good options, and right now Catherine just needed a break. Marty needed his father, whether he would admit it or not. And Eric. . .

Catherine sighed and pushed herself away from the door then headed down the hallway. She peeked in on Lindsay and found her sprawled in front of the TV watching cartoons. Satisfied, she moved down the hall to Marty's room. It looked like a clothing bomb had gone off. Whatever he hadn't packed to take to his dad's had exploded throughout the room. Clothes spilled out of open drawers, and the closet door stood open, revealing a pile of clothes stuffed in a corner.

Catherine couldn't tell whether they were dirty or clean. With another deep sigh, she began to pick them up. Just another area she was failing in as a mother. It was easier to do it herself than to fight with her son about keeping his room clean. What was it they said, pick your battles? It seemed there were too many to choose from when it came to her teenage son. "Fasten your seat belt Katie-Girl, cause yer headin' into the teen war zone." Her dad's voice from a few years ago came back to haunt her. "Raising teenagers is an awful lot like dancin' in a minefield. I know. I raised four."

"Okay, Da, but it can't be that bad."

No. It was far worse than she ever imagined. She snapped the sheet over the bed. Marty's sheets were clean at least. He had only spent one night in his bed since she'd washed them. More often than not he fell asleep on the couch. Another battle she'd lost. She yanked the covers up smoothed his bedspread, then took another look around the room. She stacked his books on his desk and straightened the papers then moved to clean off his dresser. She lifted a pair of dirty socks off a framed photograph and used them to clean the dust off the lamp and the corner of the dresser. She picked up the frame and stroked the face of the sleeping baby. How long ago it seemed.

She and Eric looked so young. Marty had only been days old when this was taken. The photo sitting on Marty's nightstand spoke volumes of his desire for a solid family and his need for his dad's affection. If Eric only knew which of the photographs Marty chose to have sitting beside his bed, maybe Eric would finally see their son's great need. Catherine sighed again, sat down on the edge of the bed, and continued to stare at the picture.

Eric had been so ecstatic when he'd found out it was a boy. It was the only time she had ever seen him cry. Eric had picked out the baby's middle name. She wanted Christopher after her dad, and when he chose Martin after his own father she was surprised because his relationship with his dad wasn't the best, and she had asked Eric if they could call the baby "Marty."

Eric had been so proud! And he'd been a real hands-on dad. He didn't even mind changing diapers. He was better at putting Marty to sleep than she was, too. She remembered waking up one night to find his side of the bed empty. . . .

She stumbled from the bed, still half asleep, and staggered down the hall to the nursery to check on the baby. The door stood ajar, and in the faint glow from the night-light, she could see Eric sitting in the secondhand rocker soothing the fretful bundle in his arms. Just as she was about to step into the room, she heard his softly spoken words.

"Hey, little guy. I know life seems kind of tough right now. Your world is the now and present, and it's not suiting you much. But I promise it will get better. Shhh. It's gonna be all right."

Catherine leaned against the doorframe. In the dim light, Eric's face was in shadow. He lifted the baby up to kiss his forehead.

"I'm here for you, little guy. I always will be. That's what dads are for." He shifted the baby to his shoulder, set the rocker moving faster, and began to hum an unfamiliar tune. Catherine stepped back from the doorway. It was too precious a moment to interrupt, and she crept back to bed.

It had all seemed so perfect then. Until the arguments had started. Until the doubt and mistrust had set in. Until. . .

Catherine swiped the front of the picture and set it back on the dresser. That was all in the past. She yanked a T-shirt off the corner of the drawer and picked up the remaining clothes on the floor.

The arguments remained, but the rest was gone. A wisp of an illusion she could no longer grasp. Eric's stubborn pride had brought them to an impasse. Even if she wanted to, there was nothing she could do to change it now. She shut the dresser drawers and glanced one more time around her son's room.

She wouldn't give up on Marty. She wouldn't give up on Eric either, at least not on his responsibilities toward his son. Their marriage might be over, but she would fight to the death to get him to start being the father she knew he could be. That once upon a time he had been.

"Supper's ready!" Eric called up the stairs.

"I'm not hungry."

"Marty! Get down here before your lasagna gets cold."

Eric didn't wait for a reply. By the time he made it back to the dining room, he heard the heavy clomp of feet on the bare, wood stairs. His son was grumbling under his breath, but Eric chose to ignore it. Conversation might be limited, but at least he was coming to the table for dinner.

Eric scooped some lasagna onto his son's plate and handed him the bowl of garlic bread. He moved the bottle of salad dressing and set it beside Marty's salad bowl. "Got everything you need in your room?"

His son shrugged and stuffed his mouth with the pasta.

So much for making an effort at communicating. Catherine was wrong. Eric tried all the time to get through to the boy. His son simply didn't care. Eric picked up his fork and dug into his own meal.

They ate in silence, but at least the food had turned out. Not bad, if he had to say so himself. He could find his way around a kitchen, but he did miss Catherine's homemade bread. The frozen kind had a slight taste of cardboard to it. He looked at Marty. His mouth was full again, and he reached for his glass of milk. So much for manners.

"We'll leave for the store at seven thirty, so be sure to set your alarm."

"Whaaat? Why can't I sleep in?"

"You heard me." Eric took a drink then wiped his mouth. "Whether you like it or not, the judge says you need supervision. It's summer. With no school, you're with me, and I work for a living." He forked a bite of salad and crunched a carrot.

"Dad! You gotta be kidding me!"

"Don't worry. I'll pay you good wages. You'll mostly be a gofer, but you'll have spending money." Eric took another bite of salad and watched his son's face. "You get half your wages. The rest goes in savings."

Marty had quit eating. "No way!"

"This isn't up for debate, Marty. You aren't at your mother's now. You are under my roof, and we're going by my rules. Your probation states you need supervision. Working through the summer months will be good for you."

"That's child labor!"

"No, it's child labor if I hire you out. It's chores if you work for me."

"Dad, I'm not—"

"Okay, fine! Your only other option is a babysitter, or do I call your parole officer?" Eric rested his arms on the table and stared at his son. He wasn't thrilled about it either. He wasn't exactly excited about having an angry teenager working for him, but there really was no other choice here.

Bare wood screeched against wood as Marty shoved his chair back from the table and stood up. "Whatever." He threw his napkin on the table. "I'm full." He clomped back up the stairs and slammed his bedroom door shut.

Eric sighed. Round one to him. Or not. He looked at the half-eaten dinner and the mess left on the table. His own appetite was gone. His heart felt bruised, aching for the laughter and easy chatter of his baby girl. Or the quiet. He'd even take the mindless quiet of the empty house next to the hostility rising around him.

He rose and began clearing away the dishes. Things were definitely different now. He remembered a time when laughter and banter swirled around his dinner table. When listening to the children and his wife were the highlights of his day and the thoughts of coming home were pure joy.

He scraped the leftovers off the plates and watched as the garbage disposal chewed through a crust of bread. The motor ground as it struggled to handle the mess. His own life felt just as chewed up and spit out.

He set the dishwasher to run its wash cycle and pushed the button. He was ready for his recliner. But after fifteen minutes of channel surfing, he shut off the TV. He pilfered through his collection of history books, but he had read them all countless times. He plopped back in his chair and closed his eyes. He couldn't seem to get his mind to unwind.

He rose and headed upstairs and knocked on Marty's door. The deep *thump-thump* of the bass from his stereo was his only reply. He held out his hand to knock again and let it fall to his side. *Live to fight another day*. The advice seemed appropriate for the circumstances. He went back downstairs and headed out to the patio.

He dropped onto the padded chair and clasped his arms behind his head. Times like this he wished he still smoked. The nicotine had a way of quieting his brain, and he could see things better through the haze of smoke, but Catherine didn't like the smell, and he'd quit shortly after meeting her. He'd have walked on the face of the sun for her in those days. Back when her eyes had only been for him, before everything had drained down a hole.

The sun had set, and night was dropping like one of his grandmother's soft down quilts over the backyard. He spotted the first star, and then several others began to peek out. Too many lights to see much in the suburbs. Nothing beat the night sky at his grandparents' farm. He remembered pitching a tent with his brother Geoff on the hill overlooking the farmhouse. They'd been big-game hunters, wild and free, their imaginative adventures the stuff of books and legend. Now he was just tame and tired.

He left his chair and wandered out to check the lock on his toolshed. The door hung with a slight lean to the left, but it was secure when he tugged on it. It was too dark to fix it now, but he made a mental note to add it to his Sunday chores list. Another project to decide if he wanted to try to get Marty involved in. He shook his head. His own father hadn't given him a choice in whether he would work around the house, but with Marty it felt like he was continually doing a balancing act. Push too hard and it might shove him right over the edge. The kid seemed to be on a teeter-totter and could go either way. Eric's frustration and anger with him had shifted somehow. Tonight he felt only sadness and a deep sense of something lost and out of reach. Eric turned and headed back indoors. He could still hear the faint beat of Marty's stereo.

He locked the patio doors and turned off the lights in the kitchen and hallway. He checked the front door and made sure the alarm was set. He turned in the shadows and looked at the spotlighted portrait on the wall. Their family portrait, taken only weeks before Catherine had left. Their smiling faces hid the turmoil that would soon erupt—or had already erupted but they were trying to hide. Eric stepped closer to the picture. If you looked at the eyes, you could tell.

He reached out and drew a finger down the length of Catherine's hair. Anger surged, and he turned on his heel to shut off the lights in the living room and head upstairs. No use longing for what he couldn't have. It was all a facade anyway. That picture of the happy family. Underneath was a swirling mass of lies and deceit.

Eric took the stairs two at a time. One day he would get to the truth.

Chapter Three

Marty stumbled over the pile of two-by-fours and followed his dad through the open framework of the unfinished house. The sound of hammers, air guns, saws, and shouts of the work crew rang out through the early morning. Marty used the bottom of his T-shirt to wipe the beads of sweat already forming on his brow. He checked his iPod. He had been up for two hours, and it was only eight o'clock.

"Marty, get the box of electrical wire from the truck."

"Yeah, whatever." Marty turned his back, so his father couldn't hear the rest of his words. The old man was already on his back about being late this morning.

"And grab that plastic bag beside the box while you're at it."

He couldn't believe he was actually wishing it was time for school to start. Two weeks of working for his dad proved it was going to be a long summer. He shoved the box under one arm and grabbed the bag of supplies. He checked to make sure he'd stuffed his iPod in his pocket. At least he still had his tunes. Too bad he didn't have a phone; it would be nice to be able to text his buddies. Fat chance that would happen anytime soon. He turned to walk back to the house. What made his dad want to work on a Habitat project anyway?

Just as Marty got to the steps, he saw a tall man with light curly hair walk up to his dad and slap him on the back, knocking him forward.

"Bennington."

His dad turned around. "Hey, Trav!" He rubbed at his beard. Marty wondered if he knew how goofy he looked playing with the scruff on his face. His dad grinned at the other man. "How's it going?"

The man gave him a thumbs-up. "Great! We have another twelve volunteers coming in tomorrow, so that should put us ahead of schedule, and we'll finish this Habitat house early. Depending of course on our passing electrical codes—how's that looking, inspector?"

"No problems so far." Marty's dad glanced around the construction site and then nodded his head toward Marty. "I brought along a helper today. Have you had a chance to meet my kid yet? Marty! Get over here."

Marty dropped the box at his dad's feet, earning him a glare. He set the bag on top of the electrical wire and shoved his hands in his back pockets and looked at the guy beside his dad wearing torn jeans and a Guns N' Roses T-shirt. Who was this guy?

"Travis Jamison, meet my son, Marty. Marty, this is Reverend Jamison."

Travis held out his hand. "Everyone calls me 'T.' "

Marty watched his father frown. He held out his hand to Travis. "Cool. Nice to meet you, T."

His dad crossed his arms, and Marty saw disapproval written all over his face. "I think you'd better make that Reverend or Pastor T." Marty shoved his hands in his back pockets. He hadn't even done anything, and his dad was already on his back. He swallowed past a lump that seemed lodged in his throat and wondered for the millionth time what he had done to make his dad hate him so much.

"Chill, Bennington." Travis punched his dad in the arm. "I gave him permission."

Marty stared at Travis and felt a smug grin trying to make its way to his face. He worked hard to keep it from reaching his lips. Man, he liked this guy already. He didn't seem like any preacher he had ever met.

Travis laughed. "Now that's a compliment."

He must have muttered that one out loud. He glanced up and saw his old man look at him, and then back at Travis, then open his mouth and let out a bark of laughter.

"It's okay, kid. I thought the same thing first time I met this guy. At a Habitat project like this one. I was standing next to him when he slammed his finger with a hammer, let out a streak of cuss words, and then apologized for the next fifteen minutes."

A red flush started up Travis's neck. "Yeah, well I'm still working on that. It's a holdover from my days working on a construction crew before seminary. Won't be perfect till I get to heaven."

"I can vouch for that."

"You're one to talk!" Travis slapped his dad on the back again and motioned toward the electrical wires. "We standing around talking, or are you going to put us to work?"

This was one strange dude. A preacher who swore and could put his dad in his place. Marty felt his entire body relax in the presence of this guy. It was the first time in a very long time he felt like he could let his guard down around his father because it appeared that Pastor T just might cover his back.

At lunchtime Marty hopped in his dad's work truck. He wouldn't admit it out loud, but it hadn't been that bad of a morning. One of the guys at the site had let him use the nail gun. It was nice not being treated like a kid for once.

His dad climbed behind the wheel and spoke as he closed the

door. "We'll get some lunch, then I need to head over and pick up your sister." His dad glanced at him. "You'll be with your mom until I bring Linds back."

Marty turned toward the window. He watched the people moving along the sidewalk in front of the downtown storefronts. He wondered where they were going, all in a hurry like that. What kind of life did they have? *Better than mine.*

He swallowed down the lump that formed in his throat. It wasn't fair. None of this was fair. His parents fighting, the divorce, the constant moving back and forth was so hard. Marty remembered picnics and parties, water fights that his mom would start, and while his dad had been stern with him, he had been fair. But that world had been built on an illusion, and some evil magician had waved his magic wand, and it all disappeared. Now all that seemed to exist was hostility, frustration, and neither parent really wanted him around. He and Lindsay were shuttled back and forth like unwanted garbage, and the only time he got to see her was for an hour before they went to their separate corners of the world. It wasn't fair. Especially to her! She didn't deserve any of this.

His eyes tracked a young girl, Lindsay's age, riding her bike down the street, and he swallowed hard. The vision blurred. He blinked several times to rid his eyes of the unshed tears. He would not let his dad see him cry! But Marty missed his sister.

"I asked you if you remembered your overnight bag!" Marty startled at the sound of his dad's impatient voice. He was always harsh and critical. The words *Why do you hate me so much?* almost tumbled from his tongue. He bit his lips and mumbled instead, "I got it. It's behind the seat." What did it matter anyway? The guy really didn't care about him. He just wanted to shuffle him off on his mother—and she just dumped him back on his dad.

At least she let him use the Internet. His old man had his password protected, not like that had stopped him, but his computer was in the den, and it was hard to find any time alone there.

His dad was telling him the "rules"—like he didn't know them or something. So he had messed up once or twice. Hadn't he paid for it by now? He went to those dumb counseling sessions. He was doing everything they told him to. Why couldn't they cut him some slack?

Marty reached for his iPod and put in his earphones. It didn't do any good to try to talk to his dad. He didn't believe him, and he didn't listen to a word he said. His dad kept talking, but Marty turned up the music to shut him out.

Chapter Four

Catherine slammed on the brakes. Her tires squealed, and the puppy she had narrowly missed yelped and scrambled to the curb. She dropped her forehead to the steering wheel. Thank God the little girl standing on the sidewalk hadn't run out into the street when she called the dog. A car horn beeped, and she lifted her head. She made sure there were no more kids or dogs close at hand and moved down the street at a cautious pace.

She glanced at the clock when she pulled into the garage. She'd left Marty at home while she ran to the store. It was easier than fighting with him. She gathered up the grocery bags and elbowed her way through the back door. She set her load down on the kitchen counter and called through to the living room. No answer. She was halfway up the stairs when she heard the *wump-thump* of Marty's speakers and turned around to head back to the kitchen. She needed to conserve what little strength she had. At least he couldn't get into trouble in his room. Much.

Catherine put the frozen items in the freezer. The phone rang. "Hello." She clamped the phone between her ear and shoulder as she opened the refrigerator to put the milk away.

"Cathy, it's Mom. How's my darlin' girl?"

"Good, Mom. How's Da feeling?"

"His hip is much better. But you know how it is when Arthur Itis comes to visit. He's just. . ."

"A pain." Catherine finished the long-standing joke.

"He's feeling well enough that I'm having trouble keeping him down!"

"That's Da!" Catherine switched the phone to her other ear and opened a cupboard. An ache settled in her throat. She rolled her shoulders to release their stiffness. She should have been out to see her parents before now. Her mother's diabetes and her dad's arthritis made it difficult for them to get around. "How are you feeling?"

"Oh, I'm fine, honey."

"So what's been happening?" Catherine asked. "Heard from Carrie and Connie?"

"Your sisters are fine. As a matter of fact, I called to let you know that Connie and Tony are coming home, and we want to have a family get-together when they come. Any chance you and the kids can make it?"

Catherine's brother-in-law was a commander in the navy and was stationed in Hawaii. "When does Tony's leave start? I haven't talked to them for a while."

"They'll get here next week. I'd like to plan a day when we could all get together."

"Mom. . ." Catherine paused and opened the pantry door then shut it and leaned against it. "You know that Lindsay and Marty aren't allowed to be together for more than two hours at a time, and then they have to be totally supervised. . . ."

"I'm sorry. I forgot. But still you and Lindsay can come."

"Do you really think it's a good idea for me to come?"

"Oh, honey! You worry too much! You and Connie have talked all this out."

Catherine swallowed hard. They had, but it still felt awkward. Her sigh was loud enough that her mother picked up on it.

"You have talked it all out with Connie, right? Honey, if there are things that need to be resolved, you need to do it. You two have always been so close, Cathy. Don't let bad blood come between you girls. We know Marty's had troubles, but he's getting better now. Besides, isn't he living with Eric?"

"Yes, but he's here for a few days, and Lindsay is seeing her dad. Our schedule is just insane right now." Catherine twisted the phone cord around her finger. "I haven't talked to Connie since just after they moved."

"Well, Bethy's doing fine. All that's behind her now. Cathy, please try to come. It's been almost six years since the entire family has been together, and it would be a wonderful gift from you girls. It would be so wonderful to have everyone here. At least as many of us that can get together."

"I'll try but my schedule. . ."

"Okay, I know that's my cue to quit pushing. If you can make it, then come. If you can't, you know we still love you."

Catherine assured her mother she would do her best and hung up the phone with more force than she intended. She exhaled deeply. She really did miss her family, and it would be wonderful to see them all again, but this—thing—still stood between them. *So call her.* The last thing she wanted to do was call her sister. They had been so close until. . .

She dug into the grocery bag and began setting canned goods on the counter. It wasn't really over. They were still reeling from the effects of the whole fiasco. She stacked the cans in the pantry, knocking over the next stack of red beans. She shook her head. At the moment, the beans proved to be a pretty good metaphor for her life. What a mess. Tears blurred her vision. She straightened the cans then began to fold the bags scattered on the counter. When had it all fallen apart?

Marty wasn't a bad boy. Memories swirled of a towheaded Marty leaning over her shoulder staring in wonder and excitement at his newborn baby sister and a few years later Marty twirling Lindsay around in a circle until both of them were dizzy. They had fallen laughing to the ground. She remembered Marty wiping Lindsay's tears away when she had fallen off her bike and skinned her knees. He had picked her up and awkwardly carried her into the house.

Catherine wanted to scream, "He's not a bad boy!" In fact, that's just what he'd been—a boy. With a boy's curiosity. Whatever had happened that day—and Catherine still wasn't sure what to believe—he hadn't intended to harm Bethy. His acting out had to do with his father. Or lack of one.

Catherine turned on the tap and filled the teakettle.

She looked out the window to the backyard. An old swing set sat weathered and forlorn in the back corner of the fence. It looked like she felt, which was ancient. When she had moved into this place, Lindsay still played on it. Even Marty would sit on the wooden deck from time to time, but Linds had outgrown it, and Marty—

She shut the water off and set the teakettle on the stove then went to the cupboard for a cup and a tea bag. She walked to the foot of the stairs. Marty's music was still blasting away. He spent hours at a time alone in his room with nothing more than the music and his own brooding silence keeping him company.

She longed for the days when the two of them would curl up together on the couch and read a book, make up a story, or just talk about their day. Marty had always been interested in what she was doing. He loved making new concoctions in the kitchen and was better at baking than she was. She had often called him "my little man."

But that was then. Right now she had other things to think about. Namely dinner and whether she should call Connie. Dinner was doable. Connie was another matter altogether. She went back to the kitchen and started preparations for dinner. She tore the lettuce into little bits then sliced tomatoes and cucumbers for the salad. She sliced the carrots in time to the argument going on in her head. She should call. She wouldn't call. She should. She wouldn't.

"Oh for pity's sake, Cat, just make the call!" She wiped her hands on the dish towel and reached for the phone. She chewed the corner of her lip as she waited for someone to answer the ringing.

"Commander Lincoln's quarters. Molly speaking."

"Hey, sweetheart! It's Aunt Cathy. Is your mom there?"

"Yeah. Hang on, Aunt Cathy. Mooom. . ."

The steam gathered in the kettle, and it began to whistle.

"This is Connie."

"Hang on." Catherine reached to pull the kettle off the hot burner. "Connie? Sorry, the tea water is hot. It's Cat."

"Cathy! It's been a while."

"Yeah. Sorry about that. Mom called and said you and Tony would be home on leave."

"For three whole weeks! Can't wait."

"What? And leave paradise? I still think we should come visit you guys."

"Anytime!"

"You know you're never getting Dad on a plane, and Mom's not going to be happy unless we're all together."

"Cath—"

She interrupted her sister. "Look, Connie, I'm sorry about everything."

"Quit apologizing already. I know it's not your fault. . .and—"

"How's she doing? Bethy, I mean," Catherine interrupted again.

Connie sighed and followed Catherine's conversational path.

"Good. The move helped a lot. I think she's forgotten it, to tell you the truth. We don't talk about it anymore. How's—how's Marty?"

"Good. I mean, he's—well, he's been in counseling. He's living with his dad now, and Lindsay is with me. He's here for a day or two and then, you know, we have to swap them back and forth." Catherine blinked back tears and dunked her tea bag up and down.

"That's tough. I'm sorry for you."

She suddenly wanted the conversation with her sister to be over. "Anyway, we'll see you next week. Lindsay and me, I mean."

"It will be good to see you, sis. I mean that."

"Yes, it will. Give the kids a hug from me."

"Sure. See you next week."

Catherine hung up the phone and picked up her tea. She blew on the surface and took a sip. The sweet smell of peppermint filled her sinuses and taste buds. She set the teacup back on its saucer and got out the frying pan and hamburger meat. Dinner still had to be cooked, and she had some files to look at after dinner for work. And she needed to talk to Marty. It was going to be hard on him being sent back to his father so soon, but it would be the only way she could visit with her family. Marty couldn't come, and he and Lindsay couldn't stay at the same place, so this was the way it would have to be.

She went up to knock on Marty's door and shouted out a five-minute dinner warning. She was just finishing setting the table when he came downstairs.

"What do you want to drink? There's milk, water, or iced tea in the fridge. Get me some water, will you?"

They sat down at the table in the kitchen. The dining room was just for display these days. Marty wolfed down two burgers and had a second helping of salad, but Catherine could only manage to nibble at the cucumbers.

"How's it going at your dad's?"

Marty shrugged and kept chewing.

"Marty?"

"Fine."

Catherine watched him drink half his glass of milk without taking a breath. The boy must be going through a growth spurt. She could hardly keep him full. "Want some applesauce?"

Marty shook his head. "You gonna eat your burger?"

Catherine shoved her plate toward him. "Help yourself."

She watched him eat his third burger and gulp down another glass of milk, wishing he was as eager to engage in conversation as he was in eating.

"So, at least you're making a little money, huh?"

"I guess." He shrugged one shoulder then asked, "Mom, would you get me a cell phone if I paid for it?"

She started to say yes then thought better of it. If she wanted Eric to handle him, she'd better let him make some of these decisions. "What's your dad say?"

Marty rolled his eyes. "Whadda ya think? He says no to everything. Just because he can."

"I'm sure that's not true."

"Whatever." Marty shoved his chair away from the table.

"Where are you going?"

"To my room."

Catherine nodded at the table. "At least take your dishes to the sink."

She watched him scoop up his plate and silverware then fill another glass of milk. "Bring that back downstairs. You know it'll smell if you leave it up there."

"Yeah, yeah."

"And Marty?"

"What?" He stopped in the doorway and looked at her. His bangs shadowed his eyes. She wished he would cut his hair.

"You know I love you, right?"

He gave one nod of his head, took a swallow of milk, and

turned to go out the door. The phone rang, and Marty raced to grab it. " 'Lo?"

Catherine watched his shoulders go rigid. It had to be Eric. "Yeah, she's here." He stretched his arm out her direction. She raised an eyebrow at him.

"It's Dad. He wants to talk to you." He dropped the phone in her hand and sprinted out the door as he mumbled something incoherent.

She drew a deep breath before lifting the phone to her ear. Eric only called when there was a problem with the children's schedule. Usually it was to try to have some extra time with Lindsay.

"Hello, Eric."

"Hi, Cat." Eric cleared his throat. "Listen. . ."

She set her jaw. *Here it comes. He's going to try to weasel out of his responsibilities toward Marty.*

She sat up straight. Had she really heard him correctly? "Eric, I'm sorry, I missed that last question. What did you just say?"

Catherine heard his intake of air. One of his complaints against her had been that she only half listened to him. She guessed she was guilty of that after all.

"I said I would like to pick Marty up early. My friend Travis has invited Marty and me to go white-water rafting with a group of guys, and I need him here so we can get an early start. Any problems with that?"

Absolutely none! She wanted to sing out the words. But held herself back. She felt her heart lifting. Maybe Eric was trying after all. "No, I don't see a problem with that. Have you told Lindsay? Does Marty know?"

"Yes, I talked to Linds. She's okay with it."

She shifted the phone to her other ear. She really wanted to ask Eric about this Travis fellow. Who was he? How did he manage to get Eric to do with Marty what she had been trying all their married life to get him to do? But she knew what he would say if she asked. Instead, she asked, "Do you want me to put Marty back on the phone?"

She walked to the stairs and called up, "Marty! Your dad wants to ask you something! Grab the upstairs phone." She waited until she heard Marty's sullen hello and then pressed the OFF button and turned to the disarray of the kitchen. She smiled despite the fact that another change was coming. She wondered what Marty's reaction to his father's invitation would be and if he would share that reaction with her. She didn't have long to wait.

Marty returned to the kitchen a few moments later carrying the empty milk glass plus two dinner plates, a dessert dish, and a bowl that looked like its contents had been petrified a millennium ago.

"Christopher Martin, I have been looking for that bowl for a month." She spoke with mild reproof. Her heart was just too light to be angry over missing dishes. "Where was it?"

He sent her a sheepish grin. "I found it under my stack of Joe Boxers."

"Ewww. Put it in the dishwasher, and set the temp for scald!"

He laughed. Tears formed in Catherine's eyes. It had been years since she had heard that lighthearted giggle of his. Oh, how she missed it. She refrained from pulling him into a hug. Instead she popped lids onto the food containers and placed them in the refrigerator. Catherine's eyebrows rose when she saw Marty stacking the dinner dishes into the dishwasher. "So, what did your dad want?"

"Didn't he tell you?" Marty leaned into the bottom cupboard and pulled out the dishwasher detergent. He plopped the little pillow of soap into the tray and closed the door then leaned against the counter.

Catherine reached for the dishrag and wiped the stove. "You tell me."

"Pastor T has invited us to go white-water rafting." There was none of the usual sullen belligerence in his voice.

"So you don't want to go or anything, do you?" Catherine teased him as she poured them both a ginger ale. She handed him a glass and then sat down at the table.

His head came up, and he stared at her for a moment. "Naw." He said it with a straight face, but there was a twinkle of excitement in his eyes that couldn't be hidden. He surprised her by pulling up a chair and straddling it. "I mean, water, sun, a wild ride, all those guys taking on the river. Hanging with a dude like Pastor T. . . Well, it's more than a man can deal with."

Catherine chuckled. It was the best conversation she'd had with Marty in months. "And your dad."

Some of the joy left his face. "Yeah, there is that, too."

She regretted the remark as soon as she said it. "So who's this 'T' fellow?"

Marty's face lit back up. He swigged down the rest of his soda and reached for the bottle. "He's really cool. He's a preacher, *and* he's dad's friend."

"Really?" Catherine tried to imagine Eric friends with a pastor. She couldn't fathom it. "Nice guy, huh?"

"Nice isn't the word, Mom. He's just this really—real guy, know what I mean? He like, accepts you just where you are, and he really listens to you. It's like he knows what you are saying 'cause maybe he's been there, too."

That was just what Marty needed in his life. It was too bad he had to get it from a near stranger when his own father was more like him than either cared to admit. What did it matter where the encouragement for her son came from? She was just grateful that maybe the tide was turning for him, and finally he might have an advocate in his corner. She wondered what the weekend had in store for her son.

And for that matter, the rest of his life.

Chapter Five

"Back paddle!" Eric heard the shout above the roar of water and dug his paddle deep, pushing against the force of the churning water and the pull of the inflatable raft. His stomach bottomed out along with the raft as it plummeted beneath him before heaving upward and making contact with his backside.

"Dad!" Eric started at the sudden cry and turned to see his son plunging face-first into the seething water.

"Marty!" Before Eric could shift positions he heard "River rescue!" being bellowed at the top of a strong pair of lungs and saw the instigator of this particular trip latching onto the waistband of his son's shorts and hiking him back into the bucking raft.

Travis gripped Marty's arm for a moment until the boy regained his equilibrium. He let go of the youth and attacked the swirling water with his paddle. Even as he pulled hard on the piece of wood, he called across to Marty, "Okay?" Marty wasn't given time to respond as a wave grabbed the piece of rubber and slammed it down a channel of rock where it pinballed between two boulders.

The thunderous roar of water and the exhilarated shouts of his comrades were all Eric could discern. Straining against the only thing that kept their small craft from the mercy of the water, Eric paddled hard through the rapids. Moments later the current was spitting them out of the chasm and into calmer water.

Eric heaved a sigh and ran his hand down his face, wiping rivulets of water from his eyes and beard.

"Man, that was wicked!" Marty shoved his dripping hair out of his eyes and reached for his abandoned paddle. "Thought I was going to drink the river again."

"So how many times was that Mart?" thirteen-year-old Steve Cunningham asked as he tugged the straps on his life jacket.

"Don't know—I wasn't keeping track." Marty pulled the paddle through the water in time with the youth at his side. "Figured was less than you and more'n my old man."

"Four." Eric grinned.

"Six," Travis corrected as they steered the raft through a tranquil section in the river. Sunlight splintered on the choppy surface of the muddy water. Eric watched as the banks of the river grew farther apart. The water in this section resembled polished glass. He twisted in his seat to get another look at where they had just come from. White foam boiled at the base of the channel as the turbulent river churned over the hidden rocks. *Looks like my life.*

"How's come you can't keep your seat in the easy places, my man, but you stay put during the wild rides?" Steve squeegeed his black hair between his fingers as he addressed Marty.

"When you're good, you're good, dude."

"Uh-huh. I saw your knuckles and your face as we came through that rapid, both were the same pasty white. You were terrified of spilling out. Fear was the only thing that saved your butt."

"Yeah, but your face was as green as the water under those trees, dope."

Steve ignored his companion and shifted in his seat. "Hey,

Pastor T. Where an' when are we stopping to eat anyway?" He pulled his paddle out of the water as he tipped his head back and closed his eyes against the glare of the sun.

"When you see ten other rafts pulled up on the shore, then you'll know where and when. We better light a fire under this raft...."

"Be a little hard to do with all this wet stuff under us, don't ya think, T?"

"Watch it, boy. Show a little respect." Travis growled good-naturedly as he pulled his sunglasses off his nose and narrowed his blue eyes at Marty. He turned to Eric. "You got a smart aleck, here. Are you aware of that fact, Bennington?"

"So I'm told. What would you suggest?"

"Um...let me think about that. C'mon. Paddle hard, guys. I'm starved. Let's catch up with the rest."

The small talk and teasing continued around Eric, but he ignored them as his eyes took in the scenery around him.

In the deep shade made by the trees that marched down to the bank, water lapped quietly against the sandy shore. The sky was a deep aquamarine blue with no clouds in sight. The bright sunlight beat down on his skin warming him and drying his cotton shirt. Just the hint of a breeze lifted his hair and kept the day from being hot.

Eric breathed in deeply the scent of woods and water, liking the peace and solitude that this adventure was affording him. Lately there had been too little peace and solitude in his life. When did it all start? When did chaos break loose in his life? *With Marty.* It was when Marty had gotten into trouble. Or was it when Catherine walked out and took his life with her?

Eric's eyes roved over his son. Watching him now, it was hard to believe the grief his son had caused him and his family during the last two years. *Year and a half,* Eric corrected himself. At the moment Marty was just a kid enjoying a great day with some terrific friends. Maybe this was what he needed. Maybe all he needed was to hang out with kids that would be a better influence in his life. Maybe Marty didn't need to continue with the counseling. His behavior and attitude had improved. They had actually been able to have a conversation at times. Eric was kidding himself. The kid was on his best behavior because of Travis. He brought out the best in anyone.

Eric's eyes shifted to his friend. He smiled as he watched Travis dip his paddle in the river and drench Marty with the chilly liquid.

Marty yelled, bouncing the raft as water poured down his back. With lightning quickness he dove toward the slender man and tackled him, causing the raft to buck madly, and both of them tumbled backward into the water.

"Christopher Martin, that's enough," Eric thundered as their heads bobbed to the surface. The lighthearted joy in Marty's eyes disintegrated at the hard reprimand.

"Ease up, Dad. I asked for it." Travis's light reproof broke the tension between father and son. Travis knuckled Marty on the head before grabbing him in a headlock and pulling him back under the muddy surface. Eric was quick to note that he whispered in Marty's ear, apparently telling him to hold his breath.

Eric ran a hand down the back of his head and massaged his shoulders. *You just don't understand the violence that lives beneath the surface, T. You may think he's just playing, but is he?* Eric had been paying the consequences for Marty's bad attitude and temper. He just wanted to make sure it stayed under control. Especially since T was kind enough to invite them along on this trip.

When Travis had approached him with the details, he hadn't been enthused about the whole idea.

"Oh, come on Bennington, what's the harm? You need a break from all the confusion going on in your life."

"I can't afford to take the time, Travis. The screwups at two of the construction sites messed up my well-laid schedule for the entire summer."

Travis righted his chair, bringing it back on all four legs. "Eric, I don't think you can afford not to come. It's been months since you've spent time with Marty, except as his jailer or his boss."

Eric glared at Travis as he swiped electrical supplies off his shelf. "Nice wording. Is that the way everyone sees me? Why am I always the bad guy?"

"Look, all I'm saying is the father-son rafting excursion would be good for you both. Believe it or not, there will be other fathers looking to bond with their sons. The board thought this would work better than the tired old banquets. Your trip is paid for, so come on."

A hand grabbed the bulging side of the raft, rocking Eric from his silent reverie. Travis flung his arms over the side to hang on as they continued to float down the river. "You know you need to ease up on that boy just a little."

"I did that once, Travis. I won't make the same mistake again."

"Then maybe you need to learn when to be tough and when to ease up. He's going to end up hating you, buddy."

He already does.

"Y'know we were just having a little fun. You should really try it sometime," Travis continued.

Eric's eyes narrowed at the good-natured rebuke. "I'm here, aren't I?"

"Yes, you are."

Eric turned from watching Marty hoist himself back into the raft to stare down into Travis's suntanned face. "I am having fun. That was the point of this little father-son bonding experience, wasn't it?"

"*Bonding* being the operative word." Travis hiked himself higher up onto the inflated side and lowered his voice. "You do owe Marty an apology, Eric. He did nothing wrong."

"Neither did I," Eric growled back.

Pastor Travis raised a sandy eyebrow but remained silent. Eric hated it when Jamison did that. With just the lift of his brow he could preach a thousand sermons, and every one of them sent daggers of guilt into his heart.

Eric reached over and tugged his friend the rest of the way into the boat. He turned to see Steve and Marty with their heads together. *Probably cussing out his old man.* Eric took a deep breath.

He had to admit it had been a good day—a rare day. He and Marty had been getting along, or at least they had called a truce. He didn't want to be the one responsible for destroying it. Glancing over at Travis, he saw his friend duck his head in encouragement. Eric's mouth tightened in annoyance for a moment before he laid his paddle across his knees and reached out to touch his son on his bare shoulder. Marty stiffened at the touch, and Eric almost recanted on the thought of an apology. He glanced back a second time. With his hands, Travis motioned him to continue.

"Marty, I shouldn't have yelled at you." He watched as Marty's shoulders stiffened further. Then just as quickly the boy's body relaxed.

"Doesn't matter."

Eric settled back in his position and dropped his oar into the water. He caught a small smile quirking the corners of Travis's mouth.

"What?"

Travis lifted his chin. "You call that an apology?"

"Shut up, Jamison, or I'll take you out of the boat this time," Eric retorted.

"I'm scared. Real scared."

"You ought to be."

Silence descended, and the peace from earlier settled over them once again. Eric listened but didn't join in the light banter that floated around him. He'd never had that kind of relationship with his son. Light kidding and loving words just didn't work for them. They never had.

As he paddled in sync with the others, he realized he really was glad Travis had pushed him not only to come on this outing, but also to apologize to his son. Except for a few minutes ago, this had been the best time he and Marty had spent together in a long time—maybe ever.

"Marty really seems to be enjoying himself."

Eric started at the sound of Travis's words. He shook his head as he tossed a quick smile to the man sitting beside him. "Yes, he does. So am I. Thanks, T." He cocked his head as he studied his sandy-haired friend. "How do you do that?"

"What?" Travis pushed his sunglasses back into place with his finger before returning his hand to the oar.

"Know what I'm thinking. . . In the three years I've known you, you have this really irritating and unnerving way of reading my mind."

Mellow laughter floated up from Travis. "I'm not reading your mind. Though sometimes I wish I could. I'd like to know what goes on in the dark recesses of your brain. I just know you." There was a slight pause before Travis continued, "And maybe a little discernment of the Spirit going on. Y'know, a God-thing."

It was disconcerting to think that God paid attention to him— that He might be squealing on him to his friends. Eric shifted his gaze to the bend in the river and allowed Travis's comment to slide. He saw black dots on the embankment and pointed with the tip of his paddle. "Look."

"Our long-lost mates," Travis remarked. In a matter of moments the sounds of cheering and jeering met their ears as the others on shore razzed them about their tardiness.

"C'mon, Reverend T. We're starved." A youngster's voice rose above the rest.

Travis vaulted over the side, grabbed the rope on the front of the raft and tugged it behind him as he sloshed through the shallow water to shore. "Sorry, guys. I had to get out and guide the raft through the Rock Garden before we could continue our journey. Then Marty decided to take a swim some six times, and we were constantly stopping to rescue him."

"Why? You should have let him ride downriver on his vest after the fourth dump," sixteen-year-old Zane Pyle quipped.

Marty's mouth flew open, and Travis wrapped an arm around his neck, clamping his hand over the boy's mouth. "We needed him. He's little, but he's strong."

Marty wiggled free. "Yeah, but ask him who got his leg stuck in a hole in the river when he tried to stand on a rock to take a picture." Marty pitched his paddle into the boat.

"I was taking a picture of the clowns in the raft who managed to get it caught on a rock that was hugging the surface. And we got stuck because someone doesn't know how to steer. Eric and I had to trade places with these two jokers because we kept going through the rapids backward!" Jamison explained as he headed toward the white plastic containers holding the food.

"Which way to the restrooms?" Marty queried as he approached the circle of males lounging on the ground.

Zane tossed an arm around Marty and turned him toward the hillside. "See that stand of pine trees?"

He nodded, and Zane slid his hand from Marty's shoulder to his back and pushed him in that direction. "That'd be them."

Marty groaned. "Man, I hope I don't end up with poison on my. . .tush," he quickly amended. Laughter ensued as Marty sauntered up the hill and out of sight.

Eric rolled his eyes before moving in the opposite direction and settled on a log with a soda and a plate full of food. When Eric was finished, he set his plate aside and slipped to the ground, leaning his back against the rough bark. Marty and Steve had quickly finished their lunch and went back to the river to cool off.

"I'm hungry!" Travis dropped onto the log beside Eric. "You finished already?"

"Yup. I'm not as courteous as you, waiting until everyone else had theirs." Eric grinned up at Travis, whose mouth was fully occupied. "Of course, I'm not eating with my board of directors and needing to make an impression."

Travis cocked a brow and said around his mouthful of food, "That's what I'm doing, huh?" Crumbling his paper plate, Travis rolled to his feet and deposited his trash in one of the plastic containers just moments before one of the river guides began popping on the plastic lids.

"All right, gentlemen. Time to saddle up and get a move on. Some of us managed to throw this tour off schedule with their procrastination."

One of the river guides cleared his throat. "Yeah right! And we all wonder who that would be?"

Chuckles rose throughout the glade as Travis took the insult in stride. He reached down and pulled Eric to his feet. "Come on, old man, let's show them who's procrastinating."

Three hours later found the exhilarated but weary group of men beaching their rafts for the last time. Eric stumbled out of the rubber craft and felt his knees wobble. He flopped down on the sand. "I feel awful."

"You don't look so hot either, Dad," Marty remarked as he stood over Eric.

"Thanks, kid. Your old man needed to hear those words of encouragement." Eric looked up to see a rare grin playing on Marty's face. "This is worse than I ever felt in boot camp, and that was bad."

"Can't handle a good time anymore, old man?" Travis asked as he joined Marty standing at Eric's toes.

Eric was too weary to even come up with a rebuttal.

"Here." Travis held out his hand. "Let's go up to the buildings and shower before we meet for the cookout."

Eric looked up to see both of them reaching out to him. He took each proffered hand and moaned as he was pulled to his feet. Travis flung an arm around Eric's shoulder. "Ouch! Ease up, buddy. I got some sun."

"Sorry! You up for the reenactment in July?"

"You bet. Glad it's on the Fourth."

"Isn't that your family reunion?"

Eric grinned. "Yup."

"Grandma will be p.o.'d if we miss the reunion." Marty spoke up with a hopeful sound in his voice.

Eric glanced down at Marty. Maybe they did have something in common after all: mutual distaste for family gatherings. He shrugged. "Guess she'll have to be miffed."

Marty chuckled and moved ahead of the men.

"Marty."

He turned back to his dad.

"We don't say p.o.'d"

"Since when?" Marty retorted and took off on a run for the shower house.

Eric shook his head as he watched Marty go.

"So, you don't mind missing your family reunion?"

"Never! Those things are a. . ." Eric wasn't given a chance to finish explaining how difficult his family could be. Several teenage boys rushed at Travis with a cooler of melted ice. Eric was thankful for the diversion.

His relationship with his family was difficult enough; he didn't need Travis trying to fix it—or him. Travis liked to probe into Eric's life, but it was safe to let him only go so far. The rest was better off left alone.

Chapter Six

"Marty! Get a move on! We have to get to work!" Eric yelled again before heading for his Jeep Cherokee. Any truce he and Marty may have declared on the rafting trip was long gone. The kid was back to fighting him every inch of the way. Once more, Eric wondered if Marty's attitude was because he had stayed with his mother or if it was because of the constant shuttling back and forth. He would have made him walk to work, but he knew that Marty would never show up. Instead he called out again, "Christopher Martin, don't make me haul your butt to the Jeep!"

Marty appeared in his holey jeans and hair pulled back in a ponytail. Eric wrapped his hand around his neck and kneaded the knotted muscle at the base of his skull. It was going to be a very long, very trying day. He raked his fingers through his beard as Marty slid in beside him. "Where's your uniform shirt?"

With a smug grin and great deal of drama, Marty withdrew it from the Igloo cooler he was carrying. Eric shook his head at the wrinkles and clamped down on his lower lip. He'd already had a run-in with the kid's mother today; he wasn't about to go round two with her son.

Bennington Electric store manager, Greg Tanner, looked up as Eric walked in, producing a happy, tinkling sound from the silver bell connected to the door. Eric frowned at it as he strode toward the counter. "I'm going to rip that thing off one of these days. Whose bright idea was it to put it up, anyway?"

Greg lifted his bushy gray eyebrows and smiled at him. "I believe it was yours."

Eric returned Greg's smile with one of his own. "Next time I decide to do something that stupid, slug me, will you?"

Greg's grin widened as he replied, "Be glad to, boss."

Eric chuckled and pointed to the invoices and parts scattered on the counter. "Get back to work."

Eric tossed his briefcase aside and picked up the stack of mail his salesclerk, Tanya, had yet to drop on his desk.

"The shipment came in, so I sent Luke back to begin unpacking." Greg's eyes followed Marty as he disappeared around the corner of the lunchroom to deposit his lunch box. "Got the kid this week, I see. How's it going?"

It was Eric's turn to raise a brow as he lowered his voice. "Oh, just peachy. His mother and I managed to commence World War III, and he and I skirmished the whole way here." He tilted to the side to see Marty leaning against the back wall of the lunchroom, the top of his hoodie tugged down to hide his eyes and one foot pressed flat against the wall. His index fingers threaded through the belt loops of his jeans. He was in conversation with someone Eric couldn't see. It was probably teenager Luke Anstrom.

"Christopher Martin, get that work shirt on and that hair under a ball cap. You look like a gangbanger ready to vandalize my place. If the police come past here and see you, they'll have you arrested simply because you look suspicious."

A deep chuckle rose from Greg's barrel chest. Eric shifted his gaze back to Greg as a smile worked on the corner of his own mouth. "Kids these days! I swear if my grandfather were alive and saw the way that kid looked, he'd disown me!"

"Lindsay back with Cath?"

Eric nodded as he looked down at the mail he held and began riffling through it. Greg was just about the only person on the face of the earth that Catherine let call her Cath. He had been with Eric from the time Eric was just a young snot-nosed kid out of the military doing electrical odd jobs. Eric had changed old ladies' lightbulbs and rewired outlets just trying to keep food on the table. In fact, it was on just such a job that he met Greg, who in turn convinced him to start his own business. When it grew from electrical jobs into a supply store, Greg had stepped into the position of store manager. It had worked out well for both of them.

"Tell you the truth, there are more than a few days I wish I had custody of Lindsay and Catherine had him." The look on Greg's face made Eric look up. He swore beneath his breath. Marty and Luke had come from the back room, and from the expression on Marty's face he knew the kid had heard every word.

Luke reached a comforting hand toward Marty's shoulder. Marty shrugged the hand off his shoulder, spun on his foot, and jogged back down the hall. Eric wasn't sure, but he thought for just an instant he saw tears in Marty's hate-filled eyes.

Heat flushed Eric's face as guilt caused his stomach to clench for just a moment, but it was true. He had never been able to get close to Marty, not even when he was small. As a toddler and elementary-age kid, he had been a mama's boy, tenderhearted and whiny. Then he had grown into this belligerent, angry, and violent bully that nobody wanted to be around. Eric hated the thought, but he was glad the court had ordered Marty and Lindsay separated. It was better that Marty wasn't in the same house with his daughter.

Luke was staring at Eric with barely concealed condemnation. "He feels bad enough. You didn't need to make him feel worse."

Luke was a conscientious worker and Eric admired that, but he was a sensitive young man, and that tender heart oftentimes grated on Eric's nerves, as it did now.

Eric sighed as his annoyance at losing control got the better of him. "I am not paying the lot of you to stand around and sympathize or psychoanalyze Marty. I have a shrink back in Dayton who does that for him. Luke, you got that inventory put away yet? No. I didn't think so. Go get it done."

He stuffed the mail beneath his arm, jerked the briefcase off the counter, and headed down the hall to his office. As he passed Greg, he saw the older man's raised brow and pursed lips, but by this time Eric really didn't care whether Greg approved of the way he handled his employees. And at the moment Marty was an employee at Bennington Electrical and Supply.

Eric sat down hard in his leather office chair and massaged his temples. His headache usually didn't begin until after lunch, when the world began to run amok.

"Jerk," he mumbled to himself. "When are you going to get a handle on your emotions? Will you ever learn how to deal with people? So go apologize to Luke." He rose from his seat just as the phone rang. By the time he finished with the call, fished out several blueprints, and went through his client's contract, several hours had passed. He was refilling his coffee cup when his salesclerk bounced into the office. Eric swallowed the burning liquid as the familiar tug to let his eyes travel over Tanya Ambrose's well-developed frame pulled at his self-discipline. Instead Eric turned and reached for the contract. He closed his eyes as he lifted his face toward her and opened them to lock gazes with her large brown eyes. Tanya Ambrose was no innocent, but she was far too young and—perky—for his taste. *No, she isn't, and that is my problem.*

"Ella just called off work. She has to take hubby to a doctor's appointment this morning, and since she was going to leave early today because of her grandson's ball tournament, she decided to just take the whole day off." She popped her gum, and Eric winced.

"Do that again, and I'll make a no gum-chewing policy for this establishment." Totally unrepentant, she planted a rounded hip on the edge of his desk. Eric suddenly felt the need to rummage through the opposite desk drawer. He yanked it open and was vibrantly aware of her body and her perfume wafting through the air. *Don't these women know what they do to us when they do that?*

"Sooo, can I have the day off, too? I mean if it's okay for her to take off whenever she wants and for whatever the reason, then can I?" She was baiting him. If he didn't know better, he'd have sworn that Tanya and Marty had had their heads together.

"No, and that"—Eric pointed his finger at her rounded hip still planted on his desk and then to the chair across from him—"goes in there." He watched as she moved off the desk to lean back against the doorjamb. "So you sure I can't have the day off?"

"No, and don't ask about Ella either. When you've worked here as long as she has, then I'll think about giving you special considerations, too."

He looked down at the electrical schematic on his desk. When she didn't move, he allowed his eyes to travel over her curves to lock with her dark eyes. He cocked an eyebrow at her. "Something else you needed?"

"Yeah. Ella—"

Eric stood to his feet and placed a hand on her shoulder, giving her a slight push to redirect her down the hall in an effort to forestall the argument he knew was coming. Tanya and Ella had declared war the first day he'd hired the younger woman. Ella had ten years of doing things her own way, and Tanya's gum-snapping suggestions were a daily irritant. He had to admit that Tanya was one crackerjack sales assistant, and he needed her. Ella was as sharp and efficient an administrative assistant as they came. On days like this, he would have fired them both if he thought he could find any woman who wasn't more trouble than she was worth.

"Let's see if Luke unpacked that shipment so you can get those shelves stocked."

Greg forestalled the trip to the warehouse by bellowing through the back door of the sales room, "All available salesclerks to the front of the store."

The only available salesclerk was Tanya. Eric followed her out, and while she went to one customer, Eric moved to help a grandmotherly woman standing uncertainly at the front desk. By the time he had finished with her, he realized he was running late for an onsite meeting with Miles Tipton.

His irritation slipped out in profanity. He couldn't afford to lose this contract. It consisted of two housing developments in two different towns. One was the Loring project, where he had sent Thomas Miller and Marty to go work today, and the Minion Development. There was a total of seventy-five houses being built in those two sites. The contract would keep him and all his men working through next summer and bring Bennington Electric to the forefront of the housing-development business. That's why he had done whatever it took to get the subcontracts from Miles and Miles of Houses.

If he could do a good job and prove to the world that not all subcontractors are as shady as the contractor they work for, then he would be set for life. At least that was his long-term plan. If things fell in the toilet at this point, he might as well go back to changing lightbulbs for little old ladies.

He jogged back to Ella's office to see if she had all the estimates and contracts bundled together for this meeting. He was frantically rooting through the papers on Ella's desk when the phone rang. He cut off the oath that rose to his lips and yanked up the phone, taking a calming breath before speaking. "Hello, Bennington Electric."

"Eric. It's Mom. I sure didn't expect you to answer the phone. I thought you had an office girl to do that for you. What's her name again?" Her light laughter raked on his already taut nerves.

"Ella, Mom. Her name is Ella." His voice was terse in his own ears, and he knew if he didn't tame it down he would be in for a lecture. Eric forced himself to count to ten slowly, very slowly. "And she is hardly a girl. What can I do for you?" He dropped down in Ella's chair and continued to sort through the piles, hunting for the elusive paper that he needed. He checked the desire to slam the phone in her ear as his mother rambled on with family gossip.

"Mom...," he tried to interrupt her. He took another calming breath, but felt the irritation coiling around his already tense muscles. All he needed right now was his mother's fussing at him about the family's failures. He tuned back into the conversation in time to hear her trying to guilt him into spending more time with the family. It never seemed to matter that he was almost forty years old with a life of his own.

"Eric, please take some time from your busy schedule and drop by. You really need to spend some time with your father. He's still not feeling well, and I just know that you'll cheer him up." *Cheer Dad up?* That was a laugh. Nothing he had ever done had ever cheered up his father, except when he had moved out of the house. *No, Mom. I won't cheer Dad up. I'll cheer you up. Why don't you just say it?*

She seemed to have changed tack. "You work too much. I think I would leave a man who worked twenty out of twenty-four hours, too."

Eric winced at his mother's barb and shifted the phone to his other ear. Her light laughter rippled over the phone again. "I'm sorry, but you know what I mean. Eric, you work much too hard, and it's not good for a man or his family. Is it this weekend Catherine gets Marty?"

She knew it wasn't. He loved his mother. He really did, but there were days when she drove him positively nuts. Today was one of them. He really didn't have time for this. His words were sharp to keep her from going into her favorite diatribe. "It's next weekend. Listen. . .I need to go. I have a meeting I am already late for. . . ." His resolve collapsed against her sigh of defeat. "Look, I can't make it for dinner, but I'll come as soon as I can close the store."

He heard her sigh again and knew she would give in as well. "Oh, all right. I guess that's the best I can hope for. We'll save dessert until you get here, and Eric? . . . Please let's try to keep Marty reigned in. Your father doesn't need to be upset any more than he has been about these tests the doctor ordered. He's been so tired lately, and I don't think his color is good. . . ." What she really meant was, "Keep your son out of trouble and out of his grandfather's way" because she didn't want to play peacekeeper. Well, neither did he.

Eric held back a long-suffering sigh and murmured a noncommittal reply as his mother continued her list of complaints. It wasn't that he was unconcerned about his father's health. His mother just had a habit of repeating herself. They had covered this ground fifteen minutes ago when he first answered the phone.

"Okay, Mom. Uh-huh. Mom, I really have to go." In his frustration, he replaced the phone harder than he intended, and it fell off the desk. As he put the phone back in its cradle, he realized he hadn't even told her good-bye.

"Oops, maybe I should come back later."

Eric glanced up to see the swish of a blond ponytail leave his office. "Tanya! Wait." He caught up with his salesclerk in the hallway. "Ella needs the receipts from Wednesday to finish the month end. Are they still out front?"

"Why? She isn't here today."

Eric glared at her, and she had the grace to look abashed. "Sorry. They're right here, boss." A sheaf of papers waved in front of his nose. "I was just gonna ask you if you'd seen where the old. . .

I mean, I couldn't find last month's inventory in Ella's office, and I wondered if you knew where she kept it."

Eric frowned at the young woman's sauciness. "Tanya. . ." The phone's ringing interrupted his mild rebuke. "Get the phone, would you?"

"Whatever." She answered the phone and immediately handed it to him. "It's for you."

Eric watched her leave his office before turning his attention to the call. "Bennington here." It was Miles Tipton. He glanced at his watch and winced. He was really late. Eric just started to apologize and was about to make a suggestion of them meeting at a local diner midpoint from the store and the construction site when Miles interrupted him with a torrent of angry words. Miles was in rare form as he denounced Eric and his crew. Something major must have happened at the Minion subdivision site for Miles to be this up in arms.

"Miles. . ." Eric raked his fingers through his hair and tried again. "Miles, I said—"

The irate voice on the end of the phone bulldozed over his efforts to communicate. As the man paused for breath, Eric intervened. "Miles, I promise you that I will take care of it personally. I am on my way to the site right now. I will have it corrected by the end of the day." Eric shifted the phone to his other ear. Miles was beginning to calm down. "Miles, we've had a good relationship up to this point. I am not going to do anything to ruin it. Yes, I understand. . . . Yes, I know you are on a schedule. I said I would take care of it. And I will. I'll be there. . . ."

He glanced at his appointment calendar. He had the whole following week scheduled. He ran his finger down the page of his daily planner. Everything he had prioritized that morning just went up in flames.

Eric heard the definite click on the other end. He swore violently as he slammed the phone down and stabbed the intercom button.

"Which site is Thomas working at today, and who's with him?"

"Loring's and Marty. I think they are working on house number six. Why?" the female voice on the other end wanted to know.

"Never mind why! When they get back, send them to me. . . . No, never mind. I'll take care of it."

He pinched the bridge of his nose before running his hand down over his beard. Shoving back from the desk, he paced the confines of his office as a means of physically releasing the tension that was throbbing through his veins.

He grabbed his coat and hard hat before bellowing down the hall, "I'm going to the sites!" He slammed out the back door.

Heads would roll.

Chapter Seven

"Oh man, we're in trouble for something," Marty mumbled as he glanced out the square hole and paused in tacking the electrical wiring to the ceiling joist over his head. His father's red Cherokee spewed mud in all directions as it tore through the construction site and slid to a stop in front of the windowless building.

Marty shivered more from trepidation than from the cool damp air coming through the window frame. He had hoped he wouldn't see his father until evening when they would ride home together in stony silence, and then he could retreat to his bedroom and hide there until morning light.

He shivered again as his dad's voice thundered through the skeletal structure of the three-story house. "Miller! What the devil is this?" His dad stalked through the framed building ripping dangling wire off the walls and drooping strands from the ceiling. He was on a rampage. Again. Marty closed his eyes to squeeze back the sudden tears that threatened him. His hands began to shake, and he looked around for a place of escape. Marty had never seen his father so angry. He knew his old man had a temper, he'd even triggered it from time to time, but his father had amazing self-control and never, ever went on a rampage. Marty shuddered. Maybe he could disappear and not take the blame for whatever had his dad so fired up.

"What's up, boss?" Apparently Tom hadn't seen his father undo in seconds the work that had taken them three hours to do.

"I just left the Minion site. Would you care to hazard a guess as to why I was there?"

Thomas Miller shrugged. "Couldn't tell you, boss."

"Because I got a call from Tipton, who was. . ."

Marty's eyes widened at the words his dad used to describe just how angry this other fellow was. He pushed against a stud and looked at his companion. Tom seemed unphased by the entire episode.

His father continued. "I have spent three hours reworking the entire schedule!"

Miller shrugged. "What's that got to do with me?"

His dad's hand lashed out and yanked a blue plastic outlet box from the stud. "This," he shouted, "does not go here!"

"Hey! I just strung that!" Miller protested.

"And I unstrung it!" the old man bellowed back. "You have all the outlet boxes too high up on the wall! And only half the amount that the houses require! On top of all that"—his dad moved close, and his voice rose in volume—"you are using the wrong gauge of wire, you idiot!"

"No I'm not!"

His dad took a deep breath and closed his eyes. Marty watched as he slid his fists into the pockets of his pants.

"Six houses at the Minion Development have to be entirely restrung. Six! Because you used the lightest gauge of wire on every electrical box. You put too much of a load on the circuits, and you used the wrong light switches in three other houses."

"Wait a minute. . . . We did those houses by the book! We left there Friday with no complaints. Tipton was on the site all day. We didn't have any complaints before. The man is obviously trying to scam you." Miller tried to smooth his boss's ruffled feathers. "He probably doesn't want to pay the bill he owes for the work we did."

"I saw the work myself!" Eric threw up his hands. "When I send you out on a job, I expect you to read the schematics and follow those directions explicitly."

A vein popped on Tom's neck. "Marty and I worked our heads off to get that place done for him on time, just like you said."

"I saw it! With my own eyes, Miller. It was the worst work I have ever seen in my life. Teenagers could do a better job. Were you drunk?"

"Hey, don't lay this all on me. Teenagers *were* doing the work. I wasn't the only one there. Shawn and Marty were there, too. I let them string some of the wire. If the work was shoddy, then there's your answer."

Marty opened his mouth to protest, but his dad saw him and held up his hand to stop him. "Marty is just the gofer, and Shawn is still an apprentice."

"Hey, this isn't my fault. You give me slackers to do the work, and that's the result you get."

"You are the supervisor. You're the one who signs off on all jobs completed. You're the one who gets the bigger paycheck. It's your responsibility to oversee any work that's done and make sure it's done right."

"I did my job. It's your kid who didn't pull his weight." Tom stripped off his tool belt and slammed it onto the two-by-four lying across the sawhorses.

"That's not true! I never strung stupid wire by myself," Marty protested.

His dad glared at him and shook his head. Marty clenched his jaw shut then watched in amazement as his father went toe-to-toe with the surly employee. His dad stepped forward and poked a finger in Tom's chest. "He's not the slacker—you are. He's done everything he's been told to do on the job. In fact, he'd make a better supervisor than you. At least I can trust his work, and I know he's on time."

Tom pushed Eric's hand from his chest. "I don't need to take this! You're just protecting the kid cuz he's your son."

"No, Miller. I told you, this was your last chance. You blew it. Your work is shoddy. You miss work, and half the time when you are here, you're intoxicated. Yet somehow you weasel your way into keeping your job."

"This is a bunch of bunk!" Tom stomped toward the door, kicking a piece of electrical wire out of his way.

"You either repair all the work on your own time, or you are fired."

"Don't bother firing me—I quit!" Tom called over his shoulder.

The whole argument was over in seconds, and Marty was still reeling from his dad sticking up for him. His dad swore and kicked at a pile of construction dust. "Come on, kid, let's get to work. You start ripping all the yellow gauge wire off the walls while I get my tools from the truck. Maybe we can get at least this house whipped back into shape. Then I'll have to figure out how to get the last six houses redone without setting everyone else back by months."

"Dad. . ."

His father turned to him.

"I—I didn't know it was the wrong stuff. I just did what he told me to do."

Eric nodded and moved toward the doorframe. "I know, Mart. It wasn't your fault this time."

Marty clenched his jaw. *This time*. This time wasn't his fault, but every other time was.

Neither of them said much as they went to work. Except for a couple of breaks his father insisted that he take, Marty worked silently and steadily with his dad throughout the day. It was pretty amazing watching him. He only looked at the blueprints once and then set to work. He was neat and fast. Marty was impressed, though he'd never tell his dad that. Every muscle in Marty's body ached as he stumbled to the truck. All Marty wanted to do was get a shower and head to bed.

He looked back at his dad as he barked out, "Oh great!"

"What?"

"We still have to go to Grandma's."

Chapter Eight

If Eric thought his day couldn't get much worse, he was wrong. He was better off without having to keep cleaning up the messes Miller had made, even if he had to finish the job himself. He could deal with the delays at the work site, rush-hour traffic, and Marty's protests about having to go to his grandparents' home. He could handle his mother's complaints about not being there for dinner; he could even handle his father's disapproval; but seeing his sister at his mother's dining-room table almost made him turn tail and run.

His mother must have seen the look on his face because her hand suddenly snatched out to grab his sleeve to keep him from leaving. "Eric, this feuding with your sister has gone on long enough. It's been more than a year since we've been able to have any kind of family get-together."

"Yeah, well, I hope you told your daughter that."

"Eric. . ."

He ignored his mother's stern warning and continued, "Geez, Ma, why didn't you tell me she was coming?" *I would have stayed home.* Her hand tightened on Eric's arm. For a second, Eric thought she was going to squeeze the back of his neck like she had when he was a kid, but her grip finally relaxed.

"Exactly why I didn't tell you. You might as well hear the rest of it. Your brother is here, too. It's time this family started acting like a family again. Your father has not been feeling well, and I think you owe it to him to quit this foolish squabbling among yourselves and act like the grown-ups you supposedly are. Although I'm beginning to wonder, after the grief the three of you have put us through this year!"

"Mom, I didn't start any of this."

"I don't care who started what, Eric Martin Bennington, and I'll tell you who's finishing it—I am. Right now. Now get in here." She presented a ramrod back to him, turning when she had taken only a few steps. "And you *will* keep a civil tongue in your head." Eric slumped against the hall wall. Suddenly he was eleven years old again. He hated this feeling of impotence that dogged his heels every time he stepped back into his childhood home. How was it that every time he walked back into this house, he felt like he was ten again? Regardless of what had happened with his siblings, it was always his fault because he was the oldest.

Eric hadn't seen his sister, or his brother either for that matter, in months, and as little as possible before that. A year ago his sister had gotten a crazy idea into her head that he had hurt her when they were kids. Eric figured the wacko therapist she had gone to filled her head with her so-called "buried" memories. What a load of bunk. He'd never hurt her, and he certainly hadn't done the things she'd accused him of—

"Eric? Are you coming, or are you going to sulk against the wall all evening?"

He took a deep breath as his mother's words chided him. It wasn't going to get any easier, so he might as well get it over with and follow his mother into the dining room. If he stalled any longer, he wouldn't put it past her to come back to the hallway, grab him by the ear, and drag him to the table.

By the looks of the littered table, they had long ago finished dinner. Eric walked past his father's chair and headed for the least likely hot spot. Probably no seat was safe from the human time bombs seated around the table, but he chose the empty seat beside Marty. The buzz of conversation lowered a few decibels, if any, at his arrival. His son and niece were already bickering about who should help their grandmother clear the table, Geoff and his father were in a deep discussion about city politics, his brother-in-law was wiping the hands and face of his youngest daughter, while Mallory went back and forth through the swinging kitchen door helping bring in dessert.

Eric was grateful that a general greeting covered his hellos to everyone. He reached for the blueberry cheesecake in the center of the table. It was his favorite. His mother had also made chocolate cake, Mallory's favorite, and what Geoff had dubbed the "world's best" pecan pie. She was covering all the bases.

For Alecia Bennington, food was the answer for all the crises life could bring. Perhaps it was because she had been raised on a farm in a family of eleven children. Food brought sustenance, comfort, and family togetherness.

If only it were that easy.

His father turned to Eric as Geoff went to the kitchen to see if there was ice cream in the freezer.

Here it comes.

"So, Eric, how's the business doing?" his dad asked. Eric's head began to throb.

"Fine, Dad." Hoping his father would stop there for once, Eric helped himself to more cheesecake and sipped his coffee, but pretending to be busy with his food didn't stop his father.

"Those new contracts coming along all right?" Martin Bennington leaned back in his chair and struck a match to relight his pipe for his after-dinner smoke. "I talked to Loring's brother-in-law down at city hall this past week. Said Roger wasn't too happy with the work being done on his house." His father sucked on the end of his pipe until the tobacco was glowing red then snuffed out the flame on the matchstick.

Great, just what I needed—Dad and city hall getting involved in my business. Eric tried to restrain his impatience. "It's under control, Dad. Loring's a hothead, but I can handle him. Besides, he was probably grousing about the head contractor, Miles Tipton." *Drop it, Dad.*

"Mhmmn." Martin puffed his pipe. "Guy you been working with for a while, isn't it?" He spoke with his pipe still inserted in his mouth.

"Yeah. He's okay." Eric stabbed at the last of his cheesecake. His father's expectations had always been unreasonable, and now that he had retired he had become nearly obsessed with Eric's store and business. It was all he wanted to talk about. Just once, Eric wished his father would tell him he was doing a good job. Just once. But it never came. Instead all he had were constant "suggestions" on how it could be run better. It was bad enough when they were alone, but he usually did it in the presence of other people, particularly his near-perfect little brother, "Golden Boy Geoff." Eric didn't particularly relish the idea of the whole family being party to one of his lectures. Although Mallory and Geoff would probably enjoy the show.

"Daddy, at least let Eric finish his dessert before you grill him."

Eric's dessert fell off his fork. He had expected something from Mallory—a crack or snide remark—but certainly not her defending him. He scooped the cheesecake onto his fork with his finger and shoved it in his mouth to keep from staring at his sister dumbfounded. Since when did she champion him? Now if he'd been Geoff. . .

"I'm sure our big brother can handle himself. Always has." Geoff reseated himself at the end of the table.

His jet-set, playboy brother oozed success. Eric doubted he had anything less than an eighty-dollar shirt in his closet. Even his casual clothes screamed "money!" Eric had been in his apartment once, and it looked like a magazine layout for Most Eligible Bachelor.

Before Eric could think of a suitable retort for his brother, Mallory interjected again. "Oh, knock it off, Geoff. Like you're perfect!" The look on his brother's face was priceless. Probably matched his own. Mallory and Geoff had always stood up for each other, setting him up as the bad guy. Time and again he had taken the blame and the end of his father's belt for their mischief. Eric couldn't remember a time when his sister had taken his side against Geoff's—in anything.

Before either of her stunned brothers could reply, Mallory herded her daughters, Renee and Angel, to gather their things together. "Thanks for dinner, Mom."

Alecia came from the kitchen, wiping her hands on her apron. "You have to leave already? I just made more coffee."

Jake Carlisle, Mallory's husband, came through the swinging door behind Alecia and kissed her on the cheek. "It's getting late." He rubbed the top of Renee's head, ruffling her hair. "And someone needs a bath, I think."

"Daad!"

There was a general exodus; Geoff followed Jake and Mallory out, citing an early flight to catch in the morning. He was a hotshot computer whiz, and his company flew him all over the world to troubleshoot their equipment. Alecia told Marty his grandfather had gotten a new computer, and he disappeared to "check it out." Quiet descended on the three remaining adults.

Eric needed to be heading home as well. Tomorrow would arrive too soon with its long trip to Marty's counseling session, yet he remained where he was.

Alecia poured Eric and his father more coffee and began to

gather up the last few things on the table. His father seemed content to smoke his pipe, and Eric considered the evening. No nasty accusations, no raking over dead coals. No wild abuse stories. Mallory seemed to have come back to her senses. It hadn't been as bad as he had anticipated and certainly much better than he would have guessed when he found out his whole family was going to be present.

Eric found himself studying his father and actually seeing him for the first time since he'd arrived at the house. He looked as tired as his mother had claimed. Alecia was a worrier, and the tendency to dismiss what she said was an ingrained habit, but for once she might be right. Thin blue veins protruded starkly from the back of his father's hands and up his leathered arms. Heavy folds of skin bagged under his eyes, which lacked his normal luster of determination. He had given up far too easily about Tipton. Eric was waiting for the other shoe to drop, but his father just continued to sip his coffee and puff on his now-cold pipe, like he lacked the energy to try to pursue the subject.

His mother was still moving back and forth from the kitchen, but slower now, as if she had used the last of her reserves to gather her family all under one roof and keep them from one another's throats.

Eric frowned at the dark liquid in the bottom of his cup and took the last bitter swallow. When had his parents grown old?

Chapter Nine

Eric's eyes veered from the road for a brief moment as he checked his watch and fumed as the rush-hour traffic snarled around them. From the passenger seat, the heavy beat of a muffled bass thumped in the air. Eric reached across the space, jerked the iPod out of his son's hand, and fumbled with it until he found the OFF switch. Silence filled the air, but only for half a beat. "Hey! I was listening to that!" Marty yanked off his earphones and sent a withering look in his father's direction.

"Unfortunately, so was I. How you can listen to that stuff blaring in your ears at such high decibels is completely beyond me."

Marty grabbed for the player. "It's mine. I want it back."

"Tough."

"Dad," Marty wailed. "That's not fair. I want it now."

Eric slid his eyes from the heavy traffic to glare at his son. "Instead of listening to all of that trash, why don't you think about your session tonight."

"It won't matter what I say—I won't be believed." Marty flopped back in his seat, folding his arms as he sulked. He curled up against the door and stared out the window.

Eric glanced again at Marty. Gone was the little boy with golden hair throwing a ball and running beside their border collie. Gone was the happy innocence of sun-filled days, firefly catching nights, and weekends spent teaching his son to fish. Gone with the rest of his old life—his home, his wife. Even the image of sitting on the porch watching their grandchildren that he'd imagined would fill his old age had gone up in smoke.

Eric swallowed hard. Now all there seemed to be was pain, anger, resentment, heartache, and grief. Marty now carried a chip on his shoulder the size of New York City and a truckload of resentment toward his father. Eric wondered if Marty blamed him for Catherine uprooting him and Lindsay and moving to another part of the state. Probably. Was his bad attitude and getting into trouble his way of getting even or getting attention as Catherine had said? Eric didn't know. All he knew was the mess his family was in and the impossibility of finding a way out.

God knows why I even bother! As far as Eric could see, these months of counseling had been a total waste of time. If he had his way, he wouldn't be taking time away from work to travel two hours round-trip just to take his son to see a shrink. A good swift kick in the pants when he was younger would have done him a whole lot of good. Catherine had babied him. She seemed to think that her form of discipline was better than the way Eric's parents raised him. *I got cuffed a few times. It never hurt me.* Except when it hadn't been he who needed punishing.

Finding a parking lot in the complex took more time than Eric had allowed for, and he checked his watch anxiously. He hated being late for anything, even for something as distasteful as his son's counseling sessions. "C'mon kid, get a move on. We're running late as it is. Let's get this over with."

Eric watched as his son sauntered out of the car and flipped the collar of his leather jacket up around his ears. Marty tugged a comb out of his pocket and pulled the length of his dark blond hair back in a ponytail. In an instant, his whole look and demeanor changed from a sulking child to a defiant, swaggering know-it-all. Eric rubbed his aching forehead. It promised to be a very trying evening.

Brown metal folding chairs were interspersed between an assortment of patched and shabby easy chairs and placed in a semicircle in the room they entered. Ten of the twenty members were already there. The evening began with a general overview and plans for the upcoming group therapy sessions.

Because of business commitments, he and Marty had missed several counseling appointments, but Eric still felt he knew the room, the other parents, Neil Osbow the counselor, as well as each one of the boys, inside out. Had it really been more than a year ago since that first meeting?

Eric checked his watch once more. Only half an hour into the session and Marty had already decided to cause trouble. Eric ran a hand down through his beard as he stared at the others in the room. Were they as frustrated with all the whining and defensiveness as he was? He wanted nothing more than to slap a confession out of his son. He jammed his hands into the pockets of his khaki pants, effectively distorting the neat creases.

"Aw, I don't know why I even have to be here. No one ever listens to me. Nobody believes anything I say." Marty's face flushed with unconcealed rage. He folded his arms across his chest and stared at the toe of his shoes, refusing to meet the looks of the others in the room.

In a quiet, but firm voice Neil spoke from across the room. "Yes, you do know why you're here. You sexually abused your cousin. You're here to get the help you need, and we are all doing our level best to teach you how to take responsibility for your own actions. Marty, you want to act like the victim. Well, guess what? You are not the victim. None of you here are the victim. You lay the blame on the victims. You lay the blame on your parents, you lay the blame on society, school, the world, your dog, or an insect that bit you moments before you offended one of your victims. But the reality is, you are to blame. Not your victims, not society, not your parents, or your school, or the dog, or whatever other excuses you use. The fact remains that you decided to do what you did. You made the choice, and now you must live with the consequences of your actions. I'm here to see that you take responsibility and take the help that is being handed out.

"Now, Marty, let's start over. You want and need to draw attention to yourself. You used your charm and charisma to gain sexual satisfaction and the feeling of power that came from being able to pull a fast one on an unsuspecting victim. Isn't that right?"

"No!" Marty sent Neil a withering look before dropping his head to stare once more at the maroon carpet. "I didn't do anything to no one."

One of the boys in the group piped up. "Face it, Marty, you're a liar. You've never told the truth the whole time you've been in group."

Eric's eyes narrowed in defense of his son. "That's like the pot calling the kettle black, Grant. You've done your fair share of denying the truth all along."

Their counselor held up his hand before leaning toward Marty. "We're just trying to help you. But every time you lock down that anger, you are refusing our help."

"I didn't ask for your help!" Marty sat forward in his chair.

"Yes you did. The moment you laid a hand on an innocent victim you were screaming out for help. Now you've got it." Neil nodded his head. "Use it."

Marty jumped to his feet. "I didn't do anything to her! There isn't anything wrong with me."

The group of twenty groaned in unison. Eric's stomach lurched as he heard the hard, defiant words coming out of Marty's mouth once more.

"I hate this, and I hate you!"

Neil shrugged his shoulders, further inciting the teen. "We don't really care whether you hate us or not. I've got a job to do, and you've got no choice."

"I got yanked from my home. I got stuck with my dad. I had to leave all my friends. I have to work with my dad. I hate stringing electric wires through other people's houses. I can't even keep the money. I'm not allowed to listen to my music on the job, in the car, or in the house. No matter what I do, it's never good enough to meet with his approval. I have a curfew of eight o'clock. Eight o'clock! I'm treated like a freakin' baby. I'm not allowed to do anything. Nobody listens to me." His son swung around to face him. "I can't do anything to please you! And because of you, I can't even see my baby sister!" Marty's screams of pent-up rage were met with silence.

Hard, bitter, hate-filled eyes a thousand years old drilled into Eric's. "I hate you! I hate you! I hate you! You drove us out of the house. You pushed Mom away. It's all your fault, and I hate you!"

Eric swallowed hard. He hadn't known it was this bad. What had he done to deserve this? He was a good father. He couldn't help it that the boy's mother and he couldn't get along any more. *Sure, I'm strict, but I want the kid to get past his mistakes, take responsibility, and be more than his old man ever was.*

Neil turned to Eric. "Anything you'd like to say to your son?"

Eric sighed, but shook his head. What could he say that would possibly make a difference?

Grant's mother lifted her hand. "I've got something to say." Her dark brown eyes held no warmth as they raked across each boy seated in the circle. She leaned forward with the intensity of her words. "For the last eight months I have sat and listened to every one of you whine and complain and bellyache because of what was taken from you. I've heard Neil fighting you every step of the way. Well, let me tell you what you stole from your

75

victims, what you did to each one of them. I can tell you because I was a victim. I was raped when I was sixteen. He took from me my dignity, my power over my own life. He stole from me peace and hope and deposited in their place a lifetime of fear, confusion, anger, even hatred. He left in his wake of destruction all of his evil, all of his fear, and all of his pain. He fed off of my fear to relieve his own. I am sick to death of hearing about what was taken from you. Live with it. We have to."

Eric blanched at the hard, cold words pouring from the seemingly demure woman across the room from him. He suddenly felt sick to his stomach, and every muscle in his body responded to the flight or fight adrenaline coursing through his veins. Since he could do neither, he sat with rigid limbs while the blood pounded in his temples.

"It's not my fault." Marty's outburst came after twenty minutes of sulking silence. Eric's patience with his son was running thin. The driving rain was making the asphalt slick and treacherous, and Marty's belligerent attitude was making his head throb.

"Okay, son, you want to tell me what all this is about?"

"That freakin' counselor thinks he knows everything! Well, he doesn't. He doesn't know. . ."

"Marty!" Eric faced the angry teenager, reprimanding him for the use of his language. "Just the facts, please. Don't embellish it. What happened in your session with Neil?" After waiting an hour and a half for Marty to finish his individual counseling, he was in no mood to hear his son's attitude.

"Neil jumped my frame about something." Marty's mumble was nearly indistinct.

"What?"

"Aw, nothin'. You'd take his side anyway." Marty turned his shoulder and stared out the window.

"What, Marty?"

"Nothin'!"

"So this is what I'm paying big bucks for? Nothing?" The urge to rant and rave was difficult to subdue, but actually getting through to his son was more important. "What's the matter, can't you handle a little criticism from your counselor?"

"That so-called counselor doesn't know squat! I wasn't watching anything that bad."

"What were you watching?" Eric sent a questioning look toward the youth beside him. Marty's sullen expression had not changed. His jaw jutted forward in a defiant arch, daring his father to question him further. "Son, I didn't hear your answer. What were you watching?"

Eric could see the battle going on inside Marty. When he finally mumbled an answer, Eric nearly swerved off the road. "You what? What were you doing with an X-rated movie on your iPod?" He snorted in disgust at his son's stupidity. "Where's your head, boy?"

"But, Dad—"

He steamrolled over his son's whining protest. "After all the trouble you've been in, you'd think you'd have the brains to realize what a stupid move that was. The last thing you need is to be caught with something like that. Don't you get it? You are this close to ending up in a detention home. Think, Marty, think. No wonder you're in so much trouble. Of all the stupid moves. Why would you mess around with something like this? And where did it come from? Did you get it from Grant? Who bought it for you? Answer me!"

"You did."

"What?" Eric's head snapped around to glare at his son. "Don't get smart with me, boy. I guarantee you, I am not in the mood."

Marty sat up and faced his father squarely. Eric nearly recoiled at the rage that seethed beneath the young man's normal mask of assumed indifference. "You bought it, Pops." Marty's voice sneered contempt at his father. "I uploaded it off your computer."

Chapter Ten

"My only goal here is to crash this program." Catherine balanced herself against the edge of the desk. The part-time student programmer's eyes widened at the words. Good. She had his attention. Maybe the changes she had been working so hard to implement in the last two years would start with the new programmers and not the old-timers. Lord knew she was making about as much headway with them as she was with Eric.

"Caleb, I am going to teach you how to correctly test a system. We are going to break every code that we can. In IT development we don't test to see if the program works, we test to break it so that by the time it gets to our users we know that our program is solid."

Catherine smiled as she studied the young man before her. He was one of the brightest young people she had met in a very long time. She liked his initiative. He not only knew how to program software in the latest program language, but he also had a knack with people. He knew how to build relationships; and he was outgoing, creative, and extremely capable. She hoped her boss would hang on to him after he graduated. Administrative Computing needed him. Especially with the new software systems the university was looking to implement in the next two years. It gave her a headache just thinking of the amount of work and overtime she would be logging. She hoped that by the time the programs were installed Marty would be off probation and her relationship with Eric would be more manageable. If not, her family might be visiting her in a rubber room.

"Catherine," Caleb protested, "I do solid work."

She shook her head, refocusing her attention on her office partner. He folded his arms across his chest and tilted his head in that slightly defiant way that Marty did when he was justifying something. She realized that he thought she was disagreeing with his assessment.

She grinned to disarm his defenses as she spoke. "I know you do, Caleb, but what I want to teach you is not about how good you think your work is. It is about giving the end user rock-solid programs. The difference in testing to prove that it works and testing to make sure it doesn't break is what good testing is all about."

His brows drew together behind his stylish lenses as he stared at the lines of numbers, letters, and phrases that were a programmer's second language. His concentration reminded her of Marty. Her son had looked just like that when he was building his models and designing three-story mansions out of LEGO blocks. She swallowed hard, moved off the desk, and shoved her hands into her pockets as she leaned against the wall.

"Sooo, you want me to intentionally crash what you and Philip and Daniel just spent six months building?" Caleb asked.

He really did remind her of Marty. *"Sooo, Mom, you really want me to crash into your car?"* ten-year-old Marty inquired with a look of hope and disbelief. *She nodded and laughed at the look on his face as she turned the wheel of her bumper car.*

"Yep."

Caleb moved. "Okay. How do we do that?"

She blinked, and her little boy disintegrated before her eyes.

She pulled out the chair next to Caleb's and began to explain the process of testing she wanted from him. Catherine watched as he furiously typed his notes.

She paused to let him catch up. "So, you wind up testing every branch, every combination of conditions, even the most outlandish, because we know that a missing period or semicolon can change everything." Too often it was easy to miss those minute differences on a computer screen. *Just like in real life. We see what we want to see.*

Catherine continued her instruction. "When that happens, we assume that our code is correct, and that is why you need to test everything; even what you think is obviously correct code. If it gets to the end user and they break it, I am not going to be happy." She frowned at him and made a swatting motion in the air before his face. He laughed, and she chuckled as she pointed at his computer. "Get to work."

Catherine returned to her desk with a sigh. She picked up the picture and studied the face smiling back at her. It was her favorite picture of Marty. He'd been eight when his uncle Jake had captured the precious moment. Marty, blond hair streaming toward the floor, was anchored upside down in his father's strong embrace. He was laughing so hard that his eyes were mere slits and his mouth a jack-o-lantern grin of pure and glorious joy.

Funny how getting impossible projects moved from dead center seemed easier than a civil conversation with the man who was giving his son a raspberry on the belly in the picture before her. Catherine sighed again and heard an echo across the room. She turned toward Caleb.

"Problems?" she asked.

"Man, this is tough." Caleb turned toward her. "I have a list this long"—he spread his hands apart from shoulder to desktop—"and I've only tested the first of maybe fifteen test conditions."

Catherine chuckled. "Grueling, isn't it?"

"Tell me again why we have to do this?"

"Because the programmer that the end user—in your case, financial aid—will trust the most is the programmer who does this kind of testing. Because if we don't find all the places it can break, the user will."

The phone interrupted her impromptu lecture, and she shook her head and mumbled beneath her breath as she reached for the receiver, "But no matter how thorough we are, they'll find a way to break it anyway." End users and husbands both seemed to have a way of breaking down what seemed solid.

"This is Catherine Bennington."

"Mom?" Her heart thudded heavily in her chest at the sound of her son's voice. He rarely called her at work and never when he was with his father.

"Marty?" She fought down the tremor that shook her hand and fought for a lighter tone. "What's up?"

"Mom, can I stay with Dad over the weekend?"

Shock rippled through her. Marty never wanted to stay longer at his dad's. She smiled and was ready to voice her joy at the change in their relationship when Marty interrupted. "T's church is having a youth lock-in."

"Marty, I . . ." Fear rippled down her spine. Church outings. That is what began the last two-year nightmare.

"C'mon, Mom. Please? T really wants me to come." How could she tell him no when being with Reverend Jamison just might be what finally got through to her son, and for that matter, her son's father?

She glanced up as her office door opened, and Daniel peaked around the corner. He saw she was on the phone and forked invisible food into his mouth and took an imaginary drink before cocking a questioning eyebrow at her. She wiggled her eyebrows in return. On the other hand—well, the possibilities were endless.

Chapter Eleven

Y ou sure this is a good idea?" Eric stood in the doorway of the church's gymnasium. A large group of teens were milling around, high-fiving and greeting each other.

"Hey, Mr. Bennington! Where's Marty?"

Eric recognized the youth from the rafting trip. Steve something or other. He nodded over his shoulder. "Getting his stuff from the Jeep."

Travis patted the youth on the back. "Why don't you go help him?" He turned to Eric. "Don't worry so much, Dad. He'll be fine. He's a big boy now."

Eric shook his head. "T, you have no idea. The kid just cannot stay out of trouble."

"Then this is the right environment for him, Eric. We have tons of chaperones; they're going to play hard and work hard. We'll wear them out."

"I don't know about this all-night thing."

"He's not a two-year-old, Eric. Somewhere along the way you have to start trusting him."

Eric frowned. "Trust has to be earned."

"Sometimes kids live down to the expectations put on them."

Heat flared up Eric's neck. "You saying this is my fault?"

"Easy, Bennington. I'm just saying that you need to give him room to do the right thing."

"Even if he's failed to show he can act appropriately?"

"Especially then. Everybody deserves a second chance."

Eric turned at the sound of running feet. Steve and Marty burst through the door. They brushed by the adults and headed over to the Ping-Pong table. Steve flipped Marty a paddle, and soon they were in a head-to-head battle with a crowd of encouragers.

Eric shook his head. "You just don't get it, Travis. The kid just got caught with porn on his iPod—he'll likely get six months or more probation added on to his sentence."

Travis laid his hand on Eric's arm. "Come on down to my office for a few minutes. The youth leaders have this thing organized." He led the way down the hallway and unlocked the door to his office, motioned Eric to an easy chair, and closed the door.

Travis sat down on the chair next to Eric. "Is he still going to counseling?"

"Yes. He'll probably have another six months of that added on as well. Then they'll do an evaluation for the court." Eric clasped his hands behind his head. "That kid!"

"Hey, 'that kid' is just that—a kid. He's getting help, and we need to support and love him while he gets things figured out. Pornography is just the symptom, not the root of the problem."

"That sounds like psycho mumbo jumbo to me. I hear enough of that stuff at his family counseling sessions."

"Any of it getting through yet?" Travis grinned.

Eric frowned. "Are you back to blaming me?"

"No." Travis shook his head. "Just saying you might need to look at your own life and what you may have passed down to your son."

"Like what?"

"Like..." Travis paused then blew air through his lips. "Like... is pornography something you deal with?"

His friend's piercing eyes sliced right through him. Eric turned his head and shrugged. *"Nothing wrong with a little look, son."* His dad's voice echoed through the years. At six, Eric had believed him. He hadn't gotten in trouble like Marty had though.

You didn't get caught.

Eric shook his head. "I'm an adult—it's different."

"Not at all. Any kind of pornography at any age is destructive." Travis leaned his elbows on his knees. "In so many ways! It demeans women and children, but it also destroys those who get sucked into its addiction." He turned to look at Eric. "It's a vortex of evil."

"You're gonna tell me you never looked at a dirty magazine or watched an X-rated movie?" Eric laughed.

"No." Travis dropped his head and clasped his hands. "I'm gonna tell you that this is a battle I've fought most of my life. I'm talking from experience now. I'm telling you what I know to be true from my own life."

Eric dropped his arms. "You're kidding, right?" A pastor who admitted to struggling with porn?

"It almost ruined my marriage. I was so steeped in it I didn't realize how emotionally abusive it made me to my wife." Travis sat back in his chair. "She gave me an ultimatum—counseling or move out." He smiled. "Made me stick to it, too."

Eric shifted in his chair. This side of Travis was surprising.

"Look, Eric. I'm telling you all this to let you know I understand the battle, but it's worth the effort to get free from the addiction." He put his hand on the back of Eric's chair. "But I won't kid you. I don't believe you can lick it without God's help."

Eric stood and paced the room. He really didn't want to hear this sermon. This was about Marty, not about him. "I don't have an addiction. I'm just a normal man with a man's desires."

"Just think about what I said." Travis stood. "I'll be here if you need to talk." He walked to the door.

"Look, right now I just need you to talk to Marty."

Travis paused with his hand on the doorknob. "Of course." Travis turned around and nodded his head. "But don't be fooled, Eric. This is just as much about you as it is about your son."

Travis said good-bye to Eric, reassuring him once again that Marty would be well cared for, and watched his friend leave with one last look at his son. *Father, use my words. Let him remember only what he needs to hear. Draw him to Yourself.* There was always this tug-of-war within himself. Had he said too much? Or too little? Travis willed himself to leave it in God's hands and began to pray for an opportunity to speak with Marty sometime during the long night.

The opportunity came about four in the morning. Travis was in the kitchen getting another cup of coffee. Good thing he could sleep tomorrow. It would take him a day to recover; bouncing back from a sleepless night took a little longer now. Just as he finished adding cream and sugar Marty came in, smelling of sweat and still bouncing with energy despite the hour and the long night of activity. Travis smiled into his cup. What he wouldn't give to have that kind of energy again.

"Steve said there were still sodas and snacks in here."

Travis held out his coffee mug toward the refrigerator and counter. "Help yourself." He took a sip of his coffee. "How's it going?"

"Great." Marty's response was muffled from inside the refrigerator. He popped the tab of a cola and took several swallows before reaching for a handful of cookies. He grinned at Travis with his mouth full.

Travis set his coffee down and hopped up on the counter. "Take a seat."

Marty looked at him as if to ask if he was serious then jumped up onto the opposite counter when Travis nodded his head. He grabbed another handful of cookies.

"You seem to be enjoying yourself with the rest of the kids. You should hang out with us again sometime. We're working on the gym, doing some remodeling and painting to make it into a youth center for the community. We have a couple of donated pool tables to put in there as soon as we finish the rooms." Travis took another sip of his coffee. "You interested in helping us?"

"Cool." Marty pitched his empty soda can into the nearby trash can. "Gotta check with my old man—" He glanced at Travis. "Uh, I mean my dad. He'd probably say yes if you asked him though."

"I can do that, but I think he'd rather have you talk to him."

Marty rolled his eyes. "You mean *he* wants to talk. He's not much into listening—except to the sound of his own voice."

"It's tough not being heard. I hope that doesn't discourage you from trying."

"I have tried!" Marty jumped down from the counter. "I told you—he won't listen. Nobody listens to me! They don't believe me."

"Then talk to me, Marty." Travis slipped off the counter. "I'll listen to you."

Marty shrugged his shoulders and stared at his feet. "You probably won't believe me either."

"Try me. Marty." Travis put a hand on the teenager's shoulder. "Tell me what happened."

"You want the truth?"

Travis nodded. "Truth always works best—no matter how painful it might be."

Marty looked Travis in the eye. "It's not me that's going to find it painful."

Chapter Twelve

Lindsay tucked her jeans in the drawer and closed it with her hip. All her clothes were put away and her room was clean; now maybe her mother would let her get on the computer.

She found her in the kitchen. "Mom, can I do some research on the computer?" Her cousin Molly had told her that using "research" was a good way to get permission. Parents loved that kind of thing. "Dad told me about a new historical site for the Civil War, and I wanted to check it out."

Her mother mumbled and knelt at a bottom cupboard. She pulled several pans out of her way. "Linds—get that big pot for me, will you?"

Lindsay leaned to stretch her hand as far back into the tight corner space as she could. She grabbed the handle and pulled it forward. "This one?"

Her mother thanked her and put the pot on the stove.

"Mom? The computer?"

"What? Oh. Research for your history project. Okay, but just the one site—don't go surfing around the web."

"Geesh, Mom. You've got parental controls all over the place.

What are you worried about?"

Her Mom twisted around to give her a glare.

"Okay, okay. I'll 'be careful'!" She wasn't a baby anymore, although her mom treated her that way sometimes.

Lindsay booted up the laptop. She went on Facebook and updated her status then checked their e-mail account and looked for the link her dad had sent. It was a pretty cool site. It had maps and old pictures, even journal entries.

The computer binged, and she saw there was an instant message on Facebook. It was Marty.

> Marty: *u there?*
> Lindsay: *hey Marty!*
> Marty: *Zup?*
> Lindsay: *wyd?*
> Marty: *huh?*
> Lindsay: *what are u doing?*
> Marty: *not 2 much*
> Lindsay: *dad let you on comp?*
> Marty: *he had an errand—get to be home alone!*
> Lindsay: *lucky u*
> Marty: *u doin ok? did u have fun at g'ma quinn's?*
> Lindsay: *yeah—why couldn't u come?*

The cursor on the laptop continued to blink in the little box, and Lindsay wondered if he was still there. It didn't say he'd gone offline though.

> Marty: *ptls*

Lindsay frowned. She didn't recognize the letters.

> Lindsay: *what's that?*

Marty: *parental stupidity*

Lindsay wanted to laugh, but it hurt too bad. They should all be together. She wanted to tell Marty that, but before she could type anything another message popped up.

Marty: *don't worry about it, Linds—it'll be ok*
Lindsay: *that's what dad says—idk if I believe him*

Lindsay typed another message.

Lindsay: *donovan asked about you*

The cursor blinked on the computer as Lindsay waited for Marty's reply.

Marty: *what'd he say?*
Lindsay: *that you better not say anything*

Actually, what he'd told Lindsay was that she "better keep her mouth shut"—but she didn't know anything to blab about. She moved her fingers across the keyboard.

Lindsay: *what'd he mean by that?*
Marty: *Nuthin—dnt wry bout it*

Marty never told her anything. He thought she was a baby.

Marty: *& Linds—stay away from him*
Lindsay: *y?*
Marty: *jdi*
Lindsay: *what?*
Marty: *JUST DO IT*

Lindsay: *don't get mad at me*
Marty: *I'm not mad, Linds—I'm just trying to save your bacon. Donovan has. . .*

Lindsay waited for the rest of his message, but nothing came.

Lindsay: *has what?*
Marty: *Issues—leave it at that*

"Lindsay! Supper's ready." Her mother's footsteps came down the hall.

Lindsay: *p911—gotta go*
Marty: *cu*

Lindsay closed her Facebook tab. "Coming, Mom." She clicked out of the Internet and then shut off the computer. What had Marty meant by Donovan having "issues"? Lindsay didn't care for him much, just because her cousins Molly and Bethy said he was so mean. She didn't have much to do with him, and as far as she was concerned, it wasn't a problem to stay away from him. But why?

Maybe if she asked her mom, she would let her Skype her cousins later. Maybe they could answer some of her questions. The thing was—everybody got upset when she asked questions. Nobody told her anything. But that just made Lindsay more determined. She *would* find out what everybody was hiding.

Chapter Thirteen

A five-hundred dollar fine plus court costs! I hope you're satisfied, Catherine."

Anger bubbled its way through Eric's bloodstream. He could feel his body temperature rising, threatening to blow his self-imposed composure. Not wise, considering they had yet to leave the courtroom and the intimidating presence of the judge who had just ripped him to shreds for his "blatant disregard" of the court's ruling.

"You still don't get it, do you, Eric?" Catherine shook her head at him and marched through the door.

Eric watched in fascination as strands of her hair swung outward then cascaded back into its chic style. He repressed the urge to touch its silkiness. He didn't know which made him angrier, the fact that she could still make him want her or her indifference to that fact.

"I didn't do this as some kind of revenge. I did it so you'd wake up and realize how much your son needs you."

"My son?" Eric's voice rose as his emotions, already pummeled by the morning's confrontation, intensified. He pulled her arm and turned her toward him.

Catherine pointed a slim, manicured fingernail at his nose. "Don't, Eric. Don't even try to go there." Tears—from anger or sorrow, Eric couldn't tell which—formed at the corners of her eyes, and she turned her head away from him. "I've told you a thousand times—there wasn't anyone else."

If only I could believe that. There was never a question of him loving his wife—he just couldn't trust her. *If I had, would you have stayed, Cat?* The strength of his desire surprised him. Two and a half years and the hurt—the anger—were as fresh as they had been the day she had called it quits.

Their argument had carried them to the foyer of the courthouse, and Eric tugged on Catherine's elbow to pause her descent of the marbled steps to the front door. The continuous flow of people moving past them paid scant attention as they hurried to get on with the business of their day. Eric pulled Catherine out of the way of the oncoming pedestrian traffic. Catherine jerked her elbow out of his grasp, the flash of her eyes and tilt of her chin giving him a distinct warning to back off.

Eric crossed his arms and leaned against the massive pillar supporting the upper balcony and faced the little spitfire in front of him, hands on her hips as if ready to draw twin pistols straight at his head—or was it his heart? Flaming arguments were legendary in their ex-marriage. Their making up had been just as passionate as their fighting had been. Eric tried to squelch his urge to "kiss and make up," reminding himself that it would never happen now.

"Look, Catherine, let's just try to focus on the issue at hand here. You keep spouting off about how Marty needs attention, and yet you want to give up permanent custody of him. Tell me how that makes any sense? You accuse me of abandoning my son—how is this any different?"

"I've already talked to Marty. He doesn't necessarily agree with me, but he understands why I'm doing it."

"Agree with you about what?"

Catherine tugged at the flower on her silk blouse, and Eric wondered if she had done it purposely. It was a vivid red. Had she dressed for him? Eric had always loved her in red.

"He doesn't think you want him around. I told him you were preoccupied with business, that having custody all the time might wake you up to the responsibility of being a father." Her voice softened, almost pleading with him. "He needs you, Eric."

"He needs a good swift kick in the pants! Or better yet, a belt to his backside. You're too soft with him, Catherine. You always have been."

"You make me so mad I could scream, Eric Martin Bennington!" Catherine clutched at her hair. "Are you that blind or merely stupid?"

Eric threw up his hands. "He is totally disrespectful of any authority, he was constantly in trouble at school, broke probation, and getting him to be serious about any counseling is a joke!"

"If you'd *take* him to his counseling sessions, maybe it would do some good. That's why we're here today, isn't it?"

"Look, I have a business to run. A business, I might add, that provides not only for Marty and his counseling, but for you and Lindsay, too. And this business with Marty is taking more and more financial demands. And that"—Eric leaned forward—"is why I'm spending longer and longer hours at work. So I've only missed what was unavoidable—it's not like it only takes a few minutes! And anyway, why am I the one who always has to take him?"

"I've been to sessions with him, Eric. The ones you have missed have been with the family counselor. I'm not at fault here—you are."

Fault. Blame. It seemed as if the latter part of their marriage had been centered in those two areas, who could lay the most blame on the other. Today, though, Eric was determined to win that battle. "Yeah right. According to you, I'm always the one at fault. Get real, Catherine."

"You're the one that's pretending here, Eric. You're good at it. You tell yourself something often enough, and in your mind it becomes fact. The truth gets buried somewhere under all the lies and pretense, and you begin to believe your own fabrications."

"That's a load of bull!" Eric nearly snorted. "You're a good one to talk about lies, Cat." Had she ever been truthful with him? The inner war continued to rage inside of him, years after the fact. He still could hear her sobbing denial. *"It's not what you think, Eric. Honest."*

Catherine lifted her hand then let it drop, as if she was too weary to argue or else it didn't matter anymore.

Anger twisted inside Eric. "I *saw* you with my own eyes." His wife in another man's arms. Young and foolish and crazy in love, he had tried to believe her, but he had known from the start the danger in trusting her.

"You saw what you wanted to see, Eric, just like you always have." Catherine's voice rose with renewed vigor. "Play whatever games you want with me, it doesn't matter." She poked at his chest, emphasizing her next words. "But Marty is your son. Your responsibility. It's time you grew up, Eric!"

"Grow up, son! Quit being a sissy." His father's words from the past collided with Catherine's. *"Learn some responsibility, boy!"*

"Quit changing the subject." Eric's chest muscles tightened. "You're the one who wants to paint the truth."

"All right, all right! So you saw Joe kissing me, Eric. . . ."

Kissing. Kissing led to. . . Eric fought the memories that he had tried for years to keep at bay. *Twisted sheets, writhing bodies. . .*

Eric halted his thoughts; he couldn't allow himself to think about that.

". . .but if you'd walked in thirty seconds later, you would have seen me slap him. *That's* the truth." Catherine slid her fingers through her hair and groaned softly. "It's *over*, Eric. Drop the obsession. You'll never believe me anyway. I am so tired of defending myself for a crime I didn't commit. And I'm tired of you blaming Marty for something he had nothing to do with."

Eric tugged on his beard, telling himself to count to ten, to pull himself together, to not lose control. "You've never given me credit, Catherine. I've done everything I can to raise that boy right."

"*That* boy, Eric?" Catherine held up her hand. "Never mind. Just forget it. You may not be ready to accept it, Eric, but there is nothing you can do to change it. You have custody of Marty. You have to take him to counseling. You'd better just learn to deal with it!"

Before Eric could let loose the string of words that came to his mind, his ex-wife's high heels were tapping toward the steps. Then she stopped, twirled around, and came back to face him.

"Eric, you don't believe Marty is your son? Fine! Have a DNA test done." The *click-click* of her heels as she hurried down the stairs punctuated his heart beating and the question lingering in his mind. Eric slumped against the pillar.

Whose son was he?

Chapter Fourteen

Eric slapped the palm of his hand against the cold stone he had been leaning against. He kept running into the same wall. He knew what he saw, yet he so desperately wanted to believe Catherine. Maybe he should have the test done. Get it over with once and for all.

Just like her to bring all this up now. And that judge! As if he didn't have enough to deal with already. Everybody was on his back. He checked his watch. He was already late. He was supposed to be on-site twenty minutes ago. He yanked on his tie that with each passing hour felt more like a noose and headed for his truck.

He had started out this morning with high hopes of making the judge see reason. He was only one person, could only be in one place at one time. But he had the luck of pulling down a hard-nosed judge who didn't understand the real world. Who would've thought the guy would stress the "priority of family" and prattle on about today's youth being left to raise themselves?

Spare him the platitudes! His family was his priority. That's why he busted his back working like he did, trying to run a business and support his family. He cursed Catherine, the judge, and every other unreasonable person he had known. Which just about covered every authority figure he'd ever met. He slammed on his brakes as the car in front of him stopped for a yellow light. The noon traffic was doing nothing to improve his mood.

Okay, so maybe he shouldn't have had his mother take Marty to his last two sessions. But cut a guy some slack—he was under a little stress here. There were more problems with the Minion Development, and Tipton was breathing down his neck about the inspector due on the site next week.

Eric reached for his cell phone and jabbed in the numbers to the office.

"Eric, where are you?" The unflappable Ella sounded distinctly flustered. "Mr. Tipton called. He was, uh, well let's say, highly perturbed that you weren't at your meeting. He said to, uh, blankety-blank forget it because he didn't have time to waste waiting for you to show up. I guess he'll call you later."

Great. Just what he needed. Eric told Ella he wouldn't be back to the office for a while and only just managed to refrain from throwing his cell phone against the passenger door. Instead he gave a few terse orders for Luke and Marty and made sure Shawn and Greg were still on their job then hung up.

Eric blasted his horn at the Honda Civic that cut in front of him, receiving a rude gesture in return from the driver.

Now what? Just once he would like to leave the whole mess behind—the problems with business, irate and sassy employees, rebellious son and unreasonable wife—make that ex-wife. One day, one afternoon even, not to have to think about it. He deserved it, didn't he?

He felt defiant and reckless. Eric reached for his cell phone.

Travis dropped the memo on his secretary's desk and closed the office door. Friday was Sally's half day, and the church building was quiet—no ringing phones, no appointments scheduled. It was his favorite time of the week. His "prayer siesta" he called it. Normally he would spend several hours in the solitude of the sanctuary, but when Eric had called him, he had changed his plans. Flexibility was a must in the ministry. He glanced at the clock in the foyer and decided he had fifteen minutes or so before he had to leave to meet his friend.

Walking into the silent auditorium, Travis let his hand drift against the well-worn backs of the old wooden pews as he made his way down the aisle toward the front. While there were more recent additions to the church, this part of the structure was more than one hundred years old.

Travis had been pastoring this church for ten years now, yet this sacred spot never failed to move him. He slid onto the polished wood and smoothed his hands across the top of the pew in front of him. Several years ago there was a contingent in the church that lobbied for new padded pews. While one part of him acknowledged that furniture had nothing to do with worshipping God, Travis had been secretly pleased when the congregation had chosen to keep the long oak benches.

His own ancestors had never been a part of this place, but Travis knew that the roots of his spiritual heritage were here. Maybe because it had been his first pastorate, where he and his wife had begun their ministry together—so many years ago now!

His journey of faith had gone through rough terrain in this place. He leaned against the curved back of the satiny surface and looked at the stained-glass window high above the choir loft depicting Jesus' crucifixion. There were thirteen windows altogether telling the story of Christ from His birth to resurrection. Just recently a restorer had come to replace several sections that needed repairing, but overall, the windows had survived the years well.

Travis glanced around the auditorium. Perhaps that was what

he loved best about this place. The air seemed to be permeated with the lingering perfume of faithful prayers, joyous praise, and honest searching. Each time he sat here like this he was reminded of the generations that sat here before him. He was "surrounded by so great a cloud of witnesses" as the writer of Hebrews put it.

A deep ache, familiar and persistent, came with the reminder that he had no children, this side of eternity, to pass on the heritage of his faith. *"It was a boy, Mr. Jamison. Do you want to see him?"*

"One day, sweetheart. I'll see you both again one day." The murmured words echoed off the high vaulted ceiling.

But God had given him spiritual children, Travis reminded himself. Many of them sitting right here in these pews Sunday after Sunday. Some were of the community, never setting foot in the doors of his church, but ones he was called to minister to nonetheless. And some, like Eric, were not yet God's child.

Reminded of his appointment to meet his friend for the Civil War swap meet, Travis knew there was only one way to prepare for the time ahead. He bowed his head and began to talk with his heavenly Father.

By the time Travis and Eric were on their way to Richland County Fairgrounds, it was just after noon. Travis had been surprised Eric wanted to go; the last they had discussed it he said he just didn't have time. Travis glanced at his friend's discarded suit coat and tie now lying haphazardly across the backseat of the car. He wondered how the hearing had gone this morning, but hesitated to ask. Perhaps he didn't need to. Eric's scowl had already told him—not good.

"Mind if I turn this on?" Travis reached for the radio dial, not waiting for Eric to answer. It might seem a little pushy since Eric was driving and it was his car, but he was ready to take every opportunity for his friend to hear about God. "The church started a radio broadcast this week, and I haven't had a chance to hear myself yet!" He adjusted the frequency.

Eric looked surprised. "Yeah, sure. Is this one of those, 'please send money now, so we can stay on the air' schemes?"

Travis laughed. "I promise—no pleas for money! Actually, I'm doing a fifteen-minute slot each day. It's more of a devotional than a Bible study. Today I'm finishing up a series. . . ." He paused as he heard the music he had chosen for his introduction.

"This is Travis Jamison. Welcome to *The Father's Heart*. We've been talking this week about our spiritual inheritance. Colossians 1:12 and 13 says, 'Giving thanks to the Father who has qualified us to be partakers of the inheritance of the saints in the light. He has delivered us from the power of darkness and conveyed us into the kingdom of the Son of His love.' Have you been conveyed into the kingdom? Do you know what it is to be a partaker of God's inheritance?"

Travis winced. He sounded too stiff, stuffy even. The microphone had made him nervous, even though he had pre-taped everything. He had redone it three times. He looked over at Eric, who was concentrating on the freeway traffic.

"Yesterday we discussed our inheritance in Christ and all that God gives us through Him. Now let's look at our 'spiritual legacy'—what we are passing on to those behind us."

"A *spiritual* legacy—now there's a concept!"

Travis waited for Eric to continue, but the only sound in the car was his own voice introducing a recording of Steve Green singing "Find Us Faithful." Travis turned the radio down a notch. "You want to talk about it, Eric?"

"Talk about what?"

"Oh, I don't know. The president's foreign policy, the *Cleveland Plain Dealer*'s review of the latest off-Broadway hit, corn prices in Idaho, what happened in court this morning. . ."

"Oh, that."

"Yes, that." Travis once again waited for Eric to continue. Getting this man to talk was harder than getting his board of church deacons to agree on anything. "Eric?"

"Hmm?"

"This morning. . .the hearing. . .Catherine?"

A deep sigh shuddered from the opposite side of the car. "Not much to tell you really. I got custody of Marty. Judge Mr. Know-It-All fined me five hundred bucks for missing a few counseling sessions. Catherine got on her high horse and rode off into the sunset." Eric sent a twisted smile in Travis's direction. "And how was your morning?"

Before Travis could actually reply, or ask any further questions, Eric turned the radio back up.

" 'Legacy' is defined by Webster as 'anything that is handed down from an ancestor, predecessor, or earlier era.' As the song a few moments ago so eloquently put it, we are—each one of us—given a legacy, and in turn each of us leaves a legacy behind us. This is true physically, emotionally, and yes, spiritually as well. God wants us to pass on what we've already inherited from Him!"

Travis reached to turn the radio down again. Perhaps it was more important to talk about whatever Eric was trying to avoid. *Help me out here, Lord.* He needed boldness, but also the sensitivity of the Spirit to tell him how much he should probe. Travis measured his next words, speaking them slowly. "Custody of Marty sounds like it might be a good thing."

"It'd be great if the boy would knuckle down and stay out of trouble. As it is. . ." Eric shook his head.

"Sometimes progress can seem slow. Marty is doing better than he was."

Eric lifted a shoulder and turned his head to look at the side-view mirror before increasing the car's speed to move over in the passing lane. "Yeah, maybe. There are just a lot of things going on right now. You've probably noticed we don't seem to communicate all that well."

"I'm sure that's discouraging, especially when you are trying so hard to be a good father."

"Seems I'm not much better at it than my old man was."

Travis strained to hear Eric's low-spoken words. He was debating what to say when he heard his radio-self quoting Proverbs 3:33 through 35.

"'The curse of the Lord is on the house of the wicked, but He blesses the home of the just. Surely He scorns the scornful, but gives grace to the humble. The wise shall inherit glory, but shame shall be the legacy of fools.'"

Eric laughed. "That's me—the legacy of a fool!"

"You're missing the point, Eric. The *wise inherit glory*; fools inherit shame. Look, I know you've struggled with your own relationship with your father. Have you considered you may be setting Marty up for the same kind of relationship with you?" Travis stared at Eric's whitened knuckles on the steering wheel. "Listen. . ." Travis hesitated, allowing his stilted radio voice to quote Exodus 20:5, "'. . .your God, am a jealous God, visiting the iniquity of the fathers upon the children to the third and fourth generations of those who hate Me.'"

Eric braked hard, throwing them both forward as he stopped at a red light. "Isn't this where we turn for the fairgrounds?"

"Yeah, it's down this road about a quarter of a mile." Travis turned his head toward Eric, but his friend refused to look at him. "What I said on the radio is true, Eric. We pass things from generation to generation. If you aren't careful, you'll pass on the same difficulties to Marty that you and your father have."

"It's too late."

"It's never too late. . ." Travis's voice broke into the conversation from the car's front speakers.

This is surreal, as if there are two of me trying to tell him the same thing! Travis strove not to let out an inappropriate laugh.

". . .you can change the legacy you leave behind! Deuteronomy 23:5 says that 'the Lord your God turned the curse into a blessing for you, because the Lord your God loves you.'"

Eric's control snapped. "It's bad enough listening to you live! What did you do, plan this sermon duet style?"

"No, but it seems the Holy Spirit did! Anyway, I make a good point. . . ." Once again, Travis let his taped message take over.

". . .no one has to leave a legacy of shame—if you are wise, if you turn to Him—you will inherit glory. His glory. Remember it is all God's doing, not ours. The key here is humility. . . ."

Eric turned the radio off. "No offense, but one of you is more than enough!"

Travis laughed. "None taken. You sound like my congregation."

They parked in front of the Exhibitor's Hall and followed a group through the front doors. Curtained booths lined the room, and the large building echoed with the noise of vendors hawking their wares. Civil War buffs bartered their uniforms, canteens, antique rifles, and paraphernalia that covered the tables set side by side in the middle of the room.

"I need a mess kit." Travis pointed to the corner to his right. "Let's start there."

Eric nodded, and they began to work their way through the crowd.

Travis nodded at some familiar faces. They didn't hit many of these Friday-Saturday swap meets, but it stood to reason they would run into the same crowd as the reenactments. Eric picked up a wooden canteen beside him. Travis stood still, pretending to be engrossed in a selection of reproductions. He was remembering meeting Eric for the first time at a Habitat build. Eric was quick-witted, sarcastic at times, but he made Travis laugh. He also had a vulnerability that he wouldn't let show, but Travis knew it was there underneath Eric's sometimes-stoic countenance. Theirs might seem an unusual friendship, too—outside the box, this friendship between a preacher and a man who had no use for God. But Travis knew that God had His hand in it.

Eric had moved to the table selling boots, and Travis followed. Travis picked up a pair of knee flap boots then set them back on the table. They were flashy, and he had a pair almost like them. He preferred the shorter brogans with pegged soles.

He slid his eyes in Eric's direction. It still surprised Travis that he was able to talk Eric into going to that first Civil War reenactment with him.

Eric slipped on a frock coat. "What do you think?"

"I like this one better." Travis pointed to the great coat with the elbow-length cape. "But the vest might be better for this hotter weather."

Eric brushed the muslin cotton on the back of the wool vest. Wooden buttons lined the front. "You have a point." He hung the coat back onto the rack and moved into the crowd.

They bypassed the ladies' dresses and found a table holding more accessories, from leather flasks to portable campstools. Travis fingered a brass belt buckle. One end of the table was arrayed with an assortment of enlisted men's hats, called kepis, and canvas suspenders. Travis watched as Eric began rooting through a large canister of buttons.

Through the years Travis had sensed at different times that Eric was searching, and there were even a few moments where he thought he could see the longing in his friend's eyes when Travis had shared with him God's unconditional love for him. But there was something blocking that relationship. Something buried deep within Eric. Something more than his estrangement with his wife and less-than-perfect relationship with his son.

Marty. Travis thought back to their conversation a few weeks before. The teen was desperate for his father's love and attention. He wanted his trust and needed his affirmation. Travis believed that Eric wanted the same thing—he just didn't know how to get there. And while Travis wanted in the worst way to fix it all for them, he could only continue to pray and allow God to work.

Eric picked up an officer's slouch hat, put it on his head, and grinned at Travis. "Nice. Fits good. My head's too big for the cap I usually wear."

Travis shook his head and refrained from saying that his friend's head was too big for a lot of things. He thought he had the answers to the questions in his life. He pretended he wasn't in pain and that he didn't need any help to "fix" things. There was a thin line drawn in their relationship that Travis couldn't cross. Too bad he couldn't just beat some sense into him. There were things Travis didn't know, things he needed to dig deeper for, but one thing was for sure.

Eric believed too many lies—about his life and about his son.

Chapter Fifteen

"Lindsay?" Catherine dropped her purse and briefcase on the kitchen counter and moved into the living room. "I'm home, sweetheart."

The muted sound of the TV came from the living room. Lindsay was sprawled on the couch, feet straight up in the air, head hanging toward the floor. She was singing along with Hannah Montana. Catherine picked up the remote off the cushion and flopped down beside her daughter.

"Annie leave already?" Lindsay insisted she could stay by herself while her mother was at work, that she was too big for a babysitter. Catherine had compromised by hiring a teenager that lived down the block to "hang out" with Lindsay in case she needed anything. The teenager had asked to leave early today for a family party.

"Hi, Mom. Yeah, she left right after she talked to you." Lindsay flipped her legs over her head and somersaulted onto the floor in front of the couch. "I'm hungry. Can we order pizza tonight?"

"Not tonight. I put a roast in the slow cooker this morning."

Lindsay frowned. "But, Mom—"

"Hey, I'll make your favorite garlic smashed potatoes, and we'll get pizza this weekend. Deal?"

Lindsay sighed and sank onto the couch beside her mother. "All right."

Catherine watched as the credits of the show began to roll and pointed the remote at the TV. "And let's turn this off."

"Mom!"

"If you don't have anything to do, I can find something for you."

"No. I guess I could play in my room. Can I get on the computer?"

"After dinner."

Lindsay continued to mutter on her way out of the room. Catherine watched her daughter's high-drama exit then hauled herself up off the couch and went out to check the mailbox. She brought a stack of envelopes in and dumped them by the phone to sort through later. She would have to write out checks tonight. She was grateful for her salary from her job. Eric still didn't know it, but all his child support was going into the children's college fund. She was footing all the other bills of this household. It was just one more thing among so many that she couldn't talk about with her ex-husband. She went upstairs to change into comfortable clothes then headed back to the kitchen to finish dinner.

Despite Lindsay's grumbles, she ate a good meal and after supper willingly cleared the table. Catherine gave her permission to use the computer and joined her in the little room she had converted to an office. While Lindsay powered up the laptop, Catherine sorted through her correspondence. She set aside the stuff that needed to be done online and got out her checkbook.

"Oh good! Bethy's online."

"Bethy?"

"Yeah, Mom—she's on Facebook now. So are Molly and Kelly."

"Just be careful what you put on there—don't fill in your profile information or give out your address."

"Mom, you worry too much!" Lindsay's hands moved swiftly over the keyboard. "We chat—or do private messages."

Catherine ripped out the check she'd just signed. "What's that?" She leaned forward to get a closer look at the computer screen.

"Oh, these are pictures they just posted. They're from Grandma Quinn's house." Lindsay double-clicked and enlarged a photo. "Look, here's a picture of you and Aunt Connie and Grandma."

Catherine stood to lean over Lindsay's shoulder. If it had to be posted for everyone to see, at least it wasn't a bad picture. Catherine's mother had one arm around Connie and one around Catherine. The next picture was of all five sisters then one of the grandkids with her parents. Catherine laughed at the last shot. "Look at your grandfather hamming it up for the camera."

"I like it when he does his magic tricks for us."

Catherine had to admit it had been good to be with her family. Even the kids had gotten along once they had separated Donovan from the girls. She and Connie had a chance to talk in private later in the evening while the girls were busy with a movie. They had taken a walk around their parents' neighborhood.

"So how's Hawaii?"

"We're settling in. It's always tough at first, but some friends of ours that we were stationed with in Virginia have just arrived."

Catherine slipped her hands in her back pockets and glanced over at her sister. "And the kids? How are they doing?"

"Truthfully? They're struggling." Connie stopped walking. "At first they seemed to be doing all right. Now Bethy seems to be withdrawing again. And Kelly and Molly—" Connie shrugged. "Maybe it's just the whole preteen and teenager thing going on. Heaven knows Donovan has gone through it."

Catherine had nodded, and they continued their walk. She didn't have any good advice for her sister. She was still working on figuring out her own kids, and that was difficult enough.

Lindsay's squeal brought her back to the present.

"What's wrong?"

"My friend Mary just 'friended' me."

"That's great, honey." She tugged on Lindsay's ponytail. "But you've got ten minutes, and then we're shutting it down."

"Mom!"

"Want to make it five?"

It was more like twenty minutes by the time she finally got Lindsay on her way to bed and had everything cleaned up. Catherine went back into the office to finish her bills online. She lifted the lid on her laptop and realized that Lindsay had left the computer on, and it was in sleep mode.

Lindsay's Facebook page was still open, and Catherine noticed the instant-message box. She scrolled up to read through it, stifling the twinge of guilt she felt. Since their family counseling sessions with Marty, she had made it clear to Lindsay that rule number one was there were no secrets. Anything she posted on Facebook or wrote in an e-mail was fair game for her parents to see. That might seem a little invasive for some parents, but after what they'd been through with Marty. . .

Each message had a profile picture by it, so it was easy to see what each person said.

> Lindsay: *hi cuz*
> Bethy: *hi linds how ru?*
> Lindsay: *gd had fun at g'mas house*
> Bethy: *ru glad ur home?*
> Lindsay: *Kinda*
> Bethy: *mu*
> Lindsay: *mu2*

Mu? Mu2—miss you, too. Got it. Catherine might need a dictionary for this texting lingo. She knew computer-speak from work, but this instant messaging with preteenager mixed in could be complicated.

> Bethy: *it's more fun at g'mas*
> Lindsay: *y? u get tgt beach every day*
> Bethy: *dumb ol donovan is here*
> Lindsay: *bros can be a pain sometimes*

Catherine chuckled. She didn't have any brothers, but sisters could be a pain sometimes, too. She'd had to referee a few fights between her kids, but overall they got along surprisingly well for their age difference. She knew Lindsay missed her brother, and she certainly didn't understand why they had to live apart. It was tough to know how much to share with her daughter, and Catherine worried a little about what Bethy might say to Lindsay. They hadn't given her any details because of her age, but she was growing up. Fast. She looked back to the messages.

> Bethy: *is marty mean?*
> Lindsay: *mean? nt rly but sometimes he takes my stuff*
> Bethy: *does he hit you?*
> Lindsay: *punches me smtms—i just tell dad*
> Bethy: *wsh i cld do that*
> Lindsay: *dz donovan hurt u?*
> Bethy: *nvr mind*
> Lindsay: *bethy?*

Catherine drew in a breath. What was going on? Maybe she was just a super-vigilant mom now, and after everything Bethy had been through, she might just be overreacting, but what if she was hiding something?

She quickly scrolled down the messages. There it was. In black and white. Catherine's heart started beating faster. She highlighted the messages and pasted them into a Word document to print them.

She would have to get to the bottom of this.

Chapter Sixteen

The hot sun beat down upon Eric's head. He lifted his captain's hat from his brow, wiped the sweat from his eyes, flipped it back onto his head, and squinted into the early afternoon glare. The rattle of swords in scabbards caught his attention as the small contingent of Civil War reenactors fell into line. He looked to his left and then to his right. Men in both Union blue and Confederate gray had joined ranks to "fight" the common enemy. He wasn't so sure about putting on a demonstration with the reenactors of the French and Indian War. It just didn't feel right to see Travis in his Southern army uniform standing in the ranks with him. For as long as they had known one another, they had stood on either end of the field, opposed to one another.

Eric smiled. Seemed he and Travis had been standing on opposite ends of just about everything from the Civil War to how to handle Marty. He wondered how Marty was faring at the family reunion. He shook his head. Now wasn't the time to think about that. Now was the time to engage the enemy.

At least on these battlefields he could see the enemy, could fight the enemy, and could live to see another day after having engaged the enemy. Out there in the world called his life, he had no clue how to survive. Strangers treated him better than the ones he loved the most. The ones he had given his love, his loyalty, his blood, sweat, and tears to had stabbed him in the back, sent lead balls of betrayal through his heart, and left him a cripple on the battlefield of his own home. He shook away the morbid thoughts.

His family wondered why he came to these reenactments. He came because out here the world made sense. It represented a simpler time. Right now he could use all the simple he could get.

He glanced around. He loved this place. Of all the reenactment camps, this one was the best. Reenactors from every era starting with Arthur and his knights all the way up to Vietnam gathered in this spot for three days to relive the history of war.

In the years he and Travis had been coming to this particular field, they had never had so small a group of Civil War reenactors that there wasn't enough men to put on a show for the onlookers. It had happened this year, and some of the men had worried that they wouldn't be able to participate in a campaign.

Early the day before, some men had wandered into their camp. They were dressed in buckskin breeches and cotton shirts of an earlier era. They carried flintlock rifles in the crooks of their arms. Travis had looked up from cleaning his weapon and invited the men to pull up a log. Eric eyed them. Marty would have fit right in with this bunch. One sported a Mohawk and another's waist-length hair flowed free in the evening breeze.

They voiced their disappointment over the low numbers of participants that had shown up this year and their frustration at not putting on a show for the guests. They had suggested that the two groups combine and fight one another. It wouldn't be the same, but at least some action would happen, and the crowds wouldn't be disappointed.

The men in Eric's gathering had eagerly agreed and after a brief discussion set about putting their plan into action. The crowd had been pleased, and the men from both parties had been ecstatic to be part of the action rather than sitting along the sidelines. They all decided they would put on another demonstration the following day, and so here they were, Travis on one side of him and another fellow by the name of Dawson Sutherland in Confederate gray on his other side.

Eric eyed the tall grasses swaying in the breeze as their drummer took his position at the head of the line and beat out a marching *rat-a-tat-tat* rhythm. The commanding officer raised his sword. Eric looked beyond the shoulders of the front line of men but couldn't see the enemy that was supposed to be taking up position on the opposite end of the field.

"I don't like this," Eric stated to the men in his company as their officer dropped his sword arm and began marching through the waist-high grass. "I'm telling you, I smell trouble."

"What makes you say that, Bennington?" the man next to Travis asked.

"Are you kidding? We're fighting French and Indian War soldiers."

"So?"

Eric compressed his lips. "Different era. Different style of fighting. We might as well be engaging the Revolutionary War group, or for that matter the Vietnam men. Tactically, they think differently. Besides, did you see that motley crew? Mohawks and floor-length hair—that, in itself, screams trouble."

Travis nudged Eric with the butt of his rifle even as he kept eyes forward and feet marching. "Play nice."

The man next to Eric laughed. "Yeah, Bennington, play nice! At least we get to play!"

"Okay, but mark my words, these guys may have let us win last night, but they won't play that nice today."

"We have it all mapped out. Both sides know what we are supposed to do."

"Hmmm. Did you reiterate that to the boys over there?

Because I don't see anyone. And there's supposed be a line of men standing in a nice neat row over there."

At that moment a bone-chilling, blood-curdling war whoop rose through the air, and an Indian popped up from the chest-high grasses, aimed his flintlock at them, and fired a shot then grabbed his blunderbuss, fired another shot, and disappeared back into the grass.

"Ambush!" Travis yelled.

Eric raised his weapon to his cheek and frantically scanned the horizon as he took aim across the meadow. *Where are they?* He could see no one.

Men in the front line dropped as an ambusher rose from the weeds directly in the path of the advancing army. Eric's jaw dropped, and a chill rose up his spine. Behind this individual enemy, a mountain seemed to rise from the foliage. The guy was easily seven feet tall and had to be that big across. The long barrel flintlock looked like a toothpick in his meaty hands. He fired a volley, and more of Eric's group fell. He was shooting blind while the smoke from fired muskets and flintlocks filled the air all around them.

The giant dropped his weapon, roared like a wounded animal, and with arms outspread, rushed from his cover straight into the front line of the Civil War men.

He's insane! Eric's hands slipped against the slick metal of the rifle as he tried to get a bead on the bear of a man rushing directly at him. Before he could fire off a shot the bear was on top of him, and he threw his hands up into the air to block the tackle. It felt as if a wooden beam hit him directly in the chest. He sailed through the air and landed flat on his back. The air rushed out of his lungs. For an instant, Eric thought he was back in high school getting slammed by the opposing team's linebacker. Eric opened his eyes and found himself staring up the barrel of a Brown Bess musket. The tip of a bayonet touched the brass button on his coat.

"Concede defeat."

Chapter Seventeen

"C oncede defeat, indeed!" Eric muttered as he sipped the steaming brew. The taste of defeat was as bitter as the coffee that Travis poured into his cup. More defeat. Just once in his life, he would like for something to go according to plan. He shook his head. Oh well, at least here it was just a game and nothing like his life.

For a moment, he leaned his forearm on the fence and stared at the pennants and streamers fluttering from the medieval tents on the other side of the park. Off to their left the sounds of cannon and mortar fire told him the World War II battle was still going strong. He hoped the American troops weren't being overrun the way their troop had been.

Eric turned around to see Travis shed his double-breasted gray coat and sink down onto the canvas cot. He pulled a tin from his haversack. "I still can't believe they won! They were outmanned and outgunned. How could we get outmaneuvered?"

Eric winced as he watched his friend nibble on a biscuit known as hardtack. He understood too well how it had gotten the nickname "Sheet Iron." You had to have teeth made of granite to eat that stuff.

"I told you those Frenchies couldn't be trusted. But did anyone here listen to me? No." Eric shrugged out of his wool coat and pulled the coarse cotton blouse over his head. He dropped onto his own camp cot.

"Boy, you really hate defeat, don't you, Bennington?" Dawson asked from the next tent. Most of the men had rolled up the sides of their canvas tents to make a canopy overhead and allow the breeze to come through.

"Yes, especially when the rules of engagement get changed!" Eric pulled out his pack to find another shirt to put on and wished he had picked up a vest at the swap meet. Eric's hand brushed against the soft, supple leather of a small book tucked beneath an extra pair of wool breeches. The old journal weighed on his mind, but he wasn't ready to look at it yet. His eyes flicked up to Travis, who had removed his knee-length boots and was massaging his instep.

"Bennington, tell me again why we're doing this. I seem to have forgotten."

Eric chuckled as he replied, "Somehow the reasons don't seem so logical when you're standing in ninety-degree weather wearing three layers of wool and being beaten by a bunch of wild renegades who don't know the meaning of a code of conduct. However, I like the sadistic nature of the Civil War, while you wanted to get back in touch with your roots."

"Ahh. Yes. I remember now. Roots are important. And every year I get to investigate mine a little more," Travis replied.

"You are as bad as Gran and Lindsay. Why you dwell in familial past is beyond me."

"Legacy, my friend. It's all about legacy. If you'd just research your heritage a little, you might be surprised at the discoveries."

"And maybe I don't want to find out either," Eric retorted.

"Afraid of what's lurking there?" Travis asked in amusement as he turned to study Eric's face.

"I am not afraid," Eric replied. *Am I? Is that why I hesitated in taking this journal Gran gave to me last week?* Eric reached in his canvas backpack and fingered the worn leather again before he withdrew his hand and stood to his feet. "I'm just not a fanatic for the past."

"Yeah right! Look around you. You are in the middle of a Civil War reenactment, and you try to tell me that you aren't a history nut?"

"Let me rephrase that. I'm not a nut about my family history. Hanging out at the family reunion is bad enough. Thank God for this enactment. It was the best excuse I could have for not showing up at the family picnic. 'Course Mom and Dad are ticked at me, but then what else is new? It's always a hassle."

Travis shook his head. "Admit it, Bennington, you're just a coward."

"When it comes to those blasted family reunions, you bet I am. Did you know that a couple of years ago Mallory practically attacked me because Marty was kidding his cousins? Last year I was ripped to shreds because I was teasing her girls. It was a good thing her husband was right there to set her back in her place. No thank you. I don't need that kind of aggravation in my life. Not now. Besides, one genealogist in the family is enough."

"Oh, who's that?" Travis dug in his bag for a worn towel and began to rub a shine back into his boots.

"Lindsay." Eric turned away to look across the field. The guns had ceased from the battle across the field, and he could see groups of people drifting toward the concession area set up not too far from the reenactment camps. He moved to the small fire by their encampment and poured himself another cup of coffee. He lifted the pot toward Travis, but he shook his head.

"So Lindsay's into genealogy? How'd that happen?" Travis drew Eric's thoughts back to their conversation.

He moved over to his cot and sat back down. "She had to do a year-end history class project and trace one parent's family tree.

She chose Catherine's family." He reached for his great coat and rolled it up and shoved it in his haversack. "Linds got an A on the project and a fever for genealogy."

Travis set his boot down and looked at Eric. "So how has that been for the two of you?"

"Good! Except now she's got me helping her trace my family tree."

"Wait a minute." Travis stood and waved his polishing rag at Eric. "How's that again? Didn't you just tell me you didn't want to know the secrets lurking in your family history?"

"Quit waving that thing in my face." Eric pushed Travis's hand away.

"So you're telling me you secretly want to know your past? You're stranger than I thought, Bennington." Travis grinned as he sat back down on his cot and picked up his other boot. "And have you enjoyed getting to know your ancestors?"

Eric rolled his eyes. "I wouldn't put it quite like that."

"How would you put it?"

"Every time she's with me, she's either asking me questions about the family or asking me to help her on the computer to research our family. After the family was split apart and the trouble that Marty got into, Linds just withdrew from us all. She stayed hidden in her room most of the time with her Barbie dolls or reading books. She was so quiet she wouldn't talk to anyone. She was becoming someone I didn't even know anymore. It took a while to draw her out again. I always loved being with that kid. She's so lovable, so easy to be with." *I wish Marty had gotten some of his sister's common sense.* Eric took a sip of his coffee and looked out across the camp. It was fairly quiet now. Most of the men were milling about their tents, small puffs of smoke rising from their individual campfires. He watched their neighbor strip down to his T-shirt, allowing his suspenders to dangle from his breeches.

"And?" Travis's damp towel brushed his face and landed at his feet. "Stay with me, Bennington."

"What?"

"Alzheimer's creeping in on you or what? You, Linds. . . bonding."

"Oh yeah. We've been spending more time together."

"So you said."

"I think the hardest part of it all was when she finally asked about Shelly."

Travis frowned. "Who's Shelly?"

Eric turned to stare at Travis. *Who's Shelly? You don't know?* No. He'd never told Travis about Shelly. *How do you tell your best friend that you mur–* Eric looked away and took a gulp of his coffee. The hot liquid burned his tongue, and he swallowed hard. "My sister, Michelle. She died a long time ago." Eric cleared his throat. "Blasted coffee's hot!"

"I hear it's good that way." Travis got up to retrieve the towel he'd thrown. "So—family, you, Lindsay, what else?"

He was persistent; Eric had to give him that. "She talked to my folks about some stuff. Then two weeks ago she called and asked me if I could take her to Gran's. She decided she needed to research my father's mother. So I took her." Eric shook his head as he restrained his laughter. "Those two! Once Gran discovered that Lindsay had a 'hankering for the past' as Gran called it, there was no stopping either of them. So I just left her with Gran for a couple of days. I figured that she could recount all of the old stories to Linds. That was always the best part of the family gatherings, even though they can get a little old with all the retelling."

Eric set his coffee down and reached into his pack for his own boot rag. He swiped at the toes of his boot. "Anyway, when I went to pick Lindsay up at the farm, I found her and Gran in the attic of the homestead."

"The attic?"

"Apparently they found a treasure trove in the old trunks that

Gran said belonged to Gramp's father and grandfather. Actually, they did find something rather interesting." Eric reached into his pack and pulled out the diary. He fingered the velvety soft deer-hide leather cover of the slender volume he held in his hands before handing it to Travis.

"Wow. This is pretty amazing."

Eric watched his friend open the cover carefully and run his fingers over the brittle pages. Whatever had possessed him to accept it? Gran had pressed it into his hands when he had dropped Lindsay off to spend the week with Gran.

"Gran thought I might want to read it while I was 'out playing war.' It was written by my great-great-grandfather." Eric took the journal from Travis's outstretched hand and rose from his cot. "I was thinking of taking my cup of coffee and finding a shady spot, preferably with a breeze, and to relax a bit before the festivities begin again this evening."

Without waiting for Travis's reply, Eric slipped out of the tent and walked toward the grove of trees. He settled against the bent trunk of a sycamore tree. For a moment he stared at the deep blue sky through the tangle of branches. He let out a breath and was surprised to find his muscles tightening. Why did he react like this? For as long as he could remember, he had always been drawn to and repelled by the past.

From his vantage point he could see people in shorts and tank tops mingle among men and women in dress of the nineteenth century. Women in long cotton dresses tended fires. In the field, a horse whinnied.

He stared at the bound leather against his dark-blue breeches. He had been reluctant to open the pages of the past, but dressed as he was in historical clothing, the timing seemed right. He slipped his reading glasses out of his pocket and turned the book toward the sunlight filtering through the trees. With gentle fingers, he opened the cover and leaned forward to decipher the elegant fading brown script on the flyleaf.

> *Artelius Sherman Bennington*
> *Meganville, Ohio*
> *December 25th, 1857*
> *I am aware of the amount of money Mother had to spend to buy me this journal. It is a most beautiful present, and I shall cherish it. I sold my sorrel to purchase a brooch I had seen her admire in Lichen's Mercantile.*

The rest was unreadable. Slowly Eric turned the pages, reading what was legible and skipping what wasn't.

> *August 2nd, 1861*
> *Word has just arrived. The southern states have declared absolution from the Union. President Lincoln has declared that the Union is in a state of war. Men are being pressed to fight the rebellion that is sweeping our land. I have enlisted and volunteered my entire stock of horses to the cause, twenty in all.*

Eric tipped his head back and closed his eyes, wondering what it was like for his great-great-grandfather. Would he have enough courage to sign up to fight in a war? Sure, he had done a stint in the army, but that had been during peacetime.

> *I have joined the Ohio 2nd Regiment Cavalry and will be taking my training at Camp Dennison. Mother sobbed against my chest when I told her of my decision. She stayed up for two days and sewed my travel attire. I told her it was not necessary, but she insisted. I leave two days hence.*

"How's it going? Discover any family secrets yet?"

Eric jumped at the sound of Travis's voice. "What?"

"Just thought I'd check on your journey into the past." Travis dropped to the ground and wrapped his arm around his knee. "Your great-great-grandfather's journal. Do you know how old that must be?"

Eric reached for his forgotten cup of coffee. "Yep. Really old."

"You know that should probably be in a museum, not on a battlefield."

"Actually, I can't think of a better place to be reading this than right here."

"Why is that?"

"Believe it or not, he fought for the North in the Civil War," Eric stated as he readjusted his reading glasses. "Listen to this.

'February 22nd, 1862, Fort Scott, Independence, Missouri. We have been entrenched for months as this skirmish drags on. We have lost good horses in our campaign, but I must say thanks be to God for keeping our men safe and in good shape. Only six have died, two mortally wounded in battle. Avery Desmond fell from his horse when struck with a bullet and was instantly killed as he broke his neck. Three men fell to Influenza. We are holding our breath that it does not turn into an epidemic. It is miserable and cold.'"

Eric turned the page. "Here's another one.

'March 2nd, 1864. I sent a letter home to Mother and one home for Frederick. I wonder how Della is? Every day I fight to remain alive so I may return for her. I have plans. I am selling my land in eastern Ohio and moving further west, perhaps on the other side of Cleveland. I hear there is good land around the Ashland area. I plan on looking into it and establishing a farm before I return for Della.'"

"Who's Della, I wonder. She must have really captured him with her charms." Travis stretched his long legs out before him and responded with a greeting to several people who wandered past.

"You'll love this. I thought it was outrageous." Eric flipped through the previous entries.

" 'March 13th, 1861. The snow is receding, spring is approaching, and Frederick has a new daughter. The first after five sons. He reminds me of my bantam rooster. Puffed up and proud. I visited the farm. Orpha is doing fine. Della is the most beautiful baby I have ever laid eyes on. I am smitten. How can it be that I have fallen in love with a mere infant and know in my heart that we will be wed when she is of marriageable age? But she is mine. I have claimed her for my bride. I told Frederick that when she turns sixteen I am going to marry her. He laughed and said, "But what if she turns out to be of ugly countenance, what then?" I said it mattered not. I am smitten, and she is mine.' "

"I had heard this story at the family picnics, but never made the connection as to who it was." Eric chuckled as he placed a leaf in the pages of the book and laid it aside. He glanced up.

Travis looked at him in stunned silence. Eric laughed. He wasn't sure which was more amusing, the family story or the look on Travis's face. It wasn't often he could make T speechless. He relished the moment.

Finally Travis sputtered, "A baby? She was just a baby, and he wanted to marry her? I know that life was a lot different back then and that older men oftentimes married much younger women, but somehow this just seems—wrong."

"Oh come on, T, I think it's funny." Eric laughed again.

The look didn't leave Travis's face. If anything, it seemed to intensify at Eric's remark. "Do you?" He shook his head as a slight tremor raked his body. "Maybe, but it just seems wrong!"

A sweat broke out on Eric's brow that had nothing to do with the stifling heat that was being alleviated by the cool evening breeze. "Okay, how and why is this so wrong?"

"How would you have felt had I known you, say, ten years ago?"

"I wish I would have."

"Now let's say that I saw Lindsay through the nursery window and announced to you that I had fallen in love with her. And I was going to wait for her to grow up, so I could marry her."

It was bad enough to think of some pimple-faced punk making moves on his baby girl, but the thought of a man his age thinking those thoughts about a little girl, his little girl. . . Eric's stomach lurched, and his fist contracted. "Point made and taken. I never thought of it like that, but it does seem perverted when you put it like that, doesn't it?"

"Yeah, it does. Did he end up marrying her?"

Eric flipped to the end of the journal, but the last entry was 1865. "According to the family legend, he married her at the age of thirty-eight. She was fifteen."

Travis bounded to his feet. "Weren't planning on portraying that character in our reenactments, were you? I'd hate to see him passing on that particular quality to my friend."

"No. He's not a guy I want to emulate." Even as he spoke, Eric felt his stomach roll again. The thought of being like that made him nauseated.

Travis clasped Eric's shoulder. "I told you delving into your past could be very enlightening."

"Dangerous is a better word." Eric shuddered at the thought. What else was lurking in the recesses of his past?

Chapter Eighteen

He's here!" Lindsay jumped up and ran to the kitchen.

Eleanor Bennington smiled at her great-granddaughter's enthusiasm. It took her a little longer to unfold herself and rise from the floor. Her stiff knees creaked as she made her way to greet her grandson. She paused in the doorway, enjoying the sight of the father-daughter reunion. Their living apart had been hard on both of them.

"Hey, Dad! Me and Gran were just going through Gramp's old trunks in the attic. Wanna see?" Lindsay tugged on Eric's arm, urging him into the farmhouse.

"Whoa! Slow down there, pumpkin." Eric halted Lindsay's rush and gave her a hug. "Did you have a good time with Gran?"

"I sure did! But everybody asked where you were. The reunion was cool though. Me and Renee got to ride Sunny and Prince, then Gran let us go swimming in the pond."

"Uncle Geoff watched the girls on the horses and at the pond. We missed you," Eleanor assured him.

Eric turned to the doorway and greeted his grandmother. He leaned down and kissed her on her cheek. "Hey, Granny. I'm sure everyone got along just fine without me."

Eleanor gripped his arms and gave him a little shake. "Eric Martin! Don't you think for a moment you weren't missed. You're part of this family, and they love you." She looked him directly in the eyes. "I love you." How she longed for him to believe that was true.

Eric grinned at her and put his arm around her back. They followed Lindsay into the living room. "So what have my girls been up to?"

Eleanor glanced up at him from the corner of her eye. He was good at evasion. Always had been, even as a little boy. She motioned Eric toward her old settee and took a seat in the bentwood rocker in the corner. She laid a small afghan across her knees and smiled at Lindsay who was kneeling at an open trunk on the braided rug in the middle of the room.

"Look, Dad—here's a picture of Gramps in his old army uniform." Lindsay handed Eric a photograph in a padded frame. He turned it over in his hands.

"I think I've seen this before. Wasn't it taken in France, right before he came home from the war?"

"We were married right after that. So long ago now." Eleanor nodded and tipped the rocker into motion. "I can't believe your gramps has been gone for almost two years."

"I miss him." Lindsay crawled over to her great-grandmother and clasped her hand. "He used to call me his lollipop and give me suckers."

Eric laughed. "He used to sneak us stuff when I was a kid and stayed here with Gran."

Eleanor shook her head. "He could be a rascal, but I miss him, too." She looked at Eric. "Did you enjoy the reenactment?" Another evasion, no doubt. And the reason he hadn't been at the reunion.

"Did you take the journal, Daddy? Can I look at it?"

"Let's wait until we get home. Why don't you go gather your things?"

Lindsay stuck out her bottom lip. "But Dad—"

"Uh-uh. No buts. We need to get home. I think we need to give Gran a break." He turned her shoulders toward the stairs and gave her a swat. "Now scoot!"

Eleanor watched Lindsay leave the room and listened to her sandals slap against her heels as she went up the stairs. Eric was wonderful with his little girl. It was such a shame he couldn't have that same relationship with his son. Or with his father.

"Thanks again for the journal."

"You're welcome, dear." Eleanor picked up a ball of yarn beside her chair. "I had a little chat with Catherine when she dropped Lindsay off." She knew she needed to be careful what she said to Eric. Her needles clicked as she began to knit. "She said that she thinks Marty has been getting help through his counseling."

Eric walked over and looked out the big picture window overlooking the backyard. "I don't know, Granny. Some days I would agree with her that he's doing better, then he turns around and pulls some dumb stunt."

"Perhaps he's just looking for some affirmation." His shoulders stiffened, and she couldn't see his face.

Eric turned around. "You have been talking to Catherine."

Eleanor stopped the rocker and peered over her reading glasses. "Have you ever thought she might be right about this, Eric? Marty seems to be seeking his father's approval. You know how difficult adolescence can be." *Oh dear boy, surely you remember your own rebellious youth!*

"I get that, Granny. I just can't get through to him. I try to talk to him, but. . ." Eric turned back to the window and pressed his forehead on the cool glass. "I think—I think he hates me."

His last words were whispered, but Eleanor heard him. She rose from her chair and hugged him. "Eric, he doesn't hate you.

He loves you. He longs to know you. Just as you've always longed to know your own father."

Eric blinked and cleared his throat. "Look, Gran—"

"My dear boy, you're the one who needs to look and see things more clearly! I know you hurt inside. I know you want a relationship with your dad and your son—and I know you don't want to hear what I'm going to say next. But I'm going to say it anyway." She gave his arm a shake. "It's not going to happen until you begin a relationship with your heavenly Father and He helps you forgive."

"He doesn't deserve—"

"I'm not talking about Martin or Marty. I'm talking about you forgiving yourself."

"Dad!" Lindsay clumped down the stairs dragging her backpack and small duffel bag. "Can you help me?"

Eric turned to his daughter. "What did you do? Pack everything you own?"

"I need all this stuff."

"Okay, I got it. Thank your grandmother, and let's get you home."

Lindsay rushed to her great-grandmother and wrapped her arms around her. "I love you, Gran! Thanks for letting me stay with you. Can I come back sometime?"

"Of course, my darling girl! Anytime. I love having you." Eleanor kissed the top of her head then narrowed her eyes at Eric. He seemed more than willing to rush out of here, but he wasn't getting off that easy. "Bring her back. And come yourself. We didn't finish our conversation. I have more things to say to you."

Eric laughed. "I just bet you do, Granny. Thanks again."

Eleanor followed them to the door and waved them off. Once again Eric was running from his problems. Her heart ached for him. He was his own worst enemy at times. He hadn't been willing to listen—at least to his grandmother—for a long time.

She moved to the stove to put the kettle on. It was more than time for a cup of tea. She got her cup and saucer from the cupboard then stood at the sink looking out over the land that had sustained them for so many years. This was home to her; she hoped she never had to leave it. In a way, Paul was lucky to be gone. At least he was in heaven, and his difficulties and trials were over.

The whistle blew on the teakettle, and Eleanor poured the hot water over a tea bag. There was only one place to go when she was troubled like this. She took her cup to the kitchen table and set it down beside her Bible. She smoothed the edges, pressing down the tape that held the binding together. She had cried many tears and prayed many prayers for her children and grandchildren, but she still had a few more left.

She opened the book to the Psalms and began to pray for Eric. How long would he continue to resist the only One who could help him? *Use whatever it takes to get his attention, Lord. Whatever it takes.*

Chapter Nineteen

Bennington Electric is on fire!"

In one instant, with one phone call, Eric's entire life altered and his well-ordered world crumbled around him.

He roused Marty out of bed. They scrambled for clothes and ran out to the Jeep; both of them were too stunned to make conversation. Marty pointed ahead at the pink glow on the distant horizon, and Eric gunned the motor. They shot into the deserted downtown area going faster than the speed limit. As he turned the corner, the cacophony of sounds merged with the kaleidoscope of color and action, leaving Eric's mind swimming and his body numb. Smoke plastered the air in an acrid curtain of black soot and gray smog as the yellow inferno before him devoured all his hopes and dreams. He screeched to a stop before the barricade and bolted from the car.

A policeman barred his way. "That's my business!"

The officer moved the barricade to the side and allowed Eric entrance, but motioned him away from the frantic activity. Eric stood in numbed silence as the roar of the burn and the shouts of the firemen washed over him. He ran his hands through his hair as his life and livelihood went up in a billow of black smoke.

"Boss? You okay?" Eric turned. Greg looked as shocked and disheveled as he felt. "That's my business. Greg, what are we going to do?"

"Man!" Greg rubbed his already disheveled hair. He had a bald spot right on the top, and the longer strands he normally combed over it were hanging off to the side. "I can't believe this!"

Eric turned as a shout from one of the firefighters came from his left. They were backing in another fire truck. "It's gone. All gone."

Greg put his hand on Eric's back, and the two of them stood in a silent cocoon of disbelief as the chaos of activity swirled around them. What more was there to say? Greg seemed as stunned as Eric felt, both of them unable to articulate the enormity of what they were witnessing. This was both their livelihoods. They'd been on the journey to get this far and now—

Now the roaring monster before them devoured that dream, leaving ashes and billowing smoke in its wake of destruction. More and more people were gathering to watch the show. Eric shivered despite the heat. What was he going to do?

"Eric?" A woman's voice invaded the chaotic world of his thoughts. "Are you okay?"

He shook his head as he turned to face his sister. Her eyes were soft with compassion as she slid her arm around his waist for a sideways hug. He stepped back and looked over his shoulder. Greg had drifted off and was talking to a man at the edge of the barricade. Firemen shouted instructions to one another above the roar of the flames and the torrent of water gushing over the structure.

"What happened?

What happened indeed? Did someone throw a cigarette into the Dumpster? Perhaps Shawn or Tom? No, not Tom. He didn't work there anymore. Was it too close to the building?

"Eric?"

"What?"

Mallory took him by the arm and led him to the curb facing the burning building. Her hand remained on his back as she pushed him down and settled beside him. "Do you know what happened?"

"No." He pulled a handkerchief out of his pocket and wiped his face. The blaze upped the temperature of the already sultry night, making it nearly unbearable. He wondered how the firemen were able to stay so near the inferno. He looked at his sister. Her hair was twisted up in a hair clip, and the faded letters on her T-shirt were OS and half a U. Both of her knees peeked out through holes in her jeans.

"How'd you know about the fire?"

"Oh, Joey was spending a couple of days with his mother. The scanner woke him up. He called Jake and me."

"Joey?"

"Jake's photo assistant. Joseph Peterson."

"Oh yeah, I remember him now. Weird guy. Where's Jake?" He couldn't believe he was having this mundane conversation with his sister while his entire life was going up in smoke.

"Home with the girls. I called Mom and Dad. They're on their way."

Eric sprang to his feet. "Why'd you do that?"

"I thought you'd want them to know." She scrambled up. "Don't be so darn defensive. I was just trying to help you out."

"How? By having you and Dad here to gang up on me?" He jammed his hands in his pockets.

"No, by trying to be here to support you. That's what families do. But then, you've never needed anyone but yourself, have you?"

"That's enough, Mallory!"

They both whirled to face the third voice that came up behind them. At his mother's reprimand, a curious feeling of warmth curled through Eric. It wasn't often when someone came to his defense.

133

His mom's blond hair had been hastily pulled to the back of her head in a loose ponytail and was tinted orange by the firelight. Eric couldn't remember the last time she had looked so frazzled. She pulled him into a hug. "It's horrible. Just horrible."

"How'd this happen, son?"

Eric stiffened. Condemnation was in his father's voice. It would seem even this was his fault. "I don't know, Dad."

Was it the sign? Did Tom replace the ballast on the sign like he'd told him to? Did the fuse kick out again? Eric had been after him to take care of it.

"Was it a short in the wiring someplace? You know what they say about a shoemaker having no shoes for his own children. The same holds true for just about everybody."

"Martin, not now."

"Just stating facts."

Eric frowned. "I said I don't know."

"Well, you needn't worry. Your insurance will take care of it. You do have insurance, don't you?"

He squared his shoulders and faced his father. In the amber glare, Martin's face appeared like something out of a Hitchcock movie. "Of course I have insurance." *Oh Lord, where's the insurance policy? Fire? Did it cover fire? I think it did. Would it cover negligence?* "Give me some credit, Dad. I have been a successful businessman for the last fifteen years."

"Calm down, and don't you use that tone of voice with me."

Eric suddenly had the sensation of being seven years old again and his dad was yanking his britches down for "sassing his mother." *"Don't use that tone of voice, boy. Don't ever talk to your mother like that."*

"Eric's had a terrible shock, dear. He just lost his business and his livelihood. How it happened seems rather irrelevant at the moment, don't you think?"

"I just wanted to make sure that you would be okay." Martin

pulled off his hat and swiped his brow. "If it was anything but an accident, the insurance won't pay."

"Just what are you accusing me of, Dad?"

"I'm not accusing you of anything. I'm simply—"

Mallory interrupted, breaking the tension that tightened between father and son. "Marty's not staying with you, is he?"

"Oh Lord! Marty!" He spun in a circle, scanning the congestion of people that had managed to form even in the middle of the night.

"He's here? You brought him to the fire? Where's your head, boy?" Martin condemned him yet again.

"Marty!" Eric's voice tried to penetrate the chaotic din. "Marty!"

"There!" Mallory pointed across the square to a small knot of people that were milling about. "Who's he with?"

Eric sagged with relief. "Greg Tanner, my store manager." He peered through the smoke that laced the streets. "And that's Luke, I think." He turned his attention back to the flaming building. The firemen were still struggling to bring the white-hot blaze under control.

"I can't believe that you would bring your son along to see your life go up in flames."

"What was I supposed to do, Dad? Leave him at home all alone?"

"He was asleep. He wouldn't have known until it was all over. It is rather a traumatic thing for a teenager to have to deal with. Don't you think?"

"So were some of the things that happened in my life," Eric snapped at his father. "I survived, no thanks to my—"

"That's enough, both of you!" Mom's voice was hard as nails. "Why is it that this family insists on constantly being at each other's throats? Martin, Eric needs you right now."

A derisive smile pulled Eric's mouth. It was short-lived as his mother spun to face him. "And you, Eric, don't need to be getting your father worked up. We came here to try to help, so get down off your high horse, and be glad that you have a family that does care about you."

Because there are children in the world who don't have any family. His mind automatically finished the well-known platitude that his mother was in the habit of spitting. There are times when being an orphan would be a good thing.

"I can't take this anymore. How can you stand to be so close to the heat is beyond me." Martin wiped his brow with the back of his hand.

"Are you okay, Daddy?"

He smiled and wrapped an arm around Mallory's shoulder. "Your old man can't take things like he used to, peanut. Walk with me to a cooler spot, and keep your old dad company."

"Daddy, you aren't old."

Their voices faded into the surrounding bedlam.

"Eric, what am I going to do with the two of you?"

"He started it."

"And I am going to finish it. You two have been at each other's throats for"—she paused—"from the moment you were born." His mom turned to watch Martin and Mallory as they walked down the street and away from the intense heat.

"I didn't ask to be treated like this all the time by him. It's not my fault." Was that him talking? He sounded just like Marty.

"I'm not so sure. You had a stubborn streak in you the size of Manhattan, and from the time you were a baby you were bucking authority. Don't you think it's time to give it up and try to make peace with your father?"

Eric clenched his fists. *Even now, it's about him. What about me? I just lost everything.*

"What will you do? About the fire, I mean."

He shrugged, kneading his temple with two fingers. "I'm not real sure at the moment, Mom, but I'll be fine. If things pan out,

I'll rebuild. Bigger, better. I'll be fine."

"I know you will be, Eric. You always are." She patted his face. "I think I need to get your father and go home. This has been hard on him, you know."

"Yeah, I know." He leaned over and kissed her cheek. "Go put Dad to bed. I'll be fine." Eric shifted and dropped down on the curb, drawing his knees close to his chest.

As dawn punched a hole in the nighttime blackness, the firemen began rolling up their hoses. The morbidly curious crowd that had gathered in the night had finally dissipated, for which Eric was grateful. He shifted back to lean against the rough concrete of Weltman's Five and Dime.

His family had gone once the flames had finally come into submission to the firemen's labor. Dad looked exhausted by the time Mom convinced him to leave the scene. Mallory had laid a gentle hand on Eric's shoulder and told him she would be praying for him. He wasn't sure whether it made him feel better or not.

Eric tipped his head back and drew in a deep breath only to have the acrid air sear a path to his lungs. He coughed.

"Dad? You okay?" Worry caused Marty's changing voice to wobble.

He opened his eyes, nodded, and reached a hand up to his son. Surprise double-timed Eric's heart when Marty took his hand. He eased down on the pavement beside Eric, eyeing him closely. "You look whipped, Dad."

"I'm fine."

"What're you gonna do?" The question came out on a whisper of air.

Eric looked down into the soot-smudged face of his son. Fear and fatigue were etched in the boy's face. "I'm not really sure."

He slid his arm around Marty. His heart nearly stopped beating when Marty tipped his head to lean against Eric's shoulder. "Don't worry about a thing though. We'll be fine. Just you wait and see."

He pulled Marty closer as the sun fought to break through the thickness of the smoke-laden sky and the last fire truck hauled away weary firefighters, leaving behind a pile of smoking rubble in the place Eric had deposited all his dreams and ambitions.

I will be fine. I will. His stomach clenched, and he fought the quiver that shimmied up his spine.

I have to be.

Chapter Twenty

The pungent scent of smoke and seared lumber rose from blackened debris that was once Eric's store. He stepped over the rubble as he made his way through the fire-devoured mess. The trucks had arrived soon after they had gotten the call about the blaze around one a.m. that morning. When Eric and Marty got there forty minutes later, the place had been crawling with firefighters, and now that the fire had been put out, men in hard hats and clipboards were filing through the chaos that had been left behind.

Eric stopped at the half-charred service counter. He wasn't sure which had done more damage—the fire or the water and chemical foam they had used to put it out. He heard a shout at the back of the building and made his way carefully through the scattered half-burned boxes of supplies. What hadn't been burned was soaked with water and littered with bits of cardboard and pieces of ceiling tiles. His well-stocked shelves now stood disheveled and half empty.

He kicked at a smashed box of melted electrical wire and stepped over an unidentifiable pile. Everything was ruined. The firemen's hoses had blown everything from one side of the building to the other. He doubted anything was salvageable from this mess.

Eric made his way to the area that had once been his office. He found a barrel-chested man in a hard hat barking orders. Sixty pounds lighter and ten years younger and he could have been a Billy Dee Williams look-alike.

"Be careful with those documents, Charles! Make sure you put cardboard between them and pack them in cotton."

The other man nodded at him and bent to retrieve a sheaf of charred papers. "There's checks here, boss." He took out a long pair of tongs and slipped them into a plastic bag and sealed it, marking the front with a pen.

The whole side of Eric's tan filing cabinet was blackened. Another man was emptying stacks of partially burned files and placing them in cartons. He lifted the box and moved past Eric.

"What are you doing with my files?"

The older man turned around. "You the owner?" He flipped back the pages on the small notebook in his hand. "Eric Bennington?" He held out his hand. "I'm the certified fire inspector for the county. Ben Cooper."

Eric nodded then shook his hand. "The fire chief said you wanted to ask me some questions." He moved over to his scorched desk. His stack of papers he'd left there yesterday was a lumpy mass of pulp. The framed photo of Marty and Lindsay had been knocked over and the glass shattered. Lindsay had drawn a picture of Eric in his Civil War uniform. One half was smeared with soot, and the other was water damaged. He reached to pick it up.

"Please don't touch that, sir. We need to gather physical evidence in here. We'll make sure you get it all back when we are done with it."

"If there's anything worth giving back to me." Eric stuffed his hands in his pockets. He looked at the blackened streak running up the wall in the corner. "The damage in here looks like it's worse than anywhere else. Is this where it started? What caused it?"

"That's what we're trying to find out."

"Why would it start in here?" Eric turned in a circle. He hadn't left anything on in here, and he knew it wasn't the wiring. The damage was really bad in the corner, but what would have caused it?

Inspector Cooper tapped the man still gathering what remained of Eric's paperwork. "Get somebody in here to get a sample of the carpet in the corner. And don't forget the subflooring and soil samples. Did you do the hydrocarbon tests?"

Charles shook a small vial at his boss. "Gonna try these new ones with the activated charcoal."

"That's fine, but make sure you get bigger samples for the lab. And make sure I have all the interview reports from the firemen that were the first responders." He turned to Eric. "Let's move outside."

They made their way back through the building; the inspector stopped to direct a man with a camera. Eric went out what was left of the front door. It looked like the firefighters had hacked their way in. He passed a man following a yellow Labrador retriever on a leash. It was moving its head back and forth sniffing the ground. Eric turned and waited for the inspector to join him.

"What's going on? What's the dog for?"

"Just investigating the fire, Bennington. That's a fire service dog. He's here to check for accelerants."

"That's why you're 'gathering evidence'? You think somebody started this?"

The inspector shifted his weight and made some scratches on his notepad. "The firemen noted that the fire burned at an unusual rate. It swept through the whole building pretty fast. One of the guys thought he might have smelled gasoline." He finished writing and looked up at Eric. "That's when they called me in. We have to move fast on these things. A lot of evidence is destroyed.

Mostly from water damage. What doesn't burn, of course."

"So that's why you're digging around in my office? You think it's arson. You think somebody started it there?"

Cooper looked at Eric without speaking for a moment. Then as if making a sudden decision said, "I don't know for sure that was the point of origin."

"I thought the point of origin was always the area that was the most fire damaged."

"Usually true." Cooper shifted his hard hat back on his head. "But I've seen fires where that's not the case. Saw one once where the fire started in the corner of the living room—a space heater was left on next to a couch. But the living room was next to a stairwell and upstairs hall. At the top of the stairs the bathroom window was open and the damage up there was worse than downstairs. Thought that might be the point of origin." He laughed. "Had us fooled for a while. So it depends on ventilation—'course that's a whole 'nother question. Was someone trying to add oxygen to spread the fire?"

Eric lifted his hand. "You're asking me?"

Cooper took his hard hat off and wiped his brow. "Just trying to do my job here. I need to ask you some questions. How did you find out about the fire?"

"Uh, I don't know." Eric rubbed his beard. "Somebody called me this morning. I didn't even ask who it was."

The inspector scribbled on his notepad and asked without looking up, "Were you the first one here? What did you notice when you arrived at the scene?"

"Just flames and black smoke. The whole place was ablaze. The firefighters were already here. Another truck got here after we arrived."

"We?"

"My son, Marty."

"If my men haven't already, we'll need to talk to him."

142

"Sure. He's around here somewhere. We really need to be getting back home. I've got some calls to make—I gotta contact my insurance company." Eric looked up at the outside of the half-demolished building. It was in an older part of town in what was once a residential neighborhood. His store had been converted from an old wooden house. It had been consumed by the fire in a hurry. A sudden spurt of anger surged inside him. Would somebody really have started this thing? Who hated him that much?

"Are you fully insured? What's your coverage on this place?" Cooper was still writing on his notepad. He looked up, staring at him when Eric didn't answer immediately. "We'll be needing a statement of your finances."

"What? You think I torched my own place? That's ridiculous!"

"Mmmh. Nothing would surprise me anymore." One of the techs from the house hollered for Cooper, and he turned to Eric before moving inside. "You can leave, but I'll be in touch later today to finish our interview."

Eric waved his hand and began to scour the bustling scene for his son. He spotted him down the block seated on a bench outside a gift store. When Marty saw his dad, he began to lope toward him.

Eric placed his hand on Marty's shoulder and steered him toward the car. "Let's go home."

"What'd you find out? Do they know how it got started? You know one of those dudes asked me about a billion questions—when'd we get here, what color was the smoke, what'd the flames look like. He wouldn't tell me what any of it meant though."

"They think it's arson."

"Somebody started it? I bet it was Tom. He was sure pi—I mean, he was plenty mad that you fired him."

Eric shook his head. "We don't know who did it—and we're not going to be making wild accusations."

Especially when Eric was likely to be the main suspect.

Chapter Twenty-One

Geoff Bennington downshifted his '55 Triumph convertible, letting it hug the bend in the road before increasing his speed on the straightaway. This was one sweet ride and one of his favorite cars. He shifted gears again and leaned his head back to catch more of the wind. Gorgeous day, gorgeous car, all he needed was a gorgeous date.

Maybe not, considering he was going to see his older brother. No woman needed to be subjected to his brother's wisecracks or foul moods. Geoff shook his head. He wasn't going to go there. Eric needed him. He had just lost everything, and he was going to need some help. The question was—would he accept it? Especially from his little brother.

He downshifted for another curve. He had argued with himself all the way over here. He and Eric had never had the best of relationships, but he was his brother. And in Geoff's world, family meant something.

He had to admit, he hadn't always felt that way. Two years ago he'd been ready to rip Eric's head off. And nearly had. The last time Geoff had been to Eric's house they'd ended up in the mother of all fights that was a culmination of a lot of years of stuffed emotions. Geoff glanced at the speedometer. It had inched up over eighty-five, and Geoff let his foot off the gas.

They'd fought over Mallory—or maybe it was over Shelly. It didn't really matter now. They both had their share of guilt about their little sisters. What his brother did to Mallory... Geoff swore out loud. Eric could be a j–

Geoff braked as he came up over the hill and nearly slammed into a slow-moving tractor. He tried to corral his thoughts. He promised himself he wasn't going to dwell on the past. Eric might have been a jerk—had proved it over and over again as they were growing up— but Geoff had determined in the last two years that he wasn't going to get into the middle of that mess. He'd already lost one sister and had certainly lost the closeness he'd once shared with Mallory.

Mally.

He whipped the Triumph around the tractor and ignored the honk of the oncoming car. *Man, get a grip!* All he needed was to wreck his car. Geoff checked his speed and drew a deep breath. He'd decided that he would concentrate on his own life and let his family worry about themselves. It had worked so far. He went to family gatherings when required, appeased his mother's pleadings when he couldn't weasel out of one of her command performances, and basically maintained the status quo.

He pulled into Eric's neighborhood and almost missed his house. He backed up and parked the car in the driveway. Well, he was here; all he could do was try. He knocked on the front door and got no answer. He tried again. He considered jumping back into his car but then realized he could hear music coming from within the house.

Marty. Eric couldn't be far. He went around the side of the house to the garage and caught a whiff of the barbecue. He unlatched the gate to the fence and stepped around to the back patio.

"Eric?"

Eric's head popped up above the grill. "Geoff? What the—" He waved a pair of tongs at him. "Just in the neighborhood, or you come to gloat?"

Nobody said this would be easy. Geoff walked over to the covered slab of concrete. "Got a beer?"

Eric was turning hamburgers. "In the fridge. You eat yet?"

"No."

"Might as well stay for dinner. You like smoked brats? There's an extra burger here, too."

"Sure." Geoff glanced at the sliding glass doors. "Marty here? I heard his stereo."

"You and the whole neighborhood." He jerked the tongs over his shoulder. "He's upstairs."

"Think I'll get that beer." Geoff made his way through the house to the kitchen. He glanced up as he passed the stairs then decided he'd better face the bear outside before he tangled with the cub. He popped the cap and took a swig before rejoining his brother outside. Might as well get it over with.

"What's the latest on the fire? You hear from your insurance yet?"

Eric let out a bark of laughter. "Thought you knew. It's arson, and they suspect I torched my own place."

Geoff pulled the bottle from his mouth. "What?"

"They think somebody used gasoline as an accelerant. The fire ripped through the whole place. Nothing's salvageable." Eric grasped one of the sausages with his tongs, and the grease sizzled as it hit the coals beneath it. "Guess I'm a likely suspect."

"Did you do it?"

Eric turned around and stared at him with a steady eye. Geoff thought maybe he'd gone too far, but his brother just turned back around. "No."

Geoff turned the sweating bottle in his hand and wiped it

146

against his jeans. This felt a little like a minefield, but he was determined to go through with it. "What about your insurance?"

Eric shook his head. "They're still 'investigating.' So I'm pretty much in the toilet until they get this thing straightened out."

Geoff leaned his shoulder against the post at the edge of the overhang. It was the end of summer, and Eric had his backyard looking pretty good. The lush green grass was cut low. He even had a few flowers blooming, and a bunch of well-trimmed bushes lined the corner of the fence. He scuffed his foot against the large crack at the edge of the concrete patio. The ground had shifted beneath it and caused the slab to slant upward. Geoff rotated back toward Eric.

"You need some cash?"

Eric's jaw tightened, and a muscle twitched in his cheek. He flipped another burger, and the grease caused a flame to burst from the coals. Geoff waited. This could go either way.

Eric pivoted on his foot and narrowed his eyes at him. "What's this really all about?"

Geoff stood with his feet braced apart. Then shrugged his shoulders. "Just here to see if you need help." *Not that you'd ever admit it.* "Why would you suspect my motives?"

"Little brother to the rescue?" Eric snorted. "I thought you were Mallory's knight on a white horse."

Not anymore. Geoff's stomach muscles tightened. He wouldn't answer that. "Look, Eric...you're in trouble. I want to help. Simple as that."

"I don't need your help. I can take care of myself." The muscles in his face went slack. Geoff thought he saw a fleeting look of sadness. "I'll be fine." Eric turned back to the grill and began removing the brats. "I really can take care of myself."

"Yeah, you'll be fine, but what about Marty and Lindsay?"

Eric turned and pointed the tongs at Geoff. "I can take care of my family. I don't need your help." He picked up the plate and headed toward the house muttering as he went. It sounded like "thanks anyway," but Geoff couldn't be sure.

Stubborn ox! Geoff followed him inside.

"Who do you think started the fire?"

"I don't know for sure." Eric set the food on the kitchen table then went to the doorway and hollered up the stairs. "Marty! Food's ready." He went to the cupboard and got out plates. "Make yourself useful and get out the ketchup and mustard."

Geoff reached inside the refrigerator then leaned over the half door. "You think you're in serious trouble about the arson? I mean, they can't prove anything, can they?"

Eric dropped the plates on the table and yanked open the silverware drawer. "You still think I did it?"

Geoff set the condiments on the table and shook his head. "Look, Eric, I'm just asking a question here. I'm not accusing you. I'm just trying to figure out what's going on."

Eric dropped the silverware on the table then went back to an overhead cupboard and removed three glasses. He slammed them on the table then slumped against the counter and stared at the floor. If Geoff didn't know better, he would almost think his big brother was scared.

"Eric?"

He crossed his arms. "I don't know, Geoff." Eric lifted his head. "I don't think they believe me."

Chapter Twenty-Two

A fine tremor shook the paper he held in his hands. Eric read the contents of the letter again. He folded up the sheet, tucked it into the torn envelope, and placed it in the back of his filing cabinet under a stack of old bank records.

It had reached him sooner than he'd anticipated. They'd told him it might take as long as two or three months because of the workload at the lab, but the results were in. He'd just read it with his own eyes. Marty was his son.

His son. Had Catherine been telling the truth all along?

Eric moved down the hall and stood at the base of the stairs. Silence greeted him, except for the ticking hall clock. Marty had gone to bed early. Uncle Ken had him out helping on the farm for the last several days. Baling hay had a way of knocking the stuffing out of even the most cocky youth.

Eric placed a hand on the stair rail and lifted his foot. At the first creak of the stair tread he paused then turned around. He had to get his head around this whole thing.

He grabbed a beer from the fridge and went out to the back patio and flopped into a deck chair. He seemed to be sitting out here a lot lately. He took two big gulps of the bitter liquid then reached his foot out and snagged the nearby chair. The legs screeched against the concrete. He propped his feet up and stared out into the night. Crickets chirped from the nearby grass. The thick humidity of the air formed sweat beads and ran down the cold bottle in his hand.

He was wrong.

There. He admitted it. But he'd seen his wife in the arms of his so-called friend. It didn't mean that he'd been wrong about that. But could he have been?

In all the time he'd been married to Catherine, this thing had been between them. At first it had almost destroyed them—and maybe in the end that's exactly what did them in. It had taken a while, but he'd finally convinced himself that he believed Catherine. Only the scene he had walked into always came back to haunt him. It stood between him and Catherine. No matter how he fought it, that nagging doubt colored his relationship with his wife. Eric now realized it had also molded his relationship with his son.

His son.

Eric's world had turned on its head with a simple piece of paper. The DNA match proved it. Marty was his. He took another swig of beer. Catherine was sure to gloat over this one.

But what did this change really? So the kid was his. Eric poked at his emotions, trying to determine what he felt. Satisfaction? Relief? Regret? His whole life was in the toilet, and he wasn't sure if this was good news or bad. He leaned his head back and closed his eyes. Marty was his son. It rattled around in his head, and he wondered what else he had been wrong about. He sat for long moments with his head in his hands. He couldn't think about that. He would not think about it. He took a deep breath and let it out slowly. Deliberately he reached for another thought, another image, and his body responded to it.

He stood to his feet. He needed a distraction. He detoured past his refrigerator and picked up a couple of beers on his way to the computer. Eric smiled in anticipation of the entertainment the Internet had in store for him.

Chapter Twenty-Three

O h great!" Eric muttered, peaking out the window next to the door. He tilted his head back, trying to down the full can of beer in one gulp. Foam trickled off his lips and into his beard. He wiped it off with the back of his hand even as the doorbell rang again. He licked his fingers and batted the top of his head, trying to push the unruly strands of hair back into place, using what Catherine called a "spit 'n' polish." Oh well, it was the best he could do on such short notice.

He flung the door open, and as Travis pivoted to face him, his eyes widened as they traveled over Eric's unkempt body. *What? It's not like I was expecting company.* He swept the door even wider and stumbled backward.

"T, my man. Come on in."

Travis stepped past Eric into the foyer. "I just got back into town from the conference and heard about the fire. I'm so sorry I wasn't here when it happened."

"You think that woulda prevented it?"

"No, but at least I could have been here to support you."

Eric shoved the door shut and waved Travis down the hall,

past the formal living room, and into his study. "Had plenty of support from the family. Ma, Pop, and Malo all came becaussse that's what families do." He endeavored to tuck his shirt back into the waist of his sweat pants and decided it would work better if he put down the can of beer. "Even ol' Geoffy-boy came by to gloat."

Travis picked up a shirt and folded it, placing it on the floor next to the high-backed leather chair. Removing a stack of mail from the chair, he laid it on the piled-up desk. "I don't think I've ever seen your office in quite this state of disarray. In fact I don't think I've ever seen you in quite this shape either."

"Life sucks."

"Eric—"

"It does, and don't you be trying to tell me otherwise. My business was burned to the ground, and I just bet that you were gonna say, 'Oh but, Eric, God loves you.' You religious people! What a bunch of nonsense."

"Actually I was going to suggest that you go a little easier on the beer. You seem to be slightly intoxicated. But then I bet you figured that one out by yourself." Travis leaned back in his chair, crossed his leg over his knee, and grabbed his ankle.

"I have a right t' be. Do you realize that a week ago I lost everything I ever worked for? Everything." Eric's anger was itching for a way to be released, and Travis seemed to be a likely candidate.

"You can have your religion! My life's destroyed. Seven people I can't pay. Three contracts I can't fulfill. No equipment, no supplies, and"—Eric yanked out his empty pockets—"no money." He reached for the stack of envelopes on his desk. "Got bills though." As his hand lashed out, it missed its target, knocking half the pile off the desk and sending a small avalanche of white envelopes cascading to the floor.

"Got child support for a kid I don't see enough, alimony to a shrew who doesn't want me, court fines, and a kid that's—" Eric stopped. He looked at Travis then repeated, "A kid that's mine. My life's been destroyed. So tell me Mr. Preacher with all the answers, what am I supposed to do?"

Eric reached for the beer on the edge of the desk. Travis leaned forward and snagged it away. "The first thing you do"—he stood and dumped the remainder of the beer onto an ivy plant in the window—"is quit drinking. The next thing that you do is go take a shower."

"Whadda you think you're doing?" Eric roared. He rushed around the desk, grabbing the front edge to steady himself when the room began to tilt.

Travis crushed the can, dropping it in the wastebasket. "You asked for my help, Eric. I'm giving it to you. After you've taken your shower, you come back down, and we will discuss the rest of the ways that we 'religious people' deal with salvaging a life that has been destroyed."

Eric glared at him. Travis pointed down the hall. His voice was quiet but firm. "Go."

Eric balked at being told what to do. Travis stood to his feet, leaned back against the cherry desk, casually slid his hands into his pants pockets, and stared Eric down. "I suggest that you make it a cold one. The shower, not another beer. I want to carry on a normal conversation with my friend when he comes back downstairs. In the meantime, I'll put the coffeepot on."

Muttering beneath his breath about overbearing preachers, Eric stumbled down the hall only to have Travis's voice trailing after him. "I heard that, Bennington!"

The icy blast of water on his head did much to destroy the fog that the beer had woven in his mind. Fifteen minutes later he was dressed in clean clothes. His breath was fresh, and his damp hair was combed. He felt much more human—and much more guilty—than he did twenty minutes ago. Eric leaned against the edge of the counter that housed the gray marble double sinks. "Bennington, you're a jerk." He shrugged at his own reflection before exiting the bathroom and heading down the stairs to the waiting pot of coffee.

Travis handed him a large mug of the steaming brew as he stepped into the large kitchen.

"Thanks." Eric reached for the coffee. "Sorry." When Travis didn't reply, he shot a quick look at him. He just stood there, waiting for Eric to continue.

Eric sipped the hot liquid, grateful for something to do with his mouth. He'd already shot it off enough.

"What happened? All I heard when I got back was that your place burned down."

"They think it's arson."

"What?"

Eric took another sip and stared at his friend, gauging his reaction. "Arson, and they think I did it."

Travis set down his cup. "No way."

Relief spread through Eric. Travis wasn't Geoff. He believed him. "Yeah. Place went up like a torch. Someone used gasoline. It's an ongoing investigation, so my insurance company says they can't do anything until it's resolved. I'm up the proverbial creek."

"Can you keep the business going?"

"For a while. Maybe."

"Eric, I'm really sorry, man."

"Yeah, well, just quit with the God talk. I'm not in any condition to handle it today."

"What can I do to help?"

Eric surveyed his friend. That was the thing about Trav. He might preach at him sometimes, but he didn't push the limit. If Eric said he didn't want to hear it, Travis backed off. He wouldn't admit it, but it was kind of comforting to have somebody who had God's ear. Eric was pretty sure God didn't want anything to do with him, but Travis—Travis was a good guy. He genuinely cared about people. And Eric had seen how he lived. Pretty minimalistic.

Eric had never said anything, but he'd watched Travis pull out his wallet any number of times and hand people money. People he didn't even know.

He'd asked him once if he realized he was probably getting ripped off by con artists. Travis had just smiled. "I'd rather get ripped off than miss a chance to really help someone. Would want someone to do the same for me. Besides—it's God's money, not mine. He takes good care of me."

The guy was a fool—but a nice one. And someone who had Eric's back. The fact that he believed him when his own family didn't—that meant something to Eric.

"I'll be okay. I just need to keep my head on straight." Eric grinned at his friend. "I'm sure you'll volunteer to help with that job!"

Eric slumped into his desk chair in his home office. He'd been at it for hours—ever since Travis had left. A surge of anger tore through him, and he shoved the stack of papers onto the floor. He hadn't felt this helpless in a very long time. He shoved back from the desk and went to the window. The list of calls he needed to make just kept growing.

He thought of Geoff's offer to help and swore. No way was he going to let his little brother come riding to his rescue. But his bookkeeper and the bank didn't make things sound too promising. Thousands of dollars were tied up in the ruined supplies at his burned-out shop. And that included the money he needed to finish up the three outstanding electrical jobs he'd contracted with Tipton.

Tipton. Eric was beginning to regret the day he'd gotten entangled with the guy. He couldn't get him on the phone, and Tipton wasn't answering the messages he'd sent. Eric had even gone by the guy's office in hopes of getting his money, but he hadn't been there.

Greg was all over his back with questions about the employees. He'd gotten a tearful phone call from Tanya wailing about not being able to make her rent if she didn't have a job. But he didn't have time to worry about Tanya. He had more important matters to figure out. Like how he was going to keep his shirt through this whole mess.

He could keep things afloat for a little while with the savings he'd set aside—but there was no way he could continue to pay employees without money coming in. And the insurance company...

Eric turned from the window and began to pace the room. He needed to get his head on straight and figure this thing out. Obviously he hadn't started the fire, but who did? Until the investigation was completed, the insurance company wasn't going to budge. Who would have done this to him?

His mind flashed to Marty—but the kid was under constant supervision except for short amounts of time. Besides, his reaction at the fire had shown Eric he was as much in the dark as he was about it. Could it have been Tom? He hadn't been able to run him down this last week either. Really, Thomas didn't seem smart enough to pull something like this off—although it was obvious they had plenty of evidence to prove it was arson.

And they thought Eric had done it. Even his family wasn't too sure. Geoff had proved that. At least his old man had stayed out of his hair the last several days.

Eric went back to the desk and sat down. His little tantrum hadn't done much to resolve the situation. He began to stack the papers he'd been working on. It was a list of his suppliers, and he'd only gotten partway through his phone calls.

What he needed was a strategy of how to get through this crisis. Eric set his jaw. He would get through it. He'd get Greg, Shawn, and Luke onsite at the projects that needed finishing, and Ella could work from home. Fortunately, two years ago she had convinced him to save their office files online, so she could

157

connect to her home computer and didn't have to work late at the shop. As for Miles Tipton...

Eric opened a file drawer and removed a slim folder. He laid it out on his desk and went back over the information he'd already read again and again. Tipton was known to wink at regulations, but Eric hadn't really believed he would cross the line. Nor did he really care, except where it concerned Eric.

He looked down at the file again. There it was in black and white. The guy was a crook—but the question was how would that affect Eric and should he do anything about it? Eric had double-checked the projects he'd done with Tipton, and they were fine. Maybe the best thing was to finish their dealings, get his money and be done with the man. Unless...

Unless Tipton had started the fire.

Eric shut the folder. He knew what was in the file; now he just needed to decide what to do with that information.

Chapter Twenty-Four

Catherine bit her lip and uncreased the folded paper. She'd been over this instant message so many times she ought to have it memorized by now. She flattened it on her desk and asked herself for the thousandth time what to do with it.

She'd asked some cautious questions to Lindsay, but she didn't want to push it because her daughter still seemed to have her innocence in these matters. Lindsay had been a little miffed that her mother had read her messages, but was open to talk about the contents. Either Catherine was reading stuff into it that wasn't there, or Lindsay didn't have a clue to what was going on with her cousin.

Catherine rubbed her temple then stared out the window of her office. The university took great pride in its campus, and the lush landscaping showed it. As a computer programmer she should be stuck in a dingy, windowless, basement office somewhere, but she had been here long enough to be promoted to a corner office with two huge windows.

Such an idyllic scene out there—flowers in full bloom, sun shining brightly—and so much chaos in her own life. Nothing had turned out the way she had planned.

Marriage to Eric had had its ups and downs, but there were long periods of time when she had been very, very happy. He worked hard at starting his own business and had sacrificed a lot for her and the kids. He was a great provider. Weekends were family time, and while he struggled with his relationship with Marty, he adored Lindsay and they had tried to do things together.

It was just that beneath the surface she knew there was a current—make that a raging torrent—of doubt and distrust. After the debacle with Joe, she had worked hard through the years to dispel Eric's needless jealousy. And it had worked for a while. They'd had Lindsay, and Eric had seemed a new man. But when Eric's jealousy had kicked in and the accusations had begun again, she just couldn't stand the weight of his distrust and suspicions anymore. And then the whole mess with Marty...

Everything had happened at once. The whole family had fallen apart—the divorce, Marty going to detention, then Eric's sister accusing him of abusing her when she was little. Eric had laughed it off, said it was more of Mallory's drama. Catherine wasn't sure what to believe. She liked Mallory, admired her even, but she said that Eric had raped her and that didn't fit the Eric she knew.

Oh, he drove her nuts, and she couldn't live with him anymore, but anyone seeing him with Lindsay could tell he wasn't that kind of man. It was true he was harsh with Marty, but he was a marshmallow when it came to his daughter. He showed too much tenderness for what Mallory said to be true.

Eric and his sister had never gotten along, but Catherine had always put that down to Mallory's being the baby and being spoiled—especially by Geoff. Eric wouldn't admit it on the pain of death, but she'd seen him watch his brother and sister, and he'd let it slip a time or two that they cut him out of their relationship. He was the black sheep of the family, and Catherine knew that most of his attitude toward them was the pain of rejection.

Especially from his dad. It was what made it so difficult for him to communicate with Marty. She'd always wondered if at the root of everything—the jealousy, the divorce, his difficult relationship with his son—Eric was afraid of being rejected all over again.

Catherine watched as one of the groundskeepers spun his riding lawn mower in a tight circle around the tree just outside her window. The hum of the engine was muted through the sealed windows and the sound of the air-conditioning kicking in.

The thoughts in her head kept going round and round, too. *Could* it be true about Eric? Did his son follow in his footsteps? The plaguing questions never stopped coming back, but Catherine's heart always responded with a resounding "no!" Not her husband, not her son.

Marty had always declared his innocence to her. She'd wanted to believe he hadn't messed with his cousin, but he'd been caught red-handed holding Bethy's panties. She dropped her head to her hands and stared at the note lying on her desk. What really happened at that church function?

She'd let the kids go with their cousins. What could be safer than being at church, right? Wrong. Her world had come tumbling down.

She spun her chair and moved to the window. The guy mowing the grass had moved on to the next tree across the quad. Four wide sidewalks converged into a wide plaza surrounded by big oak trees and stone benches. Despite the fact that it was summer break, there were still half a dozen students enjoying the afternoon sun out there today.

She leaned her forehead against the cool glass. If she were honest, her and Eric's problems had been there long before Marty got into trouble, and maybe their difficulties were what caused it in the first place. The divorce had been hard on both kids, but before that Marty seemed like a happy-go-lucky kid. Adolescence and divorce had been a deadly combination for him.

She had tried to defend Marty, tried to believe in him, but everything happened so fast. The authorities were called in even before she and Eric heard about it. "I didn't do nuthin'!" had been his only defense. Donovan had been there, too, but Marty was the one who was put in the detention center. Catherine shuddered and turned back to her desk.

No sense going back there. It had been a terrible time, and one she didn't want to relive. She pulled out her chair and sat down. Marty had been doing so much better. He still wouldn't admit he'd done anything wrong, but the counseling had seemed to help his anger. And now this. She ran her fingers over the crumpled paper.

Is it possible Marty was innocent after all? And how could she prove it without tearing apart her sister's family any more than it already had been?

Chapter Twenty-Five

A cool blast of air swept over Eric as he stepped into the shadowed interior. It was a welcome relief from the heat pulsing up from the sidewalk outside. The coffee shop was Catherine's idea; he'd rather have gone for a beer, but he wasn't about to turn down her invitation. He was too curious about what she had to say.

Overstuffed couches with tables and easy chairs were placed in strategic conversational groups around the room. He checked the room for Catherine then glanced at his watch. He was on time, and she was late. Of course. He went to the counter and placed his order then looked around to decide the best place for this conversation, whatever "this" was about.

Eric had told her now would be a good time because Marty had gone out to Uncle Ken's farm for a few days. Granny had wanted to see him. Eric grinned, and the cashier gave him a questioning look. He shook his head and thanked her. No way to explain the punch packed by an eighty-something old lady determined to have her say. Marty was in good hands.

He chose a booth along the wall. Best to be prepared for

whatever was coming. He didn't know what Catherine wanted to talk to him about, but he knew he should tell her about the DNA results. He took a drink and burned his tongue. Too hot. He liked it straight up, no fancy flavors or syrups. Just good, strong coffee.

Eric moved his cardboard cup back and forth across the table from one hand to the other. He glanced up as the door opened, but it was two older ladies with full shopping bags on their arms.

He took another drink. He wanted to be out of here in an hour. He needed to stop back in to see Ben Cooper. The fire inspector had more questions for him. Eric twisted the tab on the top of his cup until it cracked off. He was ready to be done with this.

"I'm late. Sorry." Catherine sat down on the opposite side of the booth. Her voice was breathless, and her face was shiny from the heat. A thin trickle of sweat beaded at the base of her throat, and she fanned her hand in front of her face. "Whew! It's hot out there."

Eric motioned to the counter. "You want an iced mocha?" That earned him a big smile. "Sit still. I'll get it."

He went to the counter and ordered then turned to watch his wi– ex-wife—settle onto the bench. She was still fanning her face and intermittently lifting her hair off her neck.

"Here's your iced mocha, sir. That'll be four dollars and twenty-five cents."

Eric stared at the young high schooler until he repeated the amount. He dug into his wallet for the needed bills. This was exactly why he avoided places like this. Maybe he should forget the electrical business and open a coffee shop.

He set the drink in front of Catherine, who was twisting her hair into a messy ponytail. "Maybe this will help cool you off."

"Thanks." She took a sip and closed her eyes. "Just a moment—let me enjoy my little piece of heaven on earth."

Eric chuckled and drank from his own cup. Beer may have better suited his taste buds, but Catherine was definitely a treat for the eyes. He waited for her to speak. It was her party after all.

"Eric. . ." Catherine rubbed the top of her cup with her finger. "I heard about the fire. I'm so sorry. Do they know what happened?" She looked up at him, and those clear blue eyes cut through his defenses.

"Not yet." He cleared his throat and took another drink of his coffee. It was still hot, and he welcomed the burning sensation that moved down his throat. "They're still investigating. I have to go see the fire inspector after this."

"I heard it was arson. Do they know who did it?"

"They think I did." Eric watched her eyes widen.

"That's ridiculous! You'd never burn down your own place!"

A surge of warmth radiated through Eric at her defense of him. He shrugged. "It's a bit of a mess, but I'll work it out."

She reached out and laid her hand on top of his. He looked down at their hands resting on the table between them and forced himself not to jerk away. He was glad she believed him, but he didn't want her sympathy. He slid his hand out from under hers and took another drink.

"So, what's up? What's so urgent that we need to talk about?"

Catherine drew both of her hands around her cup and stared down at it. An ache began deep in his chest. Was everything okay? Almost involuntarily he reached out and drew her chin up, so he could see her face. "What's going on, Cat?"

She took a deep breath. "Okay, Eric. Don't get mad. Just hear me out, okay?" She gave him a direct gaze until he nodded his head, and then she reached for her purse and pulled out a folded piece of paper.

"Lindsay has been instant messaging Bethy."

"Instant what?"

"You know—like e-mail, only both people are online, and you can talk back and forth. Instant messaging." She unfolded the piece of paper. "Anyway, I printed this out. I thought you should see it."

Eric took the piece of paper from her hands and began to read. It looked like some sort of coded message with letter abbreviations.

"What is this? I can't read half of it!"

Catherine gave a small laugh and took the paper back. "Most of this is just saying hi, they had fun at Grandma's, and they miss each other." Catherine moved the paper so he could look at it.

Eric still couldn't read half of it. "Is that supposed to be 'moo'?"

"MU—miss you. MU2—miss you, too. Look, this is Bethy, 'It's more fun at Grandma's,' and Lindsay asks her why—when she gets to go to the beach every day. 'Dumb old Donovan is here.' Lindsay tells her that brothers can be a pain, and when Bethy asks if Marty is mean to her, she says sometimes he takes her stuff. When Bethy asks if he hits her, Lindsay says she just tells you."

Catherine paused and looked at him as if she just made some huge discovery. Eric was confused. This was the urgent thing she needed to talk about? It was just two little girls talking. He lifted his hands and raised his eyebrows. What was he supposed to be seeing here?

"Look, after Bethy tells her she wishes she could tell her dad, Linds asks her if Donovan hurts her. Bethy doesn't answer, and Lindsay asks her what's wrong. Now look at the bottom part." Catherine held out the paper to him and pointed to the bottom of the page.

> Lindsay: *dz donovan hurt u?*
> Bethy: *nvr mind*
> Lindsay: *bethy?*
> Bethy: *he touchs smtms*
> Lindsay: *did u tell ur mom? I tell when Marty touches my stuff*

"Seriously?" Eric handed the paper back to Catherine. "I still can't read this mumbo jumbo."

"I had to look up some of this myself." She grabbed the paper. "It says, 'Does Donovan hurt you?' And after Bethy says, 'Never mind' she tries again here—'He touches sometimes.' Then Lindsay asks her if she told her mom—that she tells when Marty touches her stuff. This 'fi' means forget it. 'P911' means parental alert—a parent is coming in the room. Then Linds says, 'See you,' and Bethy says 'bbfn'—bye-bye for now."

"Okay. Two little girls have a cute little coded message telling each other hi and what a pain their brothers are. So?"

Catherine sighed and rubbed her forehead. What was she so worked up over? As far as Eric could tell, it was just the kind of note you passed in school—only it was high tech. What was the big deal?

"Eric, I think Donovan is molesting Bethy."

"What? How do you jump to that conclusion?"

"Look, she says 'he touches'—she doesn't say he touches her things. And look back here." She shook the paper under his nose. "He's hitting her. He's hurting her, Eric." She dropped the paper to the table and searched his face. "I think he's the one that molested her all along. Marty's innocent. He's been trying to tell us that. He said he didn't do it."

"Whoa. Wait a minute!" Eric shoved back into the booth. "First of all, that's a huge leap from a little girl who can hardly spell who says 'he touches'—he's probably touching her things, just like Lindsay said. And second of all—Marty isn't 'innocent'— he says he 'didn't do it' to anything that happens. He just doesn't want to own up to it."

Catherine refolded the paper and put it back in her purse. "I told my sister. I called her and told her that I think Donovan is the one who molested Bethy. I sent her a copy of this instant message."

Eric shook his head. He couldn't believe this. "Cat—"

"Eric." Catherine leaned forward. "She wasn't surprised."

"What do you mean?"

"She didn't deny it or ask what I was talking about. She just said, 'Oh no. I was hoping it wasn't that.' They've had Bethy in therapy, and her counselor has mentioned several times that there was something she wasn't telling them." Catherine reached out her hand to his again. "I'm telling you, Eric, Marty really didn't do it."

"He got caught, Catherine."

"Holding her panties, yes."

"Aren't you forgetting something? Bethy said Marty did it, not Donovan."

"What if she was too scared to say it was Donovan?"

"Why didn't he say so then?"

"He did, Eric! We just didn't believe him."

He got caught.

Eric shook his head. It made no sense. Not that he wanted to think his son was an idiot. But was making him into a coward any better? He hated thinking about this stuff. He just wanted to get done with it. Move on with his life. Not have to deal with all this crap.

All Eric knew at this moment was he didn't know anything. He looked at Catherine, gorgeous in her disheveled state from the heat and the passion of what she had been sharing. She'd always babied Marty. Was she doing it again, or was she right? He'd been wrong about Marty being his son. She was telling the truth about that. Maybe she'd been right all along—about a lot of things.

Was she right about this, too? Was his son really innocent?

Chapter Twenty-Six

Ben Cooper glanced at his watch. Bennington should be here any minute. Maybe he could finish this and get home for supper at a decent time. Marla would be pleased. He moved to the charred doorway and pulled the plastic yellow tape to the side. He'd managed to hold off the cleanup process, but they were clamoring to get started. They could wait. He still had a few more questions to ask.

He stepped over the mess in the front room. Ignoring the ruined supplies and the damaged counter that ran the length of the room, he moved straight to the back office. He wanted another look at the starting point of the fire. The smoke smell had dissipated some, but a faint whiff remained. They knew the accelerant was gas. They just had to figure out who set this place ablaze.

Eric Bennington was on his list. So was the shyster contractor whose background alone made him suspicious. All the employees' whereabouts were accounted for—except the kid—he and the dad were vouching for each other, and that hardly counted as an alibi. The question now was. . . Did the gasoline that started the fire come from the gas can they had discovered out back of the building site?

He was on his haunches examining what was left of the floor where they took their samples when he heard sounds coming from the front of the building. He went back to meet the owner, wondering if he'd brought his son along.

Bennington was alone. He riffled through the mess on the counter then kicked through the debris on the floor. He rolled over a half-burned catalog then reached down and picked up a scrap of paper and put it in his pocket. His eyes widened when he saw Ben.

"Inspector, you're already here! I saw the tape was down. When can we get started with the cleanup?"

"When we get a few more answers." Ben gestured toward the sidewalk. He didn't want this guy messing around in here. It was his crime scene until he said different. He followed the broad shoulders through the doorway and into the humid air. It was time for cooler weather, but summer was hanging on with a tight fist this year.

"I checked your bank records. It appears you tried and couldn't get a loan. Business not doing so well?"

"Nothing like getting to the guts of it." Bennington looked him straight on. No shifty eyes. He looked more irritated than scared. "Yes, I applied for a loan. They haven't denied me—yet." He dropped his gaze and looked back at the burned-out building. "I'm sure this hasn't helped my chances any." He looked back at Ben. "I wanted to expand."

Ben pulled out his notebook and made a show of flipping through the pages. He was getting set for the real question now. He had to determine if this guy was covering for his kid—or possibly the other way around. "My notes say you and your son spent the evening together. Where were you?"

Bennington crossed his arms. "Home. Went there straight

from work. Marty works for me."

"Any possible way he could have sneaked back here?" Ben watched the man's jaw tighten. "Any reason he'd have a grudge against his old man?"

Eric looked away. "He didn't set this fire."

Not very convincing. Still, they didn't have much evidence and certainly no proof that the kid had done it. But Ben Cooper liked to follow his instincts. More often than not it led him to the truth. He flipped through his notes again then looked the father right in the eye. "We found a gas can in the area behind your shop. Something he might have had access to?"

Eric blinked but said nothing for several moments. Ben waited him out. Always better to give them room to hang themselves. They all stumbled over their lies sooner or later.

"We keep a gas can for the mower. I don't know if that one was ours or not. Marty mowed the grass around the building." He blinked again and then looked away. "My son didn't burn down my business."

"So, he didn't have any reason to?"

"I'm not saying we don't have our issues. I'm saying he wouldn't have torched this place." Eric looked back at Ben. "No way."

Ben nodded. "You mind if we speak to him directly?"

"Go ahead." Eric shrugged. "He'll tell you the same thing. He didn't do it."

Ben glanced down at his notes then up at Eric. "What did you pick up off the floor?"

Eric's eyes widened. "What?"

"You checked out the counter then found something on the floor. I want to know what it is."

Eric put his hand in his pocket and pulled out the folded paper; his eyes never left Ben's. He held it out, and Ben took it.

"A receipt for gas. Dated the day of the fire." He looked up. "Is that your son's signature?"

"Yes. But I already told you. He didn't set the fire. He mows the grass. He filled the gas tank. Doesn't mean he used it to set the fire. Probably anybody could have used it. Especially if he left it out back the way he usually does."

Ben didn't say anything. If he waited long enough, they usually filled the silence.

"He's supervised almost constantly. He was with me the whole night. I'm telling you, there was no way he could have set that fire."

Eric stood with his palms open. Whatever doubts he had about his kid, he wasn't going to change his story. Still, it wouldn't hurt to keep him guessing.

Ben made some notes then looked at Eric. "Bring the boy to my office tomorrow afternoon. I need his statement."

He watched Bennington head for his vehicle. His stride was short and choppy. Guy was torqued. But what—or who—was he angry at?

Chapter Twenty-Seven

Martin kneaded his shoulder, wondering when he had gotten so old and why his mind didn't believe what his body was telling him. The thoughts of going to the doctor the first of the month left a foul taste in his mouth. How he hated doctors.

"I don't have any idea how long I'll be." Alecia leaned across the car and cupped her hand around his chin as she drew his face toward her. Kissing his cheek, she opened the door and stepped out with the same flirty grace that had captured his heart.

"Tell Ronald I said hello. Come back when you're done. I'll be here, probably still shopping."

Martin smiled. "Probably? No probabilies to that one."

He sucked on the stem of his pipe as he watched his wife of forty-three years move with quick-mincing steps across the parking lot and disappear through the doors of the Super Walmart. His wife. She still moved in a way that set fire to his heart. She was too beautiful for her own good. Giving him five children had only upped her dress size by one. Four children, he corrected as he clamped down on his pipe with enough force to jar his teeth. She'd lost the first one, which was the one that caused them to get married in the first place. He chuffed harder on the pipe stem, sending a column of smoke bouncing off the roof of his 1979 Cadillac Sedan de Ville.

Martin pulled out of the parking lot and turned back toward the center of Dannonville. What had once been a sleepy little community in the heart of farm country was turning into a growing community of shops, restaurants, and businesses. How he ached for a less complicated time. But then, life had never been straightforward. Slowpaced, maybe, but definitely not uncomplicated. Not from the time he tried to express to his father that there was more to life than the farm and more to be seen in the world than just the community next to your own piece of land.

Truth be known, he had wanted to get away and see the world, show Alecia the world—that is, until he had seen the world with all its ugliness and depravity. When he came home, home didn't look so bad anymore. Martin chuckled. Boy, had they fought over that one! To this day he was convinced she had never forgiven him for not taking her away, but he just couldn't.

Michael had been the golden child following in his father's footsteps and winning his father's approval. Martin shook off that line of thinking as he pulled into the parking lot behind the town hall. Grabbing his briefcase and tamping out his pipe, he pocketed it as he mounted the steps and entered the building. "Good morning, Sherry. Ron in?" He addressed the town clerk as he pulled a sheaf of papers from his briefcase.

"Our illustrious mayor just happens to be in his office." She looked at the clock. "At least for the next ten minutes, before he has to be back to work. Ever wonder when this town will get a full-time mayor, one that doesn't need to hold down a real job?"

Martin chuckled. "I remember when the town clerk had to hold down a real job. When did that change?"

"When they got computers and the federal government decided

to tell the little politicians how to do their job." She motioned with her pen. "Go on back. He's not doing anything terribly important."

Ronald Greer poked his head out the door. "That's a matter of opinion. Got the zoning reports for me, Martin?"

"Yes, right here." Martin shook hands with his old army buddy, now turned mayor. Ron's hair was mostly gone as was his trim waistline. It seemed time had done a multitude of damage to his old friend. "Alecia says hi."

Ronald smiled. "How's the blond-haired beauty? Still as sassy as ever?"

"Always will be." Martin sat down opposite his friend. Alecia was still turning heads.

"Send her my love."

Fingers of insecurity wrapped around his spine and threatened to squeeze through his chest cavity. He still couldn't let go of that fine thread of jealousy. *But then you have every right to be suspicious.*

"Need your signature on these papers before we can file them in county." Mayor Greer slid the stack of computer printouts across the slick surface. He unscrewed the cap from his pen. "I was so sorry to hear about the fire at Eric's. How's he doing?"

Martin shrugged. "Hard to say with that one." *The only emotion he ever lets anyone see is his anger.* No, it was more than anger; it was rage. *Usually aimed at me.* He reached for his pipe and clenched it between his teeth.

"Uh, Martin."

He looked up as Ronald pointed to the No Smoking sign by the door. "This is a public building, you know."

"Sorry. Old habits die hard." Martin pocketed his pipe and settled back in his chair.

"So, what do you think Eric will do now?"

"Rebuild, I imagine." He was good at that. "He's got a stubborn streak in him. Gets it from his mother."

Ronald's pen scratched against the paper. "He's a fighter that one, that's for sure."

A fighter. You have no idea of just what kind of fighter he was, Ron. If he had been a little less rebellious, Martin wouldn't have needed to use the belt on him quite so often. Eric would tear through the house like a tornado when he was in a rage. Martin shifted positions and stared at the plat map on the wall. Ronald's voice penetrated his runaway thoughts. "Excuse me?"

"I said, he may be a fighter, but he may not be able to fight this one."

"What one? Ronald, what in the world are you talking about?" Martin focused his attention back on his old friend.

"I'm saying he may not be able to rebuild."

"And why not?"

"You haven't heard, then? Eric didn't tell you?"

"Tell me what? The boy tells me very little, Ron. He's a proud, private man. Doesn't want his old man's help or advice." Martin's hand began to shake. He wished he could smoke his pipe. It always helped him to unwind. He rolled his shoulders, trying to relieve the tension that coiled in his shoulder.

"State building inspector has been poking around the Minion Development." Ron leaned closer and pitched his voice lower, causing Martin to shift forward in his seat. "Seems Miles Tipton is under investigation for use of shoddy materials."

Martin's lips tightened with annoyance as he leaned back in his chair. "Is that all? We already know that, Ron. The work over at Beach City was investigated four months ago. What's that got to do with Eric and his business?"

Ronald leaned back in his padded leather chair and steepled his fingers below his chin. "Seems that the foundation of that building began cracking last month. Substandard concrete mix was used. Then we just found out that the electrician Tipton used on the Edgemont Project in Ashland was fined for not using the correct gauge of wiring."

Martin frowned. He hated gossip. Why was he sitting here listening to Greer's unsubstantiated reports? "The point of all this would be?"

"It seems that on all of these projects, Tipton has been underbidding his competition and then coming in on the bids with the use of substandard materials. He is also making it hard on his subcontractors to use materials that are within tolerance."

"Not Eric! Eric's reputation is very important to him."

Mayor Greer held up his hand. "I'm just telling you that he is suspicious by association."

Martin forced himself to remain in his seat. How many times had he told Eric that he could be in serious trouble by simple association? Reputation is everything. Who you know can make or break a man. *Eric, how many times do I have to tell you not to hang around those hoodlums from the other side of the tracks? They are nothing but trouble. Someone's going to get hurt.*

Someone did. Michelle. No. It wasn't Eric's fault. Not that time.

Martin rubbed at the pain that coursed along his shoulder and down his arm. The old war injury was rearing its ugly head. It must be going to rain.

". . .investigated."

Senility must be setting in. He couldn't keep his mind focused on a simple conversation anymore. "What?"

"Martin, you okay?"

"I'm fine. What did you say?"

"I said that because of the trouble that Tipton is in, his subcontractors are being investigated as well. Then on top of it all, the fire inspector is investigating the fire at Eric's." Ronald slid the papers back to Martin.

"Why is the fire being investigated? It was an accident."

"They aren't ruling out arson."

"Arson! Are you accusing someone in my family—"

Ronald pushed back his chair. "I'm not accusing anyone. I'm simply reporting what I've heard. But it doesn't look good for your son, in light of his association with Tipton. Tipton gets investigated, and Eric's place burns to the ground."

My son. There's a laugh. If the world only knew. Martin uncoiled from his chair.

"He'll be just fine. Don't you worry about my son. I'll talk to you later." He gathered the papers, stuffed them in his briefcase, and exited more abruptly than he had intended.

He paused outside the building long enough to retrieve his pipe and strike a match to the bowl. Pain clenched his heart. The memories wouldn't let him go. Martin may have accepted the boy into his home and given him his name, but no matter how Alecia argued that Eric was Martin's son, he knew better.

"For crying out loud, Alecia, look at him. He doesn't even look like me." He'd tried! God only knew how he had tried to make that boy a part of his life. *I loved him, Alecia. I loved him with all my heart, and then I found. . .* Martin stopped his thoughts. The two of them had worked through that a long time ago.

Martin abruptly checked his watch. An hour. He had at least an hour before he needed to be back at the store. He needed to see Eric.

Eric fumed at the car idling in front of him. He honked his horn. The light was green now. He asked himself for the hundredth time why he always caved in to his mother's pleas. More like demands. Geoff called them "command performances." Anything to make his mother happy. Although it wasn't really interfering with his nonlife right now to make a trip to his parents'. Marty was with Catherine, and Lindsay had begged to go stay with Gran again. The car behind him beeped, and Eric pulled into the left lane to make his turn.

Like he didn't have enough on his plate. The secretary that had phoned to schedule his meeting with Cooper had let it slip that the arsonist started the fire with gasoline. Eric remembered that Marty had handed him that receipt the morning before the fire, and he'd laid it on the counter. Then he spotted it on the floor in the midst of the debris and thought he could take it out of the equation. He hadn't figured on the fire inspector already being at the shop—and then Cooper had caught him at it.

Eric squealed his tires coming into his parents' driveway. His son had his problems, but no way had Marty set that fire. The kid would have had to crawl out the window, steal his car, and get back to the house before they got the phone call about the shop being ablaze.

He hit the steering wheel. Last thing he needed was for this investigation to be hanging over his head. The insurance company was stalling as long as the investigation was ongoing. Cooper had let it slip that all the employees were accounted for, so it wasn't Thomas. That left Tipton.

Eric smoothed his beard then brushed back the sides of his hair and stepped out of the car. He had to let this go right now. He could only deal with one thing at a time, and his mother had been nearly hysterical. She was insistent Eric come to their house because his father wanted to see him, and she was worried about his health. And Eric couldn't come up with a good excuse, so here he was.

His mother met him at the front door. "He's in the den."

Eric found him in his recliner reading the newspaper. "Hey, Dad." He plopped down on the couch and propped his feet on the coffee table.

"Eric! Put your feet down." Martin crumbled the paper on his lap. He pulled off his reading glasses and rubbed his eyes. His face was drawn with anger or pain, Eric wasn't sure which. He was a pasty chalk color, although Eric could see beads of sweat at his receding hairline. He really didn't look too good.

"Sorry." Eric sighed and shifted his body. "Mom said you wanted to talk to me."

Martin clunked the footrest down on his recliner. "I saw Ronald Greer over in Dannonville today. He says the fire was arson. What's going on?"

Eric tugged on his beard. He probably should have come over and told his parents sooner. He was a little surprised Geoff hadn't let the family in on what he'd found out. It would just be nice to have his own life and not have people butting into it all the time.

"Fire inspector said they think someone flung gasoline all over my office and torched the place."

"Was it you?"

Eric jumped to his feet and began to pace his parents' living room. Why did everyone believe he was guilty? Anger surged within him, and he whipped around to his father. "You think I did, so why should I deny it?"

"Look, boy, don't talk to me that way. I'm still your father."

"That's the point, Dad. I'm thirty-nine years old. I'm not a boy. And certainly not yours."

Martin's face flushed red as he rose from his chair. "You watch your tongue!"

"What are you going to do, Dad? Whip out your belt? Don't think that will work anymore."

"Why you—you—" Martin's words sputtered to a halt, and he clutched his shoulder.

"Dad?"

"What is going on here? Eric! I told you to come over to ease his mind, not get him all worked up."

"I'm fine, 'Lecia. Quit fussing." His father slumped back in his chair.

Eric took a second look at his father. His face was as white now as it had been beet red a few moments before. Remorse coursed through him. When would he learn not to let the old man get to him? It was beyond time to get himself out of here.

"Take it easy, Dad. Don't get your shorts in a twist." He held up his hands to stop his mother's reproof. "It's okay, Ma. I'm leaving." He headed for the hall and turned around in the archway. "And for the record, no, I didn't torch my own place, but thanks for believing in me." Eric opened the front door. He could still hear his parents' voices as he stepped over the threshold.

"What are we going to do with that boy, Alecia?"

"Martin—"

The full force of the door slamming closed cut off the rest of his mother's words. Eric gunned the engine and shot out of his parents' driveway. Some things never change.

Talking to his father was like talking to a brick wall. Set in his ways, he was immovable. Eric wished his dad would listen and respect what he had to say, that just once his father would believe in him and be proud of him. Instead, his dad was constantly on his case; now he was blaming him for the arson.

He fumed all the way back to his place. The thing that killed him was that his dad always believed the worst about him. He never cut him any slack. He could deny involvement in the fire until he was blue in the face, and still his father would question his involvement.

His cell phone buzzed as he climbed the front steps of his house. It was his mother. Now what? He flipped open his phone. "What?"

"Eric! You've got to come!"

"Mom?" Her next words were muffled through her sobs. "Mom, slow down. I can't understand you. What's the matter?"

"I said you have to come right away! It's your dad. He's collapsed."

"What?"

"I called 911. The ambulance has taken your dad to Mercy

Hospital. They think—Oh Eric, they think it's a massive heart attack!"

"I'm on my way, Ma. Did you call Geoff and Mallory?"

"Yes, Mallory's picking me up. We'll meet you there. Oh, please hurry, Eric!"

Eric snapped his phone shut and jumped back in the Jeep. He should never have left. He knew his dad hadn't been feeling well, but this... Eric kicked himself for aggravating his father. He knew what buttons to push, what got the old man riled, but he'd never intended to harm him.

Eric ground the gears as he shifted into second and rounded the corner. He shouldn't have gotten so angry at him. He should have— Eric cut off his fruitless thoughts. Whatever he should have done, one thing was clear.

If anything happened to his father, it was Eric's fault.

Chapter Twenty-Eight

Dead. How could his father be dead?

Eric pulled the lever on the recliner and tilted the chair back, just as his father had done only days ago. Eric closed his eyes. What was today, Tuesday? One, two, three days ago his father had been digging in the dirt, and tomorrow he'd be buried beneath it. A heart attack. Just like that, he was gone.

And it's my fault.

The doctors had assured them it was inevitable; there was nothing they could have done to prevent it. His dad had been a ticking time bomb. Eric just lit the fuse. So far no one had blamed him. Maybe it was just a matter of time.

Eric flipped the footrest down and sat forward. He reached over to pick up the book that lay on the end table. *The Civilizations of Ancient Greece.* Heedless of the worn binding, Eric flung it back on the table and looked around his parents' living room.

Nothing had changed much during the last twenty years. The carpeting had been expensive, but showed signs of wear now, its traffic patterns forever marked on its worn surface. The furniture was outdated, although the fabric was still plush. *Except for Dad's chair.* Eric smoothed the nubs of wool where his arms rested.

Clinking dishes and muted voices drifted to him from the direction of the kitchen where his mother and her sisters were washing up from the aftermath of family and acquaintances that had come to the house to offer condolences. The handful of people remaining at the house were in the basement rec room. Most of them were well-meaning, but Eric was glad for the respite from having to make conversation.

What was there to say? Even if Eric had known how to talk to him, the old man was dead now. How could he say he was sorry? Or that his dad was wrong?

Too restless to sit any longer, Eric rocked to his feet. It was too early to leave; he had promised his mother he would stay for a while, perhaps even the night. He decided to grab his coat from the closet and go for a walk.

The early fall air had a briskness to it, a chill freshness that taunted promises of winter-just-around-the-corner. Eric couldn't believe it had only been a month since the fire. In the midst of his world turning upside down the kids had started back to school. He hadn't thought things could get any worse. He was wrong.

Eric stepped off the deck, flipped up his collar to cover his ears, and headed through the backyard toward his father's fruit trees. The first flames of orange and red had already begun to light the leaves of the apple trees, gnarled and bent from the years of neglect. Eric ducked under a low-hanging branch and wandered through the long rows of uncut grass and brambles. He hadn't been back here in ages.

He wondered whether their old hideout was still standing. Eric lengthened his stride. He had been ten and Geoff seven when his dad had the playhouse built for them. When his father had cleared the land to plant the orchard, he had used the logs for their fort.

Hard to believe this tangled snarl of briars and weeds was once long carpets of mown grass. Following the faint trace of a once well-worn path, Eric fought the last of the branches reaching pointy fingers to snag his jacket.

The logs of the cabin had weathered to a dull silver gray and hung at a lopsided angle. The roof had a distinctive dip in it, but their old fort was still standing. The hinges squeaked as he pushed against the water- and time-swollen wood. Dust particles hung suspended in the air, disturbed from their long slumber as Eric stepped into the dark interior.

He was nearly eye level with the floor of the overhead loft, and impulse made him crouch down and walk over to the clouded window underneath it. He scratched at the thick dirt. Amazingly, the glass panes were still intact. Too tall to stand upright, he crab-walked to the central area of the cabin and started up the stairs. Three steps and his head was nearly to the roof, far enough to see that animals had spent more time up here than he and his brother and sisters.

"I always said it would look better with curtains."

Eric nearly lost his footing on the steps at the sound of Mallory's voice. "Dumb idea, kid."

The light from the doorway haloed Mallory's silhouette. "That's the same thing you told me twenty-some-odd years ago. I always thought it was unfair this was yours and Geoff's fort and not my playhouse." Mallory's shadowed figure moved farther into the dim room. "I couldn't even bring my dolls for fear you'd hold them captive in some Indian rampage." A loud sneeze punctuated her statement. "It's pretty musty in here. Smells like mold, and maybe something dead."

Eric nodded at the loft. "Many somethings, but a long time ago now."

"Everything seems a long time ago, yet there are moments when I feel right back in the past." Mallory spoke toward the window. "Ever feel that way, Eric?"

She sounded like a lost and frightened little girl, and Eric fought the urge to put his arms around her. She wouldn't want his comfort. "I'm not much for nostalgia. Better to be getting on with things than to dwell in the past."

Mallory's chin-length hair swung out from her face as she turned toward him. "But here you are, taking a walk down memory lane. Whether you want to admit it or not, Eric, you're just like the rest of us."

Eric stepped down to the uneven floorboards. "I was just making sure the old thing was still standing. Maybe it should be torn down."

"Always the heart of stone. Can't show any weakness or sensitivity. Even on the day before they bury your father?" His little sister's voice was edged with sarcasm. Her little digs were invariably sharp.

A heart of stone? Was that really how she saw him? He bled when cut just like any other man—he was just careful whom he let see the pain. Some people took pleasure in prolonging the agony.

"What do you want from me, Mallory? Tears? Believe me, I've already shed them."

"I'm sure you have, Eric."

"What's that supposed to mean?" Was that another slam at him? Mallory had always been able to get under his skin.

"Nothing."

Eric blew a frustrated breath from his lips and tugged his beard. He found it extremely awkward to talk to anyone in his family, but especially his little sister. She seemed to taunt him, just waiting to get his goat. When they were kids, she had always been able to maneuver circumstances so that he was the one to get in trouble. As the big brother it seemed he was responsible for his younger siblings, and woe be to him if they were dissatisfied or unhappy.

"What are you doing down here, anyway? Did everybody leave?"

"Mom sent me looking for you." Mallory moved abruptly toward the door. "Let's get out of here. It's depressing."

Eric silently followed Mallory back through the now-flattened weeds and into the orchard. He nearly ran into her when she stopped at the edge of the back lawn.

"Try, Eric. For once in your life, just try to set your egotism and self-centeredness aside." Without waiting for a reply, Mallory swiveled around and marched to the back of the house.

What was she in such a snit about anyway? Eric supposed he should try to be patient. It was hard on everyone losing Dad so suddenly, but it was especially hard on Mally. She and her father had a special bond, maybe from being the baby of the family.

Eric felt a swell of pain burning up his chest and clogging in his throat. Blinking back the sudden surge of emotion, he followed his sister.

"Who's that?" Mallory had stopped at the edge of the porch. Eric caught up with her and followed the line of her finger with his eyes. A tall slender figure with sandy hair that flamed red in the late-afternoon light had just disappeared from their vision as he made his way to the front of the house. "That's Travis. I didn't think he'd be here. Come on, I'll introduce you to him. I think you'll like him." The look she threw over her shoulder clearly told him that wasn't likely to happen. Eric hurried past Mallory and turned the corner of the house before Travis had time to ring the bell. "Hey, T. Around here."

Travis turned toward the sound of Eric's voice. Were those actually tears in his eyes? He walked to Eric and engulfed him in a hug. Eric returned the gesture with a one-handed pat then stepped to the side. He noted with some amusement that Mallory's mouth had formed a perfect little O. "Mally, I'd like you to meet the Reverend Travis Jamison. Travis, my sister Mallory Carlisle." Her jaw dropped even farther, and the little O became a big one. Eric was hard-pressed not to start laughing.

Travis stuck his hand out. "Just Travis, or T. Or, if you're stuck on formality, Pastor T or Pastor Trav will work. Personally, I hate titles. People get caught up in titles, and then you have a devil of a time getting them unstuck."

"You're the guy Eric met at Habitat and goes with to the Civil War thing?" Her voice pitched higher in amazement.

"Bennington, have you given me a bad rap?" He elbowed Eric. "You didn't tell me your sister was so pretty." Mallory blushed a deep crimson red.

Eric stuffed his hands in his pockets. "That's because she's married."

"Well, people don't get ugly just because they get married." Travis placed his hand on Eric's shoulder and changed the subject with a swiftness that left Mallory clearly bewildered.

Eric turned his head to hide his smile. Travis had a way of keeping most people slightly off balance. Eric and Travis followed Mallory into the now-deserted kitchen. Mallory looked over her shoulder. "I'm going to check on the kids." She disappeared down the hallway.

"Let me introduce you to the family. They're probably in the living room."

Subdued pockets of conversation floated toward them as they made their way through the dining room. "Pastor T!" Eric stepped back in surprise as Marty rushed toward Travis and landed weeping into his open arms. Travis pulled him tighter and whispered in his ear.

"Who's he holding? Marty?" Mallory reentered the hallway.

The words from behind Eric mirrored his own reaction. At the light nudge on his elbow, he turned toward his sister. "Yeah." He fought down the rush of emotions that suddenly blurred his vision. "I've never seen him like this before. Thank God Travis is here."

"Yes," she whispered. "Thank You, Lord."

Eric took a step toward Marty and Travis. He touched his son on the shoulder and spoke quietly, "You okay, son?"

Marty sniffled but managed a nod before bolting past Mallory. "Let him go, Mallory. He needs some time to himself." Eric's words kept Mallory in the room.

"T!" Lindsay's approach was much the same as her brother's. Travis hugged her tightly and offered her quiet words of encouragement.

"Linds. Where's Grandma?" Eric tugged on his daughter's french braid. She tilted her head back and gazed at him through her mother's eyes. "She's in the bedroom with Gran."

"Go let her know that Pastor Travis is here." Eric directed Travis into the living room to make introductions to the rest of the family.

"This is Uncle Mike, my Dad's twin brother, and his sisters, Ruth and Liz, and their husbands, Edward and Ken." With a quiet word of sympathy for each one, Travis shook their hands. "Mom's sisters, Katie and Martha. And this is the computer genius of the family, my baby brother, Geoff." Eric laid a hand on his brother's shoulder as Geoff rose slowly to his feet and hesitated a moment before taking Travis's proffered hand.

Lindsay hurried into the room followed by her grandmother and great-grandmother. Eric noted the fatigue evident on each woman's face. Although stoop-shouldered and supported by a cane, Gran looked more refreshed than his mother. There was an aura of peaceful serenity surrounding her.

It was easy to see that this day was playing havoc on his mother's emotions. Sheer willpower seemed to be the only thing holding her upright on her feet. Perhaps because the color black, although thoroughly suitable for her husband's calling hours tonight, bleached the color from her face. She graciously attempted a smile and reached her slender, manicured hand toward Travis. "Pastor Jamison, how kind of you to come."

Travis drew her toward him and kissed her temple. Eric couldn't hear his words but saw his mother nod before guiding his grandmother forward. "This is Martin's mother, Eleanor Bennington."

"Thank you for coming, Reverend."

"Travis, please, just Travis." Eleanor smiled and patted his hand. Travis continued softly, "I know how difficult it is—at any age—to lose a child."

"There aren't many things harder in this world, Travis, but God supplies us with strength for each moment."

"That He does, ma'am. That He does."

Eric could tell that his grandmother had "taken a shine," as she called it, to T. Clasping Travis's elbow, she allowed him to escort her to the sofa beside Geoff.

"Eric, will you get our coats? I believe it's time Ken and I left."

Eric turned toward his aunt. "Sure, Liz."

"They're on the guest bed, Eric, but why don't we let Lindsay get them?"

"We need to go as well." Mike put his arm around his wife, Patty, and Ruth and her husband, Edward, rose as well. "I think we'll head out, too. We'll see you tonight at the funeral home."

"Excuse me, folks. Would it be all right if I prayed with everyone before you leave?" Travis's deep voice carried over the sudden bedlam of departure.

"I think that would be wonderful." Eric's grandmother spoke before anyone else could.

Eric stood looking at the floor as his friend prayed. T had prayed in his presence before, but it felt strange that he was praying for them and in this situation. He shifted his weight from one foot to the other. The death of his father somehow still seemed unreal.

"Abba Father. I thank You that even in our darkest moments, even when we can't understand, You are there. You love us. Please send Your comfort, Holy Spirit, to these hurting hearts. Carry them in their time of grief. Help them look to You. Amen."

That was it? Eric thought all preachers were long-winded with their prayers. There was a general commotion toward the door, and he was thankful that the relatives had begun to leave. It had been a long day, and he was ready for some peace and quiet if he was going to make it through the calling hours tonight. He turned his head and found his sister's deep-green eyes staring at him. Was that some sort of entreaty? To do what?

A single tear slid down her cheek, and he looked away. It was a little too late to make peace with her now. It was too late for a lot of things.

Chapter Twenty-Nine

Mallory stepped into the muted quiet of the funeral home. She stopped, struck by the déjà vu moment of remembering her grandfather's funeral two years ago. The funeral director nodded at her, and she felt Jake's hand press against her back. He guided her down the hall. She ignored the viewing room with the casket and moved into the family waiting area. Geoff and Eric were right inside the doorway.

She stopped and tried to speak, but what could she say? Renee and Angel bumped into the back of her legs, and she laid a hand on each of their heads and pulled them close. She knew her daughters were worried about her, and she strove to reassure them. She shook her head at them and blinked back tears. Geoff put his arm around her.

"You okay, Mally?"

"Yeah." She took a deep breath and gave him a hug. She looked at Eric and let out a small laugh despite her tears. She patted the silk handkerchief sticking out of Eric's pocket. "Nice touch. You clean up good, big brother." Eric cleared his throat, and Mallory turned to look for her mother. "I'm going to check on Mom."

She was sitting with Mallory's grandmother. Mallory gave her a kiss then sat next to Eleanor. She could smell the faint scent of the lavender perfume her grandmother always wore.

Renee and Angel clung to her knees until she pointed out their cousin Lindsay in the corner and urged them to go sit with her. She wasn't sure how to help them understand what was going on. Mallory bit her lower lip and wiped at her tears. Her grandmother picked up her hand and patted it, and Mallory gave her a gentle squeeze and shook her head. Her grandmother was an amazing woman—she'd just lost her son, and she was the one holding everyone together.

She looked around for Jake and found him at the side of the room talking with Eric and Geoff then turned her head as Marty walked in. His hair was pulled back, revealing the ring in his eyebrow. He was wearing dress pants and collared dress shirt. He shoved his hands in his pockets and looked left then right, finally settling with his back against the wall near his dad. Despite his appearance, he looked more like a ten-year-old boy than a teenager.

Mallory patted her grandmother's arm then went to the door. "Hey, Marty. Grandma said there's a kitchenette down the hall with some refreshments for the family. I bet some of your cousins are down there." She watched him saunter away.

"Mallory, I'm so sorry about your dad. He was always so good to me."

"Thanks, Cat." Mallory returned Catherine's hug with one of her own. She liked Catherine. Marrying her was probably the best decision Eric had ever made. Divorcing her was one of the worst. Although that hadn't technically been his decision, and Mallory really couldn't blame Cat—still, it was a shame their marriage hadn't worked out.

"How's your mom?"

"Hanging in there. Gran hasn't left her side. I think they are holding each other up."

"Is—is Eric here?"

Mallory nodded. "Over there with Geoff."

Catherine paused on the threshold, and Mallory gave her a gentle nudge. "He won't say so, but I'm sure he'll be glad to see you."

Catherine walked over to Mallory's brothers. She hugged Geoff, earning a smile, then turned to Eric. She wrapped her arms around his neck and whispered in his ear. Eric pulled her close, his hand running up her back and under her glossy hair. He buried his face in her shoulder.

Mallory turned away. It was too hard to watch.

"Mallory, dear, how are you?" Her aunt Patty took both of her hands and pumped them up and down.

Mallory. Kiss your sister good-bye. The smell of flowers overpowered Mallory for a moment, and her hand shook. She had a flash of a memory of a small girl in a casket, still and cold. She pulled her hands from her aunt's grasp. Mallory had few memories of her sister. The hardest to bear was the one of her four-year-old self being forced by Aunt Patty to kiss her big sister in her casket.

"Mom's in there." Mallory brushed past her aunt. Pastor Jamison was talking quietly to the director of the funeral home, and she ducked her head as she passed them. She hurried out the front door, drawing in deep breaths to keep calm. Aunt Patty meant well, and Mallory was a grown woman now. She hugged herself.

"Mal?" Jake moved behind her and wrapped his arms around her. "You okay? It's cold out here."

"I'm fine." She rubbed his hands. "Just needed some air."

"They're ready for the family viewing." Jake nuzzled his chin against her hair. "Ready to go back in?"

Mallory nodded, and Jake hugged her tighter.

"I'm here, babe."

Eric stood at his father's casket and blinked the moisture from his eyes. *Dad, why couldn't you love me?* He felt a hand on his back, and he brushed his fingers across his face.

Catherine laid her head against his arm, and Eric steeled himself against the longing that welled up inside. The warmth of her earlier hug came back to him, and he stared back down at father's waxy face. He was probably more peaceful than Eric had ever seen him. Why did he demand so much? Why couldn't he have been satisfied? Why hadn't he recognized what Eric had accomplished?

"He loved you. He just didn't know how to show it."

Pain sliced through Eric. "All I ever wanted was for him to be proud of me." Eric swallowed. "Just once."

"I know." Catherine's blue eyes filled. "I know that's all you've ever wanted, and it hurts that he didn't give that to you." Her whispered words cut straight to his heart.

Eric squeezed his eyes shut.

The weight of years of trying to live up to his father's expectations and failing pressed in on him. He'd tried it all—little league, peewee football, even a community soccer league. It was never enough to get his father's approval. *He* was never enough.

He remembered coming home from his last day of sixth grade. They had just had their final awards assembly, and he clutched a blue ribbon in his hand.

"Dad? Dad! Look what I got!" He'd held out his hand to his father, knowing he would be impressed by the top award—he was the best in the whole school!

His father had been in his home office, working on papers behind his big desk. He'd taken his glasses off and inspected the ribbon. "I see. What's this for then?"

"It's for a poem I wrote. I won the contest for the whole school!"

"Poetry?"

His father had laughed. Eric would never forget the sound of it. He'd tossed the ribbon back to Eric and patted him on the shoulder. "That's fine, son. But don't give up on your athletics."

His father had gone back to his paperwork, and Eric had hidden the ribbon in the bottom of his closet. But even that hadn't stopped his quest for his dad's approval.

He stared at his father's hands folded across his chest. The ruby and gold ring on his right hand stood out against the pasty whiteness of his skin. His dad had gotten it in Korea. Eric looked back at his father's face, his eyes closed, hair combed, and cowlick sprayed in place. He had watched him smooth it down over and over again when he told his dad he was going to follow his footsteps and join the army. But even that hadn't pleased his old man.

"You should have finished college, boy. Won't make an officer now."

No, of course not. Eric had never matched up to his dad's aspirations for him.

"It doesn't mean he didn't love you." Catherine's words startled him. He'd forgotten she was there.

She meant well, but she didn't know the whole story. No one did. Eric had known his father didn't love him when he was seven years old.

He'd been excited about the new baseball mitt his dad had gotten him, and he'd run into his parents' room to tell him about how he'd caught a fly ball with it. His father was leaning over the bed, just finishing changing Mallory's diaper. Dumb sisters. They got all his dad's attention. But this was really important! He flung himself against the bed, slamming his hand still in his mitt down in front of him.

"Eric! Be careful of your baby sister."

"Dad, I caught one! It was really high, too. Coach hit one out to me, and I was right there."

"That's great, son." His dad had picked up Mallory's socks and was putting them on her feet. "Let's get your socks on, so those tootsies don't get cold, sweetheart."

His dad wasn't listening. Eric bumped his knee against the

mattress as he tried to get onto the bed.

"Be careful, I said!"

"But Dad, you shoulda seen it. All the guys clapped for me." Eric heaved himself up onto the bed. He caught his arm under his leg and turned to get free. As he jerked his arm, the weight of his body sunk the mattress, and he rolled toward Mallory. He tried to stop the downward swing of his arm, but his mitt slammed down on top of her, and she let out a wail of pain.

"Watch it!" His father's hand swooped with one motion to shove him off the bed, and Eric tumbled end over end and cracked his head against the baseboard of the wall. "Why won't you ever listen to me, boy?" His father loomed like a giant over him, his sister screaming against his shoulder. "Shh. Shhh. Mally, it's okay. Daddy's got you." He turned sideways to look down at Eric. "And you—stop crying, or I'll give you something to cry about!"

His father had walked out the door, leaving Eric backhanding his tears off his face and trying to rub the pain away.

"Eric?"

Eric blinked, and Catherine's face came back into focus. A line furrowed between her brows. "Are you okay?"

"Yeah." Eric blinked again and cleared his throat. "Yeah, I'm fine." He looked down at the cold, silent body of his father lying in his casket. Regret and longing left its bitter aftertaste in his memory. It was too late. He'd never have the chance to ask his dad what he had done to make him hate him. Or to even say he was sorry. Now there would never be a chance to make any of this right with his father. The words reverberated through his head. *Too late.*

And in the end, he killed his father. Just the way he had killed his sister.

Darkness lay across the hills of the farmland like a thick comforter. Travis looked into the clear night sky, stars twinkling like diamonds against black velvet. Calls like this one were hard enough to make, but it was especially hard when it was a friend, a friend who had no spiritual foundation. *Be with me, Father. Speak through me, Holy Spirit. Share Your love with this man.*

"Have a seat, T." Eric followed him onto the porch and nodded toward the hanging swing.

"Thanks, I think I will." Travis's weight bounced the seat backward as he sat down. Eric had been silent on the way back from calling hours. Catherine had taken Lindsay home with her, and Marty had disappeared to his grandparents' basement as soon as they'd gotten back.

Travis had been surprised that Eric had agreed to being driven to the funeral home. The fact that he wasn't striving to be in control of everything, including being behind the wheel, spoke volumes to Travis. Eric's world was crumbling. First the fire, now this. Travis hoped he wouldn't fall back on the alcohol again. *Lord, hang on to him.* His friend might be finding out that sometimes it got a whole lot worse before it got better. Still, Eric was stubborn enough to resist surrender.

His only words to him since they'd gotten in the car had been to ask if Travis wanted to hang out for a few minutes. And Travis had jumped at it, hoping he would have a chance to try to get his friend to open up. He was obviously hurting, but getting him to share it was like squeezing a porcupine—excruciating.

Everyone grieved in his own way. Travis knew that from experience. He also knew he couldn't push Eric into talking, but death had a way of making the living vulnerable. His father's death might be the very thing that helped his friend to open up.

"You cold?" Eric sat with one hip against the porch railing. His body posture looked relaxed, except for the slight jiggling motion of his leg.

"Never happen." Travis took a deep breath of fresh, soul-cleansing air. "I've always loved fall. The air seems to crystallize everything. You know winter is coming"—he burrowed his nose into the flannel lining of his jacket—"but not yet. Time speeds up and slows down all at once."

"You're weird."

"I know. . .that's why you like me."

The swing creaked rhythmically as Travis set it in motion then tucked his hands deep into his coat pockets and tipped his head to catch the brisk breeze. He sat without saying anything, letting the creaking and rocking of the swing offer its own comfort. People always expected a preacher to know the right words when sometimes there wasn't anything he could say. The living room lights winked out, and the hinges of the door groaned in complaint as it swung open.

"Lock up when you come in, Eric."

"I will, Mom." Eric rose from his position on the railing and leaned toward his mother. "Will you be all right?"

A tear slid down her cheek following the crease at the corner of her mouth. She shook her head. "I—I guess I have to be." The wobble in Mrs. Bennington's voice made her sound like an unsure child. Eric roughly cleared his throat, stepping hesitantly into the square of faint light streaming from deep within the house. Travis knew how difficult it was for Eric to deal with his mother's tears and was proud of him as he held her and let her cry. Moments later Alecia straightened and pushed away from him. "Good night, Pastor Jamison. Thank you again for coming."

Travis stood to his feet and clasped her outreached hand. "Good night, Mrs. Bennington. And you're welcome. I'll be praying for you." *Praying you make it through the long nights of no sleep, the numbness, the aching that never seems to go away, that somewhere along the line the gaping hole in your heart will be healed. Help her, Jesus.*

Alecia turned toward her son. "Good night, Eric. Don't forget to lock up."

"I won't. 'Night, Mom." For long moments Eric stared at the

closed door before turning and walking the length of the porch.

His friend paced for several minutes before Travis finally broke the silence lengthening between them. "Eric, I know that you don't share your feelings easily, but what are you thinking about?"

"We. . .had our differences, but I—I can't imagine life without him. Why did it take losing him for me to see how much she loved him?"

Travis left his place and moved beside his friend. He said nothing, simply laying his hand on his friend's shoulder.

"Why, Trav? Why did God take Dad from Mom?"

"I don't know, Eric."

Eric swung around, knocking Travis's hand to his side. "What kind of an answer is that? You're a minister. You're supposed to know all about God." Eric began his restless pacing again.

"It's an honest answer because I don't know all about God. I'm still struggling to find the answer to that one myself." Travis lowered his voice. "I'm still trying to figure out why God took my wife from me. Believe me, if I figure it out, you'll be the first I'll tell."

Eric stopped and leaned his shoulder against the white porch post. "How did you cope, T?"

"One day at a time. Sometimes a minute at a time. Even now it's hard." Travis mirrored Eric's position against the opposite pillar. "But here's what I learned. No matter how dark those moments were, and still are to some degree, God is with me through every one of them." He shook his head. "Eric, I don't pretend to know the mind of God, or why He does what He does, but I know He desires to—"

"Forget it, Travis! I know that stuff works for you, but it's not for me."

"You asked."

"Yeah, I walked right into that one, didn't I?"

"Yup, and I'll take every opportunity to share God with you that I can get." Travis let out a soft chuckle and folded his arms. There was so much more he wanted to say to Eric. But he was afraid he would just reject it all again. He wished he had more to offer his friend, but he was rejecting the One who could meet his every need.

Travis shifted his shoulder and stared out at the shadows of the tall pine tree. Its branches were dipping with the slight breeze, as if to encourage him to keep going. All of them—Eric, Alecia, Geoff, Mallory—this whole family was hurting, and he felt so helpless. It would be great if Travis could just fix things for them, but even if he could, they would miss out. The journey was part of the process.

He thought about his time with them at the calling hours tonight. He'd done what he could; Jake had even pulled him aside and thanked him, but he hadn't been much help.

"Tell me about Shelly." His own words surprised Travis; he hadn't known he was going to say that until they slipped out of this mouth. *Help me here, Lord.* Judging by the way Eric whipped around and stared at him, he may have just made a huge mistake.

Eric's eyes narrowed as he stared at Travis. "Who told you about Shelly?"

"Well, you did. At the reenactment. But just that she died." Travis moved his back to rest his full weight onto the pillar.

His friend turned back to stare into the darkness. A hoot owl sounded its eerie *whoooo*, and the rising moon defined stark silhouettes of the thinning trees.

Travis waited for Eric to respond, and when he didn't, he admitted, "Jake said something to me tonight at the funeral home. Mallory was upset, and I asked if there was anything I could do. He just said she was still troubled by her sister's death when she was little. Said her death haunted the whole family."

Eric's short laugh came out more like a groan. He rubbed at

his beard and finally turned back to look at Travis. "It was a sled-riding accident. She was seven. We were all there—out with the neighborhood kids. Except Mallory. She was home sick." Eric crossed his arms and stared at the floorboards of the porch. "We don't talk about it much."

"I'm sorry. That must have been a terrible time for your family."

"Pretty much changed everything." Eric swiveled away from him again.

Travis prayed for wisdom to know what to say. He had a sense that there was more to the whole thing. That was probably all he'd learn about it tonight, and while he didn't want to back Eric into a corner, he felt compelled to nudge his friend a little more.

"Eric, why do you think we question God only in the hard times? I've been in the ministry a long time and very few—actually no one—has ever said to me, 'Why, Trav? Why would God so choose to bless *me*? What did I ever do to deserve His goodness?'" Travis watched Eric's face harden just a fraction. The firm line of his jaw was broken as he started to speak then clenched his mouth tight.

"God is unfathomable. His ways aren't our ways. We can't figure Him out because He is so far beyond our comprehension." Travis drew a deep breath.

"Here's what I'm trying to say—God is bigger than any of us. But I know He's good, and He desires only the best for us. Our problem is our perception is skewed. We like to pretend we know more and can do things better than He can.

"Eric, I know how much pain you're in, and now isn't the time to get into a philosophical debate, but if you have no spiritual foundation upon which to stand at this moment, in the middle of this loss, you are going to crash and burn. I don't want to see that happen to my best friend."

Eric continued to stare across the front lawn. Arms crossed and turned away from him, Travis couldn't tell if his friend was rejecting what he was saying or defending himself from it. He decided to risk it.

"Think about what I said. Let me just leave you with this one verse to ponder. Psalm 28:8 says, 'The Lord is their strength, and He is the saving refuge of His anointed.' If you allow Him, He'll help you through this." Travis laid a hand on Eric's arm. "Call me if you need to talk. I'll be at the funeral tomorrow. I have to leave right away, so I may not see you, but I'll be in touch in a couple of days."

Eric nodded but refused to meet Travis's eyes.

"Okay. I'm going to head out and let you get to bed. Think about what I said. I'll see you later." Travis dug into his pants pocket for his keys as he walked to his car. As he pulled out of the drive, he glanced over his shoulder to find Eric still standing in the darkness.

Chapter Thirty

Eleanor turned the faucet to let the cold water run over the apples piled in the colander. She rubbed her knuckles. Her arthritis was bad today, but Lindsay had asked for her homemade applesauce, and it was hard to refuse her precious great-granddaughter.

"Okay, Gran. I got the peeler. Can I start now?"

"Sit up at the table, and we'll work there." Eleanor placed the colander on a paper towel in the middle of the table. Her knees popped as she settled into the wooden chair. She grasped the paring knife and slowly began to peel the first apple. "Be careful now. The peeler is still sharp—don't cut yourself."

"I won't." Lindsay's smile lit her whole face. "I can do it, Gran." She held the large red apple in one hand and attacked it with the peeler in the other. Small strips of apple littered the table between them.

"Put the peelings in here." Eleanor nudged the bowl she'd placed there earlier closer to her great-granddaughter.

"We're gonna make the best applesauce 'cuz you have a secret ingredient and you're only gonna tell me, right, Gran?"

Eleanor smiled. "Yes, I'm going to tell you, and you can be the keeper of the family recipe. But you have to promise to pass it on, so it doesn't get lost."

"I will, I promise!" The tip of Lindsay's tongue peeked out the corner of her mouth as she concentrated on keeping the peeler following the curve of the apple. Kneeling on the kitchen chair, she was nearly the same height as Eleanor. The child was growing like a weed.

Eleanor dropped the cleaned apple back into the colander and reached for the next one to peel. Life's everyday chores had a soothing rhythm about them. Peeling apples, cooking, teaching the little ones of the next generation—it all reminded her that life moved on, despite the sorrow she carried each day. How well she knew the scripture that said life was a vapor—a mist that had swept over her life and taken Paul and now Martin.

Eleanor pressed her fingers onto the table to stop the quiver she felt running through them. A mother never expected to outlive her children, but she clung to the knowledge that her Lord was still in control—that and knowing that there was more to this life than just the blink of an eye that was your life span. . . .

Lindsay's peeler banged against the side of the metal bowl. "And it's important to pass what we know on to the next generation, isn't it? 'Cuz we're all a part of the leg–legamy—"

"Legacy, child. Legacy."

"What's that mean again, Gran?"

"It means we're all part of something bigger than just ourselves." Eleanor smiled. Lindsay was like a sponge and repeated nearly everything she said to her. She shook her head. Just showed how important it was to choose your words carefully. "We don't go through life alone. The Lord meant us to be part of each other—that's why He gave us families."

"We're all part of the lin– the—what's it called again?"

"Lineage. It means the line of all your ancestors—your father and mother and grandfather and grandmother—and all the great-grandfathers and grandmothers. It's where you came from child, but more importantly—where you're headed and where your children will one day be headed."

"Heaven!"

Eleanor laughed. "That's right. Heaven. We get to heaven through God's Son, Jesus, and that's forever, so it's most important. But what we do on earth is the preparation for that time, so don't discount it, child. You're young, but God has wonderful plans for your life, and you need to follow His path."

"Gran? Do you think God's plan includes Mommy and Daddy getting back together?"

"Sweetheart, I wish I could tell you that would happen. I do know that God's plans are for the best—so yes, I think His plan was for your mom and dad to be together forever, but remember what I told you?"

"That we each get to choose what we want to do?"

"That's right! We make a choice every day."

"Like how I get to choose if I want to do what my mom and dad say?"

"Exactly!"

"I wish my dad would choose to obey God."

Eleanor sat the apple she was working on down on the table. "Why do you say that, sweetheart?"

" 'Cuz I feel better when I'm good, and I think my dad would feel better, too!"

Eleanor dropped her hands to her lap and stared at her granddaughter. It amazed her at times what came out of the mouths of these little ones. *Oh, Lord. Out of the mouths of babes— may Your will be done.* She prayed for wisdom as she answered.

"Obedience is very important in pleasing God, as well as our parents. Do you know why God wants us to do things a certain way?"

Lindsay's big blue eyes widened, and she shook her head.

"Because He knows what's best for us. Remember when I

206

told you that you couldn't light the gas fire on the stove, and then when I tried it, the flame shot up so high? You didn't know it was dangerous, but I did—that's why I told you not to do it. It was to protect you. God is like that. He wants us to live as He tells us to so we don't get hurt or find ourselves in a dangerous circumstance. Your dad—" Eleanor hesitated. How did she explain this so a child could understand it? It was a lifelong lesson.

"I think your dad has trouble believing that God wants the best for him. But he has to make that choice for himself—just the way you do. Do you remember the decision you made the last time you were here?"

"Uh-huh! I chose Jesus! 'Cuz God forgives my sins, and it feels so much better when you tell someone that you were bad." Lindsay dropped a red streaked apple in the colander and picked up another one. "Did Dad do something bad?"

"I think we've talked about this before, but we've all done bad things. That's why we need Jesus—because He never disobeyed God." Eleanor picked up a peeled apple and cut it in half to core it and slice it up for cooking. If only it was as easy to cut the bad parts out of our lives. It was easy in that it only took asking God for help, but the *choosing* to ask for help was tougher than it sounded.

Look at Eric. All these years she had watched him make bad choices—a few good ones, too, but the most important choice in looking to God as his Father—he was still struggling with that one, just as he had struggled all his life with his relationship with his earthly father. And now that Martin was gone—

The knife slipped in Eleanor's hand, sliding against the edge of her finger. No blood, thank goodness. She rested her trembling hands on the table and watched Lindsay as she worked on removing the skin on another apple.

Eleanor knew that underneath Eric's tough exterior he was as tender as that apple meat. Getting through his outer shell was going to be the hard part. She had been praying fervently for him, knowing that it would take him being desperate before he would surrender to God. He'd lost his wife, his business, now his father. What more would it take for the real Eric to come forth?

When the apples were peeled and sliced, she set them on the stove to cook. Soon their sweet aroma mixed with cinnamon filled the kitchen. By the time Eric arrived to pick up Lindsay, it permeated the whole house.

"My favorite! Nothing better than Gran's applesauce."

"Gran taught me how to make it! It's my applesauce now, isn't it, Gran?"

"It sure is! Try some of 'Lindsay's applesauce.'" Eleanor placed a bowl before Eric then joined him at the table. Eric praised his daughter's efforts then sent her off to gather her things. Eleanor waited for Lindsay to leave the room then asked Eric how the investigation on the fire was going.

"Too slow! The insurance is holding off on paying out until the investigation is done, and they can't seem to find out who did it."

"What about your business?"

"Not good." Eric shook his head. "I'm at a standstill until I can get the insurance money. I'm pretty much shut down now. Only Greg is left on the payroll." He shoved the empty bowl, and it slid to the center of the table. The spoon tumbled out and flung spots of applesauce in its wake.

Eleanor took a napkin and dabbed up the mushy liquid. "What will you do now?"

"I don't know, Granny." Eric leaned back and rubbed his forehead. "I don't know." He crossed his arms. "Why is God doing this to me?"

"Oh, Eric! You sound like God is out to get you or something!"

"Isn't He?"

"No, sweetheart, He isn't! He loves you." Eleanor folded her hands on the tabletop. Eric refused to meet her eyes. It was the same old stubbornness he'd shown since he was a toddler. "Have you ever thought that maybe He just wants your attention?"

"What?" Eric's eyes darted to her face. "He wants my attention, so He just starts destroying my life?"

"That's not what I meant, dear. He wants your attention, and as long as you believe you can handle things on your own and have no use for Him, you aren't going to give Him so much as the time of day. He loves you and wants you to depend on Him, not yourself."

"Those words sound good, Gran, but they don't hold much meaning for me." Eric shoved away from the table and began to pace her small kitchen. "It's certainly not been my experience anyway."

"What has been your experience?"

Her grandson stopped and leaned against the kitchen stool placed in the corner. He dwarfed it now, but she could remember as a young boy he had constantly tried to climb it, despite her best efforts to keep him down. He fell off it when he was three and had to get four stitches in his chin. The scar was still there underneath the bush of hair on his face. He'd been obstinate even as a child.

"Indifference." He shrugged his shoulders. "Why would God care about my life? He surely must have other, more important things to keep Him busy." He sank onto the stool and stretched out his legs.

"You're making fun, Eric, but I'm being serious." He was acting as if he didn't care, but was that longing she heard in his voice? "What makes you think God doesn't care about you?"

"Why would He? He goes His way, I go mine."

"You hit that nail right square on the head!" Eleanor smiled. "Do you know how much you are like your father?"

Eric's shoulders stiffened, and a muscle jerked in his jaw. He stood and went to the window. "I'm nothing like him!"

Eleanor watched his rigid back, remembering the stance from

his youth. Legs spread, chin jutted forward—just like Martin when he was a teenager. "Oh yes, my dear, you are very like him, as he was like his father. Stubbornness is a generational curse in this family."

"Curse?" Eric turned around. "Do you really believe such things exist, Gran? 'Sins of the fathers' and all that? Generational curses passed on from father to son?"

"I think it's very real. God talks about it in the Bible, and while I believe everyone answers for their own sins, I've lived long enough to see the spiritual impact of generations of sin being passed down—father to son, mother to son and daughter. I see myself in my children—and it's not always a pretty sight, I assure you! Surely you've seen the same in your own children, Eric?"

He gave a short laugh. "I concede your point, Granny. I see more of myself in Marty than I would like to admit."

"You always were a stubborn lad. Had trouble admitting when you were wrong."

Eric turned back to the window. She missed his mumbled reply, and just as she started to ask him to repeat it, Lindsay dashed into the room. Eleanor moved stiffly to her feet.

"Okay, Dad. I got my stuff. But Gran said I can come back and stay for a few days if you say yes."

"Sure, we'll work it out." Eric came over and gave Eleanor a hug and kiss. "Tell Gran thanks, kiddo."

Lindsay wrapped her arms around Eleanor's waist. "Bye, Gran! Thanks."

Eleanor kissed the top of her head. "Come anytime."

Eric picked up Lindsay's duffel bag and went out the door. Lindsay slung her backpack over her shoulder. She reached for the door handle then turned back. "Gran! You forgot to tell me which one was the secret ingredient!"

Eleanor smiled and bent over her ear to whisper, "It's love."

"Graan!" Lindsay wailed. "I thought you meant a real ingredient."

"It's the most important thing we put in that sauce today. Don't forget to add it to everything you do!" She rubbed her back.

Lindsay hugged her again. "I'll remember, Gran!"

Eleanor lifted a hand in farewell and pulled the screen door shut. She pulled the edges of her sweater tight around her. Time for the storm windows. She could feel the impatience of winter clamoring to arrive even though all the leaves had yet to turn.

Every season had its course to run, its time in God's plan. She wondered as she watched Eric's car bump down the driveway if he would recognize his own season of change. Only God could transform his life, and all she could do was watch.

That and pray.

Chapter Thirty-One

Travis used his shirttail as a towel to wipe sweat from his face. It was an extremely warm day for the first of December, and the physical exertion of cleaning out an overloaded garage had successfully raised his body temperature to an uncomfortable degree. He paused in the middle of yanking his outer shirt off when he heard Eric groan before swearing under his breath. Travis tucked his wet shirt in his back pocket and sighed. One of these days he was going to have to get on Eric for his colorful adjectives. It wasn't that he hadn't heard the words before, or for that matter had never used them, but they were such a part of Eric's everyday vocabulary that he was passing them on to his children and then jumping on them whenever they used them around him.

"I can't believe the junk my dad has collected. I always thought that my mother was the pack rat in the family." Eric grunted as he moved a box of tools from the corner of the garage where his dad's workbenches had always been. "She must have rubbed off on him."

"I'll have you know, young man, that it was your father who rubbed off on to me!" Alecia's voice rose in annoyance. Travis turned to see Eric's mom enter the garage through the side entrance. He hid a smile as he watched Eric stiffen at the sound of her voice before a deep stain flushed his dirt-smudged face. "Ma, you know I didn't mean anything."

Travis saw a twinkle of mischief lighten her honey-colored eyes and choked back a chuckle as her right lid slid down in a sly wink. Where had Eric ever come up with the notion that his mother didn't have a sense of humor?

"I know exactly what you meant by that crack. Sure, blame the woman for being a pack rat. Your dad accumulated more stuff than any twenty men should have." She stepped into the shadows of the garage and unzipped her faded pink jacket. Her brown slacks were worn at the knees, and tendrils of blond hair curled around her face, giving him an idea of what she must have looked like as a teenager.

"That man loved garage sales and junkyards. He was forever bringing stuff home saying, 'But Alecia, it was a great bargain.'" She shook her head in fond amusement. "Well, you made a dent. Will I need to call the trash company and have them send over a bigger Dumpster?" Alecia stepped up on the side of the trash container to see how full it was.

"I don't think so, Mom. How's it coming in Dad's study?" The box Eric was moving to the center of the garage muffled his voice.

Travis looked up in time to see Alecia flinch, and painful sorrow flitted through her eyes. He swallowed down his own emotions, remembering going through the baby things that his wife had been piling up before she died.

"Travis Jamison! You put your shirt back on this minute! You're going to catch your death of cold! Don't you know that it's the first of December?"

Travis jumped as the sound of her voice hauled him back to the present.

"I got hot." He turned to see her standing under the bare bulb, hands on her hips, a look of motherly indignation on her face.

She cocked her head and stared him down.

"Yes, Mother," he muttered and grinned sheepishly as he reached to his back pocket for his shirt.

The smile she gave him told him he had been accepted by her, and Travis's heart lifted. He smiled back at her as he tugged his shirt over his head.

"Mother!" Eric's voice held embarrassment and open rebuke. "Travis is thirty-six years old! He's a grown man!" He dropped the box and strode toward her. "Why do you have to constantly embarrass—"

"Well, I certainly didn't—"

"Ease up, Eric." Travis's voice was firm as he overrode Alecia's suddenly tearful defense. He moved to slip an arm around her slender waist. She looked as if she had been beaten and then abandoned. "I think it's sweet of your mom to worry about me." He reached down and kissed her temple. "I don't think I ever told you, but my mom died when I was seven, and I was raised by an aunt who clearly loved me but didn't know how to show that love. She was a great buddy, but not a good mom. Come to think of it, I never heard my aunt say anything like that to me, though the Lord knows I gave her plenty of reasons to rebuke me. Thanks, Mrs. Bennington."

The impish glow came back into her eyes at his words of praise to her motherly gifts. She patted him on the cheek. Travis looked out the corner of his eyes at Eric. His hands were stuffed in his back pockets. He blinked his eyes and looked away, but not before Travis caught a glimpse of what looked like longing on his face.

"You boys look like you're progressing nicely. I think I'll go in and finish my soup. How does some homemade apple pie sound?"

Alecia left amid hearty approval, and her "boys" got back to work. After clearing a space by the back wall, Travis pulled the ladder down to check the garage attic. "Lots of stuff up here yet,

Eric. What do you say I crawl up here and hand the boxes down to you?"

They lit the attic as well as they could with a spotlight they found on a shelf. That and one small window at the end wall gave Travis enough light to find his way around without stumbling. He and Eric soon found a rhythm. Travis would check the box, decide the general classification of what was in it, hand it down to Eric so he could put it in the designated area of the garage, and then move on to the next one. By emptying the upper storage space, they felt they could better assess what to do with everything.

Travis heaved a box toward the steps. "This one looks like books, magazines, that sort of thing. It looks like there are papers in here, too. I doubt if they are important, but you might want to check them out before you just pitch the whole box." The box slipped from Travis's grasp as he dropped it down to Eric.

"Look out!" The cardboard split when it hit the concrete floor, spilling books and papers everywhere. "Sorry! You all right down there?"

"I'm fine—but it might be time for you to take a break, old man!" Eric began to stack books on one side of the box and papers on the other.

Travis jumped off the second rung of the ladder to avoid Eric as well as the mess on the floor. "Let me help."

"I'll go in and get us a drink and maybe a snack as soon as we. . ."

Travis looked up as Eric paused. His friend was staring steadily at the pages he held in his hand. "What is it?" Curious, Travis twisted to get a better look. "Oh, uh. . ." A scantily dressed model posed provocatively on the cover. "Eric—"

"Don't worry. I know all about my dad." Eric's face grew red, and he continued, speaking rapidly, "I had just forgotten they were there, that's all." Eric tossed the magazine aside and began piling others on top of it.

215

"You knew they were there?"

Eric continued stacking. "Seen 'em all. First time I saw one of Dad's *Playboy* magazines, I must have been six or seven." He gave Travis a wicked grin. "Quite an education, let me tell you. Want to see one?" Eric had recovered quickly from any awkwardness he might have felt.

Travis tapped the back of Eric's head with a book he'd picked up. "No! I know all about how man perverts what God designed to be beautiful. Thanks anyway."

"So, aren't you even a little tempted?" Eric baited him.

"It was a long time ago, Eric. Once I found what God intended sex to be, I never wanted to go back to anything else."

"Come on, T, not even a little peek?" He held one of the magazines toward him.

Now what, Lord? "Eric, between those pages are nothing but lies."

"What, you think it's trick photography?" When Eric moved his hand toward the cover, Travis stopped him.

"It totally dehumanizes and demeans women. They become things, not people with a soul. That's not how God designed the physical union between man and woman." Travis struggled for the right words to make Eric understand. "Lust is never satisfied. Desire becomes what we feed our minds with. Smut"— Travis nodded toward the stack of magazines—"or the complete fulfillment and joy God designed sex to be."

Eric tossed the rest of the papers into the half-torn box. "You always manage to drag religion into the conversation, don't you?"

Travis laughed. "Not religion—God. There is a difference, you know. It's a *relationship*." He grew serious. "Eric, many people have this false idea of God as a bully who hangs over us waiting to rap us on the knuckles with a ruler if we don't obey. It's true there are consequences, and it's true that God has given us principles, or rules if you will, in His word, to obey, but not because He's a bully or power hungry or something. It's because He created us. He knows us intimately. That means He knows what can hurt us—even destroy us—and what can help us, what can give us peace and bring us joy."

Eric gathered the remains of the box and took it to the Dumpster. Travis followed him, dropping his armload of books on the corner of the crowded workbench. How much should he say? He hated being pushy, yet he knew God had given him unique opportunities to share with this man. Travis wasn't sure if it was wisdom from the Holy Spirit or simply one of his human hunches, but he often felt Eric was tormented by something.

"We've talked about this before, Eric. Pornography—and that's what those magazines are—has ruined the lives of so many people. And as I know from experience, it's addictive—and if you feed it, it will eventually end up devouring you." Eric was taking a long time to throw the box away, and Travis decided he had said enough. "If you asked your mother, I'm sure she'd tell you that it impacted your parents' lives as well."

"Mom doesn't know about these!"

"Perhaps you're right. Nevertheless, damage was done—not only to your mother, but to the six-year-old little boy who found that pornography." Eric walked to the workbench, and Travis spoke to his rigid back. "It damaged you, Eric, whether you acknowledge it or not. And it's certainly damaged Marty." When Eric didn't reply, Travis threw up his hands. "Okay, okay. I'm done preaching now. Look, how about that drink?"

Eric nodded, and Travis followed him into the house. The simmering vegetable soup made his mouth water, and after washing up they sat down to a simple lunch of soup and homemade bread. Alecia promised them warm pie when they were ready for another break.

"That was delicious, Mrs. B." Travis wiped his mouth and laid his napkin to the side of his bowl. "I'm ready to get back out there and dig in."

"I really appreciate your help, Travis." She smiled. "I'm sure Eric does, too."

"You got that right. Well, T, we'd better get at it." Eric moved his chair back from the table.

"Do you have much more to go through?"

"There aren't too many more boxes in the area above the garage," Travis reassured Alecia. "Once we get those down and sorted, it should go fairly quickly."

He and Eric began their tasks with renewed vigor. Travis was glad to see the final two boxes weren't particularly large. The smallest one he almost overlooked; it had been tucked away in the darkest corner. He took it toward the window and lifted a flap. It looked like personal letters and papers. This one might need to be put in the house for Alecia to sort through. Travis heard a car door slam and recognized Eric's sister Mallory walking up the driveway.

"Eric? How's it going?"

Travis couldn't make out Eric's brief reply. He heard the scrape of a box along the concrete floor and a subdued conversation between the two siblings. Turning his attention back to the paper he held in his hand, he saw that it was brittle and brown with age, a newspaper dated 1953. There were several more in the box underneath what looked to be love letters tied with a faded pink ribbon. Definitely a box for the house, Travis decided.

"What's this? Eric! Do you have no sense of decency?"

"Look, Mal, that's not—"

"It's filth is what it is!" The pitch of Mallory's voice made Travis cringe. "We've just buried our father, and you start bringing trash like this here? What if Mom had found it? Honestly, Eric, I thought maybe you might have matured just a little bit." Travis heard the distinct sound of rustling pages and could imagine the magazine flying through the air only to be stopped by the solid thickness of his friend. Uh-oh, they must have missed one of the magazines. Perhaps he should make his presence known, but it was an awkward situation with Mallory not knowing he was up here. Maybe he should just wait.

"Get off it, Mallory. It's not mine."

"Right." Travis was sure the obvious doubt in her voice would make Eric's blood boil.

"I said it is not mine."

"Whose is it then, Mom's?" Mallory's disbelieving voice rose another decibel. "That is so like you, Eric—try to blame somebody else for your own foulness!"

Travis rose up from his seated position on the floor, but he got no farther than his knees when he heard the sound of glass shattering. *Father, please, help them control their anger.*

Eric's string of cuss words fractured any hope of constructive communication between the brother and sister. "That piece of *filth* and *foulness*, Mallory, is your beloved saint of a father's." The hissing words sounded like more swearing.

"Daddy?" Mallory's disbelieving laugh was strangled by the fury that came charging after it. "How could you, Eric! Daddy hasn't even been gone two months! How can you even think of saying something so hateful? Daddy would never—"

"You don't have half an idea of what *Daddy* would do, do you, princess? Always 'Daddy's little girl,' the prima donna who never did anything wrong. Well, you're wrong about this, Mal."

"Eric, why are you doing this? Stop it, just stop it!" Mallory's voice was thickening with tears, and Travis rose to his feet. It might be time to intervene; perhaps a third party to witness their argument would calm things down.

"The only thing I'm doing, little sister, is helping you to see how things really are—instead of the way you like to pretend— that *Daddy* was perfect. He wasn't, you know. He had plenty of dirty little secrets of his own."

"Eric. . ." Neither of them had heard Travis descend the attic steps. Mallory's green eyes widened in alarm while Eric stiffened his arms and clenched his hands to his sides. *Help me here, Lord.* "There might be a better time for this, buddy." In the first few seconds, Travis thought his friend might actually take a swing at him, but was relieved when Eric's fists relaxed.

Mallory dropped her face into her hands. Travis laid his hand gently on her shoulder. "Mallory—" He had just begun to speak when the side door of the garage banged open.

"Mal?" Mallory's husband Jake stepped through the door followed by his mother-in-law who pushed past him.

"What in heaven's name is going on out here? I could hear you all the way in the house!" Every inch of Alecia's diminutive body was pouring out her wrath on her errant children.

Eric's hand lifted in disgust. "It's not my problem—it's hers. She's unable to face reality. Pollyanna here thinks just because she never caught the end of Dad's belt or the back side of his hand—"

"Eric. . ." Both Alecia and Jake spoke at once. Eric's mother continued, "Once, just once, can't the two of you get along?"

Mallory wiped her face with the backs of her hands. "I don't even know how we can be related."

"Maybe we're not."

"What's that supposed to mean?" Mallory's eyes darted to her mother and back.

"Eric!" Alecia warned him sternly.

Travis moved to his friend's side. "Take it easy here. I think we need to get a grip on the situation and talk about this."

"Yeah, whatever." Sounding more like his teenage son than he would appreciate, Eric shrugged Travis off and moved to the door. "It's always the same. Go ahead and listen to her, Ma. I'm going inside." The glass window rattled in its frame when he banged the door behind him.

Alecia looked to Travis as if to say "do something about this," but before Travis could move Mallory swung around and ducked through the half-open overhead garage door. "Forget it, Mom. I'm leaving. I'll be back to see you when he's gone."

Jake looked at Travis and shrugged his shoulders. "I'll talk to her, and see what I can do."

"Oh Lord. . ." Travis's whispered words were a heartfelt prayer. Not for the first time, he wished his seminary professors had taught him how to deal with such situations. He was torn between running after Eric and knocking some sense into him and comforting his mother; Mallory was gone. Travis wasn't sure Jake would even be able to talk with her.

Alecia clutched the edges of her jacket, looking toward the driveway then the house. The uncertainty on her face was too much for Travis. "Are you okay, Alecia?"

She gave a slight nod, her chin quivered, and she looked down. Travis pulled her into his arms. "Do you want me to talk to him?"

"No." Alecia pulled away from Travis. She pressed the back of her hand to the corner of her eye. "Thank you, Travis, but I can handle it."

Cowardly relief washed through him. "If you're sure, then perhaps it's best if I leave. I have some time later in the week when I can help Eric with the rest of the things here. Tell him I'll call him later." He touched her elbow lightly. "If there's anything I can do for you—you have my number."

Chapter Thirty-Two

Mallory's hands tightened into fists. She clenched her jaw to keep from screaming out her frustration into the quiet neighborhood. It would serve Eric right to have the cops come, but with her luck she would be the one charged with disturbing the peace. And her mother would skin her alive.

She paced her way halfway up the block and turned back in time to see Travis back his truck down the driveway and acknowledged his wave with a lift of her chin. Looks like Eric had even scared off the preacher.

She hadn't felt this much anger at her brother in months. She thought she had come so far in forgiving him for the past—but why did he keep blaming others for his own choices? Choices that ripped apart so many lives, including hers.

"Mal—" Jake's hand came down on her shoulder. "Slow down, sweetheart."

She whirled around. "Jake, did you hear what he said? He's blaming Daddy—who is in his grave—for his own twisted behavior."

"Honey, take it easy." Jake dropped his hand and looked out at the street as an older truck rumbled past with its muffler dangling. "Look, I know you don't want to hear this, but Eric could be right. Those magazines could have been your dad's."

"What? Jake! I can't believe you would say that." Mallory brushed the moisture from her cheek. She felt like she'd just been delivered another punch in the gut. She was still reeling from her father's death. Her family had had their difficulties, but her dad was an anchor in her life. Solid. Always there. Now she felt adrift. Lost. Alone.

No. She shook her head—she wasn't alone. God was here with her and so was Jake, who surely knew what a blow this was. He pulled her into his arms, and she didn't resist. He was here. He was real, and he wasn't going to run from the difficulty nor the pain. She wouldn't either.

"It's a hard truth, but one it's time you faced, little sister."

Mallory pulled back and saw her brother with his feet planted wide in the middle of the driveway.

Jake stepped forward. "Look, Eric. Maybe the two of you should cool off a little before you finish this conversation."

Eric snorted. "I did cool off. And stay out of this, Jake. It's time for princess here to deal with the truth about her old man."

"Eri–"

"What are you talking about, Eric?" Mallory stepped around her husband and braced her hands on her hips.

"Eric, I already told her your dad had a problem—that the magazines were his. Don't push this now. Let her deal with it."

"Why do you insist on doing this, Eric? Why? Daddy's not even cold in his grave, and you're smearing his memory!"

"You're the great 'Truth Crusader,' Mal. You say you want truth, but you don't deal with it even when it's right in your face."

"What truth? And what did you mean by 'dirty little secrets'— or is that more of you shifting your stuff onto others?"

"Here's a truth for you, Mal. . . . Your perfect little 'Daddy' nearly beat me to death. He was a hard-nosed, stubborn—"

"Eric! Keep your voice down, or Mom will hear you."

"He was never satisfied, Mallory. You're the only one who got his attention. You and Geoff. And Shelly." Eric's voice dipped. And Mallory leaned forward to hear him as he whispered, "He loved Shelly."

"He loved all of us, Eric!"

Eric's eyes narrowed. "Yeah, he loved me so much he paid for my first hooker when I was fourteen. Bet you didn't know that, princess."

Mallory sucked in her breath. Her mind was spinning. It was like trying to look through 3-D glasses at a neon cartoon. She felt like she was on psychedelic drugs.

"Eric! I think that's enough revelation for one day." Jake wrapped his arm around Mallory. "Come on, sweetheart. We need to get the girls."

She felt Jake tugging her toward the car. She turned her head to stare at her brother, feet still planted defiantly in the driveway. Was that regret she saw flickering through his eyes? Surely not. He was the devil incarnate.

Was there anything good in him worth saving?

Chapter Thirty-Three

He is the sorriest piece of work I have ever dealt with in my entire life!" Mallory exclaimed, breaking the silence that haunted them since she and Jake had left her mom's house, except for the excited chatter of the girls when they'd picked them up. They were playing in their room and occupied at least for a while.

"Mallory, he's hurting, too. Cut him a little slack."

"Cut him some slack?" She whirled around to him. "Jake, how can you say that to me? You heard him."

"Yes, and I heard you, too," Jake said as he quietly shut the door and leaned back against the kitchen counter. His face was a mask of calm serenity, polar opposite to what was coiling through Mallory's entire being.

Mallory reached for a glass in the cupboard and slammed the door. She really wanted to rip it off its hinges and fling it full into her brother's face. She lifted the faucet handle wide. Water hit the interior of the glass with so much force it spewed out over her hand and along the backsplash of the granite counter. The icy liquid flowing over her hands began cooling the fire in her soul.

"Jake, I know my father. He wasn't a vile man."

"No, he wasn't." Jake's arms slipped around her waist, and she felt his lips nuzzle against her neck. Mallory stiffened against the gentle persuasion in his voice. She pushed her back against his chest as a wave of irritation rolled up her spine. Why did he insist on seduction as a means of getting her to drop her guard?

"Stop it."

He loosened his grip but left his arms loosely around her waist. Hazel eyes darkened to blue with empathy as he searched her face.

"Babe, I know the history that is there. I know that." She dropped her eyes to the V-neck of his shirt, not wanting to see the pain he was feeling for her. "I don't want to relieve Eric of his responsibility, but in this case, Mal, he was right—your dad did have a problem with porn."

Her eyes flashed up to his, and she shoved out of his embrace. "He did not!"

"Yes, he did." Jake enunciated every word with flat conviction. "There were times when I would go down to his workroom, and I would see a magazine open on his workbench."

"My father would never do something that disgusting."

"You mean the father you believed him to be would never do something that disgusting." Jake spoke with quiet certainty.

"I can't believe you just said that, Jake Carlisle!" Mallory slammed the cup down on the counter with so much force that the plastic bottom fractured.

"Mallory, there is truth beyond our perception. Like, my old man wasn't evil—he was affected by the booze and broken by the world and the choices he made in that world."

"My father was nothing like yours! He was good and kind and loving! He never would have done the things that Eric accused him of—he didn't ogle women like that."

"Sweetheart, what I am saying is that our perceptions sometimes get in our way and keep us from facing truth. I saw my father as evil for so many years I refused to see anything good in him at all. You see your father as perfect, and he wasn't perfect. He had problems. Real problems. He was opinionated. He did dog Eric. He had one heck of a temper and—"

Bitter denial rose within Mallory, but Jake's fingers on her lips halted the angry course of words. His arms engulfed her once more as he finished. "And he was addicted to pornography."

Mallory's heart began to hammer in her chest. She shoved out of his grip. "You're telling me that my father is this evil, perverted man who couldn't control his animal lust?" She slammed open the dishwasher door.

She felt Jake's eyes watching her as she bent to remove the clean dishes. What she really wanted to do was throw every dish she had against the wall with such force that the shattering of glass would somehow cleanse the rage building within her.

"Babe, addiction to pornography doesn't mean your father is evil. It just means he's a man."

Mallory spun and stared at him. A thought too horrible rose and escaped her lips before she could stop it. "Do you?"

"Do I what?" he asked as his eyebrows rose into question marks.

A knot grew in the pit of her stomach. "You said porn makes him a man. Do you look at porn?"

"No. I said he is a man who looks at porn. I did not say that it makes him a man." Jake reached for her hands and held them tight as his eyes pinned hers with the most sincere look she had ever seen. "Listen to me very clearly, Mallory. I do not look at pornography. I don't need to." He leaned in and brushed her lips with his as his voice lowered to a whisper. "Not when I have the sexiest woman alive in my life and in my bed."

A tingle of love shimmied up her spine. Even when he was irritating, her husband had a way of making her feel as if she was the most beautiful and precious thing he had ever encountered.

He stepped away from her and leaned his hip on the counter. "But there are some things you need to understand about men, Mal. And maybe you can begin to understand your father and your brother better. Men are hardwired visually. We can't 'not look' any more than you can't 'not multitask.' "

The tingle of desire dissipated, and she threw him a disgusted look. "What's that mean? That's just an excuse!"

"No. It's the truth." He turned his gaze to the ceiling as if trying to find a way for her to understand what he was saying. She saw his lips moving and for an instant wondered if he was praying. For wisdom, for direction, or for her obtuseness?

"Do you remember the year before Renee was born?"

She remembered. It had been one of several hard years in their marriage. Not the hardest. That one had been two years ago. But they had been married for several years, and there were still no children. She could still taste the feeling of inadequacy of being unable to conceive.

"Do you remember what you said to me? How you felt this near-compulsive need to have a child? You said you felt as if your biological clock was ticking down and you had this physical drive to conceive a child?"

She nodded and wondered what any of that had to do with this current conversation.

"Sweetheart, it's like that for a man, when a woman walks within his radar range. In almost every man there is this nearly physical, compulsive need to look at something profoundly beautiful, and that profound beauty is a woman's body."

The clear-eyed, vulnerable gaze Jake fixed her with kept Mallory from snorting in derision. Was he serious? Did it really happen that way with men? Did her father and brother really feel that kind of feeling? It seemed ridiculous because she sure as heck didn't have that kind of a physical pull when she looked at her husband's body—not that it wasn't attractive, she amended to herself. She reined in her runaway thoughts to focus back on Jake's words.

". . .we feel this pull, and there is a split second between the pull and our reaction to it when a choice has to be made. Do we cave and look? Or do we fight the urge and find something else to catch our attention? It's a tough battle sometimes, Mallory. If it's our wife, absolutely." As if to punctuate the statement, Jake let his eyes roam freely over her body, causing ripples of desire to shoot through her. He grinned as if he knew exactly what that look was doing to her.

He pulled his eyes back to her face, paused for a moment, and reached once more for her hands, pressing his own into them as he drew her closer. "If it's someone else, we have to find somewhere else to fix our gaze until the impulse passes."

She suddenly remembered something and searched his face as feelings of admiration mingled with disbelief. "Is that why you suddenly look to the sky when we are walking down the street?"

He nodded. "It's a choice. Every man ultimately has to make a choice to honor his woman or dishonor her. It's that simple. For whatever reason, which by the way, we may never know, your father and your brother both got trapped by the choices they made. In choosing pornography, your dad chose to dishonor not only your mother, but his entire family as well.

"I'd like to tell you it is all a nightmarish lie, but sweetie, on more occasions than I would like to admit, your dad would pop in an X-rated video when Eric and Geoff and I were in his workshop. I was ribbed pretty hard by all three of them when I headed back indoors to find you and the girls, but all I could think about was how I would feel if it were my girls they were ogling. It made me sick."

It made Mallory sick, too. Her stomach churned at the thought that the man she had so admired all her life might possibly have been responsible for her brother's behavior, for his abuse of her when she was a little girl. No. Daddy wasn't responsible for that. Eric was.

Mallory dropped her chin to her chest and allowed the curtain of hair to fall around her. "I still can't believe Daddy would get caught up in that garbage. Eric, yes. But Daddy?"

"Babe?" Mallory watched Jake's hand move to her hair and felt his knuckles tuck it behind her ear, then it moved into her line of sight and disappeared beneath her chin. The firm warmth of his fingers brushed her skin as he lifted her face to meet the deep look of love in his eyes. "If it wasn't your father's influence, then how did Eric get addicted to porn?"

Mallory slid from his grasp and pushed her hair off her forehead. "Oh, I don't know. . . . How about those stupid boys he hung out with?" Her voice sounded belligerent and shrill. Even to her own ears she sounded like a shrew.

Jake winced and moved to lean against the kitchen counter. He stared out the window for a long moment. "Okay, babe, for the sake of argument, let's say that Eric was influenced by his friends. Let's say that one of them got hold of porn and introduced Eric to it. Do you want to know why we 'stupid boys' look at those kinds of things? Do you want to know why we 'dumb boys' ogle girls? Do you want to know why we 'idiot guys' can't keep our eyes from roaming south?"

She stared at him. Why would he put himself in that same category? He told her he had never done those kinds of things. She started to protest. "Jake, you are not—"

"Yes, I am, Mallory. When you make sweeping statements like that, you put all the male gender into the same category." He held up his hand. "Let me finish."

She huffed and moved toward the hall. The girls were running down the stairs. She was getting ready to head them off and send them outside when she heard the front door slam. They beat her to that idea. She looked past Jake's shoulder and saw them playing on the swing. She sagged against the wall. She was glad they weren't in the house where they might overhear this conversation. It wasn't something little girls should ever have to find out about.

"Fine then, go ahead and finish." She crossed her arms over her chest. It was a mannerism that Jake hated, but at the moment she really didn't care. She didn't want to think of her father doing the horrible things Eric, and now Jake, seemed bent on accusing him of.

"Here's the truth, Mallory. We look because at the very least our fathers never taught us not to look. For whatever reason, they never took us aside and talked straight to us about respecting, loving, and honoring a woman. At the worst, we had fathers who taught us by word and action that conquering a woman was the way to prove you were a real man." He moved past her, grabbed a soda from the refrigerator, and pulled out a kitchen chair.

She studied him closely. It made sense. She saw it all around her every day; with no men in the lives of children, they drifted. They were expected to figure things out themselves. She remembered back to her junior high school days when she and her friends were exploring their own sexuality. Half the things they thought they knew about boys were just plain wrong. She dropped her arms to her side, and Jake smiled at her as he held out his hand.

She took it and was drawn down to his lap and turned to stare into his warm hazel eyes. "So how did. . ."

"I escape the horrors with a father like I had?"

She nodded and brushed a lock of hair off his forehead.

"A neighbor who lived next door to us. He was my refuge and port in the storm when the storms at my house got to be too much. He taught me about so many things. Photography and women were two of the most important ones. He talked straight, too. Took me aside and gave me not just the facts of life, but the moral principles behind them. He lived it out, too. Great man. I miss him a lot."

Mallory smiled. "I'm glad you had someone in your life like that, Jake."

"Me, too." He brushed her lips with his own. They tasted like Dr Pepper.

"Unfortunately, most guys don't have a man like that in their lives. Each of us has our own demons, and if we don't learn about them and how they can affect us, then how will we ever help someone one else? If we can't see how all this has happened to Eric, then who will help him?"

"He doesn't want or need our help," Mallory retorted and felt Jake's body shift beneath her. "Frankly, I don't care if he gets any."

He placed her gently from him and stood to pace to the window. She followed his gaze and watched as the girls cartwheeled across the grass. He turned back around, moved toward the door, and paused long enough to fire his parting remark.

"Okay, then where does it stop, and what happens to Marty? More importantly, what happens to Renee and Angel as a result of all of this?"

Chapter Thirty-Four

Alecia moved reluctantly toward the house. She'd heard the kids out in the driveway, but she didn't have the energy to try to intervene anymore and had waited until she heard Jake and Mallory drive off. She felt ancient. Every bone, every fiber of her muscles ached with the burden of living. *Oh Martin, how could you desert me now?* She had no idea how to handle his son. *His* son. How they had fought over that!

She remembered Eric's bitter words only a few moments ago. Eric couldn't possibly know anything about it, could he? Martin wouldn't have said anything. Her certainty faltered, and doubts began to eat at her. If he had told Eric. . . A swift anger rose from the pit of her stomach and clogged her throat.

Alecia reached for the door. Sixty years had taught Alecia there was only one way to get through a difficult situation—keep moving and get it over with. She closed the storm door quietly behind her. She could hear Eric in the pantry off the kitchen banging doors and cupboards as he had when he was a kid throwing one of his tantrums.

His rages then had lasted long enough for him to sweep

through the house and destroy everything in his path. Alecia lost track of the number of lamps and knickknacks she had to replace. His favorite target seemed to be his brother's and sisters' belongings; and, of course, he always managed to explode when Martin was out of town. Just as well. His father would probably have killed him.

A shadow moved at the door of the pantry. Alecia's heart thumped, and she clutched her chest. But it was only Eric. He held a fifth of Jim Beam in his hand. "Found Dad's whiskey. He changed his hiding place."

"Eric..."

Eric ignored his mother and began rooting through her cupboards for a glass. "I think this little family get-together calls for a drink. Want one?" He flung his head back, emptying his glass and quickly refilling it. "Too bad Mal left. We could drink to 'dear old Daddy.'"

"She's gone now, Eric."

"Ah, now there's a cause for celebration. Join me, Ma?"

"No, Eric. I think you've had enough."

Eric filled his glass again then lifted it toward his mother. "Enough? I'm just getting started." Eric stood as if ready to defy her if she argued with him, and Alecia was reminded of the time he was two and she found him drenched with her best perfume. He had never been an easy child to raise. Resisting authority seemed to come naturally to him when he was young, and what could she do now that he was grown?

What was it they said, desperate times called for desperate measures? Alecia walked to the counter and picked up the glass he had poured for her. "Fine. Let's at least sit at the table and be civilized about it then." Grabbing the bottle off the counter, she turned to the big bay window and slid onto the bench. The shock on Eric's face was worth it. She nearly ruined the whole thing by snickering into her glass, but managed to take a small sip and wait calmly for him to join her at the table.

Eric's anger seemed to deflate like a shuddering balloon with the air rushing out. Amusement quickly replaced it as he sat down across from her. "Touché, Ma. And what shall we drink to?"

Alecia's lips quirked upward. "To family."

Eric stroked his beard. "I'd say 'good riddance,' but I have a feeling you'd throw your drink at me."

"Admit it, Eric. Deep down you love her."

"Maybe, Ma. But she lives in a fantasy world."

"What on earth makes you say that?"

One bushy eyebrow lifted, and Eric reached for the bottle. Alecia noticed his words were beginning to slur. She had rarely seen Eric drink hard liquor. Martin only kept a bottle around for the occasional after-dinner drink. Beers Eric could put away one after the other, but he had consumed quite a bit in a very short amount of time. She hoped he didn't fly into a rage again.

"Mal'ry believes what shhhe wants to belief."

"Eric, why are you so angry? Your father was—"

"You know what my father was! Why do you defend him?"

"No one is perfect, Eric. Especially no parent. You ought to know that—you have children. It's tough to always know the right thing to do."

"Yeah, well, I never did what he done!" Eric's drink sloshed when he slammed it on the table. "Maybe you loved him, Ma, and that's a good thing I guess, but. . ." Eric let out a moan of frustration. "Maybe you didn't know him as well as you think you knew him."

Oh, I knew him. Alecia's heart began to thump heavily in her chest. "I knew him, Eric; I was married to him for forty-three years." That was a long time to live with another person—to know the disappointments and heartaches, as well as sharing the triumphs. No, Martin hadn't been perfect, but then, neither was she.

Alecia studied her son. Now wouldn't be the best time to tell him how much he resembled his father. Oh, not in looks, but definitely in temperament and personality. She took another sip of her drink, savoring the burning sensation as it made its way down to her belly. What made it so hard for the men in her family to relate to their sons?

"It's different with Marty!" The intensity in Eric's voice forced Alecia to sit back in her chair. The whiskey must have loosened her tongue. She hadn't meant to voice her thoughts out loud. It wouldn't do any good to go down that road. Eric would never admit the similarities between him and his dad.

"Eric, I know there were times when your father might have been a little too strict with you."

"A little! He near beat the crap out of me."

"You were his firstborn. If he expected more of you, it was because you were his eldest son." *He was, Martin.* "He loved you, Eric."

"That's such a load of bull! He hated me."

"Eric!" Alecia attempted to soften her tone. Her anger wasn't at her son. It was at her husband. He was the one that should be having this conversation. He was the one who owed Eric an explanation. Well, maybe both of them did, but she shouldn't have to be doing this alone.

"He blamed me for Shelly's death."

The stark words sliced right through Alecia's heart. "Wh–what?" *Shelly.* "What are you talking about, Eric?"

Eric slid his now-empty glass along the table back and forth between his hands. He wouldn't look at her, and she tried again. "Eric?"

Eric stared at his hands, still moving back and forth, back and forth. "He screamed the whole way back to the hill. 'What did you do to her, boy?' I thought he'd kill me when he found her lying dead in the snow."

A muscle spasm moved along Alecia's spine. Her baby. "But, Eric—"

Eric continued without pause, the glass in his hands moving faster now. "Shook me till my head rattled. Blood everywhere, Michelle lying there, cold, so cold."

Alecia stilled his hands and caught the glass before it flew off the edge of the table. "I didn't do it, Ma. I swear I didn't." Her son's eyes were filled with tears.

"Eric, I know you didn't kill Michelle. It was an accident."

"I mean it wasn't my fault."

"It was no one's fault." *Except mine.* "She fell off the sled and hit her head on a tree or possibly a rock. They never knew for sure, but she died instantly. We never blamed you, Eric."

Eric laid his forearms on the table and leaned toward her. "It wasn't even me on the sled with her! It was Bobby Green!"

"I know. He came with his parents to see us. I always felt sorry for the boy."

"What?" Eric jumped up, and his chair tipped over and crashed on the floor. "You knew it was Bobby? All these years you knew?"

"Ow! Eric, you're hurting me."

"Sorry." Eric loosened the grip he had on her hands.

Alecia rubbed her knuckles. "We never blamed you, Eric. We didn't blame Bobby either. We told him so when he came to see us." Eric's face was void of color. "Eric?"

"You didn't blame me. You didn't blame Bobby. But why did Dad. . ." Eric's fist hit the table, and Alecia jumped involuntarily. "Why did he hate me then, Ma?"

"Eric, maybe your father didn't know how to demonstrate his love very well, but he never blamed you for Michelle's death, and he certainly didn't hate you!"

Eric slumped in his chair, and Alecia grew concerned when he was silent for several minutes. His disheveled hair fell in waves across his forehead. There were several strands of gray in it that hadn't been there six months ago. He'd aged this year, and Alecia felt the weight of all those years. It had all been so long ago.

Where in the world had Eric gotten this idea that Martin hated him? It had been a terrible time in all of their lives. Alecia had been out, came home to find Michelle dead, Geoff in hysterics, and Eric wrapped in a shroud of silence as hard as the cast they put on his arm. Alecia remembered it all—the accusations, the guilt. She and Martin had a hard time weathering that storm.

"He cheated on you."

Alecia's breathing shut down for the space of a heartbeat. Quick tears filled her eyes. "I know."

"You *knew*?"

"Yes."

"Did you also know I walked in on the—"

"Eric!" She watched him pace across the kitchen.

"In your bedroom. In your house. Between your sheets."

Alecia covered her ears and shut her eyes, trying to block out the sound, the pictures evoked by Eric's words, the memories. "Stop! Just stop it, Eric!" She took a calming breath.

"Eric, it was a very bad time for us." Guilt swamped the anger rising within her. "There were. . ." Alecia hesitated, wondering what to say. This was her son after all. "There were *reasons* for your father's affair." Reasons she couldn't begin to explain to her son, grown or not. "It was more like a fling, really. We were both at fault. We worked through it. Not like today when couples just up and leave when things get bad."

"Don't go there, Ma."

"Okay, okay. I wasn't referring to you and Catherine. It was just an observation."

"Yeah right."

Alecia watched him closely. He seemed to be recovering from his shock. Maybe it had sobered him up from the alcohol he'd consumed.

"Eric, let's not speak ill of the dead. For heaven's sake, let your father rest in peace."

Eric shook his head, but Alecia wasn't sure if he was agreeing or disagreeing.

"You know, Eric, the only thing I never could figure out was how you broke your arm."

He picked up the chair he'd knocked over earlier and shoved it into the table. "I gotta go, Ma."

"Oh. Okay." Alecia stood to her feet, almost dizzy from the abrupt change in the conversation. She watched him gather his coat and ball cap he'd left on the counter earlier in the day.

Wanting to warn him to be careful driving, to somehow reassure him, she was still searching for the right words when he slammed out the door and was gone.

Alecia gathered the dirty glasses, rinsing them and leaving them upside down in the sink. She put the cap back on the whiskey bottle and put it away in the pantry. She fussed around her already clean kitchen, straightening the dish towel that hadn't been touched, brushing imaginary crumbs from the table. Moving into the living room, she fluffed pillows that hadn't been used and adjusted already perfect curtains.

She sat down in Martin's chair and flipped through all one hundred sixty-seven channels before throwing the remote down and roaming the house again. It was too quiet, and she was too fidgety to sit. Eric had stirred too many ghosts.

Alecia went to her bedroom, avoiding the bed she now slept in alone, going straight to the back of her walk-in closet. She reached behind a stack of sweaters and pulled out an old hatbox.

Seated in her favorite rocker beside the window in her bedroom, she dusted the layer of dust off the top of the box. Undoing the string, she lifted the lid and laid it to the side of her chair.

The late winter afternoon was growing dim; she turned on the table lamp beside her and looked at the box lying on her lap. So many years. So many memories bound up in such a small space.

In spite of Eric's taunt earlier, Alecia had never been a pack rat.

Sharing a bedroom with four sisters left little room for anything unnecessary or in her father's words, "worldly." As the attic, garage, and his study testified, Martin had been the one for saving things.

Jonah and Rachel Kaufman belonged to a strict sect of Mennonites that believed photographs were vain and therefore prohibited. Alecia had no pictures of her parents nor nine brothers and sisters, nor the farm she grew up on or the surrounding hills, but she had managed to save a few mementos. She reached into the box and gently withdrew the item that lay right on top.

Mary Alecia Kaufman had won first place for the school spelling bee. She stroked the still smooth but now raveling edges of the blue ribbon. Many of her childhood memories had faded and blurred into the recesses of her past, but fifty-two years later she could still recall the joy she felt that day. Even her father's stern warning that "pride cometh before a fall" could not keep her from devouring every book her schoolteacher could find for her to read. She had hidden them in the rafters of the hayloft, swearing her younger sister to secrecy when Katie had discovered her there.

Alecia set the ribbon aside and dug farther into the box. Her first hair ribbon, which also had to be hidden but this time in the toe of her shoe, so she could take it out and wear it when she was away from the house. An old movie stub from another one of "rebellious Mary's" escapades. Her brothers Abe and Levi had caught and painfully reprimanded her for that one. "Discipline," Levi said.

Alecia shuffled quickly through the rest of the bits and pieces. None of these was what she was looking for. An envelope lay at the very bottom of the box. Inside was a single sheet of paper and a faded black-and-white photo. She traced the dark curls, the dimple on his chin, the captured eyes that she knew had been twinkling with mirth. She unfolded the letter and skimmed its contents.

*The farm is all I know, 'Lecia. . . . Why must you hunger
for the danger of the city? Everything we need is here. . . . If
I thought I could sway you, I would move heaven and earth
to do so, but I know it is in your heart to leave. . . . But this I
promise you, as I have vowed to stay pure before God, I vow
to be pure and remain faithful to you.*

Alecia ignored the crackle of the letter as she dropped her
hands into her lap. "You see, Martin? Silas was not Eric's father."
She could have proven it to him, but she had always wanted him
just to believe her, to end the petty jealousy. Martin was the one
she chose. Wasn't that enough? Besides, she couldn't take the risk
of Martin reading the whole letter.

*If he comes near you again, I'll kill him! No father should
do such things to his daughters. Run away with me. . . . The
shame is not yours, Mary Alecia, it is his, and it does not
matter to me, I swear. . . .*

She was too old to rehash the choices she had made in her life.
Alecia had chosen her path long ago, and she had only one deep
regret—one lapse in her judgment. One fateful lapse. It had cost
him his honor. It had cost her everything.

Alecia dropped her head in her hands and wept. "I didn't mean
for it to happen, God. I only went to the farm to visit Katie." But
Silas had been there, and Martin hadn't been—not for a long time.
Oh God! Why not punish me? I was the one who was guilty.

When she had gotten home, the accident had already
happened. God's judgment was final. Alecia wrapped her arms
around her waist, trying to ease the pain that never went away. *My
baby, my baby.*

Chapter Thirty-Five

Travis closed his eyes as the gut clenching began in his midriff. The image of the stoplight in his head that he had learned to trust all those years ago gave him a yellow light. Marty was telling the truth, but there was still some junk attached to it that Marty didn't feel safe to share yet.

"You say you didn't do it. I believe that, Mart." He watched the kid's shoulders sag in utter relief, and the self-imposed years of rebellion melted from his face. He looked so very young.

Travis leaned over and placed his hand on Marty's knee. "But son, the part you did play in the whole affair—you've got to take responsibility for it, or it will take possession of you. Aren't you tired? Aren't you tired of carrying all of it around on your back?"

Marty's head fell forward in a quick nod. His bangs hid his face, but Travis could sense he was ready to let go of the burden of guilt he carried. "I know it was wrong, Pastor T." He lifted his head, and his eyes welled with unshed tears. "I didn't hurt Bethy, but I didn't help her either. I watched him do it."

Travis nodded. "And perhaps got a bit of a thrill from it?"

Marty's head dropped, but not before Travis saw a stain of

pink flush his cheeks. With eyes downcast he mumbled a quiet, "Yeah."

"Do you see where all this has led, Marty? One word of enticement. One challenge. One quick thrill. You weren't the perpetrator, but you committed your own sin—acts of lying, even if you thought it was a good idea and that it would help your cousin. Acts of rebellion against your parents. There have been huge consequences in all of this, Marty. I know you feel you've been unjustly accused—and you have—but you haven't been innocent either, have you?"

"No, I guess not." Marty kicked the basketball at his feet closer to him and reached down and picked it up. He rolled it around and around in his hands. "I know it was wrong." He bounced the ball between his knees. "I should have told the truth."

Travis let him think on that a bit. Wouldn't hurt him to come to the full realization of what this meant—not just to Marty, but to Bethy and the rest of his family. They sat in the church's empty gym. Basketballs lay scattered across the cement floor. "Yes, you should have told the truth."

The game had ended long ago, and all the youth had cleared out. Travis had offered to take Marty home and had come back to the gym after saying good-bye to the other boys and their parents to find Marty ready to talk. Now the only sound was the slap of leather hitting the floor as Marty continued to bounce the ball. Travis watched tears pool against the boy's lower lashes.

"I made a mess of things, T. I know I shouldn't have lied."

"You're right, son. But telling the truth to yourself, well, that's the first step. What I have learned is we can't move forward without moving in truth. Lies get us stuck. Oh, we go on with life—but there's a part of us that can't move forward until we deal with what we've been trying to ignore or deny—they're both a form of lies."

Marty caught the basketball midbounce. "I can't fix it!"

"No, you can't. And neither can I, but God can." Travis leaned forward and swiped the basketball from Marty's hand and bounced it a few times on the floor before passing it back to him. *Ask the question, Marty. Ask the question that will open the door for me to give you what you need to know.*

"How?"

The door of the conversation had been thrust open by Marty. Travis saw the signal in his head go from yellow to green. Travis nearly sagged in relief. "How about we start with the truth?"

"Ohh-kay." Marty's response came out in a huge sigh. He began rolling the ball in his hands again. He stood and bounced the ball in the space between his feet. "Donovan and I were supposed to be outside with the rest of the older kids for game time, but we got bored, and we headed back inside to see what was left in the kitchen. We heard a bunch of giggling, so that's when Donovan got the idea to head down the hall to see what the girls were doing. The classroom door was open, so we peeked in—we almost got caught when Bethy came out—we had to hide behind the door. She didn't see us and went into the girls's bathroom. Donovan punched me on the shoulder and said, 'Let's go have a little fun.' I thought it was a dumb idea to scare Bethy, but he asked me if I was a chicken, and he grabbed my arm, so I followed him."

Marty paused, dropped back down on the bench, and let his forehead fall onto the basketball resting on his knees. "I didn't know what he was gonna do." His words came out in a choked whisper. He lifted his head, tears rolled down his cheeks, and he made no move to wipe them away. "I swear to God, T, I—I didn't know." He began bouncing the ball again.

"He slid under the stall door, whispered something to Bethy, and suddenly her panties were heaved over the stall door at me. The door came unlocked, and there they were. And I couldn't believe what I saw.

"After—after he did that to her, he laughed and said to me, 'Go ahead, she won't care. She likes it, don't you, Bethy?' He backed away, and that's when the lady came in and started screaming at us. She grabbed me and shoved me into the pastor's office and locked the door. Then they came and started asking me all kinds of questions. But Donovan—Donovan whispered in my ear as they were hauling me away. He said... He said, 'If you tell on me, I swear I'll do something to your sister like I did to mine.'"

Marty's voice broke. "I couldn't let that happen."

He looked up at Travis and hiccupped back a sob. "I just thought—you know—they'd believe me." He looked down at the ball in his hands then heaved it across the gym, and it smashed against the ball cart. "But why would they? It sounds unbelievable in my own ears, and my old man, well, he never believed anything I ever told him. I guess my mom tried, but—"

"But perhaps she hesitated because of the ways you'd been acting out before that?" Travis leaned his arms on his knees. All he could do here was pray for wisdom and the right words.

"Yeah. I guess she didn't have much reason to believe me the way I'd been acting. I was pretty mad at both of them—at Mom, but especially at Dad." His voice wobbled between anger and hurt. "Why couldn't they stay together? Why'd they fight all the time?"

"I don't know. All I know is that we humans can mess things up. Just like you and Donovan made wrong choices, your mom and dad made some, too. We all make wrong choices—most people don't like this word, but it's called sin—it's when we do things our way instead of God's way, and it's what gets us in trouble. And the consequences are serious—life and death, even."

"Wait a minute. . . . You don't know? But you're a preacher. Aren't you supposed to have all the answers?"

"I wish," Travis said as he smiled. "But then, that would make me God. No, Marty, I don't have all the answers, but I have one very good answer to all the guilt and shame you are carrying."

"Pastor T, I'm tired of living this nightmare, but I don't know how to get out of it. How do I make it right?"

Travis smiled and clamped his hand on his shoulder. "I'm glad you asked! First let me tell you, you might not get out of it, but you can get through it. So, let me tell you the secret. It won't change all the circumstances in your life—but I guarantee you it will take the weight of guilt off your back and provide you with the strength to get through this—and everything else, too."

Travis scooted closer until his knee was touching Marty's and whispered, "The secret? His name is Jesus."

Chapter Thirty-Six

Eric's work boots pounded the ground. He was running; heat seared his lungs, and he gasped to draw in air. He had to hurry; he had to save her. Shelly was hurt, crying out to him, but there was no one to help. He stumbled then fell against a giant who grabbed his arms and began to shake him hard.

Eric pulled away and began running again. He kept looking over his shoulder. He couldn't see anything, but the guy was still back there, still coming for him. He came to a door. He couldn't remember coming into the house; the hallway was dark. He turned the knob and slowly opened the door. His father and his mistress were lying on the bed, tangled in the sheets. They looked at him and began to laugh. They laughed and laughed. Eric slammed the door shut and ran down the stairs. He tripped midway and began to tumble; he was falling, falling. . .

Eric awoke with a jerk. He wiped the moisture from his chest with his hand. The sheet was wrapped around his foot, and he untangled himself and crawled from his bed.

Twenty minutes later he stepped out of the shower and toweled off. He scrubbed the towel against the mirror and leaned his hands on the sides of the sink. The dream was still vivid—the fear, the shame, the guilt. He looked at his reflection in the mirror. The man looking back at him was a stranger. He had always seen himself as a self-made man. Strong. Independent. Not needing anyone's help. He leaned in closer and stared into his own eyes. He could see the uncertainty lurking there, and he loathed it.

He shoved away from the sink and got dressed. It was still dark outside; he was waking up early every day as if he had somewhere to go, somewhere to be. He'd kept Greg and the boys busy as long as he could, but he'd finally had to let Shawn and Luke go. He and Greg had managed to find some electrical repair jobs to bring in some cash, but he'd been urging Greg to look for something permanent. His savings account wasn't going to last forever. He'd be fine once they settled the insurance.

His insurance agent had told him horror stories of having to reimburse the insurance company if they paid out too soon and decided later there was no claim. He'd assured Eric he was "lucky" to have a thorough investigation. *Yeah right!*

He switched on the light in the kitchen and started the coffee. He'd have to wake Marty for school soon. The kid was actually doing pretty good. Not that he could take any credit for it. Marty had been spending a lot of time with Travis and the church youth group. Who knew they would be a positive influence?

Eric opened the refrigerator and reached for the milk. He waited for the coffee to brew and thought about the changes he had seen in Marty in the last several weeks. His grades were good—not great, but above average. He might even go so far to say Marty was agreeable on occasion. There were still bumps in their relationship of course—but it was better than it had been in a long time. If only the rest of Eric's life would be going as well.

The whole insurance thing was a mess. When he asked the fire inspector why they hadn't caught the arsonist yet, he'd told Eric, "This isn't some kind of TV show!" They could tell it was arson; they just couldn't figure out who set the fire. No evidence to convict anyone. Seems even Tipton had an alibi.

Eric had finally run him down at his office late one evening.

"Bennington." Miles Tipton sat behind a huge oak desk covered in papers. His sleeves were rolled up, his shirt collar open. He had been in deep concentration when Eric had come in and sat back now with a dazed look on his face. He rebounded quickly. "What are you doing here?"

Eric slammed the folder on his desk. "I came for the money you owe me."

Tipton pushed his chair back from the desk. "What money?"

"The money you owe me from the last three development projects. I did. . ."

"You didn't finish the work." Tipton interrupted. "No finished contract, no money."

Eric leaned over the desk. "I want my money, Tipton, or else."

Miles leaned back in his chair, "Or else what? Who do you think you are busting in here?"

"I'm the guy you're going to answer to." Eric leaned his fists on the desk.

"Really?" Tipton snorted. "Get out of here. I'm busy." He picked up his pen.

Eric snatched it out of his hand. "Look, Miles, you owe me for the work that was done, and if you don't pay, I'll make a couple of calls about these." Eric shifted the file in front of Tipton. "I got a call from the building inspector. I know they're investigating you on the Beach City project."

Tipton leaned back in his chair and folded his hands. "Old news, Bennington. And a minor irritation. My lawyer has that situation under control."

"What about *this* situation?" Eric flipped open the file and tossed it in front of Tipton. "I know you bought off state inspectors. There's a copy of the cancelled check to prove it.

There's also a receipt of payment and receipts for the actual material you used for the Cranston building. You used substandard concrete blocks. Look—right there shows you used the wrong kind of aggregate mix."

"Where'd you get this?" Tipton picked up the file then threw it back on the desk. "Never mind. It doesn't matter. There's nothing in here to prove anything."

"Really? What about the testimony of the electrician you paid off?"

Tipton shrugged, "Take a stab at taking me to court, but unless you finish the job you won't get your money. Now, what is this really all about?"

"I want to know if you set the fire to my shop!"

Tipton's eyes widened. "What?"

"I said, did you have anything to do with torching my place?"

Tipton laughed. "Now what would I possibly gain from that?"

"I haven't figured that out yet."

"Because there is nothing to figure out. Clearly you are distraught. Finish the job and you get paid. Beyond that, I don't want to see you in here again. Now, get out of my office, Bennington. And don't come back." Tipton sat back down in his chair and scooted in toward his desk.

Eric clenched his jaw and his fist before he swept up the file, knocking the papers across the desk. "This isn't the last of it, Tipton."

"It better be! You think your business is all you can lose?"

In a whoosh, the air left Eric's lungs. He glared at the other man. "I'm telling you—if you had anything to do with setting fire to my place..."

But he hadn't. The fire inspector had told Eric the next day that Tipton had an iron-clad alibi. If it wasn't him, who was it?

And when would they release the insurance money?

Chapter Thirty-Seven

"Did you see that one, Dad?" Lindsay jumped up and down and pointed out to the net that had caught the softball she'd hit. The bat dropped and rolled to her feet, and she bent to pick it up. There was a loud *whack* as the teenager in the next batting cage smacked a ball into the net.

Eric smiled. "See? I told you choking up on the grip would do it! You're hitting great now." He brushed back the strand of hair that had fallen into her eyes. "You getting hungry? You've been at it for over an hour—it's probably time to go. How about we go home and get some lunch?"

"Can we have egg rolls?"

Eric groaned and headed for the car. "Only if you help me make them."

It took only minutes to arrive at their house from the batting cages. Lindsay chattered all the way home and through their lunch preparations. Eric was glad for the distraction. He was happy not to be dealing with the chaos his life was in. He still had decisions to make about the business, but he didn't want to think about that today. It was the weekend, and he just wanted to enjoy being with his daughter.

"Do you want sweet-and-sour sauce?"

"Yeah and don't forget the soy sauce and mustard—Mom lets me mix 'em."

Eric shook his head. Lindsay's taste buds were as enthusiastic as she was—everything from the weird and spicy to tongue-burning hot. She was definitely more adventurous than he'd been as a kid.

Lindsay had launched into a full-blown description of her teacher. ". . .and she says I can get extra credit if I do a report on our trip to COSI."

"COSI?"

"You remember, Dad—I told you we were going to the science museum in Columbus."

"Oh, that's right. You and your mom went last Saturday, right?"

"Uh-huh." Lindsay took a big gulp from her glass of milk. "Daniel took us."

"Daniel? Who's Daniel?" Eric watched Lindsay struggle to chew and swallow the bite of egg roll before she answered.

"Mom's friend. He's cool." She scooped up the sauce on her plate for another bite. "You know they got that humongous movie screen. It's seven stories high! We watched the film about the dolphins." She shoved the last bite in her mouth and spoke out of the side of her mouth. "That's what I'm gonna write my report on. Daniel says I'm smart enough to be a marine biologist when I grow up."

"I thought you wanted to be a historian and study more about the Civil War." Eric reached over and wiped up the drips of sauce that trailed from the edge of Lindsay's plate. This was the first he'd heard about a guy in Catherine's life. Was it serious?

Lindsay nodded. "I do. But maybe I could do both. Anyways, Daniel says I got lots of time to make up my mind."

"True enough, kiddo." Eric squished the damp napkin onto his dirty plate. "So—how long has this guy been coming around to see your mom?"

"I dunno. Awhile, I guess." Lindsay shrugged. "He works on computers, same as her."

Eric scooted his chair back from the table and began to stack the dishes. He had a million questions, but none a little girl could answer. Was Catherine moving on? He took the plates to the kitchen and dropped them in the sink. The silverware clattered against the stoneware. No reason why she couldn't move on—maybe it was even something he should have expected—but she hadn't given any indication that she was seeing anyone. In fact, Eric had hoped that maybe. . .

Lindsay came up beside him and set their glasses on the counter. "Maybe you could meet him, Dad. I bet he could fix your old laptop that got that virus."

"Maybe." Eric smiled and rubbed the top of Lindsay's head. "Why don't you get started on that report?" He glanced at the kitchen clock. "You can check out the museum online before Grandma comes to get you. I'll finish cleaning up." He watched her leave the room but made no move to clear the rest of the table. He was winded, like he'd taken a couple of blows to the chest. This reaction to the news of Catherine with a boyfriend surprised him. He hadn't been stupid enough to think they would get back together, had he?

He turned on the hot water and waited until a light steam rose from the faucet. He shoved each of the dishes under the flow of water then dropped it into the dishwasher. He was a fool. He'd let himself get drawn into her net all over again. She'd been so supportive and warm at the funeral home. And even before that—those moments in the coffee shop when they'd been talking about Marty.

She'd even bit her tongue from saying "I told you so" or worse when he'd admitted he had gotten the DNA results about Marty. She had laid her hand on his arm and leaned toward him.

"I'm so glad you have proof, Eric. I know the doubts tortured you."

"You aren't going to ream me over the coals?"

Catherine shook her head. "Not anymore. It always frustrated me and made me furious that you never really trusted me. And I won't deny that it would have been great for you to just believe me—to believe what I told you, but I just wanted you to have a relationship with your son. And now—" Catherine shrugged and twisted her cup around and around. "And now you have proof that he is your son. That I didn't—"

Eric drew her hand between his. "I always *wanted* to believe you, Cat. I just—"

She placed her finger on his lips. "Shhh. I know. I know that we've struggled with this trust issue for so long—but somehow now I'm just glad you know. That you can't doubt me anymore."

And he didn't. He had finally accepted that she'd told the truth all these years and that he'd hurt her. He had apologized. She'd cried. And then she'd held him at his father's funeral. He thought—

That was the problem. He hadn't been thinking at all. He'd given in to his emotions; he'd let himself believe that maybe there was a way back. *Idiot!* He scorched his fingers as the water splashed out of the glass tumblers he was rinsing, and he turned on the cold water until it diluted the burn. He stuffed them in the dishwasher and went to grab the rest of the debris off the dining room table.

He put the condiments back in the refrigerator and slammed the door shut with his hip. He was being stupid. It's not like he hadn't been through letting her go before, or even that he expected Catherine to never date again.

His mother arrived just as he finished wiping off the table. Eric let her in and led her to the living room. She looked tired. He wondered if she'd had trouble sleeping since his father died. It was hard to get used to sleeping alone.

"Where's Lindsay?"

"In the den. I'll get her—"

"No. Wait. I want to talk to you."

"Oh. Okay." Eric walked farther into the room. "What's up?"

"The last time we talked—when you were helping clean out Dad's things. . ." His mother fiddled with the handle of the purse perched on her lap. For a moment Eric glimpsed the girl she must have been. Her head was bowed, and she sat on the edge of the couch, feet together and tucked off to one side.

A flash of remorse shot through Eric as he watched his mother struggle to speak. He recalled the scene at his mother's house. He'd argued with Mallory. He'd had too much to drink. Not one of his better days. He blew out a long breath of air. "Yeah. Well, Ma, I probably said things I shouldn't have. Sorry."

His mother clenched her hands, pinching the sides of her purse together. "Eric, I know you're hiding something from me." She lifted her head and stared at him.

He shifted back into the cushions and spread his fingers on the arms of the chair. He tried not to squirm. His mother had always had a keen eye for lies, although he got pretty good at fooling her. Now was not a good time to get into this. In fact, never was probably the best time. Eric had gone over the conversation again and again, and each time he'd wondered at his outburst. It must have been the booze.

"What do you mean?"

"I mean that there is something about Shelly's death you aren't telling me, and I want to know what it is." She leaned forward. "It has to do with you breaking your arm, doesn't it?"

Eric pushed himself out of the chair. "Ma, I don't think this is the time—"

"You're wrong, Eric. Now is the perfect time. You've kept a secret all these years, and I want to know what it is."

Eric rubbed the back of his neck and turned away. There was no way he could tell his mother the truth stone-cold sober.

Chapter Thirty-Eight

Alecia watched her son pace back and forth in front of the living room windows. There was no question he was hiding something, and she was determined to find out what it was. If Martin's death had taught her anything, it was that perhaps it was time to bury some ghosts from the past.

"Eric? What are you hiding?"

"Ma, leave it alone."

"No. I won't." She had let far too many things alone through the years. It was time to resolve this. It was time to let her baby rest in peace. "How did you break your arm?"

"I didn't break my arm." Eric slumped back down in the chair and heaved a loud sigh. He put his elbows on his knees and hung his hands between his legs. He stared at the carpet then muttered, "Dad broke it."

"What?" It was the last thing Alecia expected to hear, and yet it made a bizarre kind of sense. She had been so angry at Martin, and he at her, that after they'd flung their accusations at each other about who was to blame for Shelly's death, they quit speaking to each other altogether. The hardest thing about those months of

grieving was the isolation and feeling so very alone. The silence of
the house had weighed as heavily as her own guilt.

Eric looked at her. "I said the old man broke my arm when
he grabbed me and shook me. . . . He was so mad—I couldn't
tell him what happened." He hung his head. "There's—there's
more."

Alecia took a deep breath and braced herself. He wasn't
finished. She watched him pick at a spot on his jeans and waited
for him to go on.

"I told you that Bobby Green took Shelly down the hill. But
I went down, too. On his inner tube. I'd just gotten that new sled
for my birthday—you remember? Everybody wanted to ride it, and
when Geoff left and Shelly begged me for a ride, I told Bobby that
he could ride my sled if he'd take Shelly down and let me take the
inner tube.

"I shouldn't have—" Eric flung back into the chair and covered
his face with his hand. "We started down the hill at the same
time—I hit this huge bump and went airborne, right into the path
of the sled. We collided, and Shelly—"

Alecia moved to the end of the couch and put her hand on
Eric's leg. "Go on, Eric. You need to tell it. I need to hear it."

"Don't you see, Ma? I killed her. I landed right on top of her. I
murdered my baby sister. It's all my fault. If I'd gotten help sooner.
If I hadn't fallen on her. I kept shaking her and shaking her, but
she wouldn't wake up. That's when Dad grabbed my arm and
pulled me off her. He kept screaming 'What did you do to her,
boy?' but I—I just couldn't tell him. He'd have killed me, Ma. I was
so scared. I just didn't know what to do."

Alecia was on her knees beside him. "Listen to me. It
wouldn't have mattered, Eric." She gripped his arm, turning
him toward her. Raw pain swept through his eyes. They were
both crying, and she wanted to gather him in her arms, but
even as a little boy, he had been resistant to affection. She laid

her head on his arm then raised her head to look at him.

"She died instantly. There was nothing you could have done. It was an accident."

Chapter Thirty-Nine

B en Cooper scooped the stack of papers together and tapped them on his desktop. It was always a good feeling when an investigation came to an end. This one had been rougher than most. It had taken them a while to get the evidence they needed, but they could put this one to bed now.

He stood and walked to the filing cabinet. These copies could be tucked away, and he would undoubtedly get started on the next fire investigation, but not today. Today he'd earned an early start to the weekend. He only had one errand to run on his way home.

Ben pulled up into the driveway of Eric Bennington's home. He sat for a moment looking at the two-story house. Nice, quiet neighborhood. Guy had made a decent living with his business. Maybe he could pick up and start again with the news he had to give him.

He rang the doorbell and waited. The door was opened by the kid, and Ben nodded. "Your dad home?"

"Sure. You want to come in?"

"No, that's all right. I just have some news to give him."

"Okay." The boy moved back into the recesses of the house

and hollered, "Daaad! That fire dude is here."

Ben chuckled. *Fire dude.* Marla would love that one.

"Hello, inspector. Can I help you?"

"Just stopping by to give you the result of our investigation."

Bennington opened the door wider. "Come in."

Ben stepped into the entryway. "This will only take a minute. I just wanted to let you know that formal charges of arson are being drawn against your former employee Thomas Miller."

"Tom? I thought he had an alibi."

"We did, too. That's what took us so long with the investigation. But we finally cracked the testimony of his friend who claimed she was with him the whole night." Ben grinned. "Turns out that Thomas was just as unfaithful as a boyfriend as he was an employee. Girl recanted her story as soon as she saw the picture of him with another woman."

Ben watched the man process the news. First he frowned, undoubtedly angry at his ex-employee. Then his face began to clear, and Ben could almost see the wheels turning in his mind. The investigation was done. He could get his money now.

"Does my insurance company know?"

Ben nodded. "They got the paperwork yesterday, same as the rest of the county and state offices."

"So I can expect a check from the insurance company now?"

"I would expect so." Ben turned toward the door. "But that's not my jurisdiction. I just handle the investigation. You'll have to contact your insurance company." He waved a hand over his shoulder as he headed for his car.

"Thanks!" Eric followed Cooper out onto the porch. He held up his hand then pulled the door shut as the inspector reversed his car down his drive. *Yes!* The nightmare was over. The money might not cover everything, but it would be a great start.

"Does this mean you'll be able to fix the store now?"

Eric turned to find Marty right behind him. Eric dropped down to the front steps with relief. It was finally over. He'd call the insurance company tomorrow. Maybe the check was already in the mail.

Eric breathed in the clear air and lifted his head to the warmth of sun. Winter was fading, and he could almost smell spring's arrival. Marty flopped down in the space next to him, and he watched him lie back and slide his arms under his head for a pillow as he stared at the porch ceiling. Eric shook his head at his footwear. The kid didn't seem to mind the chill and wore flip-flops no matter what the weather. Marty stretched out his legs. When had his son gotten so tall?

His son! It really was true. Eric smiled as he eyed the boy's long skinny legs poking from a pair of knee-length jogging shorts. He remembered that as a two-year-old Marty had worn shorts that hung past his knees, too. His grin widened at the similarity. He bet his son would hate being compared to the toddler he once was, but at the moment, that was the way he looked. Was it too late to connect with him? To make up for the time and distance that had come between them? Did he have what it took to make a difference in Marty's life? For the first time Eric was unsure.

Marty turned his head sideways. "So?"

"What?"

Marty rolled his eyes and enunciated every word. "Are—you—going—to—rebuild—now?"

"I—don't—know—yet." Eric answered in kind then swatted Marty's leg. "Smart aleck." A thought shimmered in Eric's mind. *Why not?* He tapped Marty's knee. "Come on, lazy guy."

Eric stood and loped around the side of the house to the shed in the backyard. He opened the crooked door and made another mental note to fix the thing, but not today. Today just might be the day he made some serious headway with his son. Eric rummaged through the plastic containers on the shelf in the back of the shed and was aware when a shadow passed over the door behind him.

"We aren't going to work this late in the day, are we?" Marty's voice held a slight whine.

Eric shook his head. "Nope. Ah, here it is." He backed out of the narrow space and turned, nudging Marty backward into the light. He bounced his old army football between his hands, suddenly confident in how to "bond," as T put it, with Marty.

"What's that?" Marty looked slightly uncomfortable as he stared at the ball in Eric's hand.

"This, my boy, was the football that won my army division league. I'd like to say I carried the ball to the end zone, but I didn't. My buddy Bill Wester did, but he was in a drunken stupor by the end of the day and never did figure out who took the ball for safe keeping." Eric chuckled at the memory and tossed the pigskin in Marty's direction.

Marty stood staring at his dad as if he had suddenly grown a couple of extra fangs. The ball slapped against his belly and bounced once against his feet. Marty dropped his gaze to his feet then back up at Eric with a question and something else Eric couldn't ascertain. "Son, it helps if you try to catch the ball with your hands and not your feet, and then you toss it back to me."

The boy, no—the young man, leaned over and scooped up the ball. It tumbled out of his hands and rolled across his feet. He made another move to gather it up, and Eric nearly laughed at the sight of the football taking on a life of its own. He opened his mouth to make a suggestion on how to pick it up, but bit his lip instead. His coaching would probably only end in failure, like so many other things he had tried to do with Marty.

Marty bent his elbow and lobbed the ball. It wobbled in the air before dropping with a thud halfway between them. He stuck his hands in his pockets.

T and Catherine both believed the relationship could be

healed. Maybe, just maybe, Eric did, too. Was this the time to try and tell him what had been on his heart? To tell him what he had learned? To let him know he believed in him after all? Where to begin?

Begin by picking up the ball. Eric loped to the dropped ball, scooped it up, and ran backward across the yard until he was about twenty feet away, then as he reached back and sent the football in a spiraling arc through the air, he said, "Marty, a while back, I got coffee with your mom." Marty's eyes dropped from following the ball spiraling past his head and locked with Eric's. Hope flared in Marty's eyes.

No such luck on what you're thinking, kid. That hope got dashed by a dude named Daniel. Even thinking the man's name left a bad taste in Eric's mouth and bitterness in his soul. The very thought of another man kissing his wife. . . *Don't go there. Stay focused.*

He watched as Marty removed the ever-present earphone and realized the kid was only half paying attention to him. He exhaled sharply and fought down his rising annoyance. *Focus. Don't let these things derail you. I can't do this. Yes. You can,* he argued with himself.

"Yeah?"

Eric pointed toward the pigskin lying at the far edge of the property. Marty shook his head and stuffed the earphone back in his ear before trudging off to get the ball. He turned back to Eric, and he started to throw the ball underhanded.

Eric shook his head. "Grab the laces on the ball, pull your arm all the way back, and put your shoulder into the release." Eric shouted what he hoped sounded like gentle coaching. He didn't think it came across that way as Marty's body stiffened, and he trudged back to the center of the yard carrying the ball. When he was only a few feet away, he flipped the ball underhand to Eric. "You were saying. . . You. . . .Mom. What's it all about?"

In an offhanded move he tossed the ball back to Marty. It dropped to the ground at his feet. *He's hopeless!* Eric was about to coach again when he saw the look in his son's eyes. He clenched his jaw. He needed to keep in mind it was not about how good the kid could toss a ball. It was about connecting. *Say what you need to say, Bennington.* "We had a long talk about you, as a matter of fact."

The boy's eye's narrowed, and a muscle tightened in his cheek. He lifted the iPod out of his shorts pocket, and Eric wasn't sure whether he turned the volume up or down.

He suddenly wanted the conversation to be over with, since it was apparent that Marty had zero interest in tossing a ball. He cleared his throat and attempted to lighten the mood. "Could you toss your old man the ball?"

Marty leaned over. He grabbed the ball and hiked it directly into Eric's face. He was surprised, and only his quick reflexes kept the end of it from gouging him in the eye. That was definitely more like it. "So, what did I do this time?" His tone was belligerent.

Eric was confused for a moment. "Do? You didn't do anything." He stared at the boy's rigid posture, and for the first time noticed that his bangs were shorter and there was a lack of silver glint in his eyebrow. When had all that changed?

"So, I'm in trouble for something I didn't do?" Sarcasm colored his voice.

Eric sucked in a breath and fought the fleeting thought to throttle his son. He let out the breath and silently counted, *One— two—three—four—five.* He could do this. "No. You are not getting in trouble. I just wanted to tell you that your mom discovered proof that you didn't do those things to Bethy that you were accused of."

"And you believe her?" Marty asked. His tone was devoid of emotion.

Eric smiled as he nodded. "And T says that he believes you weren't as guilty as the court system seems to think you are."

"You believe him, too?"

Once more Eric nodded. Why didn't he sound pleased? "I just

wanted to tell you that I believe them. That I don't think you were as guilty either." *Come on, kid. Give your old man some inkling of what you are thinking.*

"Figures," Marty mumbled as he turned away. "I'm done here. This was a stupid idea." His hands jammed into the pockets of his shorts. Eric couldn't be positive, but he thought Marty was mumbling other not-so-flattering things.

Disbelief left Eric standing with his hands spread apart. What had he said? What had he done to cause this reaction? He had dared to bare his soul to his son and received a *"figures"*? He slammed the football down, and it bounced across the yard.

"Christopher Martin!" Eric roared at the retreating back. "Stop right there and explain that attitude!"

"You don't get it, do you?" Marty bellowed back across the empty expanse. He spun on his heel and stomped back to his original spot. His hands clenched and unclenched, and in that moment Eric was convinced that Marty wanted to take him apart a piece at a time. "You self-righteous, arrogant. . ."

"Christopher Martin! Watch it!"

His internal counting was picking up momentum. At this pace he would reach a thousand and still have enough anger to take Marty out. But he needed to get to the bottom of this. Did the kid really hate him this bad?

"Now explain yourself." He expected Marty to turn in a huff and walk away. Instead his son came back at him with all the pent-up anger of a wild bull.

"You *believe* Mom."

Eric thought they had established that already.

"You believe Pastor T. You believe Linds. You even believe the frickin' fire dude. *But you never believed me!*" Marty swiped at the tears, and balled his hands into fists.

"You never gave me a reason to believe in you!" Eric shouted back.

"It wouldn't have mattered! I could never measure up! You never, ever believed a word I said! Linds could say anything to you, and you believed her! Well, guess what? I got a new Dad now, and I don't need you!" Marty's words knifed through his heart to the deepest longings of his soul and bludgeoned him to death. Not even the knock-down, drag-out fights he'd had with Cat had hurt this bad.

Eric's knees wobbled, and his legs turned to spaghetti. Marty *knew* he had never believed in his son. He didn't think his dad cared about him. Eric sank to the ground and sucked back a silent sob as Marty turned and raced through the back door, slamming it solidly behind him. Eric raised his eyes to the darkening sky.

When had he turned into his father?

Chapter Forty

"Jake!" Mallory called out as she pushed open the door leading from the garage. "Jake, we're home!" Silence met her ears as she moved out of the doorway to allow her mother to enter. She deposited her armload of packages onto the kitchen table and picked up a sheet of paper peaking from beneath a bag.

> *Babe, picking girls up from school and taking them to*
> *Kingdom Klub, will stop for ice cream after. I am going to*
> *hang out at Joey's. C'ya tonight. Love you most!*

She smiled at the note. Jake had always been a good daddy, but he was amazing now. Pain knifed through her, poignant and sharp. She still missed her daddy. She shook off the thought. She'd had a good day with her mother and was reluctant to break the spell.

The rustle of plastic caught her attention, and she turned around in time to see Alecia nudge the door closed with her shoulder. "I am getting old," her Mom remarked as she laid the packages on the table and slid onto one of Mallory's oak chairs.

Mallory grinned at the remark. "There was a time you could

shop circles around me."

Alecia smiled as she lifted a strand of bleached blond hair back into place. "Once was the time I could shop circles around everyone. Now it just makes me tired. I could use a cup of coffee." She chuckled. "Maybe an entire pot, the way I feel at this moment."

Mallory laughed. Yes, it had been a very good day. Since her father's death, her mother hadn't been quite so controlling. Mallory put on the coffee before turning to the groceries and putting them away. When she was finished, she poured two cups of coffee and set the one with sugar and cream before her mom. She took a sip from her mug before reaching for the Elder Beerman bag and lifting out a short-sleeve copper blouse and matching shorts.

"That is a wonderful color for your complexion."

Maybe her mom was softening. Maybe her grieving had allowed some of the rigidity to be broken, but since her dad's death, she seemed much more approachable. Mallory looked across the table at her mom as Alecia reached down and removed her high heels and massaged her instep.

Daddy. Could her parents' relationship have caused some of her mom's stiffness? Mallory's eyes widened at the random thought. Was it possible that Daddy wasn't the man she had always thought him to be?

She tugged the price tag from the outfit and rolled the tag into a small tube. Could she ask the questions that had plagued her for the last several months, since Eric had lambasted her in her parents' driveway? Dare she disrupt the harmony between them for the answers she so desperately needed?

She had been so glad that her mother had never reprimanded her for the way she acted all those months ago. Mallory had been certain her mother was going to lay the blame on her for the altercation between her and Eric.

"Mom, can I ask you a question?" She rolled the tag past her coffee cup and back again before reaching for the coffee.

"Mmmm?"

"Eric said some things about Daddy that really bother me. . . ."

"That's not unusual for the two of you."

Mallory ignored the sarcasm and took another sip of her coffee. "You know, when we were cleaning out your garage, Eric insisted that Daddy wasn't a good father."

Alecia's sigh sounded more tired than annoyed. "Mallory, must we rehash that day? Can't you let go of your obsession with the past?"

Mallory tried to ease the moment and hang onto the goodness of the day that was quickly evaporating. "I guess I am as obsessed with the past as Lindsay is. Mom, I know this is really hard for you, but I really am just trying to find some answers. I can let it go if I have the truth."

Alecia slid her feet back into her sandals and raised her eyes to Mallory. "What do you want to know?"

Mallory stood and went to the counter for another cup of coffee. With her back turned, she dared to ask the question. "I found Eric ogling *Playboy* magazines, and he dared to claim that they were Daddy's." Jake was sure of it, but Mallory just couldn't reconcile the thought with whom she knew her father to be. He just wouldn't—would he?

"It wasn't true was it, Mom?" Mallory faced her mother. "Did Daddy look at *Playboy*s?"

Alecia shrugged her shoulders as she sipped the steaming brew. "I don't understand what the big deal is, Mallory. Your dad has always had girlie magazines in his garage and pinups hanging on the walls. Though, I did insist that he take down the more questionable ones as Shelly got older. He eventually took the rest down when the granddaughters came along."

Mallory sagged against the counter. Daddy was addicted to porn, and her mother knew and was all right with it? It felt like her world just tilted off its axis.

"Mother! Daddy was addicted to pornography?" If Eric was right about this, then what else from that conversation might he have been right about? Jake had warned her, but she hadn't wanted to believe him. She wrapped her arms around her waist, suddenly unsure if she really wanted to know the whole truth after all.

Eric's words haunted her. *"Your perfect little 'Daddy' nearly beat me to death."*

"He claimed that Daddy beat him black and blue once. Mother, Daddy never beat me or Geoff. Why would Eric say such a horrible thing about Daddy?"

"Because he did." Alecia winced and dropped her eyes to stare at the table. When she lifted them, tears glistened on her lashes, and her face suddenly looked old and haggard. "Once. He never did it again."

"What? Daddy beat Eric? When? How? Why?" Mallory fumbled for the chair and slid into it as she stared at her mom.

Alecia's lips pursed together in a look Mallory had seen countless times in the past. She folded her hands neatly in her lap, turned slightly in the seat, and crossed her ankles. "He lied to your father. That and sassing me were the two things your father simply couldn't abide. I had money lying on the kitchen counter to pay the paperboy, and remember, you saw Eric take the money and you told Dad. He was upset. Daddy did have a bit of a temper, but when Eric kept insisting he hadn't taken the money, your dad lost control because you had seen him take the money. He never did return it. . . ."

I told Dad? But. . .Eric didn't take that money. I took the money. Fragments of memories fell in succession like pieces of a puzzle coming together. She had given the money to Geoff, and he had gone and bought them candy. They had hidden it in the springs of Eric's bed, just in case. . . . Geo had told her it was their little secret.

Mallory sat up straight in her chair as another thought bombarded her brain. "Mom, did that all happen around the time when Eric fell off the roof of the fort and had to stay home from school?"

Alecia abruptly stood to her feet and scooped up her coffee cup. She took it to the sink and ran water into it then shut the water off. Mallory stared. Her rigidly squared shoulders sagged. Not even during the days immediately following her father's death had her mother looked this beaten. She seemed to wither right before Mallory's eyes. Her voice quivered when she finally spoke.

"Yes, but he didn't fall off the roof of the fort. Your father beat him black and blue. He had welts and bruises all over his body. I tried to get him to stop, but he knocked me out of the way. As Eric tried to get away from your father, he tripped and fell down the steps. He ended up with three broken ribs and a concussion." Alecia turned around. "Your dad changed after that. It scared him so badly that he never laid a hand on your brother again."

Mallory dropped her gaze to the floor, trying to process the information. She felt a fleeting touch against her shoulder as her mother leaned over and picked up her purse.

"It's been a very long day, and I am exhausted." She watched her mother's ramrod straight back exit the kitchen and turn down the hallway that led to the front door.

In the silence that followed, the refrigerator sounded like an airplane engine taking off. Mallory dropped her head in the crook of her arms as nausea rolled her stomach. What other horrible consequences did Eric deal with because of her tattling? Memories stirred.

"Daddy, Eric won't give me any candy."

Daddy's voice roared down the hallway. *"Eric Martin Bennington, get in here! You've had it, boy."*

"Stooooopppppp. Eric, quit picking on me. . . ."

"I wasn't picking. . ."

"Leave your sister alone!"

"Daddy, wasn't Eric supposed to be mowing the lawn? I saw him

down the street hanging out with Allen Morgan."

"Eric Martin, you are grounded for a month, and you can help your grandpa at the farm for the summer. Baling hay might get the laziness out of you." Mallory smirked. A summer without Eric! Yes!

"Daddy. . .Eric said he would walk me home from school, and he never did. Is that a lie, or is that not keeping a promise?"

"Boy, if you can't be here to look after your sister, then you don't need to be here for supper. Go to your room."

"Eric's not here, Daddy. I saw him push his car out of the driveway before he started it. Why did he do that, Dad?"

"I am not waiting up for that boy. He can sleep on the porch!"

"You stole the money for Geoff?" Eric's face flushed vivid red. "I took the heat for a candy-buying spree for you and your knight in shining armor? You little witch! How could you do that to me?" Eric's hands grabbed her ankles and yanked her off her feet. She struggled.

"Oh dear Lord, that's why he raped me?" She'd been through this so many times. She wanted to forgive, had chosen to forgive, had even felt forgiveness and compassion for Eric. And then she would remember—

Mallory's heart triple-timed, and her pulse hammered in her temple. The memory flashed once more. Pain ripping through her. Rage rose on the heels of the revelation and flowed like hot molten lava, sweeping over her from the tips of her toes to the top of her head. She hated him!

"God, he *raped* me! I should hate him. He deserves everything he gets." Mallory rubbed her eyes and swept her hands through her hair.

"What about what you deserve?"

The quiet thought thrummed through her anger and persisted when she tried to resist it. "It's not the same, God, and You know it! I never did anything like that. I never would."

"No, but you would harbor hate and plan vengeance and cause more pain."

"I was just a kid."

"So was he."

"Yeah right. He was old enough to get caught up in porn. He was old enough to choose his own path. He never takes responsibility for anything!"

"What about your responsibility?" The still, small voice in her soul spoke up again.

"We aren't talking about me! I was the victim!"

"He raped you. He was beaten nearly to death. Which one of you is a victim? He hurt you. You tattled constantly on him and got him punished for things he did not do. For things you did. Which one of you is an offender?"

The hammer of truth dropped Mallory to her knees. She slid down the wall, wrapping her arms around her head as the words continued to beat against her soul. Sobs wracked her body.

"Oh Father, what have I done?"

Chapter Forty-One

Eric woke to an explosion in his head and the vile taste of leftover beer on his breath. He rolled to a sitting position and stared at the floor as the throbbing in his head pounded out a tempo with his runaway thoughts. *Loser. Failure. Jerk.*

He ran his hand through his hair and down over his beard as he stumbled to the bathroom. On the way, his toe caught in the hole of a beer can. Bending over to loosen his foot from the constricting hole, he wobbled and danced down the corridor as he pulled the can off, squashed it like a bug, and flung it down the hallway. It bounced against the wall and landed with a clink against another discarded container.

He stopped, registering the fact that his entire upstairs hallway was littered with aluminum cans. He made his way around the mess. He didn't even want to think about what the downstairs might be like. How many had he had? How long had he been on the binge? A memory danced just beyond the screen of his mind. He paused midstride and frowned, trying to capture the elusive thought. *"Eric, I didn't come here for a fight."*

Mallory. Why had she come last night? What had he said to

her? What had she said to him? More important, why had he started drinking and when? He was concerned that he had no recollection about the night before, except that a litany of negative thoughts had taken up residence in his head and not even his drinking had canceled them. *No good, sorry excuse for a man. Can't even hold your liquor.* He glanced back down the hallway. Maybe he had a good reason for not being able to hold his liquor, considering the amount of cans strewn around. Eric's shoulders slumped. His chin dropped to his chest, and he shook his head as he shuffled into the bathroom.

He leaned against the sink and stared into the bleary, bloodshot eyes looking back at him. He really did need to lighten up a bit on the booze. Where in the world had all his self-control gone? He once had been a man who prided himself on drinking and not getting drunk—keeping his cool, a civil tongue, and his violent emotions in check. Who was this shell of a man staring back at him? He leaned closer, scrutinizing the haunted, defeated face before him. *"A man who can't hold down a job is not much of a man, boy. Remember that."* *Terrible father. No good husband. Loser son. Awful businessman. Naive business partner. Hard-nosed sibling. Murderer.*

"I just wanted him to be proud of me, Ma. Why couldn't Dad ever say, 'I'm proud of you'?"

"It wouldn't have mattered." His mother's words haunted him, but he knew better. *Murderer.*

"Eric, why can't you just admit the things you did to me?" Eric jerked upright and stared in the mirror at the door behind him. Where had that come from? *"I'm not asking for my sake. Really I'm not! I want to help you, but you won't let anyone in to do that."*

"I got a whole lot more on my mind than some imagined grievance from your childhood. My business went up in smoke. My kid won't talk to me. My wife is seeing another man, and I just got word that the insurance company I placed my faith in to pull me out of this whole

mess just packed their bags and got out of Dodge with my money. So frankly, little sister, I don't give a rip about what Jesus said to you. So if you won't have a drink with me, just leave."

Eric winced. *Idiot* was too soft a word for the man he had become. He shook his head and for once welcomed the violent explosion of pain that short-circuited the litany of failures. He reached for the bottle of aspirin. It slipped through his hand and tumbled open-ended into the sink. He took a deep breath to quiet the tremble in his hand and scooped the offending white dots back into the bottle. He turned on the spigot to wash away those that were turning to mush in the puddle at the bottom of the basin. Water spewed over the black marble counter and onto the floor. Eric swore, grabbed the towel, and mopped up the mess. He started to rise and smacked his head against the underside of the counter. Swearing again, he threw the towel across the room where it landed in the toilet bowl.

His hand knotted into a fist, and he closed his eyes and began to count. He'd learned the strategy in the military, and it had served him well through the years. *One. . . Okay, man, get a grip. I can't believe the insurance company just locked their doors without a word! Two. . . You gotta pick up Marty from Mom's. Three. . . What you are dealing with is the aftereffect of the booze. You can do this.* No money. Not now, not ever. What in the world was he going to do now? *Count, man, count. Four. . . Focus on the moment. Just clean up the mess. It's not that hard.* He felt his emotional chaos retreat back into the hole from where it erupted.

But like some wild animal, it remained hidden just below the surface. He looked at his reflection again and reached for his electric razor. Lord, he was glad his kid hadn't been around to see what he had dissolved into. Scruffy was an understatement as he realized how much he had let himself go in light of all the things that had happened to him. Looking as he did now would only invoke another lecture, or worse, his mother's pity and then a sermon on the need for some self-respect. He didn't need any of those things.

He trimmed the contours of his beard. The mundane act soothed his ragged emotions, and he loosened the firm hold he had on his otherwise obsessive thoughts. Foggy images floated in his mind of his sister's surprisingly compassionate eyes and sorrowful tones. She had handed him an envelope with his name on it.

"I wrote this letter, Eric, to tell you that I hate what has been happening to you and wish with all my heart I could make some of your pain go away, but that doesn't change all the things you did to me."

Eric jerked as the fiasco with his sister from the night before snapped clearly into focus. He glanced at his reflection and let a string of profanity fly. He'd cut a swathe in his beard from high on his cheekbone to the top of his chin. Something deep inside him snapped. He let out a roar, and with it the wild animal found an escape route as all the years of reigning in his emotions unleashed its fury.

Travis heard the sound of bedlam from the front porch. Smashing wood, shattering glass, and something like the roar of some wounded beast rose from the recesses of the house. *Eric!* Travis tried the door. It was locked. What was going on? He tried the door again. It was definitely locked. Was someone in the house? He leaned against the glass and tried to peer through the skylight beside the door. It looked like Eric's house had been vandalized or burglarized. Was the burglar still there? He stumbled over part of a tree limb as he dashed around the back of the house. Was Eric fighting for his life? What if something happened to him? Dread slammed into the apprehension and created the kind of terror he had only known once before, when his wife and son had died.

Travis pushed against the glass door and glanced around the normally neat kitchen. The trash can was overturned. Dirty dishes were stacked in the sink, on the counter around the kitchen, and piled on the stove.

The sound of splintering glass filled the air. A bellow like a wounded animal rolled down the hallway, and Travis's heart pounded against his rib cage. He kicked the tipped-over trash can out of his way and raced from the kitchen. He ran down the hallway and skidded to a stop just inside the living room.

"Eric!" Travis bellowed at the top of his lungs. "Put that down!"

Eric froze midswing. The fireplace poker stopped just short of smashing into the large portrait of Eric's family. Eric was standing on the sofa in nothing but a pair of pajama bottoms. Sweat covered his torso and dripped off his disheveled hair. He looked like some kind of barbaric Neanderthal; his chest heaved, and he swayed back and forth on his precarious perch.

"Have you lost your mind?" Travis lowered his voice a decibel, but the shock remained. Eric jerked. His muscles bunched, and he spun around. Eric gripped the poker and for a split second, Travis wondered if he needed to hightail it out of the room before it was hurled his direction. Eric shuddered, and Travis watched as Eric visibly pulled his rage under control. He swiveled away from Travis.

A second shock wave curled through Travis. Did he really see what he thought he had seen? A clean-shaven face riddled with toilet-paper dots? "Eric?"

The way Eric had kept his beard neat and trim all these years always made Travis suspect that it was a thing of pride, perhaps a mark of manhood for Eric.

"Leave me alone." His friend's voice was sullen, but Travis recognized the undertone of guilt and mortification.

"What happened?" Travis's eyes swept across the room, *bedlam* and *mayhem* were too nice of words to describe Eric's living room. The terra-cotta lamps that had graced the ends of his sofa were now unrecognizable shards of broken clay. The end tables and coffee table were now splintered wood. The deep-brown lampshades looked like brown smudge spots on the carpet. The credenza that held the array of family photos was swept clean and its contents a shattered heap upon the floor. Bric-a-brac was strewn from one end of the room to the other. Broken glass was everywhere. Travis's eyes stopped on the doorway leading to Eric's home office. It was a mirror image of the state of the living room. He hated to think what the rest of the house looked like and was glad that Marty was with Alecia and Lindsay was with her mom. Now he seriously needed to know what caused this rampaging maniac to emerge, though he had his suspicions.

"Eric?"

"I said just leave me alone!"

"No."

Eric's face turned red, and the veins popped out in his neck as he bolted from the couch. His hands closed in a fist around the piece of iron in his hand.

"You are not going to use that on me, so why don't you just drop it now?"

Eric stood before Travis, his nostrils flaring as the muscles jerked and twitched throughout his body. *Man, I hope you don't swing that thing at me. God, a little assistance here would be a wonderful thing about now.*

The rage deflated as Eric's shoulders sagged, and he dropped the poker. It landed with a dull thud in the carpet. His tone was flat. "Just get out of my face and out of my life." He took a step away from his previous perch, and Travis held up his hand to stop him.

"Buddy, if you come any farther away from that sofa, you will do serious damage to your feet."

"Don't really care."

Travis sighed more in amusement than frustration. "I do.

'Cause I'll be the one to have to bandage those size-twelve puppies." He shook his head as Eric glared at him with barely held restraint. "You know, your son is more like you than you realize. At this moment, you look just like him."

Eric's shoulder's stiffened and just as quickly slumped again. "What are you doing here?"

Travis inspected the chair for slivers of glass before sitting down. "We were going for breakfast. So, what happened?"

Eric shrugged with the same belligerent mannerism as his son and stared down at his hands.

"You might as well come clean with me because I am not budging until you do."

Eric's eyes swept upward to meet Travis's and then landed back in his lap. Travis read the myriad of conflicting emotions. *It hurts to see him like this, Father. So broken. So easy to be fixed if he would just turn to You. Let me push him.* A red light flashed in his mind. *Okay, okay. I'll listen.* But he really needed to see what God was seeing to know how to continue because the state Eric was in. . . He had to admit he'd never been nervous before in his friend's presence.

What do I ask? Travis leaned back in his seat and crossed his ankle over his knee before lacing his fingers behind his head. "What set you off?"

Eric mumbled, and Travis leaned forward.

"What?"

"I said I shaved off my beard by accident!"

A smile started somewhere in the pit of Travis's stomach, and he had to catch it before it reached his eyes. *So, this is it, huh, Lord?* The beginning of the final breaking. . .

Nothing worse than a man who loses control over his own razor. What a way to finally bring this man to his knees—with his beard.

Chapter Forty-Two

So how did you learn to control that raging beast? Because I surely never saw 'Hurricane Eric' before," Travis said as he nudged pieces of glass away with his foot.

In a flash, Eric was back there. Sixteen years old—and in a red-hot rage.

Suddenly his arms were pinned to his side in a vicelike grip. He was yanked off his feet and pinned against a granite hard chest. Fear choked out the rage. He knew what was coming. It had happened before. Eric struggled violently to get away from the grasp. Devoid of any leverage, he was at the mercy of the older, stronger arms.

"That's enough."

He squirmed and struggled harder. He tried biting the work-worn hands, but they were down too far away from his mouth. He tried kicking, but his legs swished through empty air.

Before he knew what exactly had happened, he was flying through the air, all arms and legs. He had just enough time to suck in a breath before he landed in the chilling water of the cattle trough. The icy liquid quenched his fiery emotions, and he came up sputtering for air. As the water dripped from his bangs into his eyes, he tried to make out the masculine figure who stood towering over him.

Calm, measured tones drifted over him as Gramps said, "I told you, that was enough." The old man's mouth was set in a hard straight line, much like Eric's father's, but there was a twinkle of understanding shining in his blue eyes. His large hand reached out.

Eric grasped it, and just as unceremoniously as he went in, he was yanked from the galvanized tub. "Let's take a walk." They walked in silence until they reached the ridge that overlooked the western boundary of the farm. Gramps clambered up onto one of the ancient glacial rocks and stared for long moments, lost in some distant memory.

"Son, you have got to learn to control that temper of yours before you hurt someone, or it kills you."

"I didn't do—"

Gramps cut him off and stared him down. "Yes. You did."

Eric felt a growing urge to explain. "But, Gramps, I couldn't get the bolt loose off the baler control panel. What was I supp—"

Gramps jumped down from the rock. "That give you the right to destroy another man's property? Eric, son, today it was the baler, tomorrow a helpless animal, then what?"

"But I didn't do. . ."

The older man turned to face Eric full-on. His voice remained quiet, but his tone was getting harder by the second. "Listen to me! If you don't get control over that rage that is seething in your soul, it will consume you, and there's only one way it will eventually go down. Someone's going to get hurt." Gramps ended on a tired sigh. "I know."

That last phrase captured Eric's attention at last. He watched as his grandfather turned back toward the ravine below them. He thought he saw a tear in the man's eyes. A tear. Gramps never cried.

Gramps cleared his throat and turned back around. "Eric, every Bennington man has to learn to control the wild emotions that rage in him, or they will kill someone. I know. Because during the war, I killed a man."

Eric's eyes narrowed in confusion. "Well yeah, you were in World

War Two after all."

"No, son, that is not what I'm talkin' about. We were in France, just ready to cross the border into Germany, and a comrade of mine happened to see the picture your grandma sent to me. He made a few comments I didn't take kindly to—a couple of rude references about her body. I told him to knock it off. He did. But as we were trapped in a foxhole together, pinned down by enemy fire for four days, each of us decided to write one last letter home—you know, in case we didn't make it.

"I had run out of paper and asked my buddy for a sheet. It was then I discovered him writing a letter to her, asking if he could meet up with her if we got back from the war. Said I was seein' a little dark-haired French girl, and he believed it was over between us. Jealousy overwhelmed me and. . .there was a struggle and. . .I shot him. It was easy enough to cover the fact being in the middle of a war and all."

Eric's eyes widened as the news sunk in. Gramps?

Gramps scuffed the toe of his boots in the dirt. The move reminded him of Geoff when he got a scolding. Gramps straightened and stared straight into Eric's eyes. "When I got home, I was learning how to be a civilian again, and I nearly killed another man. It scared me so bad that I could do something like that again. . . . I know what that horrible anger in your gut does to a man. Scared me even more when I realized my jealousy and temper had been passed down to my boy. Scared me so bad that I did whatever it took to kill that raging beast, and I never told anyone what I had done in the war."

Gramps laid his hand on Eric's shoulder. "Until today I have never told another living soul. Not your father. Not your grandma. Nobody. And I want it kept between the two of us."

Gramps trusted him with a secret. Pride and pain swelled together in his heart. "I won't tell." Eric's promised whisper floated between them, and the old man nodded.

Eric cleared his throat and asked, "What'd you do, Gramps? How'd you learn to control it?" He'd cleared his throat again, trying to remove the thickness that kept swelling to the surface.

"I turned to Jesus. I knew He was the only One who could forgive a sin I couldn't confess to anyone. He was the only One who could understand the emotions that churned in my gut. So I turned to Him, and I clamped down hard on my boy because I saw so much of myself in him and knew the path he would walk if he didn't change. But you know your daddy."

Eric's hands clenched fists full of dirt. Yes, he knew his daddy, only too well.

"Martin was a wild thing. By the time he was an adolescent, he was battling the same thing. It took the military to make a man out of him. Did him a world of good. Was a changed man after he came home from the service. Was the best thing in the world for him, though I hated the thoughts of him joining the very place where I had done such an awful thing."

If his father had changed after the service, what had he been like before?

Gramps's words curtailed Eric's runaway thoughts. *"Son, I am telling you all this because you need to find your path out of this destructive pit. I know what I'd like to see for you, but you are nearly a man, and you need to make the choice for yourself."*

Gramps clamped his hand on Eric's shoulder. It was strong, warm, and a stabilizing force after the bomb his grandfather had just dropped. And in a heartbeat, Eric knew the course his life would take, and maybe, just maybe, his father would be proud of him.

"So because of that conversation you went into the military and found a release and a discipline to control your anger." Travis's words snapped him back to the present.

Had he spoken the memory out loud? He must have. He hadn't breathed a word of that story to anyone. Ever. Until this very moment. *Failure. Can't even keep a promise to a dead man.* His stomach clenched, and he wanted to swear and start swinging again.

"Know what I think?" Travis asked, breaking the long silence that hovered between them.

"That I am the biggest idiot on the face of the earth, and you are wondering why you ever decided to befriend a loser like me?" Eric muttered as his eyes swept across the debris left in the wake of his temporary insanity. He felt lower than the underside of a slug.

"Well, that thought did flit through my head." Travis chuckled. "But no, I was actually thinking that it might do you good to just get away for a few days."

Eric shook his head. "I can't."

"Why not?"

"Because now's not the time to take a vacation."

"I didn't say it was a vacation. I said you needed to get away."

Eric held up his hand. "My life is in the toilet, and I have decisions that I have got to make."

Travis was nodding. "Exactly why you need to get away. You need to get some perspective in your life."

"How, by getting in touch with my inner self? I did that and look around you." Eric could hear the sarcasm in his own voice and winced at it.

Travis laughed outright at that. "Okay. So I go with you to make sure you don't destroy some other place as well."

"I've got a mess here I have to clean up."

Travis looked around the room. "No kidding." Eric frowned, but Travis continued, "But a big broom and a couple of extra arms will have it cleaned up in no time."

"That's not what I meant." Eric felt his resolve hardening until he saw the tears in his friend's eyes.

"I'm scared for you, Eric. If you keep going this way with no rest and no time to grieve the losses in your life, all of this"—Travis swept his hand around the room—"will happen again, and maybe next time Lindsay or Marty will get caught in the crossfire. Deal with it now."

The image knifed fear into Eric's heart, but the earnestness in Travis's voice formed a lump in Eric's throat. He didn't know what to say or do. Looking into himself and trying to find some clarity to his life terrified him.

He shook his head in one last-ditch effort. "I have Marty...."

"He's staying with your mom." Travis stared long and hard into Eric's eyes.

Travis finally broke the silence. "You have really been under it, my friend. Marty. Your dad. The fire. Any one of those is enough to break a man. All together, well, it's enough to make a man break everything in his house. So, here's what we do. You pack your gear tonight and head to my fishing cabin in West Virginia. You can be there by sundown. Get some rest, do a little early morning fishing.

"I'll clear my calendar and follow you down. I can be there by late morning. We'll do some fly-fishing and some talking where the only thing that might overhear us is a loon and the deer. You spend some time with yourself, and I will spend some time with my heavenly Father. Deal?"

Chapter Forty-Three

Eric pulled into the welcome center just over the state line to stretch the kinks from his back and grab a cup of coffee before continuing to the Jamison homestead. The drive to West Virginia had been uneventful. He reached into his Jeep for the map wallet stashed neatly in the door's pocket. Travis laughed at him for not using a GPS, but each time he'd used one, it had taken him around in circles. He smoothed the road map out on the hood and squinted as the late-afternoon light reflected off the white background, sipping his coffee as he examined the route. One, two hours tops and he should be there. He pulled the directions that Travis had given him from the front pocket of the vinyl folder, and another piece of paper fluttered to the asphalt.

Eric's brows pulled together in a puzzled frown as he bent to retrieve it and noted his name written in Mallory's elegant script. How had his sister's letter gotten in with his maps? He'd thrown it on the counter when she'd given it to him and left it there. He turned the envelope in his hands as if that simple gesture would reveal the answer he sought. It must have been hiding under Travis's printed directions and map to the cabin. His friend's words echoed through his mind. *"Eric, whatever is between you and your sister, you really need to work through it. She is the only sister you've got. Treasure that, and cherish her. You will never know how much I regret not having my wife here with me. Work it out."*

It was just his luck he would have to grab her letter along with the map. He might as well see what sort of entertaining fiction she'd dreamed up this time. He unfolded the multiple sheets of paper.

Eric,

> *I know that I'm probably not being fair to you by writing this letter instead of speaking to you face-to-face. Call me a coward, but I'm truly tired of the squabbling, bickering, backstabbing, and hatred that have been between us for as long as I can remember.*

Eric's heart pounded as he leaned back against the side of his Jeep.

> *We've been playing these roles all our lives, and frankly, I'm sick to death of it all.*

"So am I, Mal, so am I. So why don't you just let it go and leave me alone?" He nearly crumbled the letter and tossed it in the trash can nearby. The next words kept him from doing just that.

> *I need to apologize to you.*

Apologize? Mal didn't do things like that. Not the Mal he'd grown up with, but then that Mal would never have been with him at the fire either. That Mal would have gloated over his failures. Maybe she had changed.

I've had to do some serious soul searching, praying, and repenting since our fight. Jake made me take a long, hard look at myself, and it wasn't a pretty picture. You were right, you know, when you said that there were many times I asked for the treatment I got from you. Not intentionally, and no one deserves, ever deserves, to be treated the way you treated me, but I did go begging every time that I tattled on you about stupid things.

Eric fought to get air past the fist-sized lump that grabbed his throat. He turned to the last page to examine the signature at the bottom. Who was it that had really written this letter? Not Mallory. She wouldn't admit to making a mistake, would she?

That was Mallory's signature, no doubt about that. No one could sign her name like she did. He knew. He'd tried. In fact he'd gotten quite good at forging his parents' handwriting, even Geoff's, but he'd never been able to copy hers.

There were more times than I care to admit that I took great delight in watching Dad give you the belt. I always felt vindicated when he did that for all the horrible stuff you made me endure. I won't rehash the junk again. We've already ground that one into mincemeat.

Long-forgotten memories rose like ghosts from a foggy mire. Eric shuddered and jerked away from the truck like it had become electrically charged with high voltage. "Mal, I swear, I don't know how you managed to put these ideas into my mind, but I never did that kind of thing to you! Never."

His fist clenched around the paper. Another phrase caught his attention as the words crumbled together. He smoothed the sheet back out. Hating himself for insisting on finishing this fable, he continued reading.

*What I didn't realize was the part I played in the awful
cycle of abuse that our family was trapped in. I don't know
why Dad treated you like he did.*

"Dad"? Not "Daddy"? Maybe something he'd said got through
her thick skull after all.

*All I know is that I used it to my advantage, and Jake
made me see that in this scenario I was an offender, as
horrible in manipulating the situation to my advantage as
you were in manipulating me. I am so sorry!*

Mal sorry! Mallory never said she was sorry. Not to him,
anyway. At least not unless their mother caught her in the very act
of being a jerk and forced the apology out of her. It always sounded
hollow in his ears, and not at all sincere. The words blurred. He
raked his hand across his eyes.

*"Don't be a crybaby. Big boys do not cry. Only girls and sissies do
that. Real men don't cry."* His father's stern voice still rang in his
ears.

Travis's voice intruded. *"You're wrong, Eric. Real men do cry.
Real men aren't afraid of showing their vulnerability to themselves,
their loved ones, or their God. Real men express their emotions and are
never ashamed of the things that have touched them deeply."*

Eric massaged his suddenly throbbing temple and downed the
last of his now-lukewarm coffee.

I'm tired of laying blame.

"Good! I'm tired of being blamed for everything that has ever
gone wrong in this family. We all lived in it. We all made a mess of
it. Quit blaming me!" He tossed the letter into the Jeep where the
fluttering pages settled against the leather seat. He climbed in and

slammed the door. "Quit thinking. Just get to Travis's cabin and unwind. Forget about everything."

Eric turned up the radio as he pulled onto the freeway. Regardless of how he tried to shut down his brain, he found himself sucked into a vortex of memories that threw him thirty-some odd years into the past.

"Uncle Mike, why does my dad hate me so much?" There was a wobble in the child's voice.

Mike started before reaching down and ruffling Eric's hair. "Eric, he doesn't hate you."

"Yeah he does. He never says, 'Good job, Eric.' Nothing I do ever pleases him. Why can't I please him? I don't think I'm even his kid. He told me once that his kids don't act like I do. What did he mean, Uncle Mike?"

Eric shook off the memory as he reached for the directions to Travis's cabin. Mallory's words stared him in the face.

I just want this family to begin to heal. To live in truth, walk in truth, face the truth.

He threw the paper across the seat. "You want the truth, Mallory? The truth is our father is a lying, no-good human being who never cared for anyone, or anything, but himself. He lied to us. He cheated on Mom; he pretended to be so perfect, so loving. I hate you, Dad. I hate you with everything that is inside of me."

His left hand clenched the steering wheel while his right hand groped for the elusive directions. Finding them, he read the exit number and realized he had just passed it. He jerked on the turn signal. He swung through the no U-turn strip and headed back the way he had come. Catching the correct exit, he followed T's directions to the mining community of Adler Falls.

His head was throbbing. His eyes hurt, and his gut was tied in knots. Eric pulled in front of the dilapidated grocery store and went in search of some aspirin. Buying them and a six-pack of beer, Eric returned to his vehicle and downed four aspirin with a can of beer. Somehow it failed to satisfy. Those things that once brought him pleasure now had a bitter taste. He snatched up the offending letter. If he finished reading it, he could toss it and be rid of the fire boiling in his veins.

You know, Eric, I just want our family to be free. Truth is the only way for that freedom to come. It's not pretty. It's definitely not pleasant. It's not easy, either, but it is possible. All I want you to do is face the truth.

"What truth, Mal? Your truth? If the family is as screwed up as we both believe it is, then your version of the truth is just as screwed up as mine. So why should I possibly believe you?"

He looked up only to find an old lady staring at him as he argued with his invisible sister. He turned away as heat burned beneath his skin. "Thanks, Mal. Make me look like a fool. You always were good at that." He muttered beneath his breath, careful to keep his lips from moving. The old lady continued to stare. Eric grabbed a cold beer and raised it in salute to her, eyeing her with a long, hard stare. She dropped her gaze and hurried down the street, her cane tapping out an uneven rhythm.

Face the truth. Face the past. Face yourself, and face your God. I want to see you free of the rage that has riddled your soul all your life. Is it too much to pray for—this breaking of the generational curses that have been passed down through our family for so many years? I don't know where it started, but I can tell you where it can end. It can end with us.

"Yeah, sure it can, sis. Always the one with her head in the clouds."

*What Gramps passed down to Dad, and Dad passed
down to us, is a lifetime of shame and the repercussions of that
shame. The Bible calls it a legacy of fools and it is.*

Had she been talking to Travis? He'd said something similar
to that on his radio program. At the time, Eric thought it had been
just preacher jargon; now he wasn't so sure. Travis's words came
back with haunting clarity. *"It is a generational curse that gets passed
down from parent to child until it becomes so ingrained that it is all a
family ever knows. It has been handed down by parents who refuse to
walk in the light of God's Word and refuse to be held accountable by the
light of God's Truth."*

Truth. What was truth? Whose truth did he listen to? He
tipped his head back and pinched the bridge of his nose before
screwing his courage up to finish the letter.

*Yes, I listened to Gran, and yes, for the first time in my life
I began to see that there was another side to Gramps. Yes, I also
am beginning to understand that there was a dark side to our
father as well. Shame has become our inheritance. It's a fool's
legacy that is being passed down to us, and if we aren't careful,
through us. As long as we refuse to acknowledge the part that
we all played in this handing down of sin in our lives, it will
continue to be passed along for generations. When will it end?*

*I no longer want that legacy for our family. I want the
legacy of glory that is available to us by God. I want our
homes blessed for being homes of justice. I want God to give
us grace, and I want our inheritance to be that of glory that
comes from acknowledging what only God can do.*

*So please do this one thing. Think about our childhood in
relationship to your children. Look at what we lived through;
look at it through the lives of your kids.*

Eric reached for another beer, popped the tab, and took a long swallow. It wasn't good either. He arched it over his head out the window and made a perfect slam dunk into the trash can nearby. He gritted his teeth, determined to finish his sister's stupid letter and continue on to the cabin. "Get it over with, Mal. Just finish your long-winded story and get it over with."

You said, "We were just playing. It was cowboys and Indians." Imagine if it were Lindsay that was tied up by Marty.

Eric's hand clenched.

Look at the difference in our ages and our sizes. We were comparable to Marty and Lindsay. What would you have done to Marty had you discovered your daughter tied to a tree?

"Kill him. Because no son of mine would act like... Oh God, I sound just like Dad."

You said, "But you could have gotten out of those ropes anytime you wanted." How? Eric, I wasn't even old enough to tie my shoes. How was I supposed to get loose? You left Geo and me tied to those trees for hours! Hours, Eric, because you went off and forgot about us. What would you have done had you found Lindsay like that—naked and scared? You would never have let Marty get away with the excuses that you have used with me. Never! What would you do if someone did to Lindsay what you did to me?
You said, "I never hurt you." What a lie! What about the bruises, the busted ankle, the shame, the rage, the promiscuity

*I had in college because I was exposed to sexual filth at such
an early age? You said, "You could have told."*

Eric nearly bolted from the truck as his own hate-filled voice
whispered in his mind. *"You cry, you tell, I'll kill the cat. You ever tell
Dad or Mom, I'll hurt Geoff. You pretend everything is all right, or I'll
find a way to shut you up for good."*

He ground gears as he pulled out of the parking space and
spun tires in an effort to physically leave his past behind him. The
last sentence of her letter followed him all the way up the logging
road.

*For the sake of your life, think about what I said, and
for the sake of your children, think about what is true; I'm
praying for you.*

The logging road was dark and formidable in the late-
afternoon light. Eric rolled the window down to allow the wind
to cleanse his mind. The day was sultry with the humidity high
enough that Eric believed he could squeeze water from midair.

The narrowness of the path reminded him of Aunt Liz's cabin
on Percy's Island. A tangle of wild vines snaked from the trees they
possessed. Eric shuddered despite the heat of the late afternoon.
As he pulled in front of the two-story log cabin, he tried to quell
the shiver that scaled up his back. The building was far too similar
to Aunt Liz's for comfort. He never liked that place, though he
wasn't sure why.

"Okay, you're here. Make the most of it." Eric reached for
his leather suitcase and the rest of his beer. Setting them on the
ground, he went around to unload his fishing tackle. T had told
him there was a great stream for bass fishing on the far end of
the property. Grabbing up his stuff, he readjusted his fishing pole
under his arm and got a firmer hold on the case of beer.

The forest beyond the cabin was a dim, gray-green barrier in the early evening light. The recess beneath the second-story porch appeared as an endless black hole, except for a strip of white suspended from the rafters. Eric squinted. What was that? He moved closer. The shape gave way to details. A hammock.

Mallory's voice came to him from out of the past. *"But Eric, I don't want to play pirates. Aunt Liz will be home soon. You'd better let me go before she gets back!"*

Eric hurried up the steps, tossing his stuff inside the door and reaching for a light switch. *Click.* Nothing happened. He flicked it several times. "Great! Just great! Now I know why he insisted I come. To fix his electrical problem. Well, I won't be staying that long."

Eric stumbled his way through the twilight darkness to the fireplace. There had to be matches around here. His hands swept across the mantel and knocked a box onto the floor. He had just located the errant box as lightning illuminated the interior of the cabin.

Striking a match, he discovered the grate laid out and waiting for a flame to ignite it. He touched the match to the tinder and watched as tiny flames devoured paper before moving on to the oak logs. The flickering light spilled warmth throughout the structure. Eric grabbed an oil lantern from the shelf next to the window and lit it before going off to explore.

The bedroom sported a huge, four-poster bed made from native timber and covered with a psychedelic comforter. He set the satchel on the bed and drew out his shirts to hang in the closet. In the bathroom, he tossed his shaving kit on the counter next to the sink.

Maybe Travis was right. Maybe this would be his haven of rest. God alone knew that he needed some time to unwind and make some decisions about his life. His business was destroyed, his reputation was down the toilet since the fire investigation, he was nearing bankruptcy, and whatever hope he had ever had for getting back with Catherine had been dashed like a ship against the rocks.

Eric headed back down the stairs, stared at his beer, then grabbed a can and settled onto the overstuffed sofa. Kicking off his shoes, he tried to let his mind drift off to nothingness, but the cacophony of voices in his head was like an orchestra warming up before a concert. Fragmented conversations blended and blurred until he thought he would lose his mind. Eric bolted to his feet. "Stop it! Just stop!"

Rain slashed against the windowpane as the wind knifed through the chinking of the log cabin, moaning like a disembodied spirit haunting this last place of refuge. Eric spun around. Where had that come from? That haunting cry of fear and pain? Forgotten fragments of memories snagged in his mind like fish caught on a hook. Sweat broke out on his brow. *Mallory's high childish screams pierced the air as Eric pressed the muzzle of his BB gun to her temple. "Don't scream an' don't move."*

Eric recoiled as a fireball of lightning fell from the sky while a simultaneous crack like a discharging .22-gauge rifle shattered the night air.

"It was loaded, Eric! How could you put a loaded gun, even a BB gun, to your sister's head? Didn't you know that thing could kill her?"

Uncle Ken shook his shoulders. "I have to tell your father about this stunt, Eric. I don't want to, but he has to know because frankly I don't know what to do about this."

An eleven-year-old voice pleaded with his uncle. "Don't tell! Please, Uncle Ken, I was just playin'. He'll kill me if you tell. I promise I won't let it happen again. I promise!"

Eric pressed his palms against his eyes. He perused the small stack of books on the shelves in an effort to sidetrack his skittish mind. He swore as he tossed one aside. "This is no haven. This is becoming my worst nightmare. What was I thinking? I hate the woods. I hate spending the night surrounded by nature, and I hate log cabins. I've got to get out of here." Peering through a sheet of water, he tried to assess his situation. His chances of making it back down to the main road didn't look too good. A loud boom reverberated beyond the log walls. He rubbed his neck. Maybe he should think about it.

Why had he thought spending time at Travis's West Virginia cabin would solve all his problems? At the moment it was only compounding the pandemonium within his life. *"Eric, you need time to unwind. To think. To just get away. Use my homestead. It's a great place to get a good perspective on the world."* His friend's words ricocheted in his mind.

"Yeah, sure, Travis," Eric mumbled as he moved restlessly from the door into the firelight's glow. "How? By getting stuck here until next spring? I don't think so, buddy." Eric poked the dying embers back to life and tossed another oak log onto the fire. He sank down in the rocker that faced the fireplace. Sparks flew, and flames licked over the wood, casting their dancing light into the room and chasing shadows into its corners. The wind howled like a woman in torment, and Eric flinched as if he'd been struck.

"Eric! Stop it! Stop it! Please, stop. Please! Mommy and Daddy will be back soon. Please! I promised you I wouldn't tell. I really won't."

He shoved his hands in his pockets, feeling the crumpled paper of Mallory's letter. *"Eric, you raped me!"* The almost-forgotten memory of Mallory's phone call a year ago cascaded through his mind, filling his entire being with revulsion.

"NO! I never did that. Mallory, whatever else you believe, I never hurt you like that!" Eric shot to his feet. He swallowed hard and ran a hand through his hair. "I've got to try and get down this mountain before the storm strands me here. This isn't the place to try and put my life back together." Eric would never have come here if he had known this cabin was a mirror image of Uncle Ken and Aunt Liz's place.

Was the storm letting up? He paced the confines of the cabin like an angry tiger as the minutes ticked away. Why had he thought that this was a place of refuge? Eric paused. "Okay, I'm outta here." He swung around, galloped up the stairs, and yanked his small leather case from beneath the bed.

Another volley of lightning flashed across the sky. He grabbed his satchel, pulled his shirts from their hangers, and stuffed them into the bag along with his jeans and toiletry kit. A clap of thunder sounding like leather hitting skin jolted Eric's nerves, and he hastened his movements. *"How many times do I have to tell you to quit picking on your sister? Every time I turn around it's 'Daddy, Eric's picking on me. Daddy, Eric won't leave me alone. Daddy, he took my doll.' I'm sick of it, boy."*

Eric glanced out the window. The chances of making it down the road in one piece were slim. His fingers raked through his hair. He'd never been overly fond of storms, but he'd done a good job of keeping his fears from the light of day. Now it seemed his worst fears were determined to penetrate through the walls he'd built around his mind. This storm rocking his world was the worst he'd ever lived through, and as lightning pierced the sky, he wondered if he'd ever actually get out of it with his sanity intact. He shoved the rest of his belongings in his case, snapped it shut, and jogged back down the steps. After dousing the coals and double-checking the fireplace, his eyes swept the cabin one last time before zipping up his raincoat and switching on the flashlight he'd found near the door.

The wind ripped the door from his hands and fired stinging pellets of rain against his skin. Bending against the gale-force winds, he inched his way along the upper-story porch to the stairs. The trees around the cabin were nearly doubled over and taking the brunt of the storm. The flash of lightning sent him straight to his past.

Thirteen-year-old Eric huddled against the wall curled in a ball to shelter himself from the pelting rain and shook in his thin jacket as he stared in bewilderment at the door that refused to open with the turn of his key. Tears mingled with the rain as he crawled to the swing and pulled his coat over his head to ward off what rain he could. Thunder crashed. Lightning fingered the sky, and he whimpered in fear. "Dad, I'm sorry. I only missed my curfew by four minutes. I'm sorry. It won't happen again."

Eric shivered against the memories that were determined to destroy his well-ordered domain. He climbed into his Jeep Cherokee and shook his head, flinging beads of water throughout the interior.

The world was illuminated by a wash of glaring white. A shrouded human struggling to rise was clearly visible beneath the raised front porch. Eric's breath caught, and the hair rose on the back of his neck. "It's just the hammock." He sagged against the seat as he clutched his chest.

"Want to have some fun, little brother? Trust me, you'll love this. Climb in the hammock. Ready? Okay, hang on. Wait till it unwraps, that's the cool part. Oh, quit being a baby. You're not really hurt. You didn't fall that far. Besides, the rope around your leg caught most of your weight anyway."

Eric reached for the key in the ignition. "You've got to quit watching those thriller movies, old man."

The blinding sheets of water pouring from the sky diffused the twin beams of headlights to a ghostly glow. Eric backed around and began a tortuously slow descent down the winding road. When the rain began letting up, he sighed and felt his shoulders begin to relax. The Jeep slogged through the deepening mire that moved like thick lava down the ruts.

"Two more miles. Only two more miles," he muttered beneath his breath. With every mile of distance put between him and the cabin he breathed that much easier. He was reaching to turn the radio down when the sight before him caused him to slam his brakes and grip the wheel with both hands. The Jeep slid sideways, sending a spray of black muck over the windshield. Eric pounded the steering wheel in impotent fury and swore. "This is just great!" The tiny rivulet of a stream that meandered down the gully and across the road a mere two hours before was well on its way to becoming a raging torrent of water.

He stared at the foaming brown water and shook his head. Eric roared into the night, "I can't believe this! There's no way I can cross that." He slammed his hand against the horn. "I don't want to spend a night in that cabin, but do I want to sleep in the Jeep? I guess I go back." Shifting gears, tires spun fruitlessly as they tried to get a grip in the slime. He shifted into four-wheel drive and pumped the gas. The Jeep moved several inches before bogging down and spinning furiously. He pumped the gas, causing mud to splatter onto the roof.

The wheels continued to spin. Eric swore once more. He jammed the gears from REVERSE to FIRST and back again in an effort to rock the vehicle from the viscous goo.

Muttering words that his father would have found offensive, Eric shifted into first gear again and nudged the gas pedal. "Come on—move!" The Jeep crept slowly into the brown water. The tires gripped the rocky riverbed. The pent-up breath that he'd been unconsciously holding eased out as the headlights revealed the bank on the other side. From out of the blackness something slammed against the side of the truck. Eric felt himself being swept along on a spinning journey downstream some thirty feet before the Jeep lurched to a sudden stop.

Eric was thrown tightly against his seat belt. The vehicle had been deposited in a quagmire of mud. He turned the ignition, but the only sound the engine made was a grumble of complaint before it died completely. The drumming of rain on his roof and the rush of water beneath him echoed hollowly around the interior of the vehicle.

Eric's fist came down hard on his horn, but its feeble little bleat only increased his wrath as a horrific picture crammed his mind. Mallory's eyes were pools of terrified deep, deep green. Unable to utter more than a tiny groan from beneath the duct tape, tears coursed down her cheeks as he fell on top of her. Bile rose in his throat. Pushing the door against the crush of water, he stepped midthigh into the icy whirlpool. It was the only thing that saved him from being violently sick.

"It didn't happen! I have been watching too many shows on HBO, that's all. It did not happen!" Despite the hard shove with both hands, the door refused to close. "I can't even slam the door!" His frustration was being eaten by other, more violent emotions.

Using the truck as leverage, he pulled himself forward through the swirling water to the front of the Jeep where the right bumper was embedded into the bank of the river. A slurping sound rose from the mud with each step. His stomach rolled as the memory of his sister with his brother filled the screen of his mind. Eric strained his powerful thigh muscles against the pull of the water and silt on the river's bottom, losing a boot in the process. It took a long moment for his brain to process the mundane information. Then he bent to try to retrieve it, but the darkness of the night and the clouded water defeated him.

"Forget it! It did not happen! Just move, Bennington. Just keep moving. One more yard and you'll be out of the worst of it." Eric turned toward the elusive bank, but the suction from the slime and the turbulence of the water was making it next to impossible. Encouraging himself to keep going, Eric grabbed at the tall grasses growing on the bank and tried to hoist himself closer to the solid ground. The grass uprooted from his excess weight, and he slid back into the icy water. Taking one step forward, he was hauled up short by the inability to move his foot. Just as quickly, it snapped loose as he jerked it upward, leaving his right boot behind in the death grip of muck trying to drag him back.

Cursing as he stepped on loose stones beneath his stocking feet, he tottered and managed to grab hold of a root sticking out from the overhang. Hand over hand he hauled himself up and out of the water. Scrambling up over the edge of the bank, he lost his balance only to fall face forward in the mud.

The years of pent-up rage exploded, and he slapped the ground, spraying mud all around him. All he'd ever wanted was for the pain to stop. For his dad to love him as much as he loved Mallory. To just once be the light of his father's pride like Geoff. He'd taken the blame for them all his life.

"What have I ever done to deserve any of this?" Eric bellowed at the top of his voice. Peals of thunder and flashes of lightning were the only answer to his rage-filled cry.

"The curse of the Lord is on the house of the wicked...the wicked... wicked." The scripture Travis had shared on the radio echoed with the reverberating thunder. *"It says, 'Shame shall be the legacy of fools'—be careful not to leave that kind of legacy to your children."*

Travis's gentle voice came to him, *"Isn't God awesome—look at the rest of the verse. God blesses the home of the just! He gives grace to the humble! No one has to leave a legacy of shame. If you are wise—if you turn to Him—you will inherit glory. His glory. Remember it is all God's doing, not ours. The key here is humility. A vulnerable heart. Because vulnerability—admitting the truth about ourselves, who we are, and what we have done to others and then agreeing with God about it—is the only way we can ever approach Him."*

Eric dropped his head toward the ground. He *was* a fool. And what kind of legacy did he have to leave to Lindsay and Marty? Look what he had already passed on to his son! A litany of accusations ravaged his mind. *Look at who you are! Look at what you have done! What kind of a person would do those things to his own sister? His own brother? Do you know what you are?*

"Go away!" Eric screamed at his tormentors, but they refused to leave, and no one came to his aid. He unleashed the full fury of his anger against the muddy riverbank. His fists pounded the gravel-laden ground, banging against rocks and roots. Years of tightly restrained guilt and fear unleashed tears of pain that mingled with the pouring rain as sobs tore at his throat. "Gran says You are there! Travis says You are a God who helps. . . . Well, where were You when my life was being shredded?"

Only the rumbling of thunder met his ears, infuriating him even more. "God! Answer me! What do You want from me? ANSWER ME! What do You want?"

"Truth."

Eric's head snapped up. He looked around, peering into the darkness for a form, a shape, a figure to go with the commanding voice. There was none. Chills fingered up and down his back.

"What truth? Whose truth?" The similarity of the conversation with Mallory on this very subject was more than eerie. It was downright unnerving.

"My truth."

The words filled the whole of his world and rumbled against the thunder echoing in the sky.

"What about Your truth?"

The images ripped violently through his mind, causing Eric's stomach to clench and churn before it finally emptied in one great upheaval. Shelly lying stark and unmoving in a puddle of bloody slush. A hand moving fast and furious toward his face. A belt whipping outward. Rage-filled fists and hate-filled thoughts toward his baby sister. Mallory tripping against his outturned boot. Her bloody lip. Shrieks of horror. Terror-filled eyes. Soft arms grasped in his hard, unyielding hands. Mallory's small, soft body beneath him as he threw her to the floor. The unrelenting kaleidoscope of scenes mercilessly inundated him. A chant of words took up residence in his soul. "A child abuser, a sexual offender. A rapist."

Visions too powerful to ignore flattened his will to move and threatened to bury him alive.

"God! No! I never did those things! It wasn't me! Make them stop! Make it stop!"

"Face the truth." The words hammered in rhythm with the images.

Eric slid back down the muddy bank and curled up in a ball in the icy water's edge as he was assaulted with the memories of who he was and what he had done. A whimpering sob escaped his lips. "Oh, God! What have I done? What have I done?" Tears poured as unrelenting as the rain. "I'm sorry. I am so—so sorry. What have I done?" He wrapped his arms around his head. "It won't go away. I can't fix it! I can't make it go away."

"You are right, Eric. You can't make it go away. No one can make what has happened go away. Only I can redeem what man has soiled. Only I can help you face your past. If you let Me, son, I can redeem the legacy of the fool you have been and give you an inheritance of My glory. But you have to let Me in.

"I can redeem it. If you let Me."

Eric lifted his eyes. The dark clouds were parting; dawn was lighting the eastern sky to a pearl gray.

Eric sobbed. "I don't know how to begin."

"I know you don't. But I do. It begins with acknowledging Me as greater than you. Take My hand. The process will be slow, but the glory will be worth it, son."

Pink and violet fingers branched through the breaking clouds, signaling the dawning of a brand-new day. Eric reached up to the fingering light and felt a hand pulling him back from the brink of hell.

Travis turned onto the unpaved road that would take him to his cabin. Not for the first time, he wondered how Eric had fared the night in an unfamiliar environment. Often throughout the night, he had an overwhelming desire to call his friend and just check in, but he had refrained. He didn't want to wake Eric up. The whole idea of getting away to the cabin was so Eric could unwind.

Besides, cell service was almost nonexistent on the mountain where his cabin was located. He did the next best thing. He prayed. All night long, his burdened heart rose to the Lord in petition for his friend, who was so close to the brink of either losing himself forever or finding himself completely. He prayed desperately that it would be the latter. Once more, he lifted his voice to the Lord, asking that He would pave the way for Travis to show Eric his need for a Savior. The tension that had dogged his heels ebbed from his soul, and a sweet peace coursed through him.

Travis raised his voice in praise even as he sipped his lukewarm coffee. He glanced at the dawn skies and watched as the sun rose gloriously above Wolvertine Mountain. He was thankful that the night's fierce storm had abated in the early predawn hours.

Singing at the top of his voice, Travis scanned the scenery around him and watched the dark murky waters of the swollen creek tumble along the side of the road. The sight of a red vehicle halted his words midsentence, and he tapped hard on the brakes.

Eric's Jeep Cherokee was halfway immersed in the middle of the swollen creek. A large boulder had stopped its headlong flight downriver. Its passenger side was shoved against the rock. Travis jumped from his GMC Jimmy.

"Eric!" He yelled at the top of his lungs as he slid down the side of the embankment and jumped to the nearest exposed rock. He couldn't see anybody inside, but that didn't mean anything. He wobbled his way across the rocks and scrambled up to the top of the one that held the Jeep captive. He peered into the windshield and slumped against the glass in pure relief. Eric wasn't there.

But where was he? Farther down the river? How did the Jeep get here? Eric was supposed to be in the cabin, and it was at least a quarter of a mile away from this creek. Questions consumed him.

He fought them off.

There was only one way to find out the answers. Travis scrambled back across the rocks and into his vehicle. He slammed it into gear. Travis rounded the last curve and found the drive leading to the cabin immersed in water. Thankfully, it looked like the water was already receding. Travis scanned the side of the creek, and his heart nearly exploded from his chest. He downshifted and jammed his foot on the brake pedal, spraying mud in all directions as he fishtailed to a stop.

He bolted from the vehicle. "Eric! Eric!"

Eric was lying face up on a rock beside the road. Slowly he sat up and stared at Travis. "Got here a little early, I'm glad to see."

Travis didn't know whether to laugh or cry. He slipped and slid to his friend's side. "Eric! Are you all right? What happened?"

"Wet and cold, but yes. I'm okay."

Travis inventoried his friend. Mud was drying in his hair. His soaked shirt and pants were filthy and torn. Streaks of dirt covered his cheeks, and there was a red welt just below his left eye. His knuckles were bruised and swollen.

"Oh man, you look wonderful! When I saw your Jeep in the river downstream, I was so scared." Travis hauled Eric to his feet and wrapped him in a bear hug before slapping him on the back.

"Oww. Easy."

"I'm sorry. Here." Travis opened the tailgate, yanked out a blanket, and wrapped it around his friend's shoulders. He looked down and back up into Eric's face. "What happened to your shoes?"

Eric looked down at his bare, dirty feet, and he laughed. "Same place as my Jeep. They were sacrificed to the murky depths of the water, and I expect they are nearly to Wheeling by now."

A joke? His friend must be in shock. No. His tone of voice wasn't the result of shock. It was the result of peace. *Peace?* Travis scrutinized his friend. Yes. It was definitely peace.

Travis opened the door, and Eric slid onto the seat and scooted until his back was against the other door. He tilted his head back to rest against the window and closed his eyes. "Now tell me," Travis implored. "What really happened out here last night?"

"So there you have it. All of it. Every sordid detail. So much of it I didn't even remember until last night, and I swear I never did those kinds of things again. I never hit my wife, and I never. . ." Eric paused then took in a shuddering breath. "I never touched my kids." He continued to stare past the front-seat headrest. Silence expanded around them. This was it. He wouldn't be surprised if his friend never spoke to him again.

"I believe you, Eric."

Eric tilted his head to glance at Travis. All he saw was compassion. He swallowed hard and looked down at his hands clenched in his lap. Once more silence descended between them until Eric broke it. "Do you hate me?"

"No."

"Good. I was afraid."

"That our friendship would be over? Give me a little more credit than that, Eric. I liked you before you accepted Jesus. You think I am going to walk away now that you have accepted the love of my heavenly Father? Think again, buddy. You got a long way to go, and I am going to make sure you get there successfully."

Eric turned and looked at his friend as a thought flashed through his head. He tried to keep the pain from his voice as he asked the question that had haunted him for so long. "Marty said something about not needing me anymore because he had a new dad." He swallowed hard against the tears that welled up in his throat. "Do you know anything about that?"

Travis smiled and patted Eric on the knee before handing him a cup of hot coffee. "I do. I believe you just met his new Father this morning, and He became yours as well."

Eric's eyes widened as flesh bumps rose on his arms. "Marty found God? I don't bel–" Eric stopped midsentence as the truth warmed his soul. "Amazing. My kid and me both finding our heavenly Father. There may be hope for us yet!" Eric's heart heard God speak to him again. *"Son, know this: no one is beyond the measure of My grace."*

"With God in control of your family and your life, there is more than hope. It's a sure thing." Travis clamped a hand on Eric's shoulder and spoke words Eric had longed to hear all his life. "I am so proud of you."

The words felt good, but Eric realized they didn't seem as important as they had once been. Eric drew in a deep breath. He finally knew in the depth of his heart that no one, not one person on the face of the earth, regardless of how evil he or she appears, is ever beyond the measure of God's grace. He looked up as a tear rolled unchecked onto his cheek. *Thank You, God, for never giving up on me.*

He had a new Father now—One who was in control of his future and had promised to reclaim his foolish past. Maybe he had the opportunity to change the legacy he left behind.

Somehow that was enough for the moment.

DISCUSSION GUIDE

The Legacy of Fools

Scripture: Proverbs 3:33–35 NKJV
*The curse of the Lord is on the house of the wicked,
but He blesses the home of the just. Surely He scorns the scornful,
but gives grace to the humble. The wise shall inherit glory,
but shame shall be the legacy of fools.*

Scripture references for further study: Psalm 14:1; Proverbs 17:21; Proverbs 12:15; Psalm 71:18; Psalm 145:4; Joel 1:3

What is a legacy?
What is the scriptural understanding of a fool?
What will be the spiritual inheritance of someone who says there is no God?

What legacy is Eric passing down to his children?
What specific spiritual inheritances did Martin give to Eric, to Geoff, and to Mallory?
What kinds of spiritual inheritances did Gramps and Gran hand down to Martin?

Do you see any legacies, either good or bad, handed down in your family?
What are they, and how have they influenced your life?
Where has shame colored your life?

Scripture: EXODUS 34:7 NKJV
*"Keeping mercy for thousands, forgiving iniquity and transgression
and sin, by no means clearing the guilty, visiting the iniquity
of the fathers upon the children and the children's children
to the third and the fourth generation."*

Scripture references for further study: EZEKIEL 18

*Note: A doctor recognizes that we genetically pass on our physical traits
and health issues, therefore they ask for a family history. Our families
have a spiritual history, too.*

Define generational curses.
Define generational blessings.
Is there a difference between a legacy and a generational curse and
    blessing?

Identify some generational blessings, or spiritual strengths, that
    Gramps and Gran have passed down through their family.
Identify some generational curses, or spiritual weaknesses, that
    have been passed down from Martin to Eric.
How do you see the generational curses being broken in the
    Bennington family?

What does your family's spiritual history look like? Strengths and
    weaknesses?
How far back can you trace it?
What specific curses and blessings are being handed to the future
    generation?

Scripture: 1 CORINTHIANS 4:5 NLT
So don't make judgments about anyone ahead of time—
before the Lord returns. For he will bring our darkest secrets to light
and will reveal our private motives. Then God will give
to each one whatever praise is due.

Scripture references for further study: MATTHEW 7:1–5; PSALM 96:13; PSALM 51:3–5; LUKE 6:35–38

Note: It's easy for us to judge offenders and want justice. However, we must remember that God is the ultimate judge, and He will judge everyone.

Define judgment.
How might identifying legacies and generational histories create a judgmental attitude?
How might identifying the same legacies and family histories create a less judgmental attitude?

How has Mallory's learning about her father's history changed her verdict of him?
How did Mallory's opinion of her brother change once she had all the evidence?
How did God's truth judge Mallory, and what was the end result of that judgment?

How has learning the truth of another person's story changed your verdict of them?
How have others judged you unfairly?
In what ways have you judged others unfairly?

Loving Your Enemy

Scripture: Luke 6:27–30 msg

*"To you who are ready for the truth, I say this: Love your enemies.
Let them bring out the best in you, not the worst. When someone gives
you a hard time, respond with the energies of prayer for that person.
If someone slaps you in the face, stand there and take it. If someone
grabs your shirt, giftwrap your best coat and make a present of it.
If someone takes unfair advantage of you, use the occasion to practice
the servant life. No more tit-for-tat stuff. Live generously."*

Scripture references for further study: Luke 6:31–36; Proverbs 10:12; Ephesians 5:2; 1 Peter 4:8

Describe an enemy.
What does loving an enemy look like?
Is it really possible to love an enemy?

Briefly describe some of the offenses done by the following characters:
Martin
Alecia
Eric
Marty
Catherine
Mallory
How did Eric bring out the best in Mallory?
By the end of the book, how had Eric learned to love his Father and himself?

How can you show love toward those who have offended you?
How have others shown you love when you didn't deserve it?
Is it possible for you to ever love (show mercy) to the one who hurt you the most?

Scripture: ACTS 26:17–18 NIV
*"I will rescue you from your own people and from the Gentiles.
I am sending you to them to open their eyes and turn them from
darkness to light, and from the power of Satan to God,
so that they may receive forgiveness of sins and a place
among those who are sanctified by faith in me."*

Scripture references for further study: MATTHEW 18:21–22;
MATTHEW 26:28; LUKE 7:47; EPHESIANS 4:32

Define forgiveness.

Is forgiveness a onetime shot or a process of release? Explain your
thinking.

Jesus said forgive and you will be forgiven. What might be His
point?

In *Love Me Back to Life*, Mallory believed she had forgiven Eric,
but we see in *Legacy of Fools* that she is still struggling with her
anger and wanting to get even.

Do you think Mallory has really forgiven Eric? Why or why not?

What did Mallory have to face before she was able to release Eric
into God's judging hands?

What had to happen to Eric before God's forgiveness poured over
him?

How have you voluntarily given up your right to lash back at
someone because he or she hurt you?

How did you work through the process of forgiveness? Or have
you?

How has it changed you?

*Note: At its most basic element, forgiveness is voluntarily giving up the
right to hurt someone for hurting you.*

Scripture: EPHESIANS 1:7 NLT
*He is so rich in kindness and grace that he purchased our freedom
with the blood of his Son and forgave our sins.*

Scripture references for further study: ROMANS 9:14–24; PSALM
130:7

Give a simple definition of redemption.

When you think of redeeming, what comes to mind?

Is there anyone who is beyond God's redemptive grace? Why or
why not?

Was there one character in the book that you did not want to see
redeemed?

Who and what did God use to break the foolishness of Eric's
pride?

How did God reach out to Marty?

Do you believe that your offender is beyond God's grace? Why or
why not?

In the deepest recesses of your heart, can you identify any person
that you believe is beyond God's ability to redeem? Why do
you believe that?

Do you believe you are beyond God's grace? Why or why not?

*So now there is no condemnation for those who belong to Christ Jesus.
And because you belong to him, the power of the life-giving Spirit has
freed you from the power of sin that leads to death.*
ROMANS 8:1–2 NLT

ABOUT THE AUTHORS

SUSAN STEVENS holds a Bachelors degree in Psychology and a Masters of Divinity from Ashland Theological Seminary. Her heart's passion is working with women in formational prayer. Susan lives and ministers in east central Ohio.

MISSY HORSFALL, a pastor's wife for over twenty years, is a board member and speaker for Circle of Friends Ministries, as well as the executive producer and radio host for the COF radio program. She and her husband live in Ohio and have three married children and three adorable granddaughters.

Circle of Friends Ministries, Inc., is a nonprofit organization established to build a pathway for women to come into a personal relationship with Jesus Christ and to build Christian unity among women. Our mission is to honor Jesus Christ through meeting the needs of women in our local, national, and international communities. Our vision is to be women who are committed to Jesus Christ, obediently seeking God's will and fulfilling our life mission as Christ-followers. As individuals and as a corporate group, we minister a Christ-centered hope, biblically based encouragement, and unconditional love by offering God-honoring, Word-based teaching, worship, accountability, and fellowship to women in a nondenominational environment through speaker services, worship teams, daily web blogs and devotionals, radio programs, and GirlFriends teen events.

COF also partners with churches and women's groups to bring conferences, retreats, Bible studies, concerts, simulcasts, and servant evangelism projects to their communities. We have a Marketplace Ministry teaching kingdom principles in the workplace and are committed to undergirding, with prayer and financial support, foreign mission projects that impact the world for Jesus Christ. Our goal is to evangelize the lost and edify the Body of Christ, by touching the lives of women—locally, nationally, and globally. For more information, visit www.circleoffriends.fm.

SPIRITUALITY FOR RELIGIOUS LIFE

Spirituality
for Religious Life

by
Robert Faricy, S.J.

PAULIST PRESS
New York / Paramus / Toronto

IMPRIMI POTEST
Silio Giorgi, S.J.
Rector, Pontificia Universitá Gregoriana
February 25, 1976

Copyright © 1976 by
The Missionary Society
of St. Paul the Apostle
in the State of New York

All rights reserved. No part of this book may be reproduced or transmitted in any form or by any means, electronic or mechanical, including photocopying, recording or by any information storage and retrieval system, without permission in writing from the Publisher.

Library of Congress
Catalog Card Number: 75-44594

ISBN: 0-8091-1932-3

Published by Paulist Press
Editorial Office: 1865 Broadway, N.Y., N.Y. 10023
Business Office: 400 Sette Drive, Paramus, N.J. 07652

Printed and bound in the
United States of America

Contents

To my mother

To my mother

Introduction

Spiritual theology is that branch of theology that studies practical Christian living. It is aimed not only at truth, but at practice, at the truth that is to be done, to be lived. A spiritual theology of the religious life, then, studies how the religious life is lived.

The subject of spiritual theology is not God but man; it studies man in a special way—in terms of his relationship with God. That is, it has in view man and man's world in the light of God's revelation to us in Jesus Christ. A spiritual theology of the religious life considers the religious, the world around him, and the life he is called to, in the light of the Lord who calls him.

What is important in the religious life is how that life is lived. It is a question of living, a question of conduct. But how we live depends on the values we hold; conduct is based on values. And values follow from meaning; I will hold those values whose meaning I can grasp. To see meaning, to understand, means to see how things fit together. This is what spiritual theology does. It tries to express meaning.

This book is an attempt to express in words the meaning of the religious life. Since the religious life is, fundamentally, a mystery—the mystery of a personal call by God—any effort to formulate its meaning is necessarily inadequate. A mystery, after all, is some-

1

thing that we can know more and more about but never understand fully. Nevertheless, we do have a need for understanding, a need to see meaning. And that is the purpose of this book: to help men and women religious to formulate for themselves a better understanding of their life so that they can grasp more firmly the values that they hold, and so live the religious life in a more aware and a more productive way.

Much of the material presented here has been published, sometimes in a different form, in *Spiritual Life, Review for Religious, The American Ecclesiastical Review, UISG Journal,* and *The Way.*

1
Prayer

A theological approach to prayer can never be abstract. Prayer is the one theological topic that, in the whole Christian tradition, has always been written about in the concrete terms of the writer's own experience. For example, the classic theologians of prayer, John of the Cross, Teresa of Avila, Ignatius Loyola, and the great contemporary writer, Thomas Merton, have all written about prayer out of their own experience. There is no other way to speak theologically about prayer, and so, although I hope that these ideas will be generally useful, I will necessarily be reflecting on my own experience.

Personal Relationship with Christ

The place to begin reflecting on anything in the religious life is with what is most important and most central in the religious life. What is most central in the life of a religious is his or her personal relationship with Jesus Christ. Everything else hinges on that, depends on that personal relationship with Christ. Other relationships, with community, with work, with lay people, are important, but relationship with Jesus

3

Christ is of central importance. It is true, too, that my relationship with the Lord will be conditioned by many things—by my community, by my apostolate, by my temperament. Still, that relationship is central and everything else depends on it. To the extent that I am a mature religious, my relationship with the other members of my community, with persons outside the community, with my work or my studies—all these relationships will be sustained, brought together, and integrated by my personal relationship with Our Lord. Theologically, the religious life makes sense only if personal relationship with Christ is central. And, at the practical level, the religious life can be lived happily only when personal relationship with Our Lord is made central, given priority of importance, put first.

This is true because of the very nature of the religious life. It has often been said that the religious life is a state of perfection. It is more accurate to say that it is a covenant. The word "covenant" comes from the Old Testament, where God is in covenant with His people Israel. He is their God. He takes care of them and guides them. Israel, in turn, is called to be committed to God, to be His people. A covenant, then, is an interpersonal relationship in which persons give themselves to one another. It differs from a contract; according to a contract persons give something—money, for example—in return for something else, such as services or merchandise. But in a covenant, it is the persons themselves who are involved in the exchange. Friendship is a covenant. Marriage is a still deeper kind of covenant. In the religious life, a person is in covenant with God who, in and through Christ, calls that person to a special relationship with Himself. A religious is in covenant with Christ. This covenantal relationship with

Jesus Christ is the heart and the center of the religious life.

It is possible to have the attitude that what is most important in the religious life is keeping the law or the rule. If I put law at the center of my life, I am a legalist. True religious life is not legalism; it is not centered on the law or on rules; it is centered on Christ.

It is also possible to think that knowledge is what is most important in the religious life, that I am saved by what I know. I may think that what is most important in my life is education, or the knowledge that will make me professionally competent, or, perhaps, knowledge of the new theology. It is according to the nature of the religious life, however, that it is not primarily a life of learning but a life of personal union with Christ.

The fact that the religious life is based on interpersonal relationship with Our Lord is, furthermore, what distinguishes the religious life from magic. The religious life is not a magical routine that we go through in order to control God. God is not an object, and He cannot be manipulated. The religious life is not a union with God in which God is considered to be a powerful force to be controlled and manipulated. It is, rather, a union of persons, a union in which God is met on personal terms. It is true, of course, that God hears and answers our prayers. But this is not because our prayers have some magical effect and make God do what we want Him to do. Prayer is effective not because it is magic but because God hears us lovingly and, in His concern for our needs, answers our prayers.

It is, then, Our Lord who should come first in my life, not the law, and not knowledge, and not some kind of magic. What saves me is not union with law, or union with knowledge, or an impersonal union with

God that treats God as an object. What saves me is personal union with God in and through union with Jesus Christ. What is more, it is this interpersonal union with the Lord that is the main source of my personal growth and development. Modern psychology has shown us that persons grow and develop as persons only through interaction with other persons. Union of persons personalizes. I can see this, for example, in friendship. To the extent that a friendship is well-ordered and appropriate, then the friends, far from losing their identities, grow as persons precisely in function of the friendship. In marriage, too, to the extent that the marriage is based on love and sacrifice, husband and wife develop as persons not in spite of the lived out marriage union but because of that union. Husband and wife, in going out of themselves to each other, find themselves in each other and grow as persons. The fact that union personalizes is above all true of the union of the religious with God. The primary love relationship in the life of a religious is relationship with God, and this relationship is personalizing; it is the principal source of personal development.

The Condition of Personal Relationship with God

Since what is central and most important in the religious life is personal relationship with God, I can ask this question: What is the *condition* of personal relationship with God? What must I do to be in personal contact with God? What condition, being present, will mean that I am encountering God in a personal way? The condition of personal relationship with God is prayer. By "prayer" I mean *relational* prayer. I do not mean solitary reflection, or just reading and thinking; I mean a reaching out to God, a lifting of the heart and the mind to God. Prayer is necessary for personal relationship with God. The reason for this is that interpersonal relationship with God follows the general laws of interpersonal relationship. This means that my union with God must be conscious—that is to say, that it must be prayerful. And, as in any loving relationship between persons, union with God calls for communication and affectivity and spontaneity or a certain being-at-home-with-God. It requires sharing; I should bring my concerns and worries and preoccupations to Our Lord. Union with God also, like any positive relationship between persons, requires trust. Trust is especially necessary in encounter with God because it is an encounter that takes place in the obscurity of faith. All these—communication, affectivity, spontaneity, sharing, trust—add up to prayer. What is more, no interpersonal relationship can endure without sacrifice, perseverance, and discipline; so these too are needed in my prayer life.

The Conditions of Prayer

What is central in the religious life is personal relationship with God. And what is central in personal relationship with God is prayer. This leads to an investigation of the conditions of prayer. What is necessary for prayer? What are the conditions of prayer? I would like to consider prayer according to four aspects or elements of prayer. I want to consider prayer first as fidelity to God, secondly as openness or attentiveness to God, then as response to God's love, and, finally, as loving relationship.

What is the condition of prayer considered as an expression of fidelity to God? The condition of prayer as fidelity is simply spending the time and the effort. That I put in the time and the effort is certainly not sufficient; there is much more to prayer than that. Nevertheless, it is *necessary* that I spend the time and the effort; otherwise, there can be no prayer at all. In fact, there is no personal commitment to anyone or to anything without spending time. If I am committed to a person I spend time with that person. If I am committed to a project, I put in time on the project. Without time and effort, there is no commitment. When I put time and effort into prayer I am, by that very fact, saying to God and to myself that my relationship with Him is important. If I put time for prayer in first place, and—although I might miss lunch—I do not miss Mass or mental prayer, then I am saying effectively that personal relationship with Our Lord is more important to me than anything else; I am saying that He is central in my life. The truth of the religious life is not a truth to be simply spoken; it is a truth to be done. It is not enough to think or to say that God is central in my life; I must live that out; and I cannot live it out without putting prayer first on my list of priorities. Spending time and effort in prayer is the condition of prayer in its aspect of fidelity to God.

What is the condition of prayer as openness to God, as listening, as attentiveness? It is that I see myself as needing God. I have to understand myself as needy, as poor in a radical sense, as insufficient of myself. This is the lowliness that Mary talks about in the Magnificat: He has looked upon the lowliness of His handmaid. . . . He has exalted the lowly. I have to see myself as needing Our Lord. The condition of prayer as openness to God is that I be humble, that I make myself small and like a little child. This humility further requires that I face my own sinfulness; I have to accept myself as a sinner. I must understand and accept my sinfulness and see myself as someone who needs Our Lord. I can be helped to accept myself and my own frailty and neediness and sinfulness by the knowledge that God accepts me. In fact, my very weakness and sinfulness are His opening to me; my neediness is part of what makes me attractive to Him. He did not come to save the just but sinners. It often happens in families with several children, where one of the children is retarded, that the retarded child is given special love. The retarded child is often the most loved child in the family, not in spite of the fact that he is retarded but partly because of that very fact. We are God's retarded children. It is true that each of us is needy. Each of us is something of a mess, disorganized in many ways, sometimes coming apart. The very fact that I am a sinner, weak, needing Our Lord, is part of what attracts Him to me. So I can, like Saint Paul, glory in my infirmities, for God's strength is made perfect in weakness. I can, furthermore, face my own sinfulness with hope in Our Lord. Our Lord is the Savior, sent to save sinners. It is He who will pull me together and knit up the unraveled fibers of my existence. He will integrate me, give me integrity, make me whole. There are some who think that God loves them to the extent that they are perfect; that is not true. God's love for each of us is a love that accepts each of us unconditionally, just as we are. I want, then, to realize my need for God's saving love; this realization is the condition of prayer considered as openness to God. Without this lowliness, this humility, this acceptance of my own neediness, I will not be able to be open and attentive to God in prayer.

What is the condition of prayer as response to God's love for me? The condition of prayer as response is freedom. I can make a positive and loving response to another person only to the extent that I am free. What is necessary for prayer is that I be free from whatever would lead me away from Our Lord or would block me off from Him. This is a matter of detachment. I should not, of course, be detached from everything. On the contrary, I want to be attached to God, to my vocation, to my community, to helping others. But I must be free from inordinate attachments, free from any attachment to a person, thing, activity, or situation that tends to lead me away from God. These inordinate attachments are real obstacles to prayer. If I am attached to something and giving in to that attachment, my relationship with Our Lord will be hurt. I will not be free to respond to Him in prayer. My mind will be distracted by my attachment, and my heart will not be free. A common example of an inordinate attachment is this: I may be very attached to the approval of other people. I may have an inordinate attachment to praise and esteem and appreciation. I may have a great need for attention, or a need to be popular, or a need not to be criticized. Such an attachment will block me in my prayer. To the degree that I am attached to narcissistic feedback from other persons, to that degree I will lack freedom. I need, then, to recognize my attachment, to try to not act in such a way as to gratify my narcissism, and so work out my freedom. I may always have strong narcissistic tendencies, but I can learn not to give in to them and so be free to respond to God in prayer.

What is the condition of prayer as loving rela-

tionship? That prayer be a loving relationship it is necessary that it be simple. Simplicity is the condition that
prayer be an intimate loving relationship. It is not necessary to have an elaborate method for prayer. A complicated mental process is more of a hindrance than a
help. There are persons who spend almost the whole
time in their daily mental prayer reading, then applying
what they have read to their own life, then reading
more, then applying more, but without ever talking to
God or simply being with Him in His presence. Psycho-
logists say that the appropriate behavior for an adult in
an intimate love relationship is child-like behavior. The
intimate love relationship in the life of a religious, by
the very nature of the religious life, is with God. We
should be like children with God, simple and direct and
trusting. We can go simply to God, be there with Him,
share our worries and concerns and problems with
Him, ask for help, tell Him how we feel, thank Him for
His love, and try to love Him back. Prayer should not
be complicated. Sometimes reading can be helpful in
prayer, but what is read should never be the focus of
prayer. In prayer, my attention should be directed toward God; reading is a means to help me be in a loving
personal relationship with God.

The condition of prayer as fidelity is spending the
daily time and effort. The condition of prayer as
openness to God is humility. The condition of prayer as
response is freedom. And the condition of prayer as
loving relationship is simplicity.

Obstacles to the Spirit of Prayer

I would like to conclude these reflections by men-
tioning two dangers to the spirit of prayer in the reli-

gious life. First, there is always the possibility and the danger that I will not put first things first, that I will not put prayer in first place in my life. If I am to maintain a personal relationship with God, then prayer must have the priority over all my other activities. A religious is a person who puts all his or her eggs in one basket. That basket is personal relationship with God, and prayer is the condition of that relationship. One temptation, then, that has to be resisted is the temptation not to put first things first.

The second danger, the second temptation, is a greater and more subtle one. It is the temptation to dishonesty. Hypocrisy has always been a problem in the religious life; hypocrisy is, since the scribes and the Pharisees and probably before, the besetting temptation of professionally religious people. To pretend to be something that one is not—this kind of hypocrisy will always be a problem for religious. I am, however, thinking of a new dishonesty in the religious life, a dishonesty that has in recent years become a serious danger to the spirit of prayer in the religious life. I can consider this new dishonesty from the point of view of changes in the religious life. In general, there is much more freedom in the religious life than in the past. Religious are freer with regard to the permissions they need, with regard to choosing studies and jobs, with regard to many other things, and in particular with regard to prayer. This new freedom is, of course, good; it brings with it new possibilities of religious maturity and of growth in the religious life. New freedom also brings new responsibility. And where there is more responsibility there is the greater possibility of not taking responsibility, of making compromises—especially compromises regarding prayer. In other words, because

I have more freedom with regard to when and where I pray, it is easier for me to compromise. It is then possible to justify dishonestly the compromise so that I will not feel guilty. And it is precisely this dishonesty that is the problem.

I may, for example, gradually cut down on time for mental prayer and finally practically omit a daily extended time for mental prayer. If I make this compromise, I will feel guilty; I know that daily mental prayer is a necessity in the religious life, and that I should be doing it. Feeling guilty is uncomfortable, and so, in order not to feel guilty, I may try to justify my compromise. I may say to myself, "I am very busy; my work takes a lot of time; I don't have time for mental prayer. Furthermore, I don't get anything out of it. Besides that, why should I sit in chapel and talk to myself when I can be helping others and doing some good in the world? Anyway, this is the post-Vatican II age of incarnationalism and secularity and involvement in the world. Christ is important, but I find Christ in my brothers and sisters." This line of thinking is, of course, dishonest. I know I should make mental prayer, but I have talked myself out of feeling guilty because I do not.

After a while, since my justification of my compromise is flimsy, it will begin to shake. I may try to shore up my dishonest justification by making converts. So I may say to you, "If you make daily mental prayer, that's all right. That's your way. I find I don't need it myself. I find Christ in others. After all, this is the age of incarnationalism and secularity and involvement in the world." By speaking in this way, I have sown a seed of doubt in your mind. You may say to yourself, "He's a good religious, and yet he doesn't need daily mental prayer. Maybe I'm old-fashioned or conservative." The problem here is that I have been dishonest in justifying my compromise, and I have spread that dishonesty through subtly trying to make a convert.

There is a new dishonesty in the religious life that justifies disobedience in the name of freedom, that justifies defection from the religious life in the name of self-fulfillment, that justifies worldliness in the name of being relevant and, most importantly, that justifies compromises in the area of prayer. It is certainly not freedom that is dangerous, nor change, nor increased responsibility. It is a new dishonesty that makes compromises and that dishonestly justifies those compromises.

Our Lord loves me and calls me to close personal relationship with Himself. All He asks is that I take Him seriously and that I try to live my life honestly in terms of His love for me and my response to that love.

2
Faith and Integration

What is the relationship between Christian faith and everyday activity? How are these two related, my faith and my ordinary experience? Granted that faith is at least a part of my experience, how can it become a more important dimension of all my experience? To put the problem a little differently: How can prayer and other activity be integrated? How can I integrate my non-prayer activity into my relationship with God, and so make my whole life a prayer? What is the value of my work, community life, mundane activities, in terms of my relationship with God?

The "Upward" and the "Forward"

Religious today are often torn in two directions. On the one hand, they believe in God, worship Him, want to respond to His love; they take their faith seriously, and they take God seriously as personal. On the other hand, they also believe in their family, their friends, their work, the world around them; they believe in man, in man's capacity to build a better world, and in human progress, especially as these broad concepts are concretized in the particular circumstances of their

own lives. And this is the problem. There is, in the life
of many religious, an "upward" component of faith in
God, of worship, of adoration and love for God. There
is, also, a "forward" component of faith in the people
around one, in one's work, in the whole human enterprise in general and, in particular, in one's place in
that enterprise. Both of these sectors seem important.
Both directions, the "upward" and the "forward," seem
good and deserving of all man's efforts and dedication.
But they seem to be two different directions. This problem is met and handled differently by different people.
Some simply forget about God, at least for the most
part, and give themselves entirely to the "forward."
Others, a very few, use religion as an escape from the
world around them, and try to give themselves entirely
to the "upward." Most, however, try to go in both directions at once. This is not easy. It results in a kind of
compartmentalized living, where one part of everyday
life is given to God in times of prayer and worship, and
the rest is lived to some extent on a simply natural
level.[1]

   This common enough situation, being torn between
the vertical and the horizontal, between faith in God
and faith in the world, is intrinsically unstable. Even if,
in order to cope with the conflict, I organize my life
into compartments, there will remain a nagging sense
of a lack of unity. And I may, for example in a time of
dryness in prayer, tend simply to give up on prayer; not
finding satisfaction in the "upward," I may reduce that
impulse to simply formalistic observances and seek all
my real satisfaction and happiness in the "forward."
Or, I may feel that my ordinary work is always at the
level of a spiritual encumbrance; in spite of the practice
of right intentions and the "morning offering," time

spent in ordinary duties can seem to be just time taken away from prayer and adoration.

And yet the constant teaching of the Church has always been that faith should permeate all of life, that the Christian faith commitment gives the key to the on-going experience of a new life, that faith should have an all-pervasive coloration—like the experience of love. The question is not, then, whether the synthesis between the "upward" and the "forward" can or should be made, but how to make it. It is a question of practice, of living out a synthesis between the two faiths. But to live out this synthesis, an understanding of how the two faiths fit together is necessary. Practice must be based on understanding. So the question is now: How can faith and everyday experience be understood as integrated? How can I *see* the intrinsic relationship between the "upward" and the "forward"?[2] This is a matter of how I view reality.

What is needed is a faith view of reality, a faith view that works, that is operational—a view of reality in terms of which faith in God and faith in the world can be lived out in synthesis. The question can be put simply: How can I understand myself and the world around me in terms of my faith in God?

Faith as Relationship

In order to see myself and the world around me more in the light of my faith in God, I can begin by trying to deepen my understanding of what faith is. It is true that faith involves intellectual assent; faith is a supernatural virtue by which we assent to all the truths that God has revealed, accepting those truths on God's authority. However, faith is something more than assent to truth. As the word is used in the New Testament and generally in contemporary theological writing, "faith" has a more profound and richer meaning that includes, but goes beyond, intellectual assent. In the gospels, for example, and especially in Saint John's gospel, Jesus invites men to have faith in Him. This faith is a believing and also a hoping and loving adherence to the person of Jesus recognized as Savior. It is an affirmative response to God's invitation, the acceptance of God's saving love present for men in Jesus. Faith is the acceptance of Jesus as Savior, a response to Him, and an adherence to Him. This faith is not just an act or an initial commitment, nor is it a series of acts; it is an enduring relationship.

The faith relationship between the Christian and Jesus Christ is the fundamental and central relationship of Christian living. It is this relationship that organizes and sustains and gives deeper meaning to all the other relationships in the life of the Christian. And it is the faith relationship with Jesus Christ that is the principle of synthesis of faith in God and faith in the world. It is this relationship between the Christian and Jesus that is the integrating factor in daily life.

The reason that personal relationship with Jesus Christ is the synthesizing factor that integrates dedication to God and involvement in the world is this: God is present to man in Jesus, and this same Jesus is He in whom all things have been created, He in whom the world is centered and holds together. This raises two new questions: What is meant here by "world," and—most importantly—what is the basis and the meaning of the statement that the world holds together in and is centered on Jesus Christ?

Christ and the World

The two great theologians of the New Testament, Saint John and Saint Paul, although their expressions differ, both teach the same doctrine concerning the relation of the world to Jesus Christ. The world, as well as everything in it, depends on Christ for its existence, its harmony, and its meaning.

Saint John, in his gospel, identifies Jesus as the creative word of God of the Old Testament. In the first chapter of Genesis, God creates by His word; He speaks and things come to be. "God said, 'Let there be light,' and there was light."[3]

> By the word of Yahweh
> the heavens were made. . . .
> He spoke, and it was created;
> He commanded, and there it stood.[4]

God's word, furthermore, is sent for a purpose and does God's will.[5] It is a word that saves those who are in trouble.[6] In the prologue to John's gospel, the word is seen to be the Word.

> In the beginning was the Word;
> the Word was with God
> and the Word was God. . . .
> Through Him all things came to be,
> not one thing had its being but through Him.
> All that came to be had life in Him.[7]

This Word of God has become flesh and come among men so that, through men's faith response to Him, men —and through men the world—might be brought back

to the Father. Jesus has come to save the world that has
its existence in and through Him. In this way, just as it
was in and through Him that the Father started the
world in the beginning, so it is in and through Him that
God's work is being brought to completion.

This same teaching is presented by Saint Paul,
especially in the epistles of his captivity, by the use of
the metaphor of the body. Just as Christ is the head of
the Church, which is His body, so too—in a different
way—Christ is the head of the whole world, and the
world is His body.[8] As in John's gospel, all that exists
comes from God through Christ and remains in existence through Him.[9] God's plan from the beginning has
been to bring everything under Christ as head,[10] for
Christ is the ruler of everything and He fills the whole
creation.[11] All things have been created in Christ, and
through Him and for Him, and He holds everything in
unity.[12] Not only do all things exist in Christ, but it is
God's plan that "all plenitude be found in Him and that
all things be reconciled through Him and for Him."[13]
In Saint Paul's perspective, everything is seen as somehow suspended from the risen Christ, and everything
finds its existence and meaning and value in Him. And
so the world itself, begun in Christ, will—somehow—be
saved in Him; even now the whole world is groaning
toward its salvation.[14]

For both Saint John and Saint Paul, there is a certain mutuality between God and the world, a mutuality
that is in, and because of, Jesus Christ. God is not aloof
from the world, indifferent to it; on the contrary, He is
committed to the world for He is its Creator, and He is
profoundly involved in His creation through the incarnation. The world and all that is in it is of the highest
importance to God.

Yes, you love all that exists,
you hold nothing of what you have made in abhor-
rence.
For had you hated anything, you would not have
formed it.
And how, had you not willed it, could a thing per-
sist,
how be conserved if not called forth by you?
You spare all things because all things are yours,
Lord, lover of life,
you whose imperishable spirit is in all.[15]

What is more, because it holds together in Jesus
Christ, the world can be understood in personal terms.
The world is personalized by being anchored in the Person of Jesus. Sometimes theology speaks of a "cosmic
Christ," but the fact is that it is not Christ who is cosmic but the cosmos, the whole world, that is Christic, in
Christ. I can, then, be involved in the world precisely in
terms of my personal involvement with Jesus. I can
love the world and love Christ without going in two directions at once. The God of the "upward" is, at the
same time, the God of the "forward." In Him in whom
all things have been created to find their fulfillment, I—
together with all I am and all I do—can be brought
together, integrated, and find my own fulfillment.

Two Other Religious Understandings

This understanding of the relationship between
God and the world in Jesus Christ can be made clearer
by contrasting it with two quite different under-
standings of the God-world relationship: the Lutheran

doctrine of the two kingdoms, and pantheism. In Martin Luther's theology of the two kingdoms, the kingdom of Christ and the kingdom of the world are seen as in tension, in some kind of opposition, in antithesis. There is the same antithetical tension between God's rule of power in the world and His rule of grace through the gospel, between the Church and the world, and between the order of creation and the order of salvation. And there is a presupposed tension between faith and mundane experience, between prayer and action, between the "upward" and the "forward." There is much that is positive in the two-kingdom view of reality, but it leaves little place for synthesis between faith in God and faith in the world.[16]

In the view presented in the preceding section of this chapter, on the other hand, the kingdom of God and the kingdom of the world are seen as integrated in the kingdom of Christ. There is no opposition or antithesis; rather, God and the world are united in a certain mutuality in Jesus Christ, and the possibility of a lived integration between faith in God and faith in the world exists.

Another common religious world view is that of pantheism, the belief that God and the world are identical, that God is not only everywhere but everything. Pantheism is the basic belief of several religions of the Far East. Pantheistic religions always have a great reverence for the world, for they consider it to be divine. The pantheistic insight is that God is everywhere and that He is more interior to the world than the world is to itself, more interior to things and to persons than they are to themselves. This, of course, is true. But pantheism overlooks God's creativity.

To create means to make exist in its own right.

God, the Creator, holds the world and all in it in existence; He makes it to be. And in causing the world to be, He causes it to be—not Himself—but itself. This is what it means to create. Whatever God causes to be, creates, He takes to Himself; and in taking it to Himself He causes it to be itself, grants it autonomy. God has created the world, holds it in existence, and takes it to Himself in His Son, Jesus Christ.[17] God and the world are not to be identified but, rather, distinguished in their union. Just as the divine nature and the human nature of Jesus are united in one person but remain distinct, so—analogously—God and the world are united in and through Jesus Christ, but they remain distinct. Because God and the world are distinct, we can distinguish the sacred and the secular, Church and state, worship and work, the "upward" and the "forward." And because God and the world are intimately united, we can understand and try to live a union in faith between those interests and activities that refer directly to God (the sacred) and those that refer to Him through the world (the secular), a synthesis between the "upward" and the "forward," an integration between faith in God and faith in the world.

Prayer and Integration

The question still remains: Granted that an understanding of faith of how God and the world are united in Jesus Christ makes it possible to see *that* Christian faith and ordinary experience can be integrated, *how* can this integration be brought about? How can my faith be an important element, not just in my prayer, but in all my experience, a dimension of my whole life?

How can all that I am, all my activities, all my relationships, be brought together, integrated, lived out along the central axis of my faith relationship with Christ? This integration takes place for the most part in prayer.

If the core of Christian living is personal relationship with Jesus Christ, then the condition of that relationship, its foundation and its heart, is prayer. My relationship with Jesus is most personal and most direct when I am most fully given to that relationship as such, and this is when I am at prayer. It is ordinarily when I am at prayer that I am most open to the healing action of God's love for me. And so it is particularly at prayer that God's love for me, present to me in Christ, pulls me together, knits up the various poorly organized parts of myself, makes me more one, gives me integralness, integrity. When I am most present to the Lord in prayer, I am most being made whole.

This is why it is so important in prayer to be as completely present to God as possible, facing God from where—as it were—I am standing at that given moment, with all my emotions, attitudes, problems, and preoccupations at that particular time. Distractions in prayer have a serious importance here; they indicate what is on my mind, what my concerns and cares and worries are, and they provide an occasion for me to bring those cares to the Lord and to put them in His hands. The content of a distraction—what it is that distracts me—is something that remains, at least to some extent, unintegrated into my relationship with God. If it were integrated into that relationship, it would not be a distraction. I can bring the matter of the distraction into my prayer, pray about it, ask the Lord's help, refer the person or the problem concerned to Him. In this way, in my prayer, with the help of God's grace, I will be, gradually and increasingly, synthesizing my Christian faith and my everyday experience.

The most important prayer is the Mass. It is above all by participation in the Mass that I encounter God present in me and for me in Jesus Christ in such a way that my life becomes unified. The Eucharist is the sacrament of unification; it brings the individual person together. And it brings persons together, uniting them in Christ. It is, furthermore, at Mass that the opportunity is present to offer all my daily activities, together with myself, to God at the offertory, together with the bread and the wine. The bread, which "human hands have made," and the wine, "work of human hands," in the words of the offertory prayer, are the symbol of each person participating in the Mass and of each person's work, efforts, concerns, problems. The bread and wine stand for me and my involvement in the world around me. All of this, symbolized by the bread and wine, is offered to God at the offertory. At the consecration, the transubstantiation of the bread and wine into the body and blood of Christ symbolizes the transformation of my daily activities in Christ. And at the Communion, Christ makes what has been symbolized real by actively uniting all that I am and do to Him. It is in a special and profound way at Mass that the "upward" and the "forward" components of my life are brought together in synthesis.[18]

NOTES

1. See Pierre Teilhard de Chardin, "The Heart of the Problem," *The Future of Man*, tr. N. Denny (New York, 1964), pp. 260-269; "What the World Is Looking For from

the Church of God at This Moment," *Christianity and Evolution*, tr. R. Hague (New York, 1969), pp. 212-220.

2. For a treatment of a different but closely related problem, see Sr. Catherine McIntyre, R.J.M., "Man's Experience of Insignificance and the Christian Response," *Spiritual Life*, 18 (1972), 24-26.

3. Genesis 1, 3.

4. Psalm 33, 6 and 9.

5. Isaiah 55, 10-11; Ecclesiasticus 42, 15; Wisdom 9, 1-3.

6. Psalm 107, 20.

7. John 1, 1-4.

8. See H. Schlier, "The Pauline Body-Concept," *The Church*, edited at Canisianum, Innsbruck (New York, 1963), pp. 44-58.

9. 1 Corinthians 8, 6.

10. Ephesians 1, 10.

11. Ephesians 1, 23.

12. Colossians 1, 17.

13. Colossians 1, 19.

14. Romans 8, 18-25.

15. Wisdom 11, 21-27. Robert Farrar Capon writes, "The world exists by the divine *applause*, by means of the intimate and immediate delight that God has in the sons of men and in the being of everything that is. . . . He keeps it on his person, because he will not get its delight out of his system": "The Secular and the Sacred," *The Sacred and the Secular*, ed. Michael J. Taylor, S.J. (Englewood Cliffs, 1968), p. 177.

16. On the two-kingdom doctrine in contemporary theology, see especially Gerhard Ebeling, *Word and Faith*, tr. J. Leitch (Philadelphia, 1963), pp. 386-406; Heinrich Bornkamm, *Luther's Doctrine of the Two Kingdoms*, tr. K. Hertz (Philadelphia, 1966); Carl E. Braaten, *The Future of God* (New York, 1969), pp. 145-152.

17. See J.-B. Metz, "A Believer's Look at the World," *The Christian and the World*, tr. H. Wansbrough, O.S.B., edited at Canisianum, Innsbruck (New York, 1965), pp. 68-100; *Theology of the World*, tr. W. Glen-Doepel (London, 1969), pp. 13-55.

18. See Pierre Teilhard de Chardin, "My Universe," *Science and Christ*, tr. R. Hague (New York, 1968), pp. 64-66; "Introduction to the Christian Life," *Christianity and Evolution, op. cit.*, pp. 165-167.

3
Love

The purpose of this chapter is to help toward a better understanding of the meaning and place of love in the religious life. The method used here is one of reflecting at three different and connected levels on the meaning of love: (1) the natural or common sense level, (2) the level of Christian theology—the meaning of love as revealed to us by Christ, (3) the level of the theology of the religious life—what is the meaning and place of love in the context of the religious vocation?

The Natural or Common Sense Level

Only Jesus Christ has fully revealed to us what love is, what the word "love" really means, but we can make some preliminary observations at a natural or common sense level. We observe immediately that love is relational. Even love of self is relational to one's self. Ordinarily, however, love includes a going-out-of-one's-self in the direction of the other person. This relation of love can be of two basic kinds. First; there is a love that finds its delight in the possession of the person loved; its pleasure or happiness is in being with and possessing the person who is the object of love. This is a love that

27

looks for self-fulfillment through possession of the person who is loved. Secondly, there is a love that finds its delight in the delight of the person loved, that finds its pleasure or happiness in the pleasure, welfare, or happiness of the person who is the object of love. This is a love that gives itself away, a self-giving love, a love of benevolence. Usually, of course, the two are mixed. So, although it is true that all love, at least in its unconscious roots, is selfish in the sense that it is ultimately rooted in self-interest, nevertheless—in its manifestations—love can be observed to be possessive love or benevolent love or a mixture of both. Love in its manifestations is seen to be either centripetal (taking in, possessive), or centrifugal (outgoing, benevolent), or both together, mixed.[1]

A second observation is that love tends to unite people, to bring persons together "not superficially and tangentially, but center to center."[2] Love is an affective bond between persons precisely as persons; it is "the bond that draws together and unites persons among themselves."[3] It is true that people can be joined together by many things and by many feelings; people may be unified through fear, in anger, for business and mutual usefulness, or simply physically juxtaposed in the way that people on the same bus are united; but love unites persons "center to center," in a way that is more personal than other kinds of union.

A third observation is that when persons are united by love, then the persons find personal growth and fulfillment as a function of the union. Union in love personalizes. In a friendship, for example, the persons united grow and develop as persons precisely in function of the friendship, in function of the mutual support of the friendship. Again, in marriage, to the extent that the marriage is based on love, husband and wife do not lose individual identity by being united; rather, each finds his or her own identity in a fuller way precisely in terms of the union.[4]

Finally, love has an enduring quality. We do not refer to a passing feeling or emotion as love; love is a more or less permanent relation. As a result, because it is necessarily involved in a long-term process, love requires faithfulness, fidelity. Love demands at least some amount of sacrifice and renunciation of self. For example, a truly benevolent love, a love that finds its happiness in the happiness of the person loved and that has real care and concern for that person, may require the sacrifice of the gratification of the desire to possess the person one loves. Sometimes love is manifested most in "letting the other person go," as in the case of possessive parents who let their children grow up and finally leave home.

The Level of Christian Theology

God's revelation in Christ goes beyond what common sense and observation can tell us about love; reflection on Christ's teaching about love leads to a deeper and more profound understanding of what love is.[5] The teaching of Jesus is that God is our Father. He has loved us first. Love is relational, and the most important relation of love is the love with which God loves us. God's love for us is the presupposition of our love for Him and for one another. This is why we have value and can have an appropriate love for ourselves and for one another: because God so loves us that He has sent His only Son to save us.[6]

Jesus teaches us, also, that love and unity and being his disciples all go together.[7] Christians are, in fact, one in Christ; we should therefore be one in thought and in deed because we are already one in fact. The sacrament of the Eucharist is the pledge of God's love for us and at the same time the sacrament of our unity with God and with one another in Christ.

If union of love personalizes and helps persons to grow and develop, then this is above all true of loving union with God. God not only loves each one of us but He loves each one with a respect for the individual person and for that person's freedom.[8] In fact, His love creates our freedom. God is Creator, and His love, therefore, makes things to be themselves. The error of pantheism is to think that since God is so interior to persons the persons are God. Pantheism lacks appreciation for God's creativity. God, in His love for us, is so interior to us that He makes us not Himself but ourselves; His loving action in us is what gives us our personal autonomy, our freedom as persons. This creative love of God for us is especially present in Jesus, and this fact is brought out in a number of ways in the New Testament.[9] For example, in the sixth chapter of John's gospel, Jesus speaks of Himself as the Bread of Life; He says that if anyone believes in Him that person will have life in Him and even eternal life. The point is that believing in Jesus, accepting God's love for us in Jesus, and trying to respond to that love by adhering to the person of Jesus will give us life, will give us nourishment and growth and development as persons. This is why prayer is so important. The principal source of our development as persons is loving union with God present for us in Christ; it is important that the union be as human as possible, that it be conscious and explicit and loving. Conscious, explicit, loving union with God is what we call prayer.

Finally, Jesus teaches us that love calls for sacrifice and that this is shown in the fidelity that cannot be separated from sacrifice.[10] The outstanding virtue of the God of the Old Testament is the fidelity of His love. Jesus, since He is the fullness of the revelation of God, is the incarnation of this loving fidelity. The God of the Old Testament and God present for us in Jesus in the New Testament is the God of the covenant; God is in covenant with us, and He is faithful to that covenantal relationship. This is the meaning of the Eucharist: God is present with and for us in Christ in the sacrament of the new covenant. In showing us, in His love for us, that love is faithful, Jesus also shows us that the fidelity of love requires sacrifice. "Greater love than this no man has, than that he lays down his life for his friends."[11] The teaching of Jesus, both in His words and in the actions of His life, and especially in the great redemptive action of His life, His death on the cross, is that love is the greatest when it is most unselfish. When love of care and concern dominates even to the point of great sacrifice to one's self, even to the point of giving one's life, when love is most unselfish, this is when it is greatest. At its best, then, love is dominated by care for, concern for, the person loved, even at great cost to one's self. Not only is our fulfillment to be found especially in a loving adherence to Christ, but this fulfillment cannot be obtained without the cross. "If anyone would save his life he will lose it, but if anyone loses his life for My sake, then he will find it."[12] "If anyone wants to be a follower of Mine, let him take up his cross and follow Me."[13]

The Level of the Theology of the
Religious Life: Love of God

What is the role and place of love in a life of

religious consecration in celibate and apostolic community? The most important love relation is the love with which God has loved us first. The religious, in his celibate consecration, is a sign and an instrument of God's love for man. A consecrated religious witnesses to God's love for us in Christ. And, furthermore, the religious is an active instrument of that love.

The celibate religious is, by his very existence and presence, a question mark. Why is he living the life he is living? Why has he chosen to live with no wife and no children? It is generally admitted that sublimation of the sexual instinct can be healthy when it is decided on for an adequate reason. But what is the reason for the celibacy of the religious? The answer to the question is this: the religious is one of those of whom Our Lord speaks in Saint Matthew's gospel when He talks about persons who are celibate for the kingdom of God.[14] The religious by his very existence stands for and witnesses to the existence of the kingdom of God, a kingdom that is present now but that is still to come in its fullness at the end of time. By his very existence, the religious points to the kingdom and to God's saving love.

A religious is not only a witness to God's love, but an active instrument of His love. There are those who do not believe in celibacy, and who think that the religious life is necessarily a truncated life that is based on refusal to marry and so on a refusal to love. This is simply not true. The consecrated chastity of the religious frees him to be a better and more active instrument of God's love for man. Religious chastity is not a refusal to love. It is, on the contrary, a giving up of the use of the sexual instinct in order to love more and better, in order to give oneself in a special way to God and to be a fuller instrument of God's love.

What is being discussed here is not sexuality in the broad sense, but the sexual instinct. Sexuality is a dimension of human existence, and sexual identity is just as important for the religious as for anyone. A religious man does not give up his maleness, nor does a religious woman relinquish her womanliness.

Furthermore, a religious does not, of course, give up his sexual instinct. The sexual instinct remains, and a mature religious accepts it in a matter of fact way. What he does give up is its use. There are two possible misunderstandings in this area. In the first place, a religious may find marriage and sexual activity in general very attractive; in order more easily to be chaste in his celibate vocation, he might attach labels to areas that are off limits to him. He might categorize as distasteful the whole area of sexuality; this helps to cancel out the allure of the sexual realm, and makes it easier not to trespass.[15] His attitude, however, is an error, not in accord with reality. The religious gives up the use of his sexual instinct not because sexuality is distasteful, but because he sees religious celibacy as a means to an end, as a means to being a fuller instrument of God's love. Sometimes, in reaction to the kind of puritanism just described, another kind of misunderstanding occurs. When the discovery is made that sex is not after all distasteful or evil, that the puritanical error is precisely an error, it is possible to fall into the opposite error. This is a line of reasoning that says: since everyone has a sexual instinct, since sexuality is part of God's creation, some sexual activity is necessary for everyone including celibate religious. A person can make the assumption that, because puritanical reasons for religious chastity are wrong reasons, therefore there are no right reasons, and so some active use of the sexual instinct is legitimate and even necessary for religious. The second misunderstanding is, of course, as unrealistic as the first.

Celibacy is not, then, an end in itself. It is a means to an end, a means to free the religious for a greater love of God, of community, and of all men. But how can this love be sustained? Every person has a need for love and intimacy that cannot be satisfied by ordinary relationships nor even by close friendships. How can this human need for love and intimacy be filled for a consecrated religious? Only in Christ. Only Christ can fill the need of the religious for love and intimacy. The primary love relationship in the life of a religious is his relationship with Christ. This relationship is, by the nature of the religious life, central.

The primary love relationship in the life of a religious, his relationship with Christ, certainly does not exclude other love relationships. On the contrary, it sustains them and organizes them and gives them a deeper meaning. Friendships are important for religious. So are an outgoing love for everyone and a generally positive attitude toward all reality. Love of Christ directs the religious toward love of other persons, of all men, and of the entire world. The Christ to whom the religious is consecrated is the same risen Lord who is the goal of all true human progress and the focal point of the world's history and evolution.[16] He is the Christ of Saint John, God's creative Word through whom all things come to be.[17] He is the Christ of Saint Paul, in whom all things are reconciled, in whom the whole universe and everything in it holds together.[18] A religious can, then, and should love Christ and all men and the entire world in one integrated love. Prayer, community, apostolate—these are different ways of loving with a love that, because it is centered on Christ, is comprehensive enough to embrace the whole world centered on Him. To say this is not to say that love of Christ and love of other persons and of the world are the same. To say that they are the same would be to not take Christ seriously as a person. Christ is a person, and He is to be loved not only indirectly through love of others and love of the world, but in a direct and personal way.

The Level of the Theology of the
Religious Life: Community

There is a need for a clear understanding of the place of love in religious community. What is the function of love, of charity, in religious community? The function of love is unitive. Charity is what holds the community together; it is the bond of community. The unity of a religious community is a unity in Christ; it is a unity of charity. This is what distinguishes a religious community from a totalitarian society. In a dictatorship, organization is imposed upon the members of that society by authority. A member of a totalitarian society is told, from above, what to believe and how to act. His adherence to the community is not by choice but by coercion. A religious community should be a true community, and the bond of a true community is not authority but love. In a religious community this bonding love is in the context of Christ and so it is raised to the level of Christian charity.

What is the place of authority in a community of charity? Authority does not primarily have a unitive function but rather a directive function. Authority is at the service of the community. It teaches, administers, orders, and leads. Indirectly, authority helps toward unity by providing goals, helping to organize the community toward those goals, and encouraging openness, mutual respect, communication, and charity among the members of the community. But the unity itself is one of charity. Authority—whether the authority of a superior or a chapter or a committee or a large group— gives the direction. But it is only charity that gives unity.

Charity not only gives unity, but it is the key to organization. The chief problem of totalitarian societies is never over-organization; it is always just the opposite— inadequate organization. A totalitarian structure must be highly centralized. There is no place for the subsidiarity and decentralization that are necessary for a high degree of organization. Although dictatorships may seem well organized, they are poorly organized because they are overly centralized. Because they are flimsy, they become inflexible; because they have a tendency to fall apart, they become rigid. On the other hand, a community bound together by mutual affinity, by love, is strong because it is founded not on exteriorly imposed force but on interior choice. It can afford to be flexible because of its strength. There is no need of rigid structures to keep the members in line. They are free, and therefore they are responsible for keeping themselves in line. A community bound by love can, moreover, be highly organized because subsidiarity of power and authority can be observed. Power and authority can be decentralized.

But does not organization tend to stifle individuality? Even in a community of charity, does not an increase in organization mean a decrease in individual freedom, does not higher organization mean less freedom to be oneself? No. We are used to thinking of person and community as opposed notions, but this is a false perspective. Person and community are not opposed; they are correlative and directly proportional. Personal growth and community growth go together. When a community of persons is a union from the interior, from the heart, that union further personalizes the members of the community. This is most sublimely true of the union of Persons that is the Trinity. The Father, the Son, and the Holy Spirit are infinitely distinct Persons in the infinite unity of a single divine nature. When a community is one of charity, person and community are correlative and directly proportional.

In a community where there is charity, the members of the community are freer to grow and to be themselves. They have a unity which does not deter but rather enhances personal growth. If I live in a community where there is real charity, then I can be myself. I know I am accepted as a person. I am free to disagree with others in the community; I know that they accept me even though they may disagree with my ideas. Where there is charity, there will ordinarily be a great diversity of views and opinions, and there will be open discussion of differences. And the members of the community, through interacting with one another, will contribute to the growth of the community and they will grow as persons. They will be in a personalizing union with one another.

What is the source of charity in religious community? Where does it come from? The source of charity is Jesus Christ and, specifically, Our Lord present in the Eucharist. This is the teaching of the Church right from the beginning. Saint Paul says that we are one because we share one loaf. Paul intends to point out a causal connection; we are one *because* we share the one bread of the Eucharist. The Eucharist makes us one. Saint Thomas Aquinas develops this idea in terms of the sacramental grace of the Eucharist. Every sacrament has a sacramental grace proper to it. Baptism, for example, makes us children of God and heirs of heaven. What is the sacramental grace that the Eucharist gives? It is the unity of the Church, and the unity of the different parts of the Church. It is oneness in Christ. The sacramental grace of the Eucharist is community. The Eucharist, then, is a creative reality. It pulls together and unifies; it creates unity. The grace of the Eucharist is to nourish the person receiving the sacrament, to unify that person, to help the person grow toward a greater integrity and wholeness and unity of self. But the grace of the Eucharist is also, and especially, to unify the members of the community, to pull the community together and make it one in Christ.

It is Jesus Christ, especially in His Eucharistic presence, who is the source of community. He is the source of the charity that is the bond of unity in Him. This fact, that it is the Eucharistic Christ who is the center and source of community, certainly has important implications for community Mass and for common prayer as well as for private prayer. These implications will differ according to different communities and differing circumstances. But the principle remains the same: the unity of religious community is a unity in Christ, and it is a unity that is from Him and because of Him.

I would like to conclude this section on religious community with some practical principles.

The first principle is this: Just as love of God and

love of neighbor go together, so do prayer and community go together. In a community where the religious are not seriously praying, there will be little charity. Where there is real prayer, there is the possibility of real charity.

The second principle is that people are more important than ideas. Christianity is a religion not primarily of knowledge but of love, of God's love for us and the love with which He expects us to respond to His love by loving Him and by loving one another. I may disagree with the opinions or even the life style of other religious, even those I live with, but the persons themselves are much more important than what they think or even how they live. My obligation is not to imitate them, nor to agree with them, but to love them in the charity of Christ. Of course, the only real charity is charity that manifests itself, that shows others that I love them. True charity will show up, not as mere courtesy but as kindness, not as just tolerance but as acceptance, and not as simply non-interference but as helpfulness and service.

The last principle is this: Love is possible only to the extent that there is interior freedom. Everyone needs support from others. But to the extent that I am attached in an excessive degree to the approval of others, to praise and esteem, to being appreciated and paid attention to, to that extent I will not be free to go out to others in charity. To the extent that I stand on my dignity or that I am hurt when I'm disagreed with or criticized, to that extent I am not free.

And to the extent that I am attached to others in a possessive way, tending to use them as objects to gratify needs of my own, manipulating them rather than relating freely to them as the subjects, persons, that they are, I will not be free. The greatest obstacles to charity in religious community are the narcissism that demands attention and approval and the possessiveness that uses others; to the degree that neither of these is given in to, to that degree freedom to go out to others is possible.

NOTES

1. See Martin D'Arcy, S.J., *The Mind and Heart of Love* (New York, 1947, 2nd ed. 1954). St. Thomas Aquinas distinguishes love of desire (possessive love) and love of friendship (*Summa Theologiae*, I-II, Q. 26, A. 4). See also Anders Nygren, *Eros and Agape*, tr. P. Watson (London, 1953).

2. Pierre Teilhard de Chardin, *The Future of Man*, tr. N. Denny (New York, 1964), p. 235.

3. Pierre Teilhard de Chardin, *The Activation of Energy*, tr. R. Hague (New York, 1971), p. 125.

4. The principle that "union personalizes" is a key principle in the theology of Teilhard de Chardin. The reader is referred to his works: *The Future of Man, op. cit.*, pp. 52-57 and 182-184; *Science and Christ*, tr. R. Hague (New York, 1968), pp. 45-46; *Human Energy*, tr. J. Cohen (New York, 1969), pp. 65-84.

5. The classic work on "love" in the New Testament is that of C. Spicq, O.P., *Agape in the New Testament* (St. Louis, 1966), 3 vols.

6. John 3, 16.

7. John 13, 34-35; 15, 9-17.

8. "To love is to accept the freedom of the other with all its consequences, even for God"—Daniel Day Williams, *The Spirit and the Forms of Love* (New York, 1968), p. 162.

9. In particular, see St. Paul's explanation of the freedom that Christ gives in Romans 8.

10. John 13, 1.

11. John 15, 13.

12. Matthew 16, 25.

13. Matthew 16, 24.

14. Matthew 19, 12.

15. Alfons Auer, "The Changing Character of the Christian Understanding of the World," *The Christian and the World*, ed. at Canisianum, Innsbruck (New York, 1965), pp. 7-8.

16. *Pastoral Constitution on the Church in the Modern World*, Introduction, article 10: "She (the Church) likewise holds that in her most benign Lord and Master can be found the key, the focal point, and the goal of all human history." Part I, Chapter 1, article 45: "The Lord is the goal of human history, the focal point of the longings of history and of civilization, the center of the human race, the joy of every heart, and the answer to all its yearnings."

17. John 1, 3.

18. Ephesians 1, 9-10; Colossians 1, 17.

4
Consecrated Chastity and Unification

The entire Christian enterprise, the purpose and work of the Incarnation extended in the Church, can be viewed as the progressive unification of all things in Christ. In this perspective, the whole of God's creative plan can be considered as a cone of time, beginning with the creation of a disordered multiplicity and culminating in the future, at the apex of the cone, in the second coming of Christ, when mankind will have achieved a maximum of human maturity and a maximum of human unity around its center, Christ. At the end of the world, when mankind will have attained a maximum of unity around Christ, its center, Christ will definitively weld mankind to Himself, hand over the kingdom to the Father, and God will be all in all.

The Christian enterprise, then, can be seen as the gradual, progressive unification of all things in Christ. This is what Christ came for and why He will come a second time. It is why the Church exists, and it is the task of the Christian. The task of the Christian is conquest for Christ through unification in Christ.

In the Christian process of conquest through unification in Christ, what is the place of the consecrated chastity of the religious?

43

Celibacy as Loss

Chastity for the person consecrated to Christ in the religious life is negative. Celibacy means non-use of the sexual instinct and the whole sexual apparatus; it means giving up the use of the sexual side of the person. Chastity for the religious means total sexual abstinence. The religious does not, for that, become other than a human and (therefore) sexual being, but he does completely forego the use of the human sexual instinct.

The chastity of the religious, then, is loss. It is the loss of the complete fulfillment of the sexual side of his nature. Is this loss somehow made up for in the religious life? Is the sexual instinct of the religious sublimated and spiritualized and then mysteriously fulfilled in a spiritual way? No. The loss is not regained, not made up for. Fulfillment of the sexual part of human nature is found only in marriage, and the religious—in giving up marriage—gives up the possibility of the fulfillment that goes with it. It is true that the religious can find progressive fulfillment as a person through growing intimacy with God. But this does not suppress the loss of fulfillment in the sexual sphere. And it is true that the religious can find increasing fulfillment through friendship and union in community, but this fulfillment as a person does not make up for or suppress the loss of fulfillment of the sexual instinct.

The chastity of the religious is loss, and it is irreparable loss. This loss is aloneness, for it is the loss of the possibility of fulfillment of an integral dimension of man's being, his sexual nature, which is meant to be fulfilled through sexual union with another person.

The sexual instinct itself, of course, cannot be given up. It remains, and it goes into action when it is stimulated. What is given up in a life of consecrated celibacy is acting in such a way as to satisfy, to fulfill, the movements of the sexual instinct. The sexual instinct, its motions and the feelings that arise from it, are—for the religious—irrelevant. There is a need on the part of the religious for awareness of his own feelings and motives of action; when these come from his sexual instinct, they are irrelevant to his life. Although he may hear the voice of his sexual instinct, he is not listening to it. He accepts the loss of its fulfillment and the aloneness that goes with that loss.

What is the justification for a chastity that is loss and aloneness? It is this: the chastity of the religious is a means to an end. Although negative itself, the chastity of the religious is a central means to something very positive. It is a means of giving oneself exclusively to Christ and, in Christ, to others, and this is its justification. It is not a loss that is suppressed or made up for or spiritually fulfilled, but it is a loss that is justified and more than justified. It is a means to greater self-giving and so a means to greater love.

Consecration through Chastity

In the light of the fact that religious chastity is loss and aloneness, it might seem that the ideal of religious consecration through chastity is timid and pale compared to the aggressive ideal of contemporary men who want to conquer the world, to push science, technology, art, all the forms of human progress, to their furthest limits so as to dominate the world around us. It might seem that consecration to Christ through chastity tends to remove the religious from participation in the world's progress, that it is a diminution rather than a positive force, a limitation of the person rather than a principle of growth and development. Nothing could be less true. Consecration to Christ through religious chastity is a dynamic force, a force of unification.

The specific action of consecration to Christ through chastity is to unify the powers of the religious so that, rising above the multiple and disordering attraction of things, he can unify and bring to maturity his own Christian personality. This consecration is a positive and personalizing unification.

Sins against chastity can now be seen for what they really are: in direct opposition to consecration to Christ and a waste of the energy of personalization. They introduce into the depths of the person a principle of corruption and disaggregation. They destroy part of the person's potential for interior unity and for consecration to Christ.

Consecration to Christ through religious chastity is the opposite of waste. It is a unification. Consecration through chastity "knits together the fibers of the soul."[1]

And this consecration through religious chastity is not flight or withdrawal. Its main significance is not simple abstention from sexual activity, for this abstention is simply a means to the consecration itself. It is not flight but conquest, not a passive force but an active one. It concentrates God in us and in those who are subject to our influence.

Consecration through chastity is not a "refusal to love." It is, rather, an increasing refinement of the power to love. It is not weakness but strength, not flight but conquest, not waste or dissolution but a growing interior unity, not a curtailment of the power to love but a concentration of that power.

The purpose and future end-point of the Church in this world, of Christianity, is the unification of all things in Christ. This is in no way opposed to the purpose of human progress. Human progress is in the direction of the control and unification of nature under man and in the direction of the political and social unification of men. It is in the direction of greater prosperity, of increased education and culture for all men, and greater unity of all men—all this so that men can be more human. Christianity partakes in this progress and builds on it and with it. Both human progress and Christian progress are in the direction of unification, and the progressive unification of all men in Christ has the unification accomplished by human progress as its matrix. Human progress, then, is not ambiguous or ambivalent; it is the base of Christian unification. All true progress is directed to the pleroma, the final unity in Christ. Human progress and Christian progress are distinct but inseparable; they are two sides of the same coin, two aspects of man's movement through history to the fullness of the pleroma. Consecration to Christ through religious chastity is operative of personal unification and so makes the religious a better and more efficient agent of progress, of a progress that is both human and Christian and that is directed to the ultimate unification at the end of time.

Consecrated Chastity and Marriage

It is clear from these considerations that consecration through religious chastity is not a stopping short of the fulfillment found in marriage. It is a renunciation of the fulfillment found in marriage in order to go further.

Marriage is a sacrament, and the state of marriage is a sacramental state. Christian marriage is a sacrament—that is, it is a mystery and a symbol of a higher reality. It is a mystery precisely because it is a symbol of a higher reality: the union between Christ and His Church. The union between Christ and His Church will be consummated, realized, completed, at the end of time, in the fullness of the pleroma. This is why there will be no "giving and taking in marriage" in the next world: because the symbol—marriage—will have passed into the reality—the complete union of mankind with Christ.

Consecration through chastity, the deliberately chosen state of celibacy for Christ, is a short-circuiting of the symbol of Christ's union with His Church and a going around and beyond the symbol straight to the reality: direct union with Christ. The religious gives himself in a total way to Jesus Christ, and he does it in this life. This is why the commitment of the religious life is a perpetual commitment. There can be no complete self-giving "for a time." The quality of the gift of self—that it is total—determines that the gift be, not for a time, but forever.

But if marriage is sacramental, why is not the state of consecrated chastity a sacramental state? Why is the public taking of perpetual vows not a sacrament? Consecrated chastity is not a sacrament—not because it is less than a sacrament, but because it is more than a sacrament. It goes beyond sacramentalism straight to the reality that the sacrament of marriage symbolizes. Consecrated chastity is a "supersacrament."

Consecration to Christ through religious chastity is an anticipation of the end of time. The consecrated person anticipates in his total self-giving to Christ the future state of saved mankind. In this, the religious is an eschatological sign, a sign of the eschaton, of this world's end and of the things to come. But he is much more than an eschatological sign. He is a living anticipation of the term of all progress, human progress and Christian progress, and so his consecration is a direct and real contribution to that progress, to the progress of the world as it gradually converges on Christ who, although present to the world now, awaits it in the future.

NOTE

1. Pierre Teilhard de Chardin, "My Universe," *Science and Christ*, tr. R. Hague (New York, 1969), p. 70.

5
Mary, the Church, and Obedience

Mary is out of style. It has been remarked that up until this generation the Church's devotion to the Mother of God has never been seen as such an embarrassment by so many Christians at once.[1] Preachers find themselves uneasy at having to proclaim the Marian mystery, professional Mariologists are experiencing a crisis of theological self-confidence, and the entire Marian movement in the Church has been called radically into question.[2] There is a crisis in Mariology.[3] Since the close of the Second Vatican Council, there have been published very few theological treatments of Mary's mediation, her queenship, or her co-redemption.[4] Whatever the reasons, there seems to be a contemporary theological vacuum and even downgrading regarding the place of Mary in the economy of salvation. What is that place?

Mary and Salvation

Marian theology often seems a little out of focus, fuzzy to contemporary eyes. There are at least three

51

reasons for this. First, the development of Marian theology in the Church has taken place largely through the logic of symbols; that is, Mary's place in the economy of salvation has been, for the most part, studied in function of symbolic categories. In the patristic period Mary was considered chiefly as the new Eve who, by her *fiat*, opened the way to man's restoration and so counteracted the function of the original Eve who prepared the fall of man.[5] The Mary-Eve parallelism in the patristic age was accompanied by a parallelism Eve-Church based on the fact that, just as Eve came forth from the side of Adam, so the Church came forth from the side of the New Adam on the cross of Calvary. This double parallelism with respect to Eve, Eve-Mary and Eve-Church, gradually fused into the parallelism Mary-Church of the Middle Ages and of modern times. These categories of parallelism are symbolic, based on Scripture; they appear to lack precision in a theological world that searches rational explanations.

Secondly, the current theological literature on Mary, although greatly subsiding, remains vast. And, thirdly, speculative Marian theology has concerned itself since the end of the Second World War almost entirely with the search for a synthetic principle from which all theological conclusions about Mary could be deduced, for some kind of brief foundational statement about Mary on which the whole Mariological edifice could firmly and stably rest. The question has been: Why has God raised Mary to such a high place? Why was Mary immaculately conceived, assumed into heaven, made the spiritual mother of all men? This search for a synthetic principle from which could be derived all of Mary's prerogatives has been concerned more with Mary herself and her dignity than with her place in the total economy. Theologians have sought to establish Mary's dignity and prerogatives on her divine maternity, or on her cooperation in the redemption, or on both. But her divine maternity and her cooperation in the redemption have not been sufficiently studied as integral to the overall plan of salvation.

Mary's terrestrial role in the incarnation and in the redemption has been studied at great length. And her transcendent role has also been analyzed at length, particularly regarding her spiritual motherhood and her position as mediatrix of grace. But the link between the two, between her terrestrial functions and her transcendent functions, has been little studied. This, in the present writer's opinion, is the main reason why Marian theology sometimes seems out of focus: because connection between her work on earth and her work in heaven has not been adequately shown. It is just not enough to make statements such as "Mary is our Mother because she is the Mother of Christ" and "Mary is mediatrix of grace because of her suffering at the Cross."

The purpose of the first section of this chapter is to study the connection between Mary's role on earth and her present role in heaven, the connection between her function in the foundation of the Christian economy of salvation and her function in the continuation of that economy. The description and analysis of the metaphysical link between Mary's place in the foundation of God's plan to restore mankind to Himself and her place in the continuation of that plan and that restoration will, it may be hoped, result in a clarification of Mary's place in the total economy of man's salvation.

In the light of the tradition, the obvious place to begin is with a consideration of Mary's relation to

Christ and, in particular, with a consideration of the fact that she is the Mother of Christ. That Mary is Christ's Mother is the New Testament's basic datum about Mary. Further, and not surprisingly, it is the gist of the earliest references to Mary in non-canonical Christian literature and the content of the mentions of Mary in the early councils and the discussion that surrounded those councils.

Thomas Aquinas makes a metaphysical analysis of Mary's relation of motherhood to the Person of Jesus.[6] Mary generates Jesus temporally. And this temporal generation, the historical fact of the virginal conception and birth, is the foundation of a real relation of motherhood, a relation which endures permanently. The point is that Mary is now the Mother of Christ. We do not say that Mary *was* His Mother, but that she *is* His mother. Mary's relation of maternity to Christ is permanent; it endures. The act of conceiving, bearing, and giving birth to Christ is a past historical fact; it is the foundation of the relation of motherhood. But the relation, whose foundation was temporary, is permanent— just as anyone's mother is always his mother. That Mary is Jesus' Mother and will continue to be has never been contested by orthodox theologians. However, it has not been sufficiently understood in the light of the relation of mankind to Christ.

For Mary, by being the Mother of Christ, is the point of contact between Christ and the rest of men. Christ became one of us in order to make us one with Himself, and He became one of us through Mary. Just as the Son proceeds from, is generated from, the Father from all eternity, He proceeded from Mary in time, was generated from Mary in time and into the human race. The Word assumed humanity, His own and—in a sense—that of all of us, through Mary. Thus His assumption of human nature passed through Mary. Our relation to Christ as Savior is permanent since His conception. In the Incarnation, Christ related the whole human race to Himself, and this relation is permanent, enduring. The foundation of this relation, the Incarnation, is through Mary.

The relation of all mankind to Christ comes to a point in the relation of Mary to Christ. Since Christ is one of us through Mary, we are all one with Him, to various degrees, through Mary. Just as Mary's motherhood of Christ is a permanent real relation based on a temporal fact, so our relation to Christ is a permanent real relation based on a temporal fact, the Incarnation. And just as our relation to Christ, as a matter of historical fact, is through Mary, so, as a real enduring relation, it passes through Mary.

Our relation to Mary is this: she relates us to Christ. Just as, historically, Mary related us to Christ through her maternity, so she relates us to Christ in the present economy. The foundation of our relation to Mary, as relating us to Christ, is the Incarnation. But although the foundation was temporal and is in the past, the relation is permanent and enduring. Just as Mary bore Christ and is now and always His Mother, so she was the point of contact between Christ and all mankind and remains that point of contact.

All men, then, are spiritual children of Mary insofar as they are related through her to Christ. In particular, Christians are children of Mary because they are incorporated through her into the Body of Christ that is the Church. Note that we cannot say that our relation to Mary is by incorporation into Christ, that we are related to Mary as to our mother because we are incorporated into her Son. Being related to Christ is not what relates us to Mary. It is not through Christ that we are related to Mary; it is just the opposite. It is through Mary that we are related to Christ, for it is through Mary that Christ has related, and relates, men to Himself.

It would be quite inappropriate to say that we are related to Mary through Christ rather than to Christ through Mary. The former (to Mary through Christ) would put Mary above Christ or at least on the same level with Him. It would detract from the unique mediation of Christ as Savior. On the other hand, to say, as we are saying, that we are related to Christ through Mary defines Mary's role appropriately. She is not our mediator with the Father, as Christ is, but—with an entirely different kind of mediation—she mediates the relationship of each man with Christ.

All men are related to Christ, either as potential members of His Body the Church or as real members, but the relation is always through Mary. Thus Mary is, in one way or another, the spiritual Mother of all men. And this is what it means to say that Mary is mediatrix of grace. For grace is a relation to Christ, and all relation to Christ is through Mary.

To summarize: the basis of Mary's place in the total Christian economy is the fact that she is the Mother of Christ. She not only was Christ's Mother, but she still is, for her relation of maternity to Christ is a real, permanent relation. Because of her motherhood of Christ, because it is through Mary that Christ came to us in the Incarnation, it is through Mary that we are related to Christ. For just as Mary's maternity is a real, permanent relation, so is the relation of men through Mary to Christ a real, permanent relation. Because, then, we are related to Christ through Mary, we are related to Mary. And our relation to Mary as relating us to Christ designates exactly the permanent place of Mary in the total economy of salvation.

It is true that Mary is the "first of the saved," a model of Christian faith and humility and openness to God's saving grace. And so, in a special way, she is a model for all religious. She is all these things. But, besides this, she has a key role in man's salvation, a function which cannot be reduced to just being a model, to simple exemplarity. In fact, her exemplary virtues depend on her (logically prior) role, that she is the Mother of Christ and so the spiritual Mother of all men.

What is the practical implication of this theological analysis? It is this: since Mary's mediation of God's saving love and power is a fact, therefore we can have recourse to her to intercede for us. The objective fact of Mary's mediation is the condition of the subjective devotion that men can have toward her. That there is a descending mediation of God's grace through Mary implies necessarily the possibility of ascending mediation, of not only venerating Mary but also approaching her in prayer. Since Mary is the point of contact between men and Christ, not only does salvation come from Christ through Mary to men, but also the possibility exists of men coming to Christ through her. This is the theological basis of Marian piety.

Mary and the Church:
God's Will Is Revealed Incarnately

Mary and the Church are closely related in Catholic consciousness. For one thing, Christ comes to each person through Mary and so, in that sense, Mary is the Mother of the Church as well as of each of its members. Further, Mary, in Catholic consciousness, stands for the Church, is a living symbol of the Church. Mary represents the Church in such a way that, in particular, she stands for two important principles of Church authority: (1) that God's will is indicated to us in an incarnate way, through in-the-world structures, and (2) that God's authority is mediated by the Church. These two principles are, of course, important for an understanding of religious life, and especially for an understanding of religious obedience.

That God's will is revealed incarnately, through in-the-world structures, is of course basic to the whole Judaeo-Christian tradition. In the Old Testament, God reveals Himself and His will for His people through historical events. The two main themes of the Old Testament, the exodus and the covenant, are both not abstractions but historical events. Not only does God intervene in history, but the historical event itself is His revelation. The history of Israel is the history of its relationship with Yahweh, and the history of Israel's relationship with Yahweh is an ordered series of historical events that mark Yahweh's interventions in the life of His people. The exodus reveals to Israel its nature as the people of God; it is a pilgrim people, on the way, led by and guided by Yahweh; not only its direction in history, but also its strength, power and unity are from Yahweh. Israel understands its whole history as an exodus toward the Day of the Lord which will be the final divine intervention and mark history's end. The history of the world itself is seen in terms of exodus; for example, the Genesis, Chapter One, account of the creation of the world out of chaos can be read as reflecting the fact of Israel's creation out of the chaos of Egyptian bondage in the exodus.

Again, the Sinai covenant reveals to Israel its nature by revealing its relationship with Yahweh, and the main events of Israel's history are seen in terms of the covenant; thus the covenant with Israel is inaugurated with Abraham, further sealed with Isaac and Jacob, and renewed with David. The world's creation is seen not only in terms of exodus, but as covenantal. In the first chapter of Genesis, God creates light and darkness, gives them their roles as day and night, and is faithful to them; the same covenantal idea is predominant in the creation of the rest of the world, including the creation of man. Man is created in God's image and given a role—dominion over the rest of creation—and God is faithful to him. This is a reflection backward to the beginning of history of the historical event of the Sinai covenant.

In Jesus, God's revelatory Word becomes flesh, becomes incarnate in the world and in the world's history. Jesus is human as well as divine, subject in His life on earth to the conditions of history. The history of Jesus' life—what He said, what He did, how He reacted to other persons, what He underwent—is revelatory of God's love and of God's will for us. God is revealed to us through the in-the-world structures of Jesus' life and death. In Jesus, it can be seen that God has willed to reveal Himself and His will incarnately, in the world and in history. This mutuality that God has willed to exist between Himself and the world in Christ is the principle of the Incarnation, a principle that dominates God's revelation of His loving will in all of Christian history. God has revealed Himself incarnately in Jesus, and continues to reveal Himself incarnately through Jesus' extension in history, through the Church.

The Church is not outside human history any more than its founder was outside human history. The Church is truly guided and inspired by God, but the Church is just as truly fully incarnate in the world, fully human, subject to the conditions of history. Understood properly, it can be said that there is a certain in-the-worldness about the Church, even a certain crassness. The Church is from God and alive with His life, but the Church is also human.

In Catholic consciousness, Mary stands for this material, corporeal, human side of the Church. More precisely, Mary stands for the fact that God is involved in the world through historically conditioned material structures, through the Church, with its hierarchical structure and its sacraments. Just as the Word became involved in the world in Jesus through Jesus' Mother Mary, so God draws each person to Himself through the Church; in this sense the Church is the mother of every Christian (and so we say "Holy Mother Church"). Mary, then, stands for "God involved in the world through Mother," and through Mother Church.

Further, Mary represents the opaque and material aspect of this involvement; she represents the in-the-worldness of the Church. Theologically, there is something difficult and unwieldy about Mary in the economy of salvation. Her place has a certain intrinsic resistance to theological speculation; there is much that is hard to put into the clear concepts so pleasing to theologians. Yet, in the history of theology and of doctrinal development, Mary has always been a touchstone of orthodoxy regarding the principle of the Incarnation. At the Council of Ephesus, for example, adherents of

the Nestorian heresy were identified as those who separated the person of Christ in such a way that they
would not admit that Mary is the Mother of God. In
contemporary theology, some seemingly sound theories
of original sin have foundered on the doctrine of the
Immaculate Conception and had their unorthodoxy
brought to light. Theology of the Resurrection continues to examine itself in the apparently impenetrable
and certainly mysterious doctrine of the Assumption.
Mary is the guardian of the principle of the Incarnation, and today especially regarding the fact that God
speaks to man through that complex in-the-world structure that is the Church.

Mary and the Church:
God's Authority Is Mediated

Secondly, Mary stands for the principle that God's
authority is mediated by the Church. This principle,
like the principle that God reveals His will in history, is
deep in the Judaeo-Christian tradition. In the Old Testament, Yahweh speaks to His people through the
prophets and the kings. Most Scripture scholars no
longer accept the notion that the prophets were out-
siders, beyond institutional Judaism; on the contrary,
the prophetic function was to call Israel back to greater
fidelity to its institutional commitment as God's people.
The patriarchs, kings, prophets, and teachers of Israel
all find their fulfillment in Jesus, who is the supreme
mediator of God's authority. He is God's very Word,
and He speaks with authority.

The Church is the extension of Christ in our own
time, and the Church, as Christ did, mediates God's au-

thority. Mary as Christ's Mother symbolically represents in the minds of Christians the Church as Mother, and so Mary stands for the principle that God's authority is mediated through the Church. A mother is not only she who nurtures, serves, and brings up her children; she is also subject to the authority of the father. A mother's authority, then, is an authority in submission to the father. Submission to an authority in submission, to a mother's authority, is humbling. The Church speaks with a maternal authority, and this is why some find it humbling to submit to Church authority. Mary represents the Church as having authority in submission to God, as mediating God's authority.

Mary and the Church: Acceptance or Rejection?

There is a close connection between acceptance or rejection of Mary and acceptance or rejection of the Church as authoritative. In the history of the Church, opposition to devotion to Mary and opposition to Church authority have often gone together; this is no accident, for Mary stands for Church authority. It was, therefore, not surprising when American Protestant opposition to the definition of the doctrine of the Assumption went hand in hand with a great increase in vocalized Protestant opposition to papal authority. There was more to this than simply opposition to an authoritative definition of a Marian doctrine. In Protestant consciousness, as in all Christian consciousness, Mary and Church authority are closely associated. Rejection of Mary as Mother of Christians (for example, as in opposition to the dogma of the Assumption) and rejection of the authority of the Church (for example, as in opposition to the act of infallibly defining the dogma of the Assumption) are both rejection of "Mother." The rejection is inevitably of both "Mothers" together, of Mary and of the Catholic Church. The general Protestant rejection of Catholic Marian piety as "Mariolatry" and the fundamental Protestant rejection of the authority of the Catholic Church go hand in hand.

Again, and speaking in a general way, much Protestant opposition to the Catholic sacramental system, in particular to the whole Eucharistic complex including the sacrament of Holy Orders and the sacrament of Penance (both ordered in an immediate way to the Eucharist), goes with Protestant rejection of Catholic devotion to Mary. For Mary represents, in Protestant minds as well as in Catholic minds, not only the Catholic principle of divine authority as *mediated* by the Church, but also that this authority is mediated by the *Church*, comes to Christians through the in-the-world structures of the Church, comes to Christians incarnately. The Catholic sacramental system is a concretization of the Catholic interpretation of the principle of the Incarnation, and Mary—as the guardian of that principle—must be rejected along with the rejection of any concrete manifestation (such as the sacramental system) of the principle.

In the same way, separatist movements within the Catholic Church nearly always include a movement away from reverence toward Mary. Trends within the Catholic Church that attack Church authority or that attack the sacramental system (especially from the point of view of the Church's jurisdiction over the sacraments) almost always contain a marked tendency to belittle the place of Mary in Catholic practice and in theology.

In the light of history, there should be no surprise that where internal opposition to Church teaching authority and to Church jurisdictional authority over the sacraments is the strongest, there too is found both opposition to Marian devotion and belittlement of Marian theology.

Finally, acceptance of Church authority and acceptance of Mary's place in the economy of salvation, as regards both Catholic practice and theology, go together. This is inevitable and as it should be.

Conclusion: Obedience in the Religious Life

The application to obedience in the religious life is easy to make. God makes His will known to every religious through in-the-world structures and through the agents who mediate God's authority.

God speaks to us in many ways and through all the aspects of our life. He speaks to us "through the world," incarnately, according to the basic Christian principle of the Incarnation. He speaks to us through Scripture, through our study and reading, through all the people we come in contact with, through the events of our lives, through our work, through our community life.

And, in a special way, He speaks to us through religious superiors who mediate His authority. We take our vow of obedience to God, but He lets us know His will through and in our lives, and especially through our superiors.

Mary is a symbol of all this. And, moreover, she is a model of obedience through her *fiat* to the angel, through the "yes" that she said to God at the Annunciation and that she lived all her life. More than a model of obedience to God's will, she is our Mother who can help our lives to be "yeses" to God.

NOTES

1. Donal Flanagan, "A Future for Marian Theology," *Ephemerides Mariologicae*, 20 (1970), 72.

2. *Ibid.*

3. Alban A. Maguire, "Presidential Address to the Mariological Society of America," *Marian Studies*, 20 (1969), 24-25. See C. W. Neumann, "The Decline of Interest in Mariology as a Theological Problem," *Marian Studies*, 23 (1972), 12-38.

4. René Laurentin, "Bulletin sur la vierge Marie," *Revue des sciences philosophiques et théologiques*, 58 (1974), 67-102. This bulletin appears every two years; see also: 56 (1972), 433-491, and previous bulletins.

5. This Eve-Mary parallelism appears in early Church literature at the end of the *Letter to Diognetus* and in Chapter 100 of Justin's *Dialogue with Trypho*; see also: Irenaeus, *Against Heresies*, III, 22, 4, and V, 19, 1: Tertullian, *De Carne Christi*, 17. For a recent study of the Eve-Mary parallelism in the Greek Fathers, see L. Cignelli, *Maria nuova Eva nella patristica greca* (Assisi: 1966).

6. *Summa Theologiae*, III, Q. 35, A. 5.

6
The Cross and Involvement in the World

In these times the religious life in many, perhaps in most, parts of the world is suffering. There are few vocations, there are defections; there is anxiety and insecurity; and there is a weakening of hope.

I believe that the present sufferings are the birthpangs of a new and more authentic religious life. I believe that the religious life is being refounded in our time—not by us, but by Our Lord working through us.

And I believe that the Lord speaks to us now in the words of Ezekiel:

They keep saying, "Our bones are dried up,
our hope is gone; we are as good as dead."
So prophesy. Say to them,
"The Lord says this:
I am now going to open your tombs;
I intend to bring you out of your tombs, my people,
and lead you back to the land of Israel.
And you will know that I am God,
when I open your tombs
and bring you out of your tombs, my people.
And I will put my spirit in you, and you will live;

and I will establish you in your own land;
and you will know that I am the Lord.
I have said it. And I will do it."[1]

The Lord tells us that he will put his spirit in us
and we will live. What is the spirit of the Lord? What is
the spirit of Jesus?

Happy are those who know that they are poor;
theirs is the kingdom of heaven.
Happy the gentle;
they shall inherit the earth.
Happy those who grieve;
they shall be comforted.
Happy those who hunger and thirst for justice;
they shall be fulfilled.
Happy the merciful;
they shall be shown mercy.
Happy the pure in heart;
they shall see God.
Happy the peacemakers;
they shall be called God's children.
Happy those who are persecuted in the cause of
    justice;
theirs is the kingdom of heaven.[2]

The Lord tells us that he will put his spirit in us, in
the religious life, and that in this spirit we will live. We
are called, then, to a firm hope in Jesus Christ. And we
are called to live in the spirit that he gives us, the spirit
of the Beatitudes. We are, furthermore, called to live
this spirit today, in today's world, in the context of contemporary culture and facing the challenge of contemporary problems.

Involvement in the World

We are called to follow Our Lord who, as Saint Paul tells us, emptied Himself, taking the form of a servant by becoming involved in the world through his Incarnation. He entered into the world, and His life took the form of service. And He emptied Himself even further by dying for us on the Cross. Christ, by His Incarnation, life, and death, became entirely involved in the world, entered into the heart of the world, so that, risen, He has become the heart of the world. We, too, then, are called to empty ourselves in poverty of spirit, to be involved in the world in the service of others, and so to be disciples of Our Lord.

How can we do this in today's world? We are living in a world far different from that of the medieval world, or the world of the last century. It is a world that is moving rapidly into the future, and that sees itself as future directed. The Second Vatican Council's *Pastoral Constitution on the Church in the Modern World* describes the situation by saying that man has passed from a static view of the world to a dynamic view. In the Middle Ages, the age of Saint Thomas Aquinas, man saw reality as centered on the present. The world was seen as static. Progress was as yet an undiscovered idea. And the world was understood primarily as an object of contemplation—a contemplation which could lead in steps to the contemplation of God. In the nineteenth century, man saw reality as centered on the past, and he looked back with nostalgia to some past golden age. Contemporary man sees reality as oriented toward the future. He does not live in some static present, and he does not look back nostalgically to the past. He lives directed into the future. He is involved in the world, and in the world seen precisely as the-world-with-possibilities-for-the-future. He wants to build a better world. This is what motivates him and encourages him to transcend his present limitations, to move ahead, and so to grow.

The future orientation of contemporary culture is, to some extent, Christian in its origin. And it is Christian in its essence. Our religion is a future-oriented religion. In the Old Testament, Israel moves into the future led by God. The event of the exodus is the category in which God's people understand history. Just as God was with them and ahead of them in the desert, leading them to the promised land, so he leads them into the future toward the Day of the Lord. The New Testament, too, is future-directed. The Church is in history, moving toward the second coming of Christ, into the future that God holds in his hands.

The *Pastoral Constitution on the Church in the Modern World* has this contemporary understanding of reality as future-oriented. And it sees history as moving toward a future goal. The risen Christ is the goal of all history and the future focal point of mankind's progress.

In the Council documents, the Church, too, is seen as future-directed and as evolving. It is the Body of Christ, which changes, develops, evolves. Like its founder, the Church grows in age and grace and wisdom. It is incarnate in history, subject to history's conditions, involved in the world that is moving into the future.

This, I believe, is the way the religious life is to be understood, especially today. A religious congregation is an organic part of the Body of Christ, the Church. It grows, develops, evolves. It suffers, of course, because suffering is always the price of progress, and because every religious congregation is, like Our Lord was, in the structure of the Cross. The religious life today, although surely with pain and difficulty, is moving in the direction of greater flexibility of institutional structures, in the direction of greater freedom and greater responsibility for the individual religious, toward a more real interiorization of the spirit of the religious life, toward better organization, toward community bonded more by charity than by law, and toward deeper prayer and greater involvement in the world.

This is, surely, a healthy and hopeful direction. It is the direction of a fuller following of Christ.

Some might think, however, that there is an opposition between following Christ and being involved in the world. This depends on what we mean by "world." If, when we say "world," we mean the world of sin and self-centeredness, the world that is under God's judgment, the world that turns away from Christ, then we have to say that a religious is a person who flees from the world. When "world" is taken in this negative sense, the religious life is a flight from the world and from all worldliness, and a religious is a person set apart from the world to serve God.

However, the word "world" is being used here in a different and more positive sense. The documents of the Second Vatican Council, most theologians, and—often —Scripture use the word "world" in a positive sense. It is the world that God so loves that He sent His only Son to save it. It is the world that has been created in Christ and that is centered on Him. When the world is understood in this positive sense, then it is clear that the relation of the religious life to the world is a strongly positive relation. Religious are called to be involved in the world. And the response to this call to involvement in the world is part of the direction of the evolution of religious life.

It is possible, of course, to fall into two traps regarding this involvement. There are two traps that lie on either side of the main path of the development of the religious life. There is the trap of a kind of spiritual isolationism that would see following Christ only in terms of flight from the world and of withdrawal from the problems and the needs of other people. On the other hand, it is possible to go to the opposite extreme by falling into the trap of a distorted activism. The heart and center of the religious life is loving personal relationship with Jesus Christ, and the center of that relationship is prayer. It is possible to fall into the trap of underestimating the centrality of prayer in the religious life. One could stress involvement in the world in a way that would de-emphasize prayer and so cut the heart out of the religious life.

What has to be grasped is that consecration to Christ and involvement in the world are not two diverging directions. On the contrary, they are the two mutually complementary components of a complete religious life.

God is not aloof or indifferent to the world, somehow removed from it. He is deeply involved in the world through the Incarnation. It is God's involvement in the world that, in union with Him, we are called to imitate. And this is how we will live the spirit of Jesus, the spirit of the Beatitudes.

Renunciation

The life of a religious is a life consecrated to

Christ. This means a life of loving personal relationship with Christ, a life that includes both a direct personal relation to Him and a loving service of Him through the world. A life consecrated to Christ is a life of personal adherence to Him, both in prayer and in action. This loving adherence to Christ in both prayer and action means a going out of oneself to Him, a decentering of oneself in order to be recentered on Christ. Loving service of Christ necessarily means a going out of oneself to Him and to the world that is moving toward Him. It means an emptying of oneself in imitation of Him.

The words of Saint Paul to the Philippians, encouraging them to humility and to love and service of one another in imitation of Christ, are appropriate here. "He emptied Himself to assume the condition of servant."[3] There can be no loving service of Christ without this self-emptying, without the Cross. Paradoxically, a religious can find self-fulfillment not by seeking it but only by going out of himself to Christ. In Christ's own words, "Anyone who wants to save his life will lose it; but anyone who loses his life for My sake will find it."[4] And, "If anyone wants to be a follower of Mine, let him renounce himself and take up his cross and follow Me."[5] Consecration to Christ means attachment to Him and to His service. And it is in this attachment to Christ and to serving Him in the world that the religious finds detachment from his own selfishness.

Participation in the Paschal Mystery

The death of Jesus was much more than the result of evil in the world, an expiation for sin, and an example for Christians. Christ's death on the Cross meant His complete immersion in the world. For Jesus to become the keystone of the world and the Center of all things, it was first necessary that He become an element of the world, that He become incarnate in the world, involved in it. That is, so that the risen Christ could be the future focal point of the world's progress, it was first necessary that He descend into the world by becoming a man, and by living out the implications of that involvement in the world according to His particular mission and historical circumstances. And this meant, finally, as the culmination of His life of obedience to the Father by emptying Himself in the service of men, His death on the Cross. Through His death on the Cross, Christ descended into the heart of the world to be the Heart of the world. The risen Christ could not be the Center of the process of the progressive reconciliation of all things in Himself without having become immanent in the world, without having become involved in the world. And the price of that immanence was His suffering and death on the Cross. Understood in this way, the death of Jesus was the act by which He draws all things to Himself.

The Cross, then, is not only a symbol of renunciation and expiation. The Cross is the symbol of the redemptive unification of the world. It is the symbol of progress and of victory through hard work and suffering and death to self. "The royal road of the Cross," writes Teilhard de Chardin, "is no more nor less than the road of human endeavor supernaturally righted and prolonged. Once we have fully grasped the meaning of the Cross, we are no longer in danger of finding life sad and ugly. We shall simply have become more attentive to its barely comprehensible solemnity."[6]

In this world, the religious lives in the existential structure of the Cross. Nevertheless, the religious life is a participation not only in the death but also in the resurrection of Christ. The religious life is a project of unification in which the religious does all he can to unify himself and the world around him. This effort of unification ends in the death of the religious, a death that is a participation in the death of Jesus. But, by His death and resurrection, Christ has transformed death from a blind alley into a passage to glory. At my death, I will be completely fragmented, torn apart, disintegrated. And, on the other side of my death, Christ will put me together again, this time completely centered on Him.

In my life in this world, every cross that comes to me brings me a partial death, breaks me into fragments to some extent. Every failure, illness, misunderstanding, limitation, set-back, upset, trial, or pain breaks me to some degree into pieces. To the degree that I carry these daily crosses in union with Jesus, He uses them to bring me closer to Him. He takes advantage of the fragmentation of my provisory unity to put me together again in a higher synthesis, this time centered less on myself and more on Him.

In this way, the religious life is a continuous death and resurrection in union with Jesus Christ, a participation in the paschal mystery.

NOTES

1. Ezekiel 37, 11-14.
2. Matthew 5, 3-10.
3. Philippians 2, 6.
4. Matthew 16, 25.
5. Matthew 16, 24.
6. Pierre Teilhard de Chardin, *The Divine Milieu*, tr. B. Wall *et al.* (New York, 1960), pp. 103-104.

7
Change in the Apostolic Religious Life

The general tradition of the religious life in Western Christianity took shape during the Middle Ages. Not only customs and cultures have changed since then, but man's whole view of the world has been transformed. In medieval times men understood the world as a static universe without any special direction. Man's future was in the next world; his existence in this one was understood as simply a preparation for the world to come. The present world was passing away and it had no significant future; the ideas of evolution and progress had not yet been discovered. In the static world of medieval times the principal form of religious consecration was monasticism; the Christian ideal was the contemplative life, and the monastery was the ideal preparation for the eternal contemplation for which man was created.

The rise of the non-monastic, apostolic religious life corresponds with the Western world's discovery of the historical dimension of the world, of genesis, of becoming, of evolution, of social development, and of progress. But because much of the tradition of the religious life had been formed in the Middle Ages and in a monastic climate, there was a gradual but strong tendency for the non-monastic religious life to become increasingly monasticized, even in the case of a religious order like the Society of Jesus. In spite of the fact that the Jesuit spirit is in many ways a reaction against monasticism, a gradual process of monasticization took place in the centuries after the foundation of the Society of Jesus. No matter what the reason for this progressive monasticization of the non-monastic religious life, it did take place and it was general. Much of the renewal of the non-monastic religious life, a renewal which has been intensive since the Second Vatican Council, has been along the lines of a return to sources and to original charisms. Consequently, renewal has been along the lines of a demonasticization. The process of this recent, intensive renewal of the non-monastic religious life is the subject of this chapter.[1]

For the purpose of this study, it seems advisable to use the terms "apostolic" and "monastic" to describe the non-monastic and the monastic religious life.[2] It is true that one cannot strictly oppose apostolic and monastic. The monastic religious life is also apostolic even in its most contemplative forms. However, the terms "apostolic" and "monastic" can be used as shorthand words for life styles that are primarily monastic and primarily non-monastic, for life styles that are "centered" and "open," "stable" and "mobile." The phrase "apostolic religious life" will be used in this chapter to stand for the non-monastic, primarily active, religious life. It is true, of course, that there are degrees of monasticism in the religious life. If "apostolic" and "monastic" represent the two poles of religious life styles, then it is true that various religious orders and congregations find themselves at various points on a spectrum between these two poles. Between the Benedictines at the monastic pole and the Jesuits at the apostolic pole, one finds the Dominicans, the Franciscans, and many other families of religious orders and congregations. What is said in this chapter, therefore, will not apply to every religious order and congregation in the same way; rather, it will apply to all apostolic religious orders and congregations, but analogously.

A large part of the problem of change in the apostolic religious life is the problem of understanding. In order to cope with changes in the religious life and in order to guide those changes intelligently, it is necessary to see change in perspective, to have a point of view, a framework, a theory, a theology of change of the apostolic religious life. The purpose of this chapter is to outline some of the main elements of such a theology.

The Religious Life as Changing

With the Second Vatican Council, the Church has renewed its self-understanding. This new self-understanding is expressed in words in the two great documents of the Second Vatican Council, *Gaudium et Spes* and *Lumen Gentium*. In these documents, as well as in post-conciliar ecclesiology, the Church understands itself in categories that are both scriptural and contemporary. The Church sees itself not at all as a static, monolithic, primarily juridical structure, but as the dynamic, changing, organic Body of Christ. The Church is not static, but moving into the future; it is the people of God in exodus through the desert of history toward the promised land of the ultimate future. And the Church is the Body of Christ, and so follows the laws of growth of living things; since it is alive, it grows, changes, develops, evolves.

The Church is the extension, in history, of the Incarnation. And so, like Our Lord, the Church grows in age and grace and wisdom, and like Our Lord, the Church is in the world. It is true that the Church is truly from God, guided and inspired by the Holy Spirit. Just as truly, the Church is fully incarnate in the world, fully human, subject to the conditions of history. The Church is not *of* the world, but it definitely is *in* the world, incarnate in history and in culture. Christianity, then, and especially Catholicism, is not a fixed system. Catholicism is not merely a collection of truths given once and for all to be literally conserved. The Church is not an immutable, unchanging monolith, the holder of some static and eternally unchanging propositions. The Church is not outside the process of human history any more than its founder was outside human history; it is fully immersed in the world. The Church is not dead and beyond change and movement; it is alive with the fullness of life and it is evolving in the direction that God has planned from the beginning. The Church is not a static juridical structure, nor is it simply a set of spiritual impulses. The Church is not just a hierarchical part and a charismatic part. It is a living organic body.

Because it is a body subject to the conditions of history, the Church grows and develops in a groping manner, finding its way, moving forward not in a perfectly straight line but in a sometimes erratic zigzag. What is more, the Church follows the law of growth of all living things in this world, the law that there is no growth or progress without suffering. We should not be surprised when we see upheavals, dissensions, and conflicts in a changing Church. These sufferings are deplorable and to be avoided as far as possible, but suffering is the inevitable price of progress. The Church in this world is not the Church triumphant, but the Church militant, the Church in combat, fired upon, wounded, sometimes staggering, falling and rising again, the Church militant. The Church's way is the way of the Cross.

All that has been said above about the Church can be applied to the religious life in general and to each religious order and congregation in particular. A religious congregation is part of the Body of Christ, an organic part of a living entity. And so every religious congregation, too, behaves like a living thing; a religious congregation is not less alive than other organizations, but more alive because it is living with the life of the Holy Spirit. The proper analogue to religious congregations is not a primarily juridical organization like a political body, the Boy Scouts, or an industrial organization. The best analogue is biological: the human body. This is because a religious congregation is part of the Body of Christ and therefore itself is very much alive. One should not be surprised, then, that the religious life is changing; change is an essential dimension of the religious life, and of every religious congregation. Furthermore, in times of rapid evolution, the religious life in general and any religious congregation in particular suffer more; periods of rapid growth are almost always periods of intense suffering. It is no surprise, then, that in this time of intensive renewal of the religious life, many congregations find themselves in tension, even in conflict, polarized to some extent. Tension, conflict, and polarization are, surely, to be avoided as much as possible, but their existence should not be unexpected in a time of rapid change; suffering is the price of progress. This is not, of course, to say that every change in religious life is progress; it is simply to say that renewal is painful.

The Direction of Change
of the Apostolic Religious Life

Change is a dimension of all religious congregations, but the subject of this chapter is change in apostolic (non-monastic) religious congregations in particular. Can we say that there is a general direction of change? Can we say that the changes that have been taking place in the apostolic religious life, especially since the Second Vatican Council, point in a general direction? Do all these changes have a general shape, are they taking us somewhere, is there a definable direction of change? There does seem to be a clear direction of change, and this direction can be described in various ways.

For example, the structures of the apostolic religious life have become much more flexible. Fifteen years ago, it was common in most apostolic congregations that all the members rose at the same time, made mental prayer at the same hour, and in general followed a more or less monastic horarium. In most cases, this monastic horarium has disappeared from the apostolic religious life except in formation situations. Not only is the daily horarium more flexible, but other structures are much less rigid than they used to be in many congregations. Structures of government are more flexible, with increasing dialogue between superiors and subjects and greater sharing in decision-making on the part of subjects. Again, apostolic structures have become more flexible, and many religious today are finding themselves in new apostolates. In a general way, the whole apostolic religious life has moved in the direction of less rigidity, greater flexibility of the external structures of the religious life, less emphasis on conformity and uniformity, and a stronger emphasis on the person.

Correlative with the increasing flexibility of the external structures of the religious life has been an increasing freedom for the individual religious. The individual is more free, at least in an exterior way. Since the individual religious is more free, he is called to a greater personal responsibility, and this is true especially in the area of the spiritual life. Today, the vast majority of religious in apostolic congregations are personally responsible for their mental prayer, for how they live their poverty, and in many other areas. What has been happening is this: as the structure of the religious life has become more flexible, there has been a greater call to and a greater need for interiorization of the previously external structures of the religious life. The contemporary call to members of apostolic religious congregations is to live the religious life more from the heart, to interiorize the spirit of the religious life, and in a more personal way to live in a spirit of total giving of self to God rather than in a spirit of conformity to external structures. This increasing freedom and new call to responsibility are, of course, partial and indirect causes of some of the elements of crisis in the apostolic religious life today. Since renewal began, there have been many defections from the religious life, there has been some loss of hope in the religious life, vocations in many cases have dwindled, and—in some cases—there has been an increase in worldliness. These elements of crisis are not at all desirable, but they are the price one pays for freedom. If a religious is freer and therefore more responsible, that religious is also more free not to take responsibility. He is freer to make compromises, especially in the area of the spiritual life, and to dishonestly justify his compromises in the name of progress or renewal or the new theology or freedom itself. This does not mean that the direction of change is somehow wrong. It means, rather, that the direction of change calls apostolic religious to greater responsibility and, at the same time, to greater honesty.

The process of demonasticization of the apostolic religious life has been, and is, a broad one, touching all areas of the religious life. There are four areas, however, which are particularly important: the apostolate, community, dress, and prayer.

The Demonasticization of Apostolate and of Community Living

The monastic apostolate, is, traditionally, a centripetal apostolate; the monastery gathers in to itself. It is a stable center which attracts people and projects. The whole idea of the monastic apostolate is that of a center. Non-members of the monastic community come to this center to be renewed and then go out to renew the world, but the members themselves of the monastic community generally remain at the monastery, because that is their apostolic *center*. The most traditional apostolic activities for monastic congregations are, therefore, schools, publishing, and retreats. On the other hand, the apostolate of properly apostolic communities (non-monastic communities) is centrifugal; it is the members themselves of the apostolic community who radiate out into the world. It might be said that the monk is "called" and that the member of an apostolic congregation is "sent."

The monastic community creates its own environment, and it controls that environment so that it is conducive to contemplation and to living in monastic community. The apostolic community, on the other hand, rather than creating its own environment, tries to change the world around it. The apostolic community has a centrifugal apostolate. Where an apostolic community has a school, the school apostolate will not be undertaken in the same way that it would be undertaken by a monastic community. An apostolic community will be much more involved in the whole community around the school; its members will participate in other religious and civic activities in the area, and there will be more contact with the outside-school milieu of the student or pupil.

Historically, many apostolic religious congregations of both men and women found it easy to become overly monasticized because of their educational apostolate. A school is, after all, a center, and many congregations drifted into a centripetal school apostolate. Most of these congregations are now discovering less monastic ways to manage schools.

The process of the demonasticization of the apostolate of apostolic congregations is going on now. It does not mean that old apostolates must be dropped and new apostolates be begun; it simply means that overly monasticized apostolates must be adapted to the apostolic way of life.

Another important area of demonasticization is that of community living. With the disappearance of the monastic horarium has gone the disappearance of the sometimes subtly monastic structures of community life. The disappearance of a monastic framework for community living has led to the search for new bonds of religious community; there are, for example, the new emphasis on shared prayer, the increasing importance being given to community prayer of a more formal kind, greater distribution of responsibilities among the members of the local community, and the new importance of community meetings. Even misguided attempts to "find community" have had their origin in the healthy desire to interiorize the previously overly monastic and external bonds of community.

In the context of the demonasticization of apostolate and of community, there has taken place a gradual demonasticization of religious obedience. The obedience proper to apostolic communities should be and is increasingly *apostolic* obedience. The classic monastic practices of "small permissions" and of explicit commands even in small matters are proper to the monastic life; in the apostolic life, these practices tend to stifle apostolic initiative and freedom, and they become picayune, reducing religious obedience to a certain rigid formalism. Apostolic obedience is an all-pervading obedience to one's mission as that mission is indicated by religious authority. It is an obedience to being sent by the Church acting through superiors. Apostolic congregations, in demonasticizing religious obedience, are finding that religious obedience is not less important, but more important, often more difficult, and always not simply a matter of practices but an entire and absolutely essential dimension of apostolic religious life.

Religious formation and the vocation apostolate

form one area in which renewal is, for many congregations, somewhat recent. Certainly, it is necessary that formation programs be demonasticized in accord with the charism of the congregation. Formation structures need to be adapted to the exigencies of apostolic religious life. At the same time, the vocation apostolate needs to be, and in many cases is being, renewed along the lines of a greater interiorization. New efforts in the direction of vocation education are taking the form of personal encounter, small-group retreats, and "live-ins" in which young people spend some time living with a local religious community.

The Demonasticization of Dress

Most conversations about what an apostolic religious should wear begin with the information that dress is not important and then continue, sometimes in a heated way, to demonstrate by the intensity of the conversation that dress is, as a matter of fact, very important. What an apostolic religious wears *is* important because it is symbolic. Dress, for men religious as well as for women religious, is an important factor because it is an important symbol. In the apostolic religious life today, what does what one wears symbolize? It symbolizes the options that one's religious congregation has taken along the road to renewal. In the past, many religious orders and congregations which were not at all monastic nevertheless adopted monastic habits. The wearing of the monastic habit in highly non-monastic communities symbolized the overmonasticization of those apostolic communities. For example, among many congregations of women whose rule was patterned on the rule of the Society of Jesus, the religious habit was strictly monastic: bandeau, wimple, cincture, large rosary, and long skirt. Even in religious orders whose constitutions forbade the wearing of a monastic habit, such as the Society of Jesus, some kind of semi-monastic habit was prescribed for all. With the renewal of the religious life, a renewal which has in part taken the form of a demonasticization of the apostolic life, the disappearance of the monastic habit is a symbol of demonasticization and so of renewal. And this is its precise importance.

Various options have been taken. Some communities have adopted a religious dress which is not at all monastic, but, rather, adapted to the apostolic religious life. Other communities have chosen to permit their members to wear what is essentially secular dress, modified by some external symbol of religious consecration. In some congregations where many of the members are priests, those who are not priests generally wear some sort of secular dress and the priests dress as the diocesan priests of that region dress. It might be remarked that, in general, some of those congregations which were most monastic and most rigid in external structures before the Second Vatican Council have, in renewing themselves, gone far in the direction of secular dress. On the other hand some of those congregations which were less monastic and less rigid have not felt the need to go as far in the matter of demonasticization of religious dress; they have simply adopted a non-monastic religious garb. But even the most extreme reactions against overmonasticization have not been basically unhealthy; they have been fundamentally healthy reactions against the distortion of the original charism of the apostolic congregation.

Apostolic congregations have, in various ways, apostolic charisms, non-monastic charisms. And so renewal has involved a return to original charisms by way of demonasticization. At the same time, different apostolic congregations have different charisms, and so renewal has involved great pluralism. The fact that different religious congregations are different in spirit and different in life style has become a fact of life, and this kind of pluralism has been increasingly accepted. As pluralism becomes more of a reality, the differences in charism of different congregations become clearer, and it becomes easier for the individual religious to identify with his own congregation and its charism, not only with regard to what he wears but with regard to his whole way of living the religious life.

The Renewal of Prayer

The contemporary renewal of prayer in apostolic religious congregations is, in part, a result of demonasticization. Rigidity and formalism have disappeared to a large extent from the exterior structures of religious life, and, as the need has been recognized for an increase in interiorization of the religious life, the primacy of personal relationship with God has been more and more emphasized. This relationship with God, in and through Jesus Christ, is the heart and center of the religious life, and it is more and more recognized that the heart and center of personal relationship with God is prayer.

In the renewal of common prayer in apostolic religious congregations, there has been the temptation to overreact to prayer forms that might have seemed too monastic, and sometimes the need for pattern and ritual in common prayer has been lost sight of. Nevertheless, common prayer has been renewed, not only through shared prayer and through participation in Pentecostal groups, but in itself. Most importantly, the need for the support that comes from common prayer in those communities where common prayer belongs to the charism of the congregation is more and more appreciated as an activity that forms bonds of charity in Christ.

Even more important has been the renewal of personal prayer. What directions is the renewal of personal prayer taking at the present time in the apostolic religious life? For one thing mental prayer is approached, more and more, with greater simplicity; the teaching of Our Lord that we should pray with child-like simplicity has been taken with greater seriousness. As the apostolic religious life has become more flexible in its structures, it seems that mental prayer itself is becoming less structured, more free, more personal, more loving, more of an interpersonal relationship with God.

Another direction that renewal of mental prayer seems to be taking is that of greater maturity of response, a response made in interior freedom. The place of the Cross, of renunciation, of detachment from selfishness and egoism, is being more stressed now in the apostolic religious life than it was, say, five years ago; and this emphasis on renunciation in the religious life is partly a result of the need that has been felt for a greater interior freedom so that one may respond more freely, humanly, to the Lord in prayer.

A third direction of renewal in mental prayer is that of greater personal responsibility on the part of the individual religious for his own mental prayer, regarding the time spent in mental prayer, the subject for prayer, and where it is made. It is possible that this fact, that mental prayer is now more and more a personal responsibility for one's relationship with God, is the factor most responsible for progress on the part of many in the spiritual life.

Finally, in the area of prayer in the religious life in general, there is a greater sense of the need for redemption, of the need for God's help, of the fact that all religious are sinners and all need to be saved. The current crises in the religious life—lack of vocations, defections, worldliness, polarization and tensions, authority problems—have in some cases given rise to discouragement and to a crisis of hope in the religious life. On the other hand, these same crises, for many religious, have resulted in an increased sense of the need of God's help, in a greater humility regarding religious life, and in a greater hope in God for the future of their religious life.

There is one recent and most interesting development in the evolution of the apostolic religious life: the growth of the "house of prayer" movement. There are at present, it seems clear, vocations within apostolic congregations which are calls to a primarily contemplative life with a centripetal apostolate centered on the house of prayer as a locus or center of prayer. A core group remains at the house, and, often, others come for short periods of intensive prayer. Is this a return in some way to monasticism? It would seem not; the life style of most houses of prayer borrows little from the monastic tradition except the principles of the primacy of contemplation and the centripetal apostolate. This movement is probably best understood as a kind of counterweight to the rapid process of demonasticization of the apostolic religious life, as a balancing factor in some apostolic congregations. It is significant that most of the houses of prayer are now found in some congregations that have demonasticized with especially great rapidity.

Secularization

Is the present process of the demonasticization of the apostolic religious life a process of secularization? It is not a process of increasing secularism. Secularism is an ideology according to which only the secular is important; the sacred is to be eliminated from life as much as possible and, if possible, eliminated entirely.

Increasing secularism would mean, eventually, the end of the religious life. Demonasticization, then, does not mean secularism, but it does mean a certain kind of secularization. Secularization is a word used by both sociology and theology to signify the removal of the "divine" or the sacred from areas of life in which the sacred does not belong—for example, the area of civil government. In the Western world, the process which began with pagan theocracies in which Church and state were identical, and which has resulted in our time in the clear distinction between Church and state, has been a process of the secularization of the state. That is, the sacred has been removed from an area in which it did not belong: the area proper to the state. Another example of secularization is the secularization of the sciences in the late Middle Ages; as theology was gradually removed from the study of nature, the study of nature became more scientific, secular, and so the natural sciences were liberated to be more themselves.

Another example of secularization is the historical process of the secularization of nature, which has its origin in the Judaeo-Christian tradition. This tradition has always affirmed the transcendence of God and, therefore, the non-divine character of nature. The effect has been a desacralization of man's attitude toward nature, a secularization of nature which is the presupposition of the rise of modern science and technology.

In the process of secularization, sacred and secular become more distinct and more themselves. The sacred is removed from areas in which it does not belong. This frees the secular to be itself, and it frees the sacred to be itself. As Church and state become more distinct, the Church is more free in its sacred nature and mission. As the natural sciences became more secularized, theology became freer to be itself, and concerned with the sacred. And the desacralization of nature by the Judaeo-Christian tradition has progressively eliminated man from an unhealthy and magical dependence on what primitive man regarded as the divine forces inherent in nature.

It is possible, then, to understand the process of demonasticization in the apostolic religious life as a kind of secularization. The sacred in the form of the monastic is, in the process of demonasticization, gradually removed from areas in which it does not belong. Just what form this process takes depends on the particular charism of a given apostolic congregation. But it is neither false nor pejorative to refer to the process as secularization.

But is there not the danger that an apostolic congregation will become, in practice, a secular institute? Secular institutes, of course, have a different canonical status than religious congregations, but the question here is not one of juridical status but of style of life. Could not a religious congregation, through radical demonasticization and without changing its canonical status, cease practically to live the religious life and adopt a life style more suitable for a secular institute? The possibility does exist.

What is it that chiefly distinguishes apostolic religious life from the life of secular institutes? It is public witness. Apostolic religious are called to give, publicly, witness to Jesus Christ by the state of life that they visibly live. An apostolic religious, then, needs some kind of external symbol, however discreet, that is a public identification of him as a consecrated person. Further, he witnesses to the gospel by publicly living the evangelical counsels. And, finally, he further gives public witness by living poorly in a community that is poor.

A member of a secular institute, on the other hand, typically does not live in a community with a group of other members of the institute, and he does not give witness by *publicly* living in a state distinguished by the evangelical counsels. He is a layman. His witness is private.

Thus it is possible for an individual religious or even for many members of an apostolic congregation to live in a way more suitable to members of a secular institute. And this is a danger. It is part of the charism of the apostolic religious life to give a witness that is public, both on the part of individual religious and on the part of communities.

Conclusion

When a religious congregation evolves in a direction contrary to the charism of its founders, its spirit tends to become dead, and its structures tend to become rigid. It is, of course, not true that monastic structures are necessarily rigid. Monastic congregations should, obviously, have monastic structures. When these structures are in accord with the authentic spirit of the congregation, then the monastic patterns will be flexible and appropriate. Unfortunately some monastic congregations have followed the example of apostolic (non-monastic) congregations and have demonasticized. For a monastic congregation, this is to go against its basic monastic charism, and can only result in harm to the spirit of the congregation. In an apostolic congregation, however, where in the past the development of the congregation was along monastic lines, that development tended to deaden the spirit of the congregation because it was in a direction contrary to the congregation's basic charism. As a result, before contemporary renewal of the religious life began, many apostolic congregations were rigid in their external structures.

The need for new, less monastic, more interiorized structures of the apostolic religious life is more and more evident, and these structures are being more and more adopted. The new emphasis on spiritual direction and on directed retreats is one manifestation of the search for greater interiorization, for living the religious life in a more interior way, from the heart. The number of religious who are members of Catholic Pentecostal groups is another example of the search for new, more flexible, less monastic ways to live the consecrated life in apostolic congregations. A renewal of the examination of conscience and the return of many religious to more frequent confession is another example of the tendency toward greater personalization and greater interiorization of the apostolic religious life. The new stress on community as fraternity rather than institution, the increase in the application of subsidiarity to religious government, frequent meetings and sharing in responsibility and also in decision-making—these things are a result of demonasticization and indicate a search for new and more interiorized structures that are adapted to apostolic communities.

NOTES

1. Change in the religious life has frequently been presented in terms of a difference between two kinds of religious life style. See, for example, Charles Schleck, "Religious Life since Vatican II," *Cross and Crown*, 25 (1973), 60-73; Thomas Dubay, "The Religious Life: The Real Polarity," *Review for Religious*, 32 (1973), 578-586; Joan Sauro, "Religious Life: A, B, C, D, E, F, G, An Answer to Thomas Dubay," *ibid.*, 32 (1973), 851-852; Thomas Dubay, "The ABC's of Polarization," *ibid.*, 32 (1973), 1071-1074; Mother M. Claudia, "The Reform of Renewal," *Homiletic and Pastoral Review*, 72 (1972), 48-55. The point of view of the present study is more general; change in the apostolic religious life is viewed not in terms of two more or less opposed concepts of the religious life, but rather as one process in which various congregations participate in various ways.

2. The use of the words "apostolic" and "monastic" in this sense, although inexact, is convenient and not uncommon; see, for example, Louis Bouyer, *Introduction to Spirituality* (Collegeville, 1961), p. 213.

8
Happiness

Theology of the religious life appears to lack concepts with which to consider the question of happiness. This chapter tries to develop some concepts that, hopefully, can help discussion of the problem. And it is a problem. Large-scale defections from the religious life, inter-community conflicts and polarizations, and the increase in the numbers of religious who need psychological and psychiatric therapy point, as symptoms, to an underlying unhappiness among many religious.

Happiness can, for present purposes, be defined as satisfaction. This minimal and barely adequate idea of happiness has the advantage of a certain specificity. "Happiness" means different things to different people; "satisfaction," as a concept, lends itself to more precise analysis. What is satisfaction? In general, we can define satisfaction as the congruence between expectations and experience.[1] To the extent that a person experiences what he looks for, what he expects, he finds satisfaction. The concern here, however, regards not satisfaction in general, but satisfaction within a certain institutionalized life form. In the religious life, satisfaction can exist only to the degree that the expectations of the person fit the nature of the religious life, conform to the basic structure of religious consecration. The definition, then, needs extension: satisfaction in the religious life exists to the extent that experience fits expectations determined by the basic value structure of the religious life.

What is the religious life's fundamental value structure? Prescinding from differences in the spirits of religious institutes, and going deeper even than the values incarnated in religious vows, we can say that the basic value of religious life is total consecration to God, complete self-giving to God, living an entirely God-centered life. While this may not sufficiently distinguish the religious life from other states, it is, surely, what the religious life is about.

Dissatisfaction, or unhappiness, in the religious life can occur for two reasons: (1) personal expectations are not congruent with the basic value structure of the religious life; expectations are other than to live totally for God; and (2) personal experience does not fit personal expectations. Let us consider these one at a time.

Religious Anomie

If a religious man or woman does not interiorize the central value of the religious life, or to the extent that that value is not central in the religious' own interior value system, then the personal value system will be at odds with the value system intrinsic to the consecrated life. Personal expectations will not fit the consecrated life. For example, a religious may, perhaps without reflecting on it, hold as the highest value professional competence or success, security, or community relationships. In that case, personal values do not fit with the value structure intrinsic to the consecrated life. This lack of fit will result in dissatisfaction in and with the religious life. The religious may leave or, worse, remain in the religious life while not living it because not living its central value as the central personal value. The failure to interiorize the basic value of total self-giving to God is, in fact, a rejection of that value and so a rejection of the whole value system of the consecrated life. We can call this rejection "religious anomie."

"Anomie" is a sociological concept which describes a state in which a person or a group considers exertion for success meaningless because they lack a clear definition of what is desirable. Anomie can be a personal quality, or it can be a pathology of the collective normative system.[2] It is the rejection of a value system because the values are ill-defined. In times of rapid change, anomie can become widespread. It is not mere lawlessness; gangsters have codes and sanctions. Anomie means a lack of moral roots, a spiritual sterility, an absence of the appropriate values and of the necessary responsibility to live those values. Persons removed from their cultural matrix can experience anomie, and whole civilizations in which ultimate goals and values do not exist in a coherent way can fall into anomie. So can civilizations that have conflicting ethical norms or that try to make people follow unrealistic norms. Modern capitalism, for example, exerts a strain toward anomie when it demands competitive performance without clear ethical norms.

In sociology, anomie means indifference to the ethical norms of society. The sociological concept of anomie can be converted into a theological concept of religious anomie, of indifference to the religious values of a given religious group by some of its members. The cause of religious anomie is primarily the lack of a clear definition of religious values. In the religious life, religious anomie results from a lack of perception of basic values, from a failure to understand the meaning of the religious life. This breakdown in the perceived meanings that underpin the basic values, and above all the value of living entirely for God, does not seem to be at all uncommon in the religious life.

The central reality in the religious life is God and the human need for God. And yet, there do seem to be many religious who do not live solely for God and who never seriously intended to do so. There appear to be many good and capable people in the religious life who live good lives and do good work, but who have not interiorized the religious life's fundamental value structure. For example, many think that a daily life of personal prayer in loving relationship with God is not essential. They have no clear perception of the basic value system of the consecrated life, or else they see that value system daily as too difficult, too "idealistic." They aim too low and they do not live the religious life. In a state of religious anomie, they remain vaguely dissatisfied. Many of these, perhaps the majority, are not to blame; they have never understood. They could get by, supported and helped by externals, when the religious life was more highly structured. But they have passed into a less structured and more secular life style without interiorizing the values contained in the former religious community structures. They do not see clearly the goals of the religious life, and so they decide, without reflection and in a thousand small everyday matters, on a natural level and looking to their own advantage rather than to God and to His work.

Not perceiving the primary goals and values of their vocation, or understanding those goals and values as too "high" or too "monastic" or too "pre-Vatican II," they do not take responsibility for their spiritual lives. They do not realize that they are alienated from the religious life, and even from their own true selves. Erich Fromm has described alienation as that state in which a person does not experience himself as the active bearer of his own power and richness, but as an impoverished "thing" dependent on powers outside himself.[3] The alienated religious lives at a superficial level, not experiencing nor knowing to look for God and the power and richness of His love in the religious' own heart. Alienated religious, dissatisfied without really knowing why, often tend to blame superiors rather than to change, except that the most alienated, having rejected even superiors as useless, tend to blame no one.

The opposite of religious anomie is not subjection to the law or to rules; it is freedom from law by living according to the law of the Spirit. In the past, some religious lived according to the laws, following even the most minute rules, but without ever interiorizing the spirit of those rules in the form of a personal relationship with God in Jesus calling the religious to a response of loving commitment. These religious found that the law did not fulfill them as persons; it did not "save" them. And so, with time, they rejected the rules and laws as community structures became more flexible. Now they have nothing. Their opportunity is to overcome their anomie by transcending laws and rules, by accepting God's gift of freedom from the law—not the false freedom of anomie, but the true freedom that goes beyond law and exists according to the law of the Spirit. The basic law of the Spirit, for religious, is to live entirely in terms of God and the human need for God, giving themselves totally to God in Jesus Christ, and bringing God to others in various ways. The present comparative absence of community structures in the lives of many religious who live in a state of anomie is an opportunity and a call for them to live in the freedom and the maturity of total consecration to God.

There seem to be many religious who are not victims of religious anomie, who *do* understand and accept the fundamental values of the religious life, but who do not implement those values in their lives. This tendency and temptation has been with the religious life since its beginnings. The early Christian ascetics and the medieval spiritual writers called it "acedia."

Acedia

Dissatisfaction or unhappiness in the religious life can result not only from a lack of fit between personal expectations and the basic value structure of the religious life (anomie), but also from non-congruence between personal experience and personal expectations that conform realistically to the nature of the consecrated life. That is, a religious may well possess and cherish the values of the religious life but find that his or her personal religious experience does not include the experience of those values. In particular, a given person may know that the consecrated life means centering on God and on the human need for God, but that person may simply not experience relationship with God, nor the need for God in self and in others. The expectation of the experience of God lacks fulfillment in personal experience. This non-congruence between expectations and experience will result in dissatisfaction.

The possible reasons for a lack of experience of

personal relationship with God are many. A religious may be so overworked and continuously tired that there is simply too little space in his or her life for being with God other than in a more or less formalistic way, just "putting in the time." This can be true of elementary and secondary school teachers whose administrative superiors are work-oriented at the expense of the spiritual lives of the teachers. Again, physical illness can dim the experience of relationship with God. Or, a religious may find all interpersonal relationships psychologically impossible or extremely difficult, including prayer, to the point of needing professional counseling. Perhaps more common, however, is a kind of spiritual sluggishness, a torpor, an apathy toward or even disgust for the spiritual because of the effort needed for the spiritual life; this is acedia.[4]

Acedia is a disaffection from spiritual realities that the fourth-century fathers of the desert called "the noonday devil." Evagrius Ponticus considers it a special temptation for hermits and monks; the rigors of a life of penance and prayer can give rise to a spiritual tiredness, to a restless fatigue of the spirit.[5] John Cassian, the greatest recorder of the traditions of the desert fathers, treats acedia at length, going into the psychology of the will and the temptations to tepidity of spirit.[6] By the Middle Ages, acedia had come to be seen as a general temptation for all Christians, a tendency to listlessness and sloth in religion, a partial paralysis of the will in spiritual matters, a giving up on the things of the spirit. For Thomas Aquinas, acedia means a vague and debilitating sadness regarding religious goodness. He contrasts acedia with joy and with love. Christian love rejoices in God's goodness and in His gifts; acedia inclines the will away from the joy of loving God, away from spiritual goods, to a spiritual stupor that dampens enthusiasm for the spiritual life, that cuts the ground from under love of God and love of neighbor, and that views prayer, penance, and truly apostolic works as too difficult.[7] Acedia is little referred to in modern writings, although Aldous Huxley has described it as *ennui*, a deadly mixture of boredom, sorrow, and despair,[8] and Martin Marty calls it "the cancelling out of seriousness" with regard to living Christian values.[9]

Acedia is the reluctance to take responsibility for one's spiritual life, and to live what one professes, because of the effort it takes. The root of acedia seems to be not lack of motivation but, more profoundly, lack of expectation, lack of the expectation that taking responsibility and living a life entirely given to God will really result in a lived experience of relationship with God. This experience is understood as desirable, but there is a failure to hope. Acedia's roots are not so much in lack of love as in lack of hope in God, in a lack of trust that God will act, will respond.

Happiness and Rule of Life

Religious who live their vocations from the heart have a high expectancy; they expect their lives to be experiences of God. To the degree that their expectations fit the basic value structure of the religious life, and to the extent that experience matches expectations, they are satisfied, happy. Persons who are inner-directed tend to have higher expectations than those who view the main locus of control of their lives as outside themselves.[10] In the religious life, such persons have more hope in God, and this hope gives them the impetus to move toward God, to take the steps, to transcend present difficulties and to grow toward greater union with God. Their locus of control, they know, is in their own hearts; they live according to the Spirit. Sometimes they stand out; they are not conformists. Their behavior follows the basic values and goals of the religious life, and if the behavior of other religious around them does not follow those goals and values, they follow their hearts and not necessarily the aspirations or life-style of others.[11]

The conditions of happiness, or satisfaction, in the religious life are, then, two: that a person's interior value system fit the value structure intrinsic to the consecrated life, and that personal experience match to at least some extent the expectations that flow from the interior values. God has made us for Himself, and our hearts will find no rest until they rest in Him.

In order that expectations truly fit the basic value structure of the religious life, it is necessary that those expectations be expressed, take shape in some sort of behavior. Furthermore, so that experience may match expectations, some context for experience is needed. The context or framework for religious experience, a framework which is a lived expression of the hope of experiencing relationship with God, is a rule of life. A rule of life gives concrete shape to hope, and it serves as the indispensable context for hope to blossom into experience.

I can say to myself that I hope to center my life on God and on bringing Him to others, but my hope is only a wish, a velleity, not a real hope, unless I do something about it. To be real, hope needs to take shape in action. And I can say to myself that I want an interpersonal and experiential relationship with God, but my desire is weak and ineffectual unless it leads me to provide in my life a context, a framework, within which that relationship can exist and deepen. What I do to bring my hope to expression and to have a framework for experience of relationship with God is this: I have and live a rule of life.

What is a rule of life? At its most simple and most schematic, it is a kind of flexible daily schedule of prayer that incarnates a person's own spirit of consecration to God, of response to God. It includes, always, liturgy, a minimum amount of time for personal prayer, and some kind of examination of conscience. In many cases, depending on the personal and community situation, it will also include spiritual reading and community prayer. A rule of life is a concrete personal expression of hope in God; it is not a law imposed from outside, but an expression of consecration lived from the heart. Almost all religious orders and congregations wisely state, in their decrees or constitutions, a norm for daily prayer: an amount of time, at least, plus an examination of conscience. But this is a norm that is to be internalized and made one's own, not a law to be slavishly and formalistically followed.

By living faithfully a simple daily rule of life, I am reaching out to God, looking for God, saying yes to his gift of Himself to me. I expect Him, hope in Him; and my hope, which is His gift, is the beginning of my experience of union with Him.

Hope and Experience

Hope looks to the future, to the future solution to present problems, and ultimately to being with the Lord in the life to come. The ground of hope is Jesus risen, and hope is a function of interpersonal union with Him. This hope in Jesus takes shape in a life centered on Him and on the human need for Him; hope's principal form is daily prayer in the framework of a rule of life.

The core of hope is the expectation of experience of personal relationship with God in Jesus. This experience will, of course, vary from person to person, and it will be, for the same person, different at different times. It can take the form of a personal awareness of oneself as consecrated to God, as living for Him, as wholly given to Him. It can be simply a yearning for God, or it can be the special gift from God of a felt awareness of His presence. And, also, the experience of relationship with God can take place in darkness.

A dark experience of relationship with God can be painful even though peaceful. It is a small share in the Cross, and it purifies a person. It can be felt as an experience of nothing, or even as a felt sense of God's absence. And yet, it is an experience of relationship with God even though not perceived as such; it is far removed from the lethargy of acedia and the ignorance of anomie. It is in this darkness, in the obscurity of blind faith, that the virtue of hope flourishes in a secret and often imperceptible way. Happiness, understood as satisfaction, can exist in this situation only when expectations are purified. Unless the religious is docile, letting God love him or her as God chooses to at the time, uneasiness, lack of peace, and frustration can result. But when expectation becomes hope in and for God, when what is expected, hoped for, is God giving Himself as He desires, in light or in darkness, then expectations can be close enough to experience so that satisfaction in the form of peace is present.

NOTES

1. This definition comes from J. Faricy and M. Mazis, "Personality and Consumer Dissatisfaction: A Multidimensional Approach," paper delivered at the meeting of the American Marketing Association, August 1975, p. 2.

2. See T. Parsons, "Durkheim, Emile," in *International Encyclopedia of the Social Sciences* (Macmillan: New York, 1968), Vol. 5, pp. 316-317; R. MacIver, *The Ramparts We Watch* (Macmillan: New York, 1950), pp. 84-92.

3. E. Fromm, "Alienation under Capitalism," *Man Alone: Alienation in Modern Society*, E. and M. Josephson, eds. (New York: Dell, 1962), p. 59.

4. See E. Vansteenberghe, "Accédie," *Dictionnaire de théologie catholique*, Vol. II, part 2, columns 2026-2030; U. Voll, "Acedia," *New Catholic Encyclopedia*, Vol. I, pp. 83-84; E. Bardy, "Accédie," *Dictionnaire de spiritualité*, Vol. 1, columns 166-169. Also the articles by I. Colosio in *Rivista di accetica e mistica*, 2 (1958), pp. 266-287, 495-511; 3 (1959), pp. 185-201, 528-546; 4 (1960), pp. 22-33, 159-169.

5. *De octo vitiosis cogitationibus*, Migne's *Patrologia greca*, Vol. 40, column 1274.

6. Conference 10, Migne's *Patrologia Latina*, Vol. 49, columns 359-369.

7. See *Summa Theologiae*, II^a-II^{aa}, q. 35; *De malo*, 1, 4.

8. A. Huxley, *On the Margin* (Chatto and Windus: London, 1923), pp. 18-25.

9. M. Marty, *Varieties of Unbelief* (Doubleday: Garden City, New York, 1966), p. 103. See P. Elmen, *The Restoration of Meaning to Contemporary Life* (Doubleday: Garden City, New York, 1958), pp. 19-74.

10. H. Leftcourt, "Internal versus External Control of Reinforcement," *Psychological Bulletin*, 65 (1966), 206-220.

11. Externality and conformism correlate positively. See D. Crowne and D. Marlowe, "A New Scale of Social Desira-

bility Independent of Pathology," *Journal of Consulting Psychology*, 24 (1960), 349-354.

Epilogue:
Hope

The religious life is, surely, undergoing a crisis of hope. This hope crisis can be seen not only among the laity and in the Church hierarchy, who often do wonder and fear about the new directions in the religious life. It can be seen especially where this crisis of hope exists in its most acute form, among religious themselves. The root of the crisis of hope among religious is anxiety about the future. There is worry about the future of the individual religious; and so some are asking, "What will happen to me, personally, the way the religious life is changing? What future do I have?" There is worry about the future of the continued existence of some congregations: "Will my congregation, changing so rapidly, evolve right into oblivion? Am I a member of my congregation's last generation?" There is even worry and anxiety about the future of the religious life itself. "Is the religious life an outmoded and dying life-style? Will it exist in a hundred years?"

The only answer to this anxiety about the future is hope. What are the conditions of hope in the future of the religious life? What conditions make hope in our future possible? Hope has two conditions. It must be interpersonal; we can hope only in persons, not in things. And secondly, hope—to exist—must be based on the

111

assurance of an ultimately successful outcome. Hope must be anchored in the guarantee that there is a way out of present difficulties. These two conditions of hope in the future of the religious life—that our hope be in a person, and in a person who assures the religious life of a successful future—are fulfilled only in the risen Christ.

Christ risen holds our future firmly in His hands. He is God's pledge to us of our future, the future of each of us, and of all of us, and of the religious life. The risen Christ is Lord of the future. He is with us now, present to us now, and in Him present now in a hidden way is our future. Our future is Jesus Christ. In having Him, we grasp—in Him—our own future. He is the ground of our hope.

The crisis of hope in the religious life is a call to religious to hope in Jesus Christ. To the extent that we do put our hope in Our Lord and take Him seriously as Savior, we will not be timid and fearful, nor will we be rash and foolish. We will not be reactionary or rigid or inflexible; nor will we on the other hand be caught up in the epidemic thirst for the new and the novel. Rather, we will be strong, and confident enough to be realistic.